Christopher Fowler, one [...]
horror writers, is the author of eig[...]
including the bestselling *Roofworld*, *Rune*, *Spanky*, *Psycno-ville* and *Disturbia*, as well as numerous screenplays and collections of short stories. He lives and works in London, where he runs The Creative Partnership, a Soho film promotion company.

PERSONAL DEMONS

✦

CHRISTOPHER FOWLER

Library of Congress Catalog Card Number: 97–81169

A catalogue record for this book is available from the
British Library on request

The right of Christopher Fowler to be identified as the author of this
work has been asserted by him in accordance with the Copyright,
Designs and Patents Act 1988

First published in 1998 by Serpent's Tail,
4 Blackstock Mews, London N4

Website: www.serpentstail.com

Phototypeset in 10pt Sabon by Intype London Ltd
Printed in Great Britain by
Mackays of Chatham plc, Chatham, Kent

10 9 8 7 6 5 4 3 2 1

CONTENTS

PREFACE

Short stories of the fantastic are cowards' deaths, explorations of what might yet be. They are premonitions written to disturb and ultimately comfort, because they present us with the results of our darkest dreams. They help us to deal with our fears and realise our fantasies.

Kenneth Tynan said 'when the writer cares more about the audience's reaction than the truth of the character or situation, they are writing for effect, they are writing melodrama.' The problem is, many novels and short stories seem to exist for the sole purpose of producing a series of melodramatic effects. Editors often ask for a showy set-piece to be situated at the start of a novel. Anthologies look for shock-pieces. The 'new lad' school of writing precipitated by Irvine Welsh has nearly kicked everything else off the shelves. Writers of great power and subtlety are treated as creators of specialist literature because they choose to explore strange territory. Television has become the new home of a specialised form of SF, horror and fantasy, dumbed-down, safe, value-reaffirming.

Not long ago I was told that my material was 'too quirky' for mainstream America. Why didn't I develop a single theme and stick to it in order to build reader loyalty? Stephen King is the most successful author in the world. Didn't all horror and fantasy authors aspire to be like him?

Well, no.

True, some of his books have made terrific films because his stories are admirably rooted in character, and his ideas are simple, clear and strong, even if his prose is as elegant as an orthopaedic boot, but ultimately it's a parochial style peculiar to one area of the USA, and I wanted to write specifically to my own English environment. In the eighties, American concepts of dumbing down horror provided grim new benchmarks, reaching ever lower. They constituted a sacrifice of all that disturbed, discomforted or encouraged thought, and the British followed suit. Virginia Woolf said that 'the steps from brain to brain must be cut very shallow if thought is to mount them'. Some writers began providing wheelchair slopes. The genre has still not recovered, although I'm convinced that it will.

The best horror anthologies ever produced were two Panther volumes edited by an experimental psychologist, Dr Christopher Evans. In *Mind At Bay* he admits that he is primarily interested in exploring the mind's 'inner space', and that his selected tales are 'tricks to trap the brain into giving up some of its secrets'. In *Mind In Chains* he suggests the reader should use the stories 'to see what they tell him about the structure and the denizens of his own internal landscape'. These are tales that look for contact points between the horrific and the normal, where logical events lurch into alarming disarray, and all the human mind can do is try to cope.

I wonder if such anthologies would be published today.

Certainly, Serpent's Tail would be one of the few publishing houses who could perform the favour. I have to admit, I would write much darker books if I thought the market could take it. One develops a certain amount of pessimism as one grows older, not based on nostalgia for the past so much as disappointment for the future. I rarely write anything as dark as the real lives we lead; the strain, the anger, the sheer dull ache of life is not something I'd wish to catalogue. Instead, I am drawn to the exotic, and I think that is reflected in these stories.

These *Personal Demons* are linked by an interest in a perverse array of subjects, a desire to test out ideas, and a need to wander into unusual territories. I have consciously tried to avoid retreading old ground, and have presented the stories in the order in which they were written, so that you may follow a logical progression of thought, even if some of these processes appear oblique. The final story is unorthodox, but explanatory. Here you will find horror, fantasy, reality and humour; there's hardly any blood, and only a few deaths. One of the stories is even optimistic. A frequently asked question is 'What scares a horror writer?' My answer is 'the disfiguring blankness of a person with no imagination'. Anyone who has seen TV interviews with murderers and religious fanatics knows the dead-eyed look they share. These stories are in some sense about keeping the death of the imagination at bay.

So long as there is imagination, there is hope.

SPANKY'S BACK IN TOWN

1 THE HISTORY OF RASPUTIN'S CASKET

'Can't we go any faster?' Dmitry turned around in the seat, punching at the driver's fur-clad back. Behind him one of the wolves had almost caught up with the rear-runners of the sleigh and was snapping at the end of his flapping scarf.

'This is new snow over old,' the driver shouted. 'The tracks have hardened and will turn us over.'

The horses were terrified, their heads twisting, their eyes rolling back in fear of the baying creatures behind the sleigh. Scarcely daring to look, Dmitry counted seven – now eight – of the wolves, swarming so close that he could feel their hot breath on the icy rushing air. He glanced down at the terrified child in his arms and pulled the bearskin more tightly around her deathly pale face.

'We'll never make it in time,' cried Yusupov, 'it will be dark before we reach Pokrovskoye.'

They could see the black outline of the town on the horizon, but already the sun was dropping below the tops of the trees. The sleigh clattered and crunched its way across deep-frozen cart tracks, swaying perilously, the wolves howling close behind, falling over each other in their efforts to keep up. One of the largest, a fearsome yellow-eyed beast the size of a Great Dane, suddenly threw itself forward and seized Dmitry's scarf-end in its jaws. The wool pulled tight, choking him as he clawed at his throat. Yusupov yanked it away from his brother's neck and pulled hard, feeling the weight of the animal on the other end. 'See, Dmitry,' he cried, 'look in the eyes of our pursuer now!'

He released the scarf sharply and the creature fell back, tumbling over itself. But it had his scent, and would follow the sleigh into the darkness until its jaws were filled. Dmitry cradled the infant in his arms, protecting her from buffets as the sleigh hammered over a ridge of ice. They had taken her hostage to effect their escape from the private apartments of Rasputin himself, but now they no longer had need of her. After all, the casket was now in their possession, and its value was beyond calculation. He knew that Yusupov was thinking the same thing. Behind them, the wolves were becoming braver, jumping at the rear of the sledge, trying to gain a hold with their forepaws. Thick ribbons of spittle fell along the crimson velvet plush of the seat-back as the animals yelped and barked in frustrated relay.

'They will not stop until they feed,' he shouted. 'We must use the child. She slows us down.'

'But she is innocent!'

'If we fail in our mission, many thousands of innocents will perish.'

'Then do it and be damned!'

Dmitry slipped the wild-eyed girl from the bear-fur. In one scooping motion he raised her above his head, then threw her over the end of the sleigh. She had only just begun to scream as the wolves imploded over her, seizing her limbs in their muscular jaws. The two young Bolsheviks watched for a moment as the animals swarmed around their meal, the sleigh briefly forgotten. The child's cries were quickly lost beneath the angry snarling of the feed. A sudden splash of blood darkened the evening snow. The driver huddled tighter over his reins, determined not to bear witness to such events. The next time he dared to look back, all he could see was a distant dark stain against the endless whiteness, and the sated wolves slinking away with their heads bowed between their shoulders, ashamed of their own appetites.

Yusupov studied the horizon once more, trying to discern the lights of the approaching town. He was twenty-three, and had already felt the hand of death close over him. He prayed that Casparov would be waiting at the bridge, that he had found a way of evading their pursuer. It was essential for them to find a hiding place for the casket in Pokrovskoye.

'Perhaps we are safe now,' said Dmitry as the sleigh turned toward the smoking chimneys of the town. 'May we have the strength to do what must be done.'

'Our story begins in the reign of Tsar Nicholas II, in the year 1908,' said Dr Harold Masters, studying his disinterested students as they lolled in their seats. 'Starving Bolsheviks fled across Russia with a precious cargo; a jewelled casket fashioned by Karl Fabergé and stolen from Rasputin himself, its contents unknown – and yet the men in the sleigh were willing to die to preserve it. Their flight from Rasputin's secret shrine at St Petersburg was doomed, but before they were brutally murdered in mysterious circumstances, we know that the casket was passed on, to make its way in time to New York.

'In the late 1920s a family of wealthy Franco-Russian emigrants who had escaped to America on the eve of the October revolution sailed on the SS *Brittanique* to Liverpool. The ship's passenger inventory tells us that the jewel-box was in their possession then, listed as inherited family property. But following the tragedy on board their ship . . .'

The sun had set an hour ago, but the sea was still blacker than the sky. Alexandrovich Novikov stood watching the churning wake of the ship with his gloved left hand clasping the wooden railing. Powerful turbines throbbed far beneath his feet, and he rode the waves, balancing as the liner crested the rolling swell of the sea. Back in the state room his wife, his brother and his children chattered excitedly about their new life in England, trying to imagine what, for them, was quite unimaginable. They would have new names, he had decided, European names that others would be able to pronounce without difficulty. They were being given a second chance, and this time the family would prosper and grow. There remained but one task for him to accomplish; the removal of the final obstacle to their safety. He reached inside his coat and withdrew the Fabergé casket. The value of the jewelled casing meant nothing to him, for its loss was but a small price to pay for the safe-keeping of his family.

He weighed it in his hand, worried that the rising wind might catch and smash it against the side of the ship. He had drawn back his arm, ready to hurl it into the tumbling foam below, when someone snatched at his coat-tails, spinning him around and causing him to lose balance on the tilting wet deck. Before he could draw breath, the stars filled his vision and he saw the railing pass beneath his legs, then the great black steel side of the ship, as the sound of the monstrous churning propellers pounded up around him.

Sinking into the ocean, Alexandrovich Novikov was dragged under by the great spinning blades and cleft in two, the pieces of his body lost forever in the frothing white foam. On the deck he had left, the unthrown casket slid beneath a stairwell with the rolling of the ship and was retrieved by a passing steward, whereupon the alarm was raised and a frantic search begun for its missing owner.

'And so we arrive in London,' continued Dr Masters. 'The bereaved Franco-Russian family who moved there from Liverpool in 1928 planned to build property in the city – but their assets were badly damaged in the financial crash of the following year. The headquarters of their empire, a magnificent building on the north bank of the Thames designed by the great Lubetkin, went unfinished. Here, the trail of Rasputin's jewelled box finally goes cold. We have to presume that it was sold off to the owner of a private collection as the family fought debts and a series of appalling personal tragedies . . .'

The building beside the old Billingsgate Market had never been properly finished, and now its poorly set foundations had been pulled up to clear the site and make way for a new Japanese banking syndicate. It was during the third month of digging, just prior to the new concrete foundations being poured into their moulds that the little casket, wrapped in an oilskin cloth and several layers of mildewed woven straw, was unearthed. The find was briefly mentioned on the six o'clock news that night, and excited speculation from experts about what might be discovered inside.

Before the box could be opened, however, it was sent to the British Museum to be cleaned and X-rayed. From the ornamentation of an exposed corner section of the casing it was already assumed to have been manufactured by a Russian jeweller, possibly the great Fabergé himself, which made it extremely valuable and placed it in the ownership of the royal court of Tsar Nicholas. It was, perhaps, too early to hope that the box might contain documents pertaining to that fascinating, tragic family.

The casket was entrusted to an unlikely recipient, a twenty-seven-year-old woman named Amy Dale who worked at the museum. In usual circumstances such a high-profile find would have been offered for examination to one of the more experienced senior staff, but Amy was having an affair with a hypertense married man named Miles Bernardier who functioned as the present director of the excavation, and Miles was able to take a procedural short cut that allowed him to assign the find himself. This was not as dishonest as it sounds, for Amy was fast becoming recognised as a luminary in her field, and as her own department head was overseas for two months advising at an excavation in Saudi Arabia, the pleasurable task of uncovering the casket's secrets fell to her.

The night before Amy was due to have the casket X-rayed, a supposedly psychic friend from the Mediterranean ceramics department seized her hands in the Museum Tavern and warned her that something strange was about to happen in her life. She pushed a hand through her frizzy blonde hair, laughing off his prediction, and ordered up another round of drinks. While they drank and chatted, the mud-encrusted casket, sealed in a large ziploc bag, sat in a basement vault of the British Museum waiting for its secrets to be exposed to the light.

2 THE APPEARANCE OF THE DAEMON

The sun was scorching down in a sapphire sky the morning Spanky came back to town. The wind had changed direction, from the faintest breeze drifting down across the south to a fierce fresh blast that stippled the surface of the Thames and brushed against pedestrians in the Strand, ruffling them like hair being combed the wrong way.

Balancing delicately as he placed one patent black Church's Oxford-toecapped shoe after the other, Spanky walked along the electrified third rail of the London, Chatham & Dover Railway, crossed the bridge over the river into Cannon Street station and carefully sniffed the air. Beneath the fumes of the choked city, behind the oil of machinery and ozone crackle of electricity, beyond the perfumes and deodorants and the smell of warm working flesh, he caught the faintest tang of enamel and oilskin, wolf urine and sea-brine and city soil. It was quite enough to tell him that the object of his search was within a five-mile radius.

On the station platform he almost melted into the crowd,

just another devilishly handsome young man arriving in the teeming city with an unrevealed agenda. Spanky's purpose, though, was single and specific; to locate the casket currently residing in the vault at Amy Dale's department.

A smile teased those who caught his eye; he permitted himself that. He could afford to be happy, for the battle was already half-won. He had seen the girl on television, speaking nervously into a microphone, pointing back at a great hole in the ground. The network had even taken the trouble to label her for him, displaying her name and place of employment. It only remained for him to meet with the girl and explain, in calm and rational tones, that he needed her to give back what was rightfully his.

Nah, he thought, I'll just take the casket and rip her guts into bloody shreds – to teach her a lesson.

Spanky was weary of walking the earth. He loathed gravity. If only he could shed his cloak of skin, free himself of his fleshy shackles and return to the skies. It was not possible yet; he could only operate in corporeal form. And he had been here too long, so long he had almost forgotten his true purpose, shifting from one body to the next, growing careless, even being cheated and forced to flee by an idiot mortal – the shame of it! How the mighty had fallen! He had hidden in two further bodies since that humiliating day. A balding, overweight ambulance attendant had provided him with a temporary home until he found someone more appropriate. This new body had belonged to one Chad Morrison, a none-too-bright twenty-seven-year-old male model with wavy black hair, shocking blue eyes and a jawline as sleek as the contours of a classic coupé. It would certainly last him until he had reclaimed the contents of the casket. After that, he would have no further reason to return to earth and live among these miserable mortals, not when paradise beckoned . . .

Out in the street, he listened to the sounds that lay hidden beneath the belching traffic and chattering offices. Spanky's senses were attenuated far beyond mortal range. He had heard the girl speak on television. In the maelstrom of humanity he could find her voice again, as easily as plucking a single yellow flower in a forest of bluebells. Satisfied that his instincts were correct, he set off along the pavement at a brisk clip, a jaunty swagger in his step and a cheery whistle on his lips. This time he would cover his tracks as he went. A trip to the excavation was called for. Then on to the girl and the treasure.

From the Thames, the gap between the buildings was like a missing tooth. Square off-white office blocks rose on either side. Thundering drills and a pair of slender yellow cranes picked at the site like dentists' utensils.

Miles Bernardier stood at the edge of the great earth-encrusted hole and peered down on the vast rusted mesh of iron rods that were about to be buried in concrete. Time had run out. He had requested a larger excavation window, and the request had been denied. Six lousy days, was that too much to ask? The wheels of commerce would not be halted, however. The DTI was worried that a historically significant find would be announced. Building would have to be stopped while the site was evaluated, and the Japanese might get cold feet. But who knew what else lay buried in the clay? The site had been repeatedly built upon for well over a thousand years. The casket had been discovered in a pocket of air created by some broken planks just eleven feet down. Beneath the rotted wood lay a brick lining from what appeared to be a far older building, but now, with the pouring of several thousand tons of concrete, it would remain undiscovered for yet another century.

Ahead of him, a pile-driver was rising slowly in the air to drop its weight on one of the upright iron posts marking out the building perimeter. Bernardier adjusted his yellow hard hat against the buffeting wind from the river, and carefully skirted the edge of the pit. He wanted to call Amy, to see if she had started work on the casket, but the noise was too great here. He was walking back to one of the foremen's cabins when something pushed at the backs of his legs, and he slipped over on to the wet clay soil.

'Damn!' He rose awkwardly, inspected the damage, then looked about for someone to blame. There was no-one within five hundred yards, and no sound but the rising wind and the dull thud of the pile-driver. Bernardier was due to have lunch in the city today, and the knees of his suit were smeared with gobbets of mud. He wondered if there was time to go home and change. For a moment nothing moved on the construction site, save for a few scraps of birds fighting the thermals above the river. Earlier the area had been filled with workmen. Where was everyone now?

The second blow caught him hard in the small of the back, and sent him sprawling on to his face. Frightened now, he pulled himself free of the sucking mire and searched about wildly. Impossibly, the area was deserted. Clouds had momentarily darkened the sun and the site had taken on an eerie dimness, as if history had returned to an earlier time. He tried to rise from his knees, but his shoes would not grip on the slippery clay. An odd smell hung in the air, something ancient and musky. Something bad.

The third blow was to his face, and shattered both the lenses of his glasses. This time he slid straight over the edge of the hole, landing on his back at the bottom in time to see the downward arc of the pile-driver descending over him. It was too late to stop the fall of the massive steel rod, which was powered by an explosion of compressed air. The shaft slammed down, bursting his skull like a rock dropped on an Easter egg. By the time the accident siren sounded, Bernardier's twitching body had settled so deeply into the sludge that it could have been mistaken for another historical find.

◆

'Very innocent,' Gillian was saying, 'but then you always were.' Amy held the receiver away from her ear and waved a hand at her assistant. 'The heat's too high, turn it down, it'll boil over,' and into the receiver, 'yes, mother, I know.'

'And now this man you're seeing, do you really think it's such a good idea? I mean, he's not only married, he's your boss. Is he worth jeopardising your career for?'

'I think I have to be the best judge of that, mother.' In truth Miles's continual philandering had almost persuaded her to end the affair, but she refused to launch on to this conversational track as it would mean hearing a new triumphant tone in her mother's voice.

'But I didn't call for this, to criticise. Who am I, just a woman who spent eight agonising hours in labour with you. I called to say how wonderful you looked on the television. I was so proud.'

Someone had entered the room and was standing before her. Someone from outside – he didn't smell of chemicals. There was something nice in the air, old-fashioned and comforting, from her childhood. Lavender-water?

'Mother, I have to go now.' She lowered the twittering receiver back to its cradle and raised her eyes to the visitor.

'Can I help you?'

Her pulse stuttered. The man was a living angel. His pupils peered from beneath dark knitted eyebrows like twin cobalt lasers. He had a jawline you could design a car around. Navy jacket, grey T-shirt, faded blue jeans cut tight around the crotch, brown work-boots. Behind him, two secretaries were peering around the door in unembarrassed awe.

'Yes, you can,' said the vision, 'I'm looking for Amy Dale.'

'That's me,' she laughed, feeling as if she had won a prize. Her assistants melted away, afraid of interrupting something private.

It was here. He could smell it in the air, its history of viscera and madness. He could taste it on the tip of his tongue, the cuprous tang of blood and death and misery. So close, after all this time.

'Excuse me, I was expecting someone far less attractive.' He smiled and the heavens opened.

'Now why would you expect that?' she asked, flattered.

'The way Miles Bernardier described you – ' he trailed off. 'Not like this.'

The bastard, she thought. How typical of him to denigrate her to a stranger, as though he had to frighten off potential rivals.

'Chad Morrison.' He proffered his manicured hand, and she shook it.

'So, Mr Morrison,' she smiled back, puzzled by his relaxed attitude – a rare thing in a world of obsessive academics, 'what are you here for?'

'The casket,' he genially replied.

'Oh?' Her brow furrowed. Territories were jealously guarded at the museum. 'What field are you in?'

'Forgive me,' he gave his head a little shake, 'I thought Mr Bernardier had already spoken to you about this.'

'No, he's out at the excavation today.' She unbuttoned her lab coat and pointed to a glass partitioned office. 'We can talk in there.'

Seated before her, he explained. 'I'm not attached to the museum, Miss Dale. I'm mainly an adviser to auction houses in my capacity as an authority on the works of Karl Fabergé. Your director called me in to help you verify the origin of your find.'

Miles had entrusted her with the investigation. Why did he have to interfere by sending her experts? Of course, she would have had to pull in her own independent specialists, which could be a time-consuming process, so perhaps he was trying to make her job easier. The museum staff comprised many brilliant, dedicated professionals, but she was not aware of anyone with expertise in this field. Better to accept the offer. He was awfully pretty.

'Thank you, Mr Morrison. I'd be interested in your impressions of what you've heard so far, sight unseen.'

'Well.' He leaned forward a little and the scent he exuded changed. His aftershave was something spicy and musky, not at all what she expected. He looked the citrus type. 'I can forgive the Russian revolution many things, Miss Dale, but not the destruction of Fabergé. He died in exile, you know, a broken man, his art reviled by men unable to tolerate luxury of any kind. But this find is fascinating. Its placement is correct. Fabergé knew England, and was partly educated here. Such a creation would date from the time he switched from producing jewellery and cigarette boxes to more fantastical items, say the early 1880s, before he began to produce the celebrated eggs.

'A number of objects we know he personally produced have never been traced. There are catalogue numbers and full descriptions of the missing items, and one of them fits the casket's specifications. Fabergé's sons assisted him, and there was a workshop here in London, facts which would provide circumstantial evidence for the find. Of course, there were also many forgeries produced. I would have to see the piece to be more exact.'

'I'll have to verify your appointment with Mr Bernardier. Just a formality.' She smiled and raised the telephone receiver.

He loved this part. Taking a chance. Out at the edge. He could not afford to let her find out about Bernardier, not at this stage of the game. He had no supernatural powers here, only natural ones in this earthbound body, but those would be enough. Enough to fog her senses and divert the call in her brain, to make her hear another voice.

Watching him, she mechanically punched out random digits and listened. Her mouth opened, but she did not speak. He concentrated harder. Searching her for details he found the usual human pain – aching loneliness and lack of fulfilment, but also – what was this? – Miles, not just a work colleague but a lover. Miles was sleeping with her. He probed deeper into her mind. She was not happy with the arrangement, not happy at all. He was married. Not much of a lover, either. She hadn't lost very much, then. He released her. She swayed back a little, looked flustered, lowered the receiver, aware of a vague conversation in her head, unaware of the dead line. She smiled to cover her confusion.

'That all seems to be in order, Mr Morrison. When would you like to examine the casket?'

'How about right now?' he suggested.

3 THE UNVEILING OF THE SECRET

'I'm sure you understand the need for strict security in this matter,' she said, allowing a total stranger to follow her into the maze of basement corridors.

'But of course,' he agreed, sniffing the air and scenting the proximity of the treasure, barely able to contain his excitement, 'we wouldn't want just anyone walking in here.'

Amy led the way to a further green-walled passage separated from the main building by two sets of steel doors and an electronic swipe-code. 'We have to bring items from this section up personally,' she explained. 'They can't be trusted to assistants, and they're not allowed to leave our sight until they're returned.'

Beyond the doors, a series of white-walled rooms housed large square drawers with brass handles, like a morgue. Amy checked the reference number on her requisition sheet and searched the containers.

'It's over here,' he said, lifting the index number from her mind and matching it to a nearby drawer.

Amy looked at him oddly. 'How do you know?' she asked, moving past him to check. It was the right drawer. She took a key from her pocket and slipped it into the lock. The moisture-pocked bag inside gave no clue to its contents. 'You're never sure what's best with a find like this,' she said, carefully removing the bag. 'This plastic is supposed to "breathe" and sustain a natural moisture equilibrium. We could have placed it in a dry environment, but if the casket contains paper materials they could be ruined.'

He was barely listening to her. The presence of the casket had enveloped and overwhelmed his senses. It was less than three feet from him, but he could not take it from her here. There were other technicians in the secure area. He could hear their bodyweight shifting past him in the nearby rooms. Back in the corridor he had an insane thought, that he could snatch the thing from her and escape from the building with it beneath his arm. He would have to wait until he was beyond the secure area. Another problem; in this body, he could not run. Morrison had sustained a football injury that had left him with damaged tendons in his left leg. Besides, mere escape lacked dignity. He wanted them to see what they had found. Better to wait until he was alone with Amy in the lab, after the other assistants had gone for the night. It would be foolish to screw up now, for the sake of a few hours.

'It'll be some time before we reach the interior of the package,' said Amy. 'It might be rather boring for you, but you can stay and help me if you want.'

'Just tell me what to do,' smiled Spanky, removing his jacket.

By six o'clock they had succeeded in removing the outer straw wrappers and had sectioned them for dating. The oilskin, too, had been photographed at every stage, and the whole process documented. It was laborious, but necessary if mistakes were to be prevented. Amy's chaotic blonde hair had fallen into her eyes so often that she had bunched it back with a rubber band. She was hunched so far over the brilliantly illuminated desktop that she had developed a crick in her neck. A hot wire of pain scratched across the top of her shoulder blades as she sat up.

'Here, let me give you a massage. Tip your chair back.' Spanky lowered broad hands to her neck and pressed his thumbs down in a smooth circular motion.

'You read my mind. Thanks, that feels good.' She sat further back and closed her eyes. Another assistant scuttled from the room. 'At least we've only one layer to go, some kind of tissue.'

'Cloth-papers from Rasputin's apartment,' he said absently. 'He kept the casket out of the light and bound in calico.'

'You must be a really big authority on this,' she murmured, succumbing to the motion of his hands.

'Oh, you have no idea how big.'

'Pieces of hidden history . . .'

'Crossing-points of the past. Everything holds something different within. The truth becomes fabulous, and fables hold truth.' His voice had dropped to a sea-murmur. Fingers slipping over her throat.

'You soon start to see the attraction . . .'

'Attraction?' His hands smoothed and smoothed. The nape of her neck tingled, a warm glow spreading to the top of her breasts. She forced herself to concentrate.

'Of – archaeology.'

'Ah, of course.'

They were alone in the laboratory. The last assistant had quietly closed the door behind her.

'Right.' He swiftly removed his hands and shifted her chair-back to an upright position once more. 'Let's do it.'

She looked wide-eyed at him. 'Here?'

He gestured at the table-top. 'The last layer. Come on.'

Even with tweezers and generous smears of lubricant, the greased wrapping proved difficult to remove, and flapped back on to the casket lid. Amy peered through the illuminated magnifier. 'I think I've got it this time.' She gripped the tweezers more lightly.

Twined ribbons of inlaid gold surrounded an intricate frieze of dancing mythological figures. You could see no detail from studying the russet splodges on the lid, but Spanky knew that the ancient gods lay beneath a layer of grime, longing for the chance to shine again. There had been many containers across the centuries for the treasure held inside, but this was the best casket so far. Ten inches by six, and six deep, it sat on the formica-topped desk awaiting inspection, a spectacular relic from a forgotten world. They had removed soil from a tiny gold-rimmed keyhole with a water-pic. The rest of the wrapping was easier to remove. As it slid away, Amy cautiously wiped a finger across the lid, and the precious figures revealed themselves.

'It's beautiful,' she whispered.

'And we can unlock it.' Spanky opened the top button of his shirt and removed a slender gold key from around his neck. He could feel his fingers trembling in anticipation. She stared at him, then at the filigreed key. What did he mean?

'I can unlock the casket, Amy.' He could not resist sounding boastful.

'Where did you get that?' She reached up to touch the key, then withdrew her hand, as if wary of being scalded.

'It's been in my possession for many, many years.'

The casket was behind her. She positioned herself before it protectively. 'I don't understand.'

'You don't have to.'

'I can't let you open it.'

'Why not?'

'This find is of historical importance. A senior member of staff must be present.'

'Then let's send for Mr Bernardier.' If you don't mind summoning a mud-caked headless corpse, he thought, smiling grimly. The director had never known what hit him. A pity, that. Spanky enjoyed taking credit for his work.

'You know exactly what's inside the box, don't you?'

'Of course I do,' he answered. She was a smart girl. There was no more need for subterfuge now that he was so close to his goal. 'I've always known.'

'Perhaps you'd like to tell me.' She could feel her unease growing by the second. The museum was closed for the night. Only a few of the research departments scattered in the building's cul-de-sac corridors would still be inhabited by lingering personnel.

'All right. Have a seat.' Outside, the warm weather had finally broken and it was starting to rain. 'Listen carefully, and don't question anything I have to say.'

Sensing the danger she was in, Amy dropped to the chair.

'I am not like you. Not – human. I am *Spancialosophus Lacrimosa*. If you find it easier, you can call me Spanky. God had seven fallen angels. Seven daemons. Seven rogue creatures of inspiration and vengeance, banned from Heaven for refusing to worship Man. Damned to a watery limbo existence between earth and paradise. Only allowed to visit earth in the encumbrance of a mortal shell, to be entered upon the invitation of the owner. But I am not like my fellow daemons. I have little of their boundless patience. I am not content to wait forever, until God, in his infinite wisdom and mercy, sees fit to readmit us to his kingdom. And now there is a chance to do more than just return to grace. There is a chance to rule for all eternity. It's all to do with the box.'

Amy snapped around to check that the casket was still there beside her in its nest of wet straw. What if this lunatic tried to snatch it? How would she ever stop him?

'You want to see inside? Take a look.' He unlooped the key from his neck and handed it to her, savouring the moment. 'Do it,' he commanded.

The key was so worn and delicate that she was frightened

of breaking it in the lock. To her surprise it turned easily. The lubricant and the water-pic must have loosened the mechanism. And of course, it had been built by the master. With trembling fingers, she raised the lid. The interior was completely dry. Beneath several layers of fine grey silk were –

'Iron rings. Seven of them. One for each of us. The rings of Cain. Forged by Adam's first son. How is your knowledge of the Bible?' He grinned at her, inching closer to the opened casket, holding out his hand for the return of the golden key.

'Let me refresh your memory. Cain was a tiller of the ground, driven from the earth by God for slaying his brother Abel. Doomed to become a fugitive and a vagabond. Cain tried to atone for his sin by appealing to us, God's other fallen children. He brought us gifts, the rings he forged from the ore beneath his feet. But just as we despised Adam, so we despised his offspring. We refused his offer, and Cain threw the rings back into the earth.

'It took many centuries for us to truly understand the power of the rings. You see, if we had accepted them, we would have been restored to Paradise. That was Cain's gift to us, and we turned it down. It was only by accident that I discovered the truth. But by then, the rings were lost. I've tracked them through time and across the world. Now I've been here too damned long. I can't get back to my home without them. The others won't let me in empty-handed.'

Obviously the man was crazy. Amy knew that the safest solution to her dilemma was to play along until she could find a way to summon help. 'Is that what you want, to be restored to Paradise?' she asked.

'Of course. Wouldn't you?' Spanky drew a step nearer. 'Only this time, we'll have the element of surprise on our side.'

'What do you mean?'

'Well, we wish to rule, obviously. God has had everything

his way for *far* too long. You have no idea how boring He has made the celestial heavens. We'll change all that. You wait, you'll feel the effects all the way down here. It'll be like having the worst neighbours in the universe living right overhead.'

'You're mad.' She hadn't meant to say it. The words had just slipped out. He laughed at her.

'If you think what I want is so very illogical, good luck with the rest of the world. A little respect is all anyone wants.'

Amy made a grab for the casket, and was surprised when he made no attempt to stop her. Instead, he watched as she took it from the desk and clutched it protectively across her breasts, smearing mud and pieces of straw on her lab jacket.

'We'd better get going,' he said, checking his watch. 'The others are expecting us.'

'What do you mean?' She looked frantically about for someone to help her. Why was it that the one time she would welcome an interruption, none came?

'Cain protected the rings. They can only be returned to us by a mortal. Lucky you.' He grinned mischievously as he grabbed her hand and pulled her toward the door. 'You get to see where we live. You'll be the first human being ever to meet my brothers and sisters. I'm sure *Spancialosophus Dolorosa* will take a shine to you.'

4 THE DENIAL OF ICARUS

She pulled back from him. 'Wait, I have to set the alarm system. I'm the last one out.'

'You're lying to me, Amy.' He bared his teeth and yanked her arm hard. 'Don't try to trick me. I can see inside your head.'

They passed from the lab along a corridor, and on to a broad staircase. Miles should have come for her by now, but they passed no-one, not even Dr Harold Masters, who was usually making tea in the cubby-hole beside the staircase at this time of the evening.

Spanky's gripping hand felt as though it was burning into her wrist. At the main entrance, the two security guards barely looked up from their desks to wish her goodnight. Couldn't they see that she was in trouble?

The rain sizzled against Spanky's back as he strode across the museum forecourt with her. Amy maintained her grip on the casket, frightened that she would be punished if she tried to fling it away. 'Where are we going?' she gasped, frantically trying to keep up with him.

'To the departure point,' he snapped, barely bothering with her. He crossed Museum Street, half dragging her upright as she slipped on the wet tarmac. He moved so quickly that she found herself being bodily lifted by him at moments when the traffic seemed about to crash into them. Onward they moved, through Holborn and down toward the Embankment.

They were standing in the centre of Waterloo Bridge with the great rain-swollen river sweeping beneath them, broadening out on its way to the sea. 'Why here?' she shouted, the roar of wind and traffic filling her ears.

'I need a good run-up,' he replied. 'Got a tight grip on the casket?'

He checked the box pressed against her sodden breast, then produced an old-fashioned cut-throat razor from his coat and passed it to her with his free hand. 'Hold this. I'm letting go of you for a moment. If you try to escape I will kill you, Amy, I think you know that.' Spanky tore off his jacket and shirt, throwing them out into the Thames.

'I want you to take the razor and run it along my spine.' He pointed to his broad rain-spattered back. 'Do it quickly.' He snapped open the blade for her.

Shaking with cold and fear, she suppressed a shudder of

horror as she touched the blade to the point he indicated between his shoulderblades.

'You'll have to push harder than that. Pull it straight down. As deep as you can.'

Wincing, she did as she was told, pushing on the blade and dragging it down. The edge sliced smoothly and cleanly as the skin of his back opened in a widening crimson slit. Spanky was drawing breath in low, guttural gasps, part in pain, part in the pleasure of release from his confinement. As the blade reached his trouser-belt he slapped it from her hand. The razor skittered across the pavement and slid into the gutter. Swathes of blood washed across his back, diluting in the downpour.

Spanky bent forward with an agonised shout and the epidermis split further apart across his back. From within the carapace of skin, two enormous black wings unfolded like opening umbrellas. As the joints clicked and cracked, the membranes between them flexed and stretched and grew. At first she thought they were made of black leather, but now she saw that they were composed of thousands of tiny interlocking black feathers. He seized her hand and climbed on to the balustrade of the bridge, dragging her up on the ledge with him. The fully opened wings spanned a distance of eighteen feet above them.

'Hold on to your hat.' He turned and gave her a mad grin. 'Here we go.'

Amy's stomach dropped as they launched from the bridge. Intoxicated with the terror of his unbreakable grip, she screamed and howled into the racing clouds above. They swooped down to the scudding grey water, almost touching their shadow, then up and along the path of the river, moving so fast that they outdistanced the falling rain. The pain in her clutched wrist was excruciating. He turned and brought his face close to hers, shouting as the great black wings beat powerfully above them.

'You have the casket.'

'Yes,' she shouted back as they started to climb, 'I have the casket.'

'Then we can make the crossing.' He pumped his membraneous wings faster, ever faster, so that they flexed and shook from humerus to metacarpal, and it seemed that they were moving beyond the speed of earth and sea and weather and light and time.

Something bright shone in her eyes. She forced herself to look up. Ahead in the clouds, a dazzling area of light had cleared the grey rain to send a mandelbrot set of fractal colours spiralling down toward them, like pieces of rainbow glass from an exploded kaleidoscope.

'You see it?' he bellowed. 'You see it? That's where we're going. Inside there.'

'No!' she screamed, knowing instinctively that the experience would kill her instantly. This was not a sight for mortal eyes. But they were racing forward at such a velocity that nothing could stop them from reaching the area now. Piercing shards of diamond brilliance enveloped them as they left the earth behind forever and plunged into the heart of the world's existence.

And just as they reached it – it was gone. Slammed shut, vanished, the colours all disappeared, nothing ahead except endless cold grey sky.

Spanky's face was contorted in fury and terror.

'The rings of Cain!' he yelled at the heavens. 'I am returning with the rings!' Already his wings were parting with the impossible velocity, flesh and feathers tearing off in strips, revealing birdlike bloody bones beneath.

With nothing to propel them, their speed slowed. For a moment, it seemed that they were hanging in the air. 'You have the rings,' he screamed at her.

'No, I told you – I have the casket.' The box was still unlocked. She had emptied the rings out as they flew. He had not noticed. With all his energy and concentration centred elsewhere, he had not seen the seven iron bands scatter in the wind and fall back toward the river, and now the doorway home was closed once more.

A sharp crack resounded above them as the great wings bloodily shattered and folded, and with a sickening lurch they dropped back toward the earth. Spanky's anguished howling filled her tortured ears every metre of the way.

Down and down.

The glutinous silt of the river formed undulations across the expanding estuary at Dartford. It trapped all manner of debris swept out with the heavy ebb tide. It cradled Amy's unconscious body, rolling her gently against the shore until some kind old souls spotted her, and dragged her out to warmth and safety. Inside Amy's jacket they found an old casket, gripped so tightly that the corners had bruised her flesh.

Spanky's broken form had fallen more heavily and plunged much deeper, to be snagged by the twisted metal on the riverbed. Held firmly in place, Chad Morrison's body undulated against the current. His earthly form was dead, from the fall, from the loss of blood, but the daemon was still alive and imprisoned within. There was nothing Spanky could do but stare out from his blanched shell in endless horror, gripped by his prison of bloating dead flesh, held in turn by the detritus of the river, beneath that great protector of the city.

He was aware of everything, and unable to do anything. He even thought he saw one of the precious rings float by, inches from his eyes. Eventually he allowed his senses to dull and close, lulled to a dreamless sleep by the lunar tides.

Somewhere inside the wide pulsing currents of the sea, the seven rings of Cain tumbled and drifted, lost to man and lost to angels.

✦

'And that is how Karl Fabergé's most magnificent casket, so beautifully restored by Amy Dale, came to be exhibited here at the British Museum,' said Dr Harold Masters, eyeing his bored students as they sprawled and drifted in various states of semi-consciousness about the lecture room like dumped shop mannequins. Honestly, he thought, you try to bring history alive for the young, but you might as well not bloody bother.

DRACULA'S LIBRARY

From the Journal of Jonathan Harker, July 2nd 1893

I have always believed that a building can be imbued with the personality of its owner, but never have I felt such a dread ache of melancholy as I experienced upon entering that terrible, desolate place. The castle itself – less a chateau than a fortress, much like the one that dominates the skyline of Salzburg – is very old, thirteenth century by my reckoning, and a veritable masterpiece of unadorned ugliness. Little has been added across the years to make the interior more bearable for human habitation. There is now glass in many of the windows and mouldering tapestries adorn the walls, but at night the noise of their flapping reveals the structure's inadequate protection from the elements. The ramparts are unchanged from times when hot oil was poured on disgruntled villagers who came to complain about their murderous taxes. There is one entrance only, sealed by a portcullis and a pair of enormous studded doors. Water is drawn up from a great central well by a complicated wooden-pump contraption. Gargoyles sprout like toadstools in every exposed corner. The battlements turn back the bitter gales that forever sweep the Carpathian mountains, creating a chill oasis within, so that one may cross the bailey – that is, the central courtyard of the castle – without being blasted away into the sky.

But it is the character of the Count himself that provides

the castle with its most singular feature, a pervading sense of loss and loneliness that would penetrate the bravest heart and break it if admitted. The wind moans like a dying child, and even the weak sunlight that passes into the great hall is drained of life and hope by the cyanic stained glass through which it is filtered.

I was advised not to become too well-acquainted with my client. Those in London who have had dealings with him remark that he is 'too European' for English tastes. They appreciate the extreme nobility of his family heritage, his superior manners and cultivation, but they cannot understand his motives, and I fear his lack of sociability will stand him in poor stead in London, where men prefer to discuss fluctuations of stock and the nature of horses above their own feelings. For his part, the Count certainly does not encourage social intercourse. Why, he has not even shaken my hand, and on the few occasions that we have eaten together he has left me alone at the table before ten minutes have passed. It is almost as if he cannot bear the presence of a stranger such as myself.

I have been here for over a month now. My host departed in the middle of June, complaining that the summer air was 'too thin and bright' for him. He has promised to return by the first week of September, when he will release me from my task, and I am to return home to Mina before the mountain paths become impassable for the winter. This would be an unbearable place to spend even one night were it not for the library. The castle is either cold or hot; most of it is bitter even at noon, but the library has the grandest fireplace I have ever seen. True, it is smaller than the one in the Great Hall, where hams were smoked and cauldrons of soup were boiled in happier times, and which now stands cold and lifeless as a tomb, but it carries the family crest of Vlad Drakul at its mantel, and the fire is kept stoked so high by day that it never entirely dies through the night. It is here that I feel safest.

Of course, such heat is bad for the books and would dry out their pages if continued through the years, but as I labour within this chamber six days out of every seven, it has proven necessary to provide a habitable temperature for me. The servant brings my meals to the Great Hall at seven, twelve and eight, thus I am able to keep 'civilised' hours. Although I came here to arrange the Count's estate, it is the library that has provided me with the greatest challenge of my life, and I often work late into the night, there being little else to do inside the castle, and certainly no-one to do it with. I travelled here with only two books in my possession; the leather-bound Bible I keep on my bedside table, and the Baedeker provided for my journey by Mina, so for me the library is an enchanted place. Never before, I'll wager, has such a collection of volumes been assembled beyond London. Indeed, not even that great city can boast such esoteric tastes as those displayed by the Count and his forefathers, for here are books that exist in but a single copy, histories of forgotten battles, biographies of disgraced warriors, scandalous romances of distant civilisations, accounts of deeds too shameful to be recorded elsewhere, books of magic, books of mystery, books that detail the events of impossible pasts and many possible futures!

Oh, this is no ordinary library.

In truth, I must confess I am surprised that he has allowed me such free access to a collection that I feel provides a very private insight into the life and tastes of its owner. Tall iron ladders, their base rungs connected to a central rail, shift along the book-clad walls. Certain shelves nearest the great vaulted ceiling have gold-leafed bars locked over them to keep their contents away from prying eyes, but the Count has provided me with keys to them all. When I asked him if, for the sake of privacy, he would care to sort the books before

I cast my gaze upon them (after all, he is a member of the Carpathian aristocracy, and who knows what family secrets hide here) he demurred, insisting that I should have full run of the place. He is a charming man, strange and distant in his thoughts, and altogether too much of an Easterner for me to ever fully gain his confidence, for I act as the representative of an Empire far too domesticated for his tastes, and I suspect, too diminished in his mind. Yes, diminished, for there is little doubt he regards the British intellect as soft and sated, even though there is much in it that he admires. He comes from a long line of bloodletting lords, who ruled with the sword-blade and despised any show of compassion, dismissing it as frailty. He is proud of his heritage, of course, yet learning to be ashamed, contrition being the only civilised response to the sins of the past.

I think perhaps he regards this vast library, with its imposs-ible mythologies and ghastly depictions of events that may never happen, as part of that bloody legacy he is keen to put behind him. He is, after all, the last of his line. I suspect he is allowing me to catalogue these books with a view to placing the contents up for auction. The problem, though, is that it is almost impossible for me to judge how I should place a price on such objects. Regardless of what is contained within, the bindings themselves are frequently studded with precious and semi-precious jewels, bound in gold-leaf and green leather, and in one case what suspiciously appears to be human skin. There is no precedent to them, and therefore there can be no accurate estimate of value.

How, then, am I to proceed?

From the Journal of Jonathan Harker, July 15th 1893
Regarding the library: I have devised a system that allows me to create a table of approximate values, and that for now must suffice. First, I examine the binding of the book, noting the use of valuable ornamentation and pigments. Then I make

note of the author and the subject, gauging their popularity and stature; how many copies have been printed (if indicated) and where; how many editions; the age of the work and its length; and finally, content, whether scandalous and likely to cause offence, whether of general interest, usefulness and the like. To this end I find myself making odd decisions, putting a history of Romanian road-mapping before the *Life and Times of Vladimir the Terrible* because the former may be of more utility in charting this neglected territory. Thus the banal triumphs over the lurid, the ordinary over the outrageous, the obvious over the obscure. A fanciful mind might imagine that I was somehow robbing the library of its power by reclassifying these tomes in such a manner, that by quantifying them I am reducing the spell they cast. Fancies grow within these walls. The castle is conducive to them.

In my tenth week I started upon the high barred shelves, and what I find there surprises, delights and occasionally revolts me. Little histories, human fables set in years yet to be, that reveal how little our basest nature changes with the passing decades. These books interest me the most.

I had not intended to begin reading any of the volumes, you understand, for the simple reason that it would slow my rate of progress to a crawl, and there are still so many shelves to document. Many books require handling with the utmost care, for their condition is so delicate that their gossamer pages crumble in the heat of a human hand. However, I now permit myself to read in the evenings, in order that I might put from my mind the worsening weather and my poor, pining Mina.

The light in the library is good, there being a proliferation of candles lit for me, and the great brocaded armchair I had brought down from my bedroom is pulled as close to the fire as I dare, deep and comfortable. Klove leaves his master's guest a nightly brandy, setting down a crystal bowl before me in the white kid gloves he always wears for duties in this room. Outside I hear the wind loping around the battlements like a wounded wolf, and in the distant hills I hear some of those very creatures lifting their heads to the sky. The fire shifts, popping and crackling. I open the book I have chosen for the evening and begin to read.

From the Journal of Jonathan Harker, August 30th 1893
I have the strangest feeling that I am not alone.

Oh, I know there are servants, four, I think; a raw-looking woman who cooks and cleans, her husband the groom, an addle-pated under-servant born without wits who is only fit for washing and sweeping (he might be the son of the cook; there is a resemblance), and Klove, an unsmiling German butler whom I take to be the Count's manservant. I mean to say that there is someone else here. I sense his presence late at night, when the fire has banked down to an amber glow and the library is at its gloomiest. I can feel him standing silently at the windows (an impossibility, since they overlook a sheer drop of several hundred yards) but when I turn to catch a glimpse of this imagined figure it is gone.

Last night the feeling came again. I had just finished cataloguing the top shelves of the library's west wall, and was setting the iron ladders back in their place when I became aware of someone staring at my back. A sensation of panic seized me as the hairs stood on my neck, prickling as though charged with electricity, but I forced myself to continue with my task, finally turning in the natural course of my duty and raising my gaze to where I felt this mysterious watcher to be standing.

Of course, there was nothing corporeal to see – yet this time the feeling persisted. Slowly, I made my way across the great room, passing the glowing red escarpment of the fire, until I reached the bank of mullioned windows set in the room's north side. Through the rain that was tickering against the glass I looked out on the most forsaken landscape imaginable, grey pines and burned black rock. I could still feel him, somewhere outside the windows, as if he had passed by on the wall itself, and yet how was this possible? I am a man who prides himself on his sensitivity, and fancied that this baleful presence belonged to none other than my host. Yet the Count was still away and was not due to return for a further fourteen days (I had been informed by Klove), having extended his trip to conclude certain business affairs.

This presents me with a new problem, for I am told that winter quickly settles in the mountains, and is slow to release the province from its numbing grip. Once the blizzards begin the roads will quickly become inundated, making it virtually impossible for me to leave the castle until the end of spring, a full seven months away. I would truly be a prisoner here in Castle Dracula. With that thought weighing heavily on my mind I returned to my seat beside the fire, fought down the urge to panic, opened a book and once more began to read.

I must have dozed, for I can only think what I saw next was a hallucination resulting from a poorly digested piece of mutton. The Count was standing in the corner of the library, still dressed in his heavy-weather oilskin. He seemed agitated and ill-at-ease, as if conducting an argument with himself on some point. At length he reached a decision and approached me, gliding across the room like a tall ship in still seas. Flowing behind him was a rippling wave of fur, as hundreds of rats poured over the chairs and tables in a fanned brown shadow. The rodents watched me with eyes like ebony beads. They cascaded over the Count's shoes and formed a great circle around my chair, as if awaiting a signal. But the signal did not come, so they fell upon one another, the strongest tearing into the soft fat bellies of the weakest, and the library carpet turned black with blood as the chamber filled with screams . . .

I awoke to find my shirt as wet as if it had been dropped

into a lake. The book I had been reading lay on the floor at my feet, its spine split. The gold crucifix I always wear at my neck was hung on the arm of my chair, its clasp broken beyond repair. I resolved to eat earlier from that night on.

From the Journal of Jonathan Harker, September 22nd 1893
The weather has begun to worsen, and there is still no sign of the Count. Klove has heard nothing of his master, and as the days grow shorter a forlorn darkness descends upon the castle. The skies are troubled, the clouds heavier now, ebbing to the west with their bellies full of rain. The library occupies my waking hours. It is like an origami model of Chinese paper, ever unfolding into new configurations. Just when I think I have its measure, new delights and degradations present themselves. Yesterday, I started on a further set of shelves housing nautical chart-books and maps, and while reaching across the ladder to pull one stubborn tome free, triggered the opening of a mahogany flap built in the rear of the shelf that folded down to reveal a hundred further volumes.

I carefully cleared a space and set these books in stacks according to their co-ordinated bindings, and only once they all stood free of their secret home did I start to examine them.

I find delicacy escapes me at this point; they were lexicons of erotica, frankly illustrated, alarmingly detailed, outlining practices above, below and altogether beyond the boundaries of human nature in such an overt and lascivious manner that I was forced to return them to their hiding place before Klove brought me my nightly brandy, for no gentleman would wish such volumes to fall into the hands of servants.

After he had left the room I took time to examine the single edition I had left out. It was much like the others, designed more to arouse the senses than to provide practical advice concerning the physical side of matrimony. The room grew hot about me as I turned the pages, and I was forced to move back from the fireplace. The drawings were shameless, representing actions one would scarcely countenance in the darkest woods, here presented in brightest daylight. Still more shocking was my discovery that the book was English, produced in London, presumably for foreign purchasers.

While I was examining this, I began to sense the presence once more, and this time as it grew I became aware of a smell, a sweet perfume akin to Atar of Roses – a scented water my own Mina would often dab at her swan-pale neck. The perfume, filled as it was with memories of home, quite overpowered me and I grew faint, for I fancied I saw a lady – no, a *woman* – standing on the staircase nearest the windows.

She was tall and handsome rather than beautiful, with a knowing look, her auburn hair swept back and down across a dress of sheer green gossamer, with jewels at her throat, and nothing at all on her feet. She stood with her left side turned to me, so that I could not help but notice the exaggerated posture of her breasts. It was as though she intended them to incite my admiration. The effect was indecent, but nothing to the effect produced when she turned to face me directly, for the front panel of the dress was cut away below her waist to reveal – well, her entire personal anatomy. Stupified by her brazenness, wondering if she was perhaps ill, I found myself unable to move as she approached. Upon reaching my chair she slid the outstretched fingers of her right hand inside my shirt, shearing off each of the buttons with her nails. I was acutely aware that the naked part of her was very close to me. Then, reaching inside the waistband of my trousers, she grasped at the very root of my reluctantly extended manhood and brought it forward, bursting through the garment's fly-buttons. When I saw that she intended to lower her lips to this core of my being, every fibre of my body strained to resist her brazen advances.

Here, though, my mind clouds with indistinct but disagreeable impressions. A distant cry of anger is heard, the woman retreats in fear and fury, and I awake, ashamed to discover my clothing in considerable disarray, the victim of some delirious carphology.

From the Journal of Jonathan Harker, October 7th 1893
The snow has started falling. During these increasingly frequent squalls, all sights and sounds are obscured by a deadening white veil that seals us in the sky. From my bedroom window I can see that the road to the castle is becoming obscured. If the Count does not return soon, I really do not see how I shall be able to leave. I suppose I could demand that a carriage be fetched from the nearest village, but I fear such an action would offend my absent host, who must surely reappear any day now.

I am worried about my Mina. I have not heard from her inside a month, and yet if I am truthful part of me is glad to be imprisoned here within the castle, for the library continues to reveal paths I feel no Englishman has ever explored.

I do not mean to sound so mysterious, but truly something weighs upon my mind. It is this; by day I follow the same routine, logging the books and entering them into the great ledgers my host provided for the purpose, but each night, after I have supped and read my customary pages before the fire, I allow myself to fall into a light sleep, and then . . .

. . . then my freedom begins as I either dream or awaken to such unholy horrors and delights I can barely bring myself to describe them.

Some nights bring swarms of bats, musty-smelling airborne rodents with leathery wings, needle teeth and blind eyes. Sometimes the ancestors of Vlad Drakul appear at the windows in bloody tableaux, frozen in the act of hacking off the howling heads of their enemies. Men appear skewered on tempered spikes, thrusting themselves deeper onto the razor-poles in the throes of an obscene pleasure. Even the Count himself pays his respects, his bony alabaster face peering at me through a wintry mist as though trying to bridge the chasm between our two civilisations. And sometimes the women come.

Ah, the women.

These females are like none we have in England. They do not accompany themselves on the pianoforte, they do not sew demurely by the fire. Their prowess is focussed in an entirely different area. They kneel and disrobe each other before me, and caress themselves, and turn their rumps toward me in expectation. I would like to tell you that I resist, that I think of my fiancée waiting patiently at home, and recite psalms from my Bible to strengthen my will, but I do not, and so am damned by the actions taken to slake my venomous desires.

Who are these people who come to me in nightly fever-dreams? Why do they suit my every morbid mood so? It is as if the Count knows my innermost thoughts and caters for them accordingly. Yet I know for a fact that he has not returned to the castle. When I look from the window I can see that there are no cart-tracks on the road outside. The snow remains entirely unbroken.

There are times now when I do not wish to leave this terrible place, for to do so would mean forsaking the library. And yet, presumably, it is to be packed up and shipped to London, and this gives me hope, that I might travel with the volumes and protect them from division. For the strength of a library exists in the sum of its books. Only by studying it – indeed, only by reading every single edition contained within – can one hope to divine the true nature of its owner.

From the Journal of Jonathan Harker, November 15th 1893
Somewhere between dreams and wakefulness, I now know that there is another state. A limbo-life more imagined than real. A land of phantoms and sensations. It is a place I visit

each night after darkness falls. Sometimes it is sensuous, sometimes painful, sometimes exhilarating, sometimes foul beyond redemption. It extends only to the borders of the library, and its inhabitants, mostly in states of undressed arousal, are perfumed with excrement. These loathsome creatures insult, entice, distract, disgrace, shame and seduce me, clutching at my clothes until I am drawn among them, indistinguishable from them, enthralled by their touch, degraded by my own eagerness.

I think I am ill.

By day, my high stone world is once more quiet and rational. Would that it were not, for there is no comfort to be had from the news it brings me. The road leading to and from the castle is now quite impassable. It would take a team of mountaineers to scale the sharp gradient of the rock face beneath us. The Count has failed to return, and of his impending plans there is no word. My task in the library is nearly over. The books – all save one single final shelf – have been quantified and, in many cases, explored.

I begin to understand the strangely parasitic nature of my host. His thirst for knowledge and his choice of literature betray his true desires. There are volumes in many languages here, but of the ones I can read, first editions of Nodier's *Infernalia*, d'Argen's *Lettres Juives* and Viatte's *Sources Occultes du Romantisme* are most familiar. Certain medical periodicals and pertinent copies of *The London Journal* add subtler shades to my mental portrait of the Count. Of course I knew the folk-tales about his ancestry. They are bound within the history of his people. How could one travel through this country and not hear them? In their native language they do not seem so fanciful, and here in the castle, confabulations take on substantiality. I have heard and read how the Count's forefathers slaughtered the offspring of their enemies and drank their blood for strength – who has not? Why, tales of Eastern barbarism have reached the heart of

London society. But I had not considered the more lurid legends; how the royal descendants lived on beyond death, how they needed no earthly sustenance, how their senses were so finely attuned that they could divine bad fortune in advance. Nor had I considered the consequence of such fables; that, should their veracity be proven, they might in the Count's case suggest an inherited illness of the kind suffered by royal albinos, a dropsical disease of the blood that keeps him from the light, an anaemia that blanches his eyes and dries his veins, that causes meat to stick in his throat, that drives him from the noisy heat of humanity to the cool dark sanctum of his sick-chamber.

But if it is merely a medical condition, why am I beset with bestial fantasies? What power could the Count possess to hold me in his thrall? I find it harder each day to recall his appearance, for the forbidden revelations of the night have all but overpowered my sense of reality. And yet his essence is here in the library, imbued within each page of his collection. Perhaps I am not ill, but mad. I fear my senses have awoken too sharply, and my rational mind is reeling with their weight.

I have lost much of my girth in the last six weeks. I have always been thin, but the gaunt image that glares back at me in the glass must surely belong to a sickly, aged relation. I appear as a bundle of blanched sticks by day. I have no strength. I live only for the nights. Beneath the welcoming winter moon my flesh fills, my spirit becomes engorged with an unwholesome strength, and I am sound once more.

I really must try to get away from here.

From the Journal of Jonathan Harker, December 18th 1893
The Count has finally returned, paradoxically bringing fresh spirits into the castle. For the life of me I cannot see how he arrived here, as one section of the pathway below has clearly fallen away into the valley. Last night he came down to dinner, and was in most excellent health. His melancholy

mood had lifted, and he was eager to converse. He seemed physically taller, his posture more erect. His travels had taken him on many adventures, so he informed me as he poured himself a goblet of heavy claret, but now he was properly restored to his ancestral home, and would be in attendance for the conclusion of my work.

I had not told him I was almost done, although I supposed he might have intuited as much from a visit to the library. He asked that we might finish the work together, before the next sunrise. I was very tired – indeed, at the end of the meal I required Klove's helping hand to rise from my chair – but agreed to his demand, knowing that there were but a handful of books left for me to classify.

Soon we were seated in the great library, warming ourselves before the fire, where Klove had set bowls of brandy out for us.

It was when I studied his travelling clothes that I realised the truth. His boots and oil-cloth cape lay across the back of the chair where he had supposedly deposited them on his return. As soon as I saw that the boots were new, the soles polished and unworn, I instinctively intuited that the Count had not been away, and that he had spent the last six months here in the castle with me. I knew I had not imagined what I had seen and done. We sat across from each other in two great armchairs, cradling our brandies, and I nervously pondered my next move, for it was clear to me that the Count could sense my unease.

'I could not approach you, Jonathan,' he explained, divining my thoughts as precisely as an entymologist skewers a wasp. 'You were simply too English, too Christian, too filled with pious platitudes. The reek of your pride was quite overpowering. I saw the prayer book by your bed, the cross around your neck, the dowdy little virgin in your locket. I knew it would be simpler to sacrifice you upon the completion of your task.' His eyes watched mine intently. 'To suck your blood and throw your drained carcass over the battlements to the wolves.' I stared back, refusing to flinch, not daring to move a single nerve-end.

'But,' he continued with a heartfelt sigh, 'I did so need a good man to tend my library. In London I will easily find loyal emissaries to do my bidding and manage my affairs, but the library needs a keeper. Klove has no feeling for language. To be the custodian of such a rare repository of ideas requires tact and intellect. I decided instead to let you discover me, and in doing so, discover yourself. That was the purpose of the library.' He raised his arm, fanning it over the shelves. 'The library made you understand. You see, the pages of the books are poisoned. They just need warm hands to activate them, the hands of the living. The inks leaked into your skin and brought your inner self to life. That is why Klove always wears gloves in this room. You are the only other *living* person here.'

I looked down at my stained and fragrant fingers, noticing for the first time how their skin had withered into purple blotches.

'The books are dangerous to the Christian soul, malignant in their print and in their ideas. Now you have read my various histories, shared my experiences, and know I am corrupt, yet incorruptible. Perhaps you see that we are not so far apart. There is but one barrier left to fall between us.' He had risen from his chair without my noticing, and circled behind me. His icy tapered fingers came to rest on my neck, loosening the stiff white collar of my shirt. I heard a collar stud rattle on to the floor beneath my chair.

'After tonight you will no longer need to use my library for the fulfilment of your fantasies,' he said, his steel-cold mouth descending to my throat, 'for your fantasies are to be made flesh, just as the nights will replace your days.' I felt the first hot stab of pain as his teeth met in my skin. Through a haze I saw the Count wipe his lips with the back of a crimson hand. 'You will make a very loyal custodian, little Englishman,' he said, descending again.

Here the account ends. The library did not accompany Count Dracula on his voyage to England, but remained behind in his castle, where it continued to be tended by Mr Harker until his eventual demise many, many years later.

PHOENIX

It was the year 2000, supposedly the start of everything new, but everything new was already old again. True, the New Year's Eve celebrations had been noisier than most, and a bunch of people had been shot dead downtown, killed by pistols and rifles fired jubilantly in the air.

Brett Ellis had thrown a party in a marquee for two hundred people. Some of the guests were his friends. Most were colleagues. Brett was an American success story; a wealthy, handsome Los Angeles advertising executive who had made his own way up the corporate ladder. Married with a young son, the thirty-two-year-old businessman lived in a beautiful Spanish-style ranch house in the Hollywood Hills with his elegant wife Mara and Davey, who was six.

Brett was a vice-president of merchandising development for one of the new multimedia agencies now controlling American advertising. He had a reputation for being a hard negotiator, and for getting what he wanted. Remembering his own humbler beginnings, Brett simply wanted the best for himself and his family. His life was comfortable and predictable. He did not fear his enemies (of whom he had plenty) because he was at peace with himself and sure of his abilities. He was a little smug, perhaps, a little too complacent. In a town like LA, that didn't exactly make him a criminal.

He certainly never paid much attention to the increasing number of homeless people on the streets, or the escalating incidents of violence he saw on the news. In his determination to assure himself that life was perfect, he had even managed to turn a blind eye to the obvious evidence that his wife had taken a lover.

Then one day, Brett became aware that someone was following him, a shabby little man in a beaten-up red Volkswagen. The car was parked outside his office for a whole day, and parked outside his house while Brett and his wife were throwing a birthday party for Davey. When Brett ran out to speak to the driver, he pulled away from the kerb with a squeal of tyres.

Brett called the cops. He was not prepared to take chances. He gave the police a full description of the man, but they told him they couldn't do anything unless he had been physically threatened. They had bigger problems to deal with. There were riots brewing once more in downtown LA, had been ever since New Year's Eve.

Brett lay in wait for his stalker. He finally trapped him one evening when the day's suffocating heat broke in a cataclysmic rainstorm. Mara had taken Davey to the movies in Westwood. She hated driving anywhere in the rain. Brett was not sure she knew how to operate the windshield wipers. He saw the VW parked across the street when he got up to fetch a soda, and ran outside in his socks, surprising the driver, who was dozing at the wheel.

Frightened, the old man told Brett his name was Elias. He worked at the Church of the Phoenix downtown, and he had been following Brett for several months.

'What the hell do you think you're doing?' shouted Brett, losing his cool. His socks were soaked, and the stormy weather had given him a headache. When the old man refused to answer, Brett reached through the open window of the car and grabbed him by the collar. 'I swear I'll break your neck. Do you know what this is doing to me?'

'I don't mean any harm,' begged the oldster. 'I have to be here. I have to watch over you.'

'What are you talking about?' He loosened his grip on the shirt, frightened that he might really break the frail old man's neck.

'You're one of the Chosen Ones,' Elias replied, 'as inscribed by the prophecies of Nostradamus and the Book of Daniel, and revealed in the doctrines of the Phoenix.'

Brett should have walked away then, but he didn't. He hesitated a moment too long, and ended up staying to listen. The Chosen Ones, explained the old man, were a handful of decent law-abiding people who would lead the church – and indeed the whole world – into a pure new era of goodness and natural harmony. Clues and signs in certain church texts led the way to Brett's door. There were other Chosen Ones in the world who would help him to achieve this grand goal of world improvement at the start of the millennium, but he had to be patient. Perhaps Brett would like to come along to the church some time and join in one of the services – they would be very honoured to have him. In fact, some of the hymns were about him.

'Just how am I supposed to change the world?' he asked against his better judgement. It was kind of flattering, the idea of being worshipped.

'Well see, it's not possible to reveal the answer yet,' said Elias. 'We're still waiting for a further sign.'

Elias explained that he was honoured to have been chosen to monitor Brett's movements, and to make sure that no harm came to him before his appointed time to act. In the eyes of his church, it was a privileged position to be in. He told Brett to think of him as a guardian angel.

Clearly, Elias was a nut.

But, Brett decided, he was a harmless one. It fed his ego to know that people were singing his praises, even if they too were all nuts. No-one ever sang his praises at work. However, he warned the little man that if he caught sight of him again, he would call the police to the church and have him arrested for harassment.

'Go on, get out of here,' said Brett, releasing his grip. Elias started the engine. Before he drove off, he leaned from the window and handed Brett a card with the address of the church printed on it. 'You must watch for the signs that you have been chosen,' he exclaimed. 'They will be natural symbols of peace and harmony, and they'll be surrounding you in ever greater force until the appointed time!'

'And don't let me catch you near my property again!' Brett called back. Sure, he thought, shaking his head, I'll keep an eye out. Meanwhile, stay the hell away from me.

Over the next few weeks, he worked long, late nights on a TV campaign his team was developing for a new kind of cola. The primary-coloured commercials they produced together were vacuous and irritating, and somehow seemed to provide an ironic comment on his empty life. Lately he noticed Mara was seeing more of her fancy man, even though she insisted she was visiting a friend in the Valley. After the campaign was delivered, he decided to take the family on vacation to Hawaii. Hiring a yacht, they headed out into the seas around Maui, even though Mara hated the ocean. Brett hoped the enforced intimacy of the boat might help them get back together.

One morning he was swimming aimlessly in the calm clear waters when his wife leaned over from the deck railing and called urgently to him. 'For God's sake, Brett,' she shouted in agitation, 'don't move a muscle!'

All around him, numbering in their thousands, poisonous jellyfish had gathered. The Portuguese men o' war gently bobbed in gelatine star clusters. Gingerly, he pushed his left arm through the water, nudging them aside. Then his right. He made no sudden movements. It was important to do nothing that would scare them into stinging.

Incredibly, he managed to reach the boat completely unharmed. The family watched as the jellyfish gently dispersed like an expanding universe.

Other oddities occurred that spring. One night they were drawn from the house by a scrabbling noise above them, and found birds of every imaginable species landing on the roof. Two days later, a vast brown swarm of bees surrounded the car as he waited in traffic at the corner of La Brea and Melrose. Other drivers got out of their vehicles to watch and take photographs. The bees massed noisily, dancing back and forth on the hood of the Mercedes before dispersing into the sky. Shiny-backed beetles swarmed in the basement, much to Mara's consternation. She shivered in horror as their iridescent bodies rippled crossing the floor. 'Looks like you've developed an affinity with nature, honey,' she half-joked.

It wasn't just living creatures that were affected, either. Technology started behaving strangely, too. Brett's infrared laptop began to pick up odd scrambled signals whenever he was around. One morning it beamed a huge file of biblical gibberish into the RAM of his office computers, crashing the system. The next day he was working on the laptop when his spreadsheet fuzzed away into the ether, to be replaced by a badly drawn image of a bird bursting into a blaze of flame. The repair shop could find nothing wrong with it. They suggested that maybe someone was playing a practical joke.

The episode with Elias had itself become something of a joke in the Ellis household, but it was one that stopped being funny the very next night. Brett had given up waiting for Mara to come home and was getting ready for bed. He was standing in his darkened bedroom when he suddenly had the feeling he was being watched. Pulling his T-shirt over his head, he walked to the windows and looked down into the scrubland beyond the back yard. As his eyes adjusted to the dark, he saw dozens of people standing among the trees and bushes, motionless and silent, staring up at his house. In the flickering shadows they looked like statues. Presumably they were all members of this crazy church. The sight chilled him to the bone. For the first time he felt that something genuinely weird was going on. Furious, he rang the number Elias had given him.

Over at the Church of the Phoenix, Elias answered the call.

'Keep your congregation the hell away from my house,' warned Brett, 'or I'll get a restraining order put on you and your "church". I'd like to know what your leader thinks about this.'

'We have no leader.' The old man spoke so softly it was difficult to hear him. 'I know it must all seem very strange to you.'

'Then perhaps you'd like to explain what's going on.'

'I can't talk on this line. There's someone else in the building, and I think he's listening in. I'm in great danger, Mr Ellis. I've received the true sign at last, only . . .' he paused uncomfortably, 'only it wasn't at all the sign I'd been expecting, and now I think something terrible is going to happen. I've been so blind. I've been used, Mr Ellis, duped. My life may even be at risk. I need your help. I can't trust the congregation here any more. Please meet me somewhere and I'll explain.'

'I'm not going to meet you, not now, not ever,' Brett replied, slamming the receiver down, even though Elias sounded genuinely terrified.

On the TV news the next morning, the Ellis family heard how a man's body had been found hacked to pieces and thrown in a dumpster. A short-order cook had discovered the corpse in the car park of a sleazy strip-joint near the airport. As they watched the screen, a photograph of Elias appeared inset in the corner.

Feeling partly to blame for the death of a man who only

wanted to watch over him, Brett decided he had to do something. He did not want to spend several hours in a police interview room. The LAPD still had a long way to go to win respect from the local populace. Instead, he decided to head downtown and pay a visit to the church.

As his shiny blue Mercedes coasted the intersections across town, Brett began to realise how far away he had grown from his roots. He never visited areas like this any more. His life was a rat-run from home to the agency and back. The strangeness of the streets and the people bothered him. He eventually located the clapboard church on a dusty litter-strewn backstreet. It was one of many fringe denominations that existed in the run-down Spanish area. Apart from two teenaged boys hanging out beside an abandoned truck, there was no-one around. Brett double-checked the alarm on his Mercedes.

The door of the church was open. Inside it was clean and smartly kept, lit by natural light alone. An attractive young woman in jeans and a white T-shirt stepped out of the shadows by the vestry, making him start.

'I'm Lisa Farrell,' she said, brushing her hair from her eyes and shaking his hand. Her voice surprised him. She had a middle-class English accent. 'I know who you are. We all do. Come in back, I'm making some tea.'

'I only recently joined the Phoenix,' she explained as they sat across from each other, sipping from hot mugs. 'I have to get this tea sent out from London. You can't buy it here, and it still doesn't taste right because of the water.'

'I heard what happened to Elias.'

'It's a terrible world, Mr Ellis.' She shook her head in bewilderment and sipped. 'The police say they have some leads, but I'll be very surprised if they do.'

'Aren't you rather a long way from home?'

'My father invited me over. He lives here with his new wife. Originally I had only planned to study Phoenix for a sociology project, but I came to believe in quite a bit of what they were teaching.'

'And what is that, exactly?'

'Elias and his followers believe in the eventual heavenly redemption of mankind. From their own "scriptures" and other archive sources, they've selected a group of people who are somehow going to lead the world into a new dawn of enlightenment.'

'How convenient. Just in time for the new millennium.'

'That's right,' she said, missing the irony in his voice, 'commencing in this year of 2000. They have dates for each of the big events, worked out accurately to the hour.'

'I guess they failed to predict the murder of one of their members. Tell me something I'd like to know, Lisa. Why have I been selected for a part in all of this? I'm an advertising executive, not a politician. Even if such a crackpot theory had some grain of truth, how could I have any influence on world events? I met Mel Gibson once at a premiere. That's about as far as I go in the "six degrees of separation" chain.'

'Well, there you have me. Elias didn't tell his congregation everything.' If she didn't know, she didn't seem particularly curious, either. 'Your future has already been decided for you, Mr Ellis, just as it has been decided for me and everyone else. All you have to do is go along with it. Decisions will be made for you that are entirely beyond your control.'

Lisa did not look or sound crazy. Despite his scepticism at her blind faith, he found himself drawn to her. She was very attractive. She replaced her mug and rose, holding out her hand once more. 'Now, if you'll excuse me, it's been a long day, what with the police . . .'

As he left, looking back at the shabby little church from his car, he noticed the iron phoenix on the roof that acted as a weather vane. He did not expect to see it, or Lisa, again.

But the strands of a strange fate were shaping themselves around Brett.

For some time he had been thinking of moving the family out of Los Angeles and starting afresh elsewhere. His company had a vacancy in their Chicago office. The move would force Mara into a decision about their relationship. Brett discussed the possibility of a transfer with his boss, and two weeks later was in the middle of making all the appropriate arrangements when his son suffered an odd accident. Davey was kicking a football around in Griffith Park when a bird became trapped in a wire-mesh compound where leaves were being burned.

Trying to rescue the panicked creature, whose wings were alight, the boy's face and arms were seared. His nanny, who had only stepped away from his side for a moment, managed to drag him clear of the fire, saving his life.

The doctors told Brett that his son could not be moved from his hospital bed. The family's relocation would have to be delayed, or possibly even cancelled. Brett resigned himself to staying in LA, at least for the immediate future.

It was an odd feeling, that his life was somehow no longer his own. He could find no way to explain it, nor his decision to contact Lisa Farrell and ask her about Elias. Specifically, he wanted to know what the old man foresaw that made him locate Brett in the first place.

Lisa asked if they could meet at her apartment; she had something to show him. She lived in a rented mock-Tudor Santa Monica condo of astonishing ugliness just behind the freeway. Here they knelt on the kitchen floor going through stacks of Elias's documents and hard-copy computer files. Brett was amazed that the old-timer had even known how to switch on a computer.

'All churches are on-line these days,' Lisa explained. 'You should take a look at the fringes of cult worship on the internet some time. Talk about scary. There's a group of obsessives who translate prophecies, supposed "seers" who monitor signs of the coming cataclysmic change. They mostly preach new age gobbledygook, but there's this one priest among them who refers to the Book of Daniel, the only book of the apocalypse in the Old Testament – Revelations is in the New – and he points out that Daniel dreamed of four beasts who came to lay waste to the peoples of the earth. He and Elias found corroborative evidence from a variety of independent sources pointing to four people who will eventually change the fate of the modern world. Not by healing or restoring faith, though, but by "a cleansing test of righteous fire".'

'Are you trying to tell me . . .'

'That's right, Mr Ellis,' said Lisa with a smile. 'You're one of the four horsemen of the Apocalypse.'

'The sixth chapter of the last book of the New Testament, The Revelation of St John the Divine, tells of the seven-sealed scroll held in God's right hand. When the first seal is opened the four horsemen will appear, and represent the hardships the world must face before judgement, specifically conquest (pestilence), famine, war and death. The horses are white, red, black and yellow-green.

'The world as we know it will then cease, wiped free from the poisonous effects of humanity so that life has a chance to grow anew. That's why nature has been reacting so favourably to you, Mr Ellis.' Father Matthew paused before a bush of English tea roses and checked the buds for damage. The manicured emerald lawns behind the church seemed to be the only green life left in this part of the San Bernadino Valley. The priest was clearly ill, and walked with difficulty. His skin was the colour of the pale dead petals that littered his rose beds. 'The final cataclysm will be triggered by events occurring to four people in four different locations,' he continued. 'We know that one of those locations is Los Angeles. Even the stars foretell this. The area is pinpointed by everything from ancient biblical scrolls to NASA maps.' He paused for breath, leaning on Lisa's arm. 'Any one of the acts occurring around the world could lead to a catastrophic disaster, but all four deeds must occur in order for the conditions of the Apocalypse to be fulfilled. The writings are most specific on this point.'

Brett tried to tell himself that this was absurd, insane. But facts fitted with a terrible inevitability. This was the news the priest had broken to Elias that had led to his death; that he was not guarding a latter-day saint but protecting someone destined to participate in the world's destruction.

'If you and Elias knew about me, who are the other three chosen "horsemen"?'

'One is a woman working for the World Health Organisation in Africa. Another is a European minister of trade, currently residing in Brussels. The third is a Chinese military leader.'

'Then I'm the odd one out.'

'It would appear so.'

'Who do you think killed Elias?'

'When I told him the truth, that he was protecting a man who would eventually be instrumental in destroying civilisation, he was horrified by his misunderstanding of events. Obviously he was murdered by someone who wants to protect you.'

'Your life could also be in danger.'

'I suppose so, but I don't think you'll hurt me. I haven't very long to live.' The priest guided them to an arbour shaded from the fierce valley heat, sat in his favourite armchair and fell into an uneasy doze.

Mara simply refused to listen to her husband, citing his behaviour over the last few weeks as a form of mental break-down. 'For God's sake, will you just listen to yourself?' she cried, pacing the lounge. 'You're talking about astrology, predictions of fate! It's ludicrous, Brett! Your son is lying upstairs in a state of trauma and you're running about all over town taking advice from these – cranks!' A sudden thought occurred to her. 'Are you giving them money? Are they getting funds out of you for all this mumbo-jumbo?'

'You've seen the signs, Mara! You've been there when it happened!'

'I want you to see someone, Brett, get some professional help. Until you do, I can't talk to you. You're not making any sense. Try to see things from my point of view. I'm as upset about Davey as you, but this is – no way to react.'

'I have to go on with this, Mara.' He shrugged, picking up his jacket. 'I believe it. I just know it's all true.'

That night he stayed in a West Hollywood hotel. The next morning, he began researching the church's accumulated evidence in order to discover how the other three 'horsemen' might unwittingly change the world.

The information was surprisingly easy to come by. All three cases were well-documented in the international press. It was simply that nobody had thought of connecting them.

The Chinese military leader was a member of the new hard right, an anti-semitic fascist currently precipitating a dangerous conflict with Russia and the USA over failure to declare unofficial chemical warfare sites – there was no doubt that he was the Horseman of War.

The Belgian minister had agreed to allow the creation of an amalgamation of charities that would distribute food mountains to starving areas – but the man he had gullibly entrusted with the task was a crook, now facing trial. The scheme had gone broke, stranding millions without food – he had to be the Horseman of Famine.

The woman in Africa was a doctor's assistant, moving from town to town trying to cure sickness, but without realising it she had been causing fresh outbreaks of a particularly virulent form of bilharzia, the second most widespread illness in the world. It was a water-borne germ, and she had been discovered accidentally spreading the lethal new strain as her medical convoy moved across the plains, their jeep-tracks filling with water, the virus following in the path it created. Newspapers reported that the disease had caused such depopulation in certain areas that opportunistic dictatorships were moving into power – the poor woman who unwittingly started this was without doubt the Horseman of Conquest.

Which made Brett Ellis the Horseman of Death.

Brett realised that the church's idea of a 'fresh start' for the world involved burning away the existing debris of humanity. According to Father Matthew, there were plenty of priests who were perfectly happy with the idea. No wonder Elias could be so easily sacrificed. Uppermost in Brett's mind was the need to discover what single act he could be responsible for that would lead to destruction on a massive scale, but it was hopeless. He had no idea where to begin. He tried using news networks sited on the internet. He trawled the LA newspaper archives. He attempted to check out the other three 'horsemen', and even managed to reach the medical team travelling with the WHO, but they were unable to return any of his calls. The other two were even less reachable. For all of the world's advances in global communication, it was still virtually impossible for an ordinary citizen to access people in power.

At night he studied Elias's teachings. According to the church's documentation the Awakening of Daniel – the final dying moment of the human world – was due to take place at midnight just five days from the present date.

Tired and heartsick, he was preparing for bed when Mara knocked on the door of his study. 'I thought you might be interested in the health of your son,' she said, remaining on the far side of the room, her hands at her sides. 'The doctor came while you were out. Davey's going to be fine. The shock to his system is subsiding, and it seems likely he'll make a full recovery. I want to take him away from here, Brett. And I don't want you to stop me.'

'I won't do that if you tell me where you're going,' said her husband. 'I don't want to lose what we have as a family.'

'It's a little late for that, don't you think? You don't need us, Brett, you never have. You only ever think about yourself.' Her hands shook. She left the room before she started crying.

She and Davey left the house three days later, on a warm autumn morning with the faintest hint of winter chill in the shadows.

He tried calling Lisa half a dozen times, but there seemed to be something wrong with her phone. In the afternoon he drove over to her apartment and found the front door wide open. The hallway was deserted. It was the kind of condominium where nobody ever saw or heard anything. In the bedroom a chair was upturned, and clothes were hanging from closet drawers. There was broken glass on the floor of the kitchen. It didn't take a genius to work out that Lisa had either been abducted or had left in a hell of a hurry. He wondered if the same zealots who had murdered Elias had now made off with the old man's most attractive disciple. He called the police on his mobile, told them what he thought had happened and asked them to check out the building. He refused to leave his name and address, which was stupid; they could easily trace his mobile.

He arrived back at his house to find the lounge filled with the members of the Church of the Phoenix. The maid had let them in. The praying men and women were now wearing white robes, in accordance with their instructions from the Book of Revelations. There were even little kids draped in cut-off bedsheets. Their numbers had certainly grown. It seemed more and more people were being converted as the foretold time approached.

'Join us!' they cried as he tried to disperse them. 'Stay and pray! Stay and pray!' Listening to their cries made him realise that there was a simple way for him to defeat the prophecy and forestall his fate. All he had to do was leave town. He couldn't influence history if he wasn't in the foretold place at the right time, could he?

Shoving the tiniest bedsheeted members of the church from his front door, he returned to the lounge and tried to call the police, but all the LAPD emergency lines were busy. Next he tried to purchase a flight out of the city, only to find that his credit card numbers had apparently been changed on the booking computer.

'That's impossible!' he complained to the girl at the airline office. 'Check them again, will you?' As he held on, he accessed his personal identification numbers on his home PC files. They all seemed in order. But as he watched, the numbers of his accounts flickered into serials of random lettering, and these in turn were replaced with a single word – PHOENIX.

He stared at the word in disbelief. It was as if everyone and everything pointed in one direction, toward the fulfilment of his destiny, no matter how terrible that might prove to be.

Stopping only to throw some clothes into a suitcase, he descended to the garage and revved up his Mercedes. There was more than one way to get out of town. He drove down from the hills, across Hollywood heading for the Santa Monica Freeway, and was just approaching the on-ramp when he saw a motorcycle cop approaching in his rear-view mirror. The cop gave a whoop of his siren and made a gesture to pull over.

Brett wearily coasted the car to the side of the road and turned off the engine. The cop dismounted and approached, shaking his pant-legs free, taking his time.

'I wasn't speeding, officer,' Brett called out, leaning from the window.

'Maybe not, sir, but you weren't telling anyone where you

were going, either. You just changed lanes back there without any indication.'

'Did I? I'm sorry, I didn't realise – I'm in kind of a hurry . . .'

The cop made no move to write him a ticket, but just stood there, staring down at the car. His glasses reflected Brett's sweating face. 'I'm afraid I'm going to have to take you in,' he said finally.

'What do you mean?' he asked, incredulous. 'Can't you just write me out – '

' "*And I looked, and beheld a pale horse,*" ' said the cop, ' "*and his name that sat on him was Death.*" Get out of the car, sir.'

Brett had only a second to make his decision. He slammed his foot on the accelerator and fishtailed on to the freeway ramp in a plume of blue smoke before the cop had a chance to run back to his bike. As he tacked across the busy lanes and the Mercedes' powerful engine gave a guttural roar, he knew he had to get out of town fast, but how? Heading down the freeway, it seemed as if everyone was watching him. The guy in shades in the convertible, the gardeners in the truck with rakes on the roof, the family of Born-Agains in their RV, everyone was goading him on. Who could he trust? Worse still, it looked as if the other drivers were laughing at him, knowing that he couldn't escape. Was he losing his mind?

There was no time to think. Behind he could see the flashing blue lights of two motorcycle cops as they wove smartly through the traffic toward him. Ahead, two lanes of the freeway were closed for repairs. Pulsing electric arrows were redirecting columns of vehicles. Already, the traffic was starting to back up. He slowed down and swung hard right on to a downtown off-ramp, his tyres screaming as they fought to grip the edge of the curve. Before the bikes had a chance to catch up, he pulled down into the shadows beneath the freeway bridge and killed the engine. Dust sprayed around the car. He stayed there for some while with his head resting on the wheel, sweat dripping into his eyes.

Brett punched out the number of his office and waited for his secretary to answer, but the call was switched over to her voicemail. That was strange – Irene hardly ever left her post during the day. Suspicious, he quickly rang off. He rolled the Mercedes into a backstreet and tried to formulate a game plan. He had no functioning credit cards and about forty dollars in his pocket. It was 11.45 a.m. He had until midnight to prevent the prophecy of the Book of Daniel from fulfilling itself.

The owner of the used car lot was naturally suspicious, but not so suspicious that he was going to pass up the bargain of a lifetime. After all, the guy's papers were all in order, every Mercedes service scrupulously entered in the logbook. If he wanted to trade it for a clapped-out '79 Oldsmobile Cutlass convertible and a fistful of bills, why argue?

Brett headed for the airport in his downgraded new car, tearing the price stickers off as he drove, but the freeway was at a standstill. It seemed as if the whole city was gridlocked. In desperation he considered driving to Long Beach and chartering a boat, but even that option proved impossible. The traffic was flowing in one direction only, and it was not the direction he wanted to go. Resigned to being grounded in LA, he figured that the best thing would be to find Lisa; she seemed to be the only one who might have an idea of what would happen to him. As he headed into Miracle Mile, he was amazed to see the church's symbol painted everywhere – on buildings, cars, sidewalks, even on people's clothing. The cryptic symbol looked more and more like a giant bird in a ring of flame. It was as if the entire city was going crazy, as if everyone wanted this cleansing apocalypse to occur.

The Cutlass coasted past crowds of worshippers gathered along the sides of the road. They made the salute of the church as he passed, the sign of Daniel Waking. It was almost as if they had been expecting him to pass along this route. He tried tuning the radio. LAX was shut for some reason. Airport security hoped to have the terminals open soon. According to an international news report, China had made a threatening gesture toward the West, expelling all US diplomats. A local news report said that mobs were stoning the office buildings in Century City because they were shrines to Mammon, places that would not survive the coming cleansing. The news announcers didn't even sound that worried.

He parked the car at a motel and took a walk through the thronging streets. A group of teenagers stood huddled together in the distance. As he approached, he saw that they were cutting the sign of Daniel into their right hands. At the next corner a sea of bloody palms passed lightly over him in a grisly wave of worship. He pushed against the rising tide of fanatics, all moving in a single direction, and passed a crowd gathered around a TV store window. On the multi-screens they stared at horrific footage of people rioting for food in the East; it appeared that the work of at least one of the horsemen had been carried out successfully. A newsreader announced that the new hard-right Chinese leader had taken advantage of this growing dissatisfaction with Western policies to stage a military coup against Russia, and would challenge the USA over the secret missile sites; clearly, a second horseman's work was paying off.

When the transmission fuzzed and dispersed across twenty identical screens, the international news footage was replaced by one of the 'lifestyle' cola commercials produced by Brett's company. The crowd hissed angrily.

The phonecall startled him. He felt in his jacket for the mobile and checked the number, but failed to recognise it.

'Brett, it's Lisa.'

'Lisa! Where are you? I went over to your apartment. I was worried sick.'

'I had to leave quickly – one of the neighbours – it was becoming too dangerous to stay there. I tried calling you but there was something wrong with the phone system.'

'I know, I had the same problem. Where are you now?'

'At my father's building downtown. There are mobs of people outside, just hanging around the entrance. There's been no trouble yet, but it's only a matter of time. Everyone's wearing these *robes*.'

'Give me your address, I'll come and get you.'

He reached the building a little before three, entering the deserted building from the underground carpark. The silence came as a shock after the chanting in the streets. Carefully, he made his way to the seventh floor. Lisa was there to meet him at the elevator bank, and rushed thankfully into his arms. She was clearly terrified.

'The world's going mad,' she said, 'I've been watching the news broadcasts. There was a report from the WHO about the new strain of bilharzia spreading overseas. All of the horsemen have been called into action except you.'

'In a few hours this – celestial deadline – is going to be met, and I still don't know what role I'm supposed to play.'

From below came a distant crash of sheet glass. 'We have to get out of LA,' he said, taking her hand. 'I have a car in the basement.' He looked around at the deserted office floor. 'Where the hell is everybody?'

Lisa shrugged as she stepped into the lift. 'The police chief has declared a state of emergency, and at the same time he's appealing for calm, don't you love this town? Everyone's been sent home. I heard someone say there are roadblocks all around the city. We'll need to cut through back roads. How's your driving?'

'Listen, Lisa, maybe you should leave by yourself. You're in danger so long as you're near me.'

She grabbed his hand and pulled him into the elevator. 'I'm not afraid of being with you.'

The new religious zealots were terrific with matters philosophical, but not so hot at building roadblocks. The Oldsmobile crashed through the oildrum-and-fencepost cordons that had been set up, and soon headed out on to the freeway, which was now curiously deserted. The road ahead was wide open and clear all the way. Los Angeles was disappearing in their rear-view mirror. As the sun started to set, Brett began to believe that the final part of the prophecy would not be fulfilled, and that they had averted the end of the world.

They kept the radio on as they drove. The US military had issued China with a deadline to declare all covert missile sites and chemical weapons factories. Clinton was demanding an immediate answer. The roads remained strangely empty. As night descended, the suburbs fell away and the desert appeared. On the other side of Palm Springs, Lisa took over the driving so that Brett could reread Elias's notes.

'We're going to need gas soon. Can't I slow down for a while?' she asked. 'This wheel is making my arms stiff. Surely we're safe now.'

'Use the cruise control. And keep your eyes on the road.'

As they drove, they saw vast burning pyres in the hills, signs that the population had instinctively prepared themselves for a cataclysmic event. He counted over a dozen glowing patches on the horizon.

The car radio was now their only link with the outside world. Its announcers continued to report on the deteriorating situation between the world powers. China had its missiles trained on Russia and was prepared to use them if their demands were not met.

The road ahead appeared ever more brightly lit. There were torches lining either side of the freeway, like burning spears on the approach to an ancient city. Puzzled, they sped on past the darkened countryside below.

'We have to stay in the desert until the deadline has passed,' said Brett. 'It's the only way to be sure. The priest said all four horsemen have to act or the Apocalypse can't occur. Where are we now?'

'The last time I looked we were about thirty miles east of some town called Plaster City. I can't read the map in this light and the glovebox bulb isn't working. Where on earth did you get this car?'

Around the next bend, crimson accident flares were spread before a stack of crushed vehicles spread across the road.

'Shit! Hold tight!'

Slamming on the brakes, Brett carommed the car side-on into the flames and veered off at a fast-approaching junction of the freeway. Suddenly there were people lining either side of the connecting road, waving, cheering and making the hand-salute of the church. It felt as though Brett and Lisa were making their entry into Rome. In fact, they were about to enter the city of Phoenix.

The car radio had been operating below Brett's hearing threshold for several miles. Now it boomed into fresh life as the announcer spoke of one last hope for peace; a few minutes ago the Chinese had said that if they were provided with a positive, conciliatory gesture from the leader of the US military within the hour, they would halt their planned strike action on the Russian seaboard. So there was a slim chance of salvation!

'Did you hear that? There's still a hope!' He turned to Lisa, and one glance at her unguarded face told him all he needed to know.

No-one could look so disappointed at the news. He had

been duped. She had deliberately led him out here. She saw him looking and stared blankly back.

'This is where you need to be in order to fulfil the prophecy,' she said simply.

He looked up at the road ahead, and saw that once again they had entered a deserted stretch of highway. A sign above him read YOU ARE NOW ENTERING PHOENIX CITY LIMITS. Puzzled, he accelerated – and suddenly on the ramp below the car he saw dozens of police motorbikes crossing in formation. A motorcade was passing beneath the empty road. Brett started to brake, trying to make sense of what he saw, but with a feral cry Lisa stamped her shoe over his, forcing his foot down. The Oldsmobile rocketed ahead to vault the off-ramp barrier and smash down on to the central passing limo of the motorcade, flipping both vehicles and turning one into a thundering ball of flame. A roar of triumphant applause grew from the reappearing crowds.

Hurled from the Oldsmobile, Brett spiralled away in a bellowing sea of flame-lit faces.

Slowly, painfully, he returned to consciousness.

He was stripped to the waist, lying on a warm granite slab that formed a dais in the middle of a field near the freeway. He was surrounded by thousands of celebrating people. Fires filled the horizon. He could smell barbecued chicken in the air.

Lisa, Mara and his son checked with each other to see who would go first, then stepped bashfully forward in turn. Davey's arms were unbandaged, and completely unmarked. He gave a Candid Camera kind of smile and shrugged. Brett's work colleagues were there. So were most of his friends and family.

'You did it, Brett!' Mara cried happily. 'You fulfilled your destiny as the Horseman of Death!' There were whoops and hollers. Everyone was joyous. The noise was like a hundred sitcom audiences cheering the entrance of a sexy woman.

'I don't understand,' he croaked weakly.

They tried to explain that he had hit the motorcade bringing the military heads back from Nevada. A simple accident on the road to Phoenix – that was all he had been needed for. They all talked at once, and weren't sure if he could hear them.

Now the only remaining moderate military leader was dead, Lisa explained. No answer could go back to the Chinese. She felt bad about killing Elias, but he'd had a good life. Hadn't it all turned out for the best? She poured him a plastic beaker of Californian champagne, but he knocked it out of her hand.

The apocalypse ran a little late. It was some time after midnight that the sky from the East began to light up with the arcing trails of the arriving missiles. Lisa gripped Brett's arm and told him not to worry.

'Your destiny isn't ours,' she said sadly. 'You and your three partners will live on, through destruction, death and decomposition. You'll see it through – right through – to a time of rebirth and regeneration. Then you'll be released from your earthly duty, to return to dust.'

As the world erupted around him, Brett demanded to know why he was chosen, out of anyone in the world.

Lisa stroked his face gently. 'Don't you know that the greatest harm can only be carried out by the blind?' she whispered, kissing his forehead as the cleansing conflagration filled the sky.

Brett stood naked at the centre of the blinding sun, the brightest light in the universe, his limbs outstretched, the living personification of Leonardo Da Vinci's drawing of Man. Like the phoenix he would die and be reborn in flame.

Around him he could see four galloping stallions of fire, racing like missiles. And through them, the merest glimpse of something else, the world far into the future, a world that was green and clean and pure, ready to begin again.

UNFORGOTTEN

It cannot think, fanciful to imagine it could, for how would so many millions of lives make themselves heard, distilled into a single voice? But if – just if – there was such a thing as a collective intelligence, what would it be saying now, the voice of London?

During the trial of Captain Clarke at the Old Bailey in 1750, the court became so hot that the windows had to be opened, and the foul germ-laden stench from nearby Newgate Prison that blew in killed everyone sitting on the window-side of the court – all forty-four people.

'How much do they want for the sale?'

'Three hundred and seventy grand. That's what they figure it's worth at today's prices.'

'I'm in this business to make a living, not to be bent over a table and fucked stupid.'

'I'm sorry, that's what their man told me to tell you.'

'Well, you can tell them – ' The door opened behind Marrick and his exhausted secretary stuck her head into the room. Marrick nearly fell off his chair trying to see who it was.

'For fuck's sake, Doris,' he exploded, 'will you stop creeping around like Marley's fucking ghost?'

'I'm sorry, Mr Marrick, I'm about to vanish for the night,

and your wife is here.' Doris tossed the information into the room like a lit firecracker and beat a hasty retreat.

Marrick banged his chair upright. 'Harrods must have declined her credit cards again. This is all I fucking need. Excuse me, gentlemen. Jonathan, see if you can talk some fucking sense into the sales agent. Try to make him see that I'm not a completely heartless bastard. You know – lie.' The door slammed and he was gone in a cloud of acrid cigar smoke.

Jonathan Laine didn't much like his boss; the man had no respect for anything or anyone. Adrian Marrick trampled a path through life in a cheap suit, shouting and shoving all the way. The technique worked, up to a point, but Jonathan could not see the company expanding beyond this dingy Holborn office. There were barriers of class in the city, invisible lines that could not be crossed by a marauding loud-mouthed oik from south London.

Jonathan was not complaining; at the age of fifty-seven he was at least still employed and making a subsistence wage. His boss was just past his twenty-fourth birthday, and although it sometimes seemed strange to be working for such a young man, Marrick possessed a cunning far beyond his years. He could even be fun in an appalling way – chain-smoking, swearing, drinking and dealing through the property market, and he was a good teacher so long as you remembered to isolate the immoral and illegal elements of his advice. His observations about his fellow man could be jaw-droppingly crass, and yet there was often a horrible accuracy to them. He was part of a new generation whose tastes were decided by price. 'You owe us, old sport,' he would say in one of his magnanimous after-dinner moods. 'We're burying the past, chucking away the old rules. Giving commerce a chance to breathe.'

Jonathan considered himself to be a reasonably moral man. He had never meant to end up working in a place like this.

The pleasures of his life stemmed from peaceful pursuits, his interests inclined to classical studies. He had always held an unformulated plan in his head, to succeed as some kind of architectural historian. Instead he had married young, looked after his parents, raised a child, suffered a nervous breakdown. He had been sidetracked by his need to make money, distracted by the fuss of living, misrouted from his original goal. And now, here he was in the centre of one of the most historically important cities in the world, and the only work he had found since the death of Connie was in property speculation, helping to asset-strip and destroy the very thing he cared about most dearly. A typical Gemini trait, he thought, to be both destroyer and creator. Well, one day he would find a way to repay the debt, redress the balance. Until then . . .

He turned back to a desk smothered in unprocessed documents. Darren, the office junior, was laboriously clipping surveyors' reports together and arranging them in files. Today's problem had been growing for a while now. The building in question was a run-down Victorian house presently occupied by an electrical appliance contractor. The freehold was owned by the Japanese property conglomerate Dasako, and the lease had been granted on a short-term basis that was now reaching an end. Jonathan's case notes ran to dozens of pages. Marrick was desperate to purchase the building outright because it stood between two other properties he owned under different company titles. Individually neither was worth much above land value, but collectively they represented a highly attractive proposition. Jonathan assumed that ownership of the third property would increase access to the other two, but Marrick had never explained why he wanted to own such a large chunk of property. He never explained anything. He was guided by an unerring instinct for making money.

Jonathan was sure that Dasako had no knowledge of Marrick's involvement in the surrounding offices; the names on the company records would mean nothing to them. Even so, their asking price for the soon-to-be-vacant property was way too high. The area would not support such a valuation. There had to be a reason for pricing themselves out of the market, but what could it be?

'Tell you what,' said Marrick in the pub later that evening, 'I've got an idea,' and he threw Jonathan a crooked grin which normally meant something dishonest was coming. He made a meaty fist around the handle of his pint, his rings glittering like gold knuckle-dusters. 'Get me the plans for the city block, would you?'

'The whole block?'

'Yeah. There's something I remember seeing the last time I went over the place. I've got a feeling we can stitch up these tossers without moving a fucking muscle.' He drained his glass and banged it down, then felt his jacket for his cigars. 'Three hundred and seventy K for an almost derelict building, bollocks! I know their fucking game.'

'You think they're going to find a new tenant?'

'Nope,' said Marrick, lighting up an absurdly large cigar. 'Of course not. Crafty bastards have other plans. They're gonna get it listed and restore all the original features.' He sucked noisily at the stogie.

'How can you be so sure?' asked Jonathan, shifting beyond his boss's smoke-ring range.

'Ah, well you see, while you're still snuggled up in bed in your pyjamas dreaming about retirement, I'm up with the fucking larks collecting information, and I hear that Dasako are currently employing the services of a design company that specialises in restaurants. Fucking great big Conran-style eateries that seat 700 diners at a time. If they get a restaurant in that space and it's a success, we'll never fucking get them out.'

'So what do you propose to do?' asked Jonathan. He ran

a hand through his straggling grey hair and waited while his employer picked flakes of tobacco from his lip.

'I'm gonna buy 'em out, pull the whole lot down and resell. It's worth fuck-all as it is. The upper floors are falling apart. Just get me the plans of the block.'

The teeming humanity that passes through London as the centuries rise and fall! The sheer weight of life borne by such a small area of land! The city transforms itself from a Roman capital with an amphitheatre, forum and basilica, its Temples of Mithras and Diana giving way to the spired cathedrals of Christianity. Walls, gates and defences rise, parish churches are built over Saxon villages, medieval commerce packs the streets with wood-beamed houses, and the kaleidoscope of history spins wildly on through coronations, insurrections and disharmonies, mutiny and jubilation eliding past, present and future. And through these pululating voices one word is heard most clearly; Charles I, stepping up to his execution before jeering crowds in Whitehall, turns to his bishop-confessor and cries 'Remember!'

When old London Bridge was widened in the 1760s, it was realised that the new footpath would have to cut through the hundred-year-old tower of St Magnus the Martyr on the eastern side of the bridge. Incredibly, Sir Christopher Wren had built the church in anticipation that this problem would occur a century later, and had already provided the tower's arches with removable sections to create such a passageway.

London's building plans are a mess. The Second World War saw to that. In some parts of the capital virtually every other building was destroyed in the firestorm of the Blitz, and the once-elegant streets gaped like the rotten teeth of a corpse. Between 6.00 p.m. and 9.30 p.m. on Sunday, 29 December 1940, the second great fire of London occurred when the

German Luftwaffe dropped 127 tons of high explosive and more than 10,000 incendiary bombs on the city. A famous photograph of that night shows St Paul's rising unharmed through a raging sea of flame.

Jonathan looked up at the squat brown building standing between two fifties' office blocks and tried to imagine how it had been that terrible night; the din of tumbling masonry, the blasts of the firefighters' hoses. He had been two years old and living far away, in north Yorkshire. London Can Take It – some motto. But the city had managed it in the past, so many times, surviving the plagues and the fires only to be brought to its knees at the end of the twentieth century by traffic and developers. A city as old as Christianity itself was fighting for its life. Jonathan pulled the camera from his jacket and snapped a few shots; the grimy storefront with the yellow plastic sign reading AIKO ELECTRICS, the four floors of crumbling Victorian redbrick (third and fourth clearly on the verge of collapse), the ill-fitting modern roof, what an invisible, unimpressive – and unlisted – building it was. Perhaps it deserved to be pulled down. It wasn't always a good idea to cling to the past. Marrick would have no qualms about demolishing the Albert Hall if it suited his plans.

But then he looked up at the building again and tried to imagine it restored and filled with people. That was when he noticed the details; the dusty turquoise glazing bars on the tops of the third-floor windows, the swagged ornamentation on the broken rainwater head at the top of the drainpipe, the rusticated keystone above the archway leading to the building's side-alley, and he realised then that a magnificent building was hiding behind its wounds and beneath a caul of dirt, that it could all be restored, because it had been a restaurant once before, long ago, and Dasako had spotted it even if Marrick hadn't. On the pavement was another tell-tale sign; a shattered section of black and white mosaic in which the name of the establishment would have been set in curlicues of brass. And most miraculous of all, there on the wall beside the door, a battered cone of blackened metal, a snuffer! These rarely-spotted pieces of street furniture were used to extinguish the tar-covered brands of the linkboys who escorted the restaurant's visitors through the unlit streets. Dasako's architects had seen all this. The Japanese respected the traditions of the past. With patience and planning, they would allow this building to spring to full-blooded life once more, filled with gaiety and beauty. Its restaurant would stand as a magnificent testament to the pleasures of the past, and the possibilities of the future.

But there was something else here as well, something that could only be seen away from the light, something less wholesome and only just hidden from view. Jonathan could feel the strange sensation creeping across him like a storm cloud obscuring the sun. There was something here that hid within the bricks. The weight of history was giddying, and he felt suddenly sick. He ceased pacing in order to catch his breath, then walked on past the central building, turning the corner at the end of the block. Three buildings constituted its longest side; the other three sides were shorter, comprising two buildings each. The one in the centre of the long side, the building owned by Dasako, grew narrower toward the rear and was truncated to allow a central courtyard within the block, although according to Marrick little evidence of this could be seen from its windows, the courtyard having been largely built over.

Jonathan looked up at the rapidly darkening sky and felt a speck of rain. At his back, traffic thrummed endlessly around a one-way system toward Hackney Town Hall. He realised with a start that he was standing near the spot where he and Connie were married. The little church had been demolished in the seventies to make way for wider traffic lanes. In his mind's eye he saw Connie turning on the steps and crying delightedly, confetti drifting from her shoulders as a passing car sounded its horn in celebration. Harder to see her now, of course; harder each day to capture each retreating memory.

He pocketed the camera and turned his collar up, preparing for his next stop – the building registry office just behind Lombard Street. Why did Marrick want plans for the entire block? What was going through his mind? Sometimes his cunning displayed the most surprising lateral thinking. As he headed for the Old Street tube station, the only certainty Jonathan had was that money would once more change hands in deceitful circumstances.

London is an old, old woman, heartsick and tired. Her aches have now grown into a solid constant pain, nagging and unrelieved. To have survived the poverty, the misery, the riots, the ravages of sickness and disaster, to have outlived the numbing terrors of the bombs – and for what? To see the city's heart torn out and cast aside, to see her body desecrated and her soul destroyed. She has always fought back, but now her fighting days are at an end, and the battle is all but lost.

There is little that is truly Christian about London. Hawksmoor's churches have long been noted for the strange profanity of their design, but there are many acknowledgements of other gods. The building of Bush House will never be completed. If you walk through the western colonnade which connects the Strand to the Aldwych, you'll see that one of the building's columns has an incomplete capital in order to comply to an old adage: 'Perfection is an attribute of Allah; Impiety to achieve perfection.'

Jonathan had to support the drawer of the plans chest on his bent knee in order to remove the architectural layouts without damaging them. They appeared to have been drawn in the nineteen thirties and poorly updated in the late fifties. Presumably there were earlier versions stored somewhere, but nobody seemed to know where. The paper was fine and brittle, carelessly stored beside a radiator for too many years. He gently laid the plan to one side for photocopying, and noticed the scrap of map wedged beneath it. It was old, certainly early nineteenth century. His finger traced a path across botanical gardens in faded emerald ink, through the fields of Kensington, over meadows and market gardens to the straggling canalways and riverbanks of North London. He loved maps. To be perched dizzyingly high in the clouds from the cartographer's viewpoint, peering down across a metropolis that is trapped forever in a single moment . . .

'Are you going to be much longer with that?' A listless secretary clumped past. There was a vague, unfocussed hatred in her eyes, a suspicion of age, of gender, of everyone and everything. Jonathan so often saw it in the eyes of the young. He reluctantly closed the drawer and rose. He could spend all day here, sifting through the blueprints of the past, but Marrick would have a heart attack. As soon as his copies were ready he folded them into his case and stepped back into the penetrating rain.

He found the drawing at his local library, in a book on Edwardian London. An attenuated young lady in a peach-coloured gown with a fur collar was alighting from a carriage on the arm of her evening-suited beau. In his free hand, the man held a top hat and a pair of white gloves. Rain glossed the street. The restaurant before them was a shimmering wall of light. Great chandeliers sparkled above the elegant dining lounge. The maître d' stood beneath a silvered canopy awaiting the new arrivals. A copperplate sign was illuminated by rows of dazzling bulbs: *La Belle Epoque*. Of course. The place was world-renowned. Jonathan pored over every detail. You could even see the snuffer beside the entrance. It all looked so – what was the word? *Swanky*. An Americanism, of course, but quite old and entirely appropriate. He savoured the picture, longed to tear it out and hide it inside his overcoat. Instead he rose and returned to his cold flat above the fishmongers in the high street, to pass the evening in his books and his dreams.

'Piece of piss,' said Marrick, wiping a chunk of bread around his plate and popping it in his mouth. 'Between the end of Aiko's lease and Dasako's application for listed building status, I bunged an offer in to them. Two hundred and sixty K.'

They were having lunch several weeks later in a vast and deafening Wardour Street restaurant. Marrick hated the food but ate here because it was fashionable. The hard wooden seats were designed to discourage lingerers, and Jonathan had to shift awkwardly about to stop his legs from going numb. 'I don't understand,' he said as the appalling truth sank in. 'Why would they have accepted such a bid?'

'Because they can't build a restaurant there any more. No fucking planning permission. Modern laws require safety exits, and they ain't got any.'

'I'm sure I saw an alleyway at the side of the building. Couldn't they have applied to make use of that?'

'Could have done if it was theirs, old fruit, but it's not. It belongs to the building next door, my little auction-purchase. Their bloke contacted me and tried to get the right-of-way signed over.'

'And what happened?' asked Jonathan, dreading the answer.

'I told him to fuck off, obviously.'

'But surely they can appeal?'

Marrick looked at him suspiciously and seemed about to speak, then changed his mind. 'No,' he said finally, raising his glass and draining it. 'They can't appeal. How can they build exits when the only other properties bordering theirs are mine? Anyway, the deal's already going through. Their hands are tied good and proper. They'll find some other dump to tart up. I'll have all three buildings down within a month, crash, bang, bosh, clear the space and flog it off as office units. I feel like celebrating. Let's get another bottle of this, if we can find a fucking waiter.'

It made perfect sense, of course. He'd seen it on the map, but had chosen to ignore an obvious truth; the three properties were worth more knocked flat and sold in newly arranged packages of landspace. The packages could be tailored to suit modern business requirements. London's existing old buildings found it difficult to incorporate the conduits that were required to carry computer cables.

In Jonathan's mind the golden windows of *La Belle Epoque* dimmed, the glittering crystalline structure dismantled itself and disappeared into the night, leaving behind a deep, dirty pool of shadow. He could not bring himself to hate Marrick; he was merely disappointed that the past had been cheated out of a chance to return.

The spirit of London sinks from a powerful roar of flame to a single glowing ember, and soon that too will be extinguished. For cities, like people, must eventually grow old and die. Even a city as ancient as this . . .

Scotland Yard, named after the palace where the kings of Scotland lodged when visiting London, is founded on the site of an unsolved murder. Mutilated portions of a woman's body were secreted on the building site in the 1880s, and the officers of the CID were never able to discover the identity of the murderer or his victim.

Jonathan turned on the desk light and tilted back the green glass shade, then unfolded the photostat across the cleared surface of his desk. Marrick was planning to inspect the vacated premises with him tomorrow. After that it was simply a matter of sorting out the paperwork and waiting for the demolition order to be cleared. He withdrew a magnifying glass and checked each of the rooms and staircases in turn. Something about the map bothered him. Or rather, something about the way it matched the experience of actually visiting the property. He checked the specifications of each of the buildings against the photographs he had taken, but the anomaly eluded him. Why couldn't he see it? Something was wrong, something at the heart of the land itself. He removed his reading glasses and massaged the bridge of his nose. Perhaps the answer would come to him tomorrow. He refolded the map, switched off the desk-lamp and wearily headed for bed.

'I don't know why they had to turn the fucking lights off,' moaned Marrick as he and Jonathan passed beneath the cracked AIKO sign and entered the ground floor of the building. 'Look at it out there, ten in the morning and you'd think it was fucking midnight. Did you bring a torch?'

'Yes. The main staircase is to the rear of this room.' Jonathan clicked on the flashlight and raised its beam. The showroom had been stripped to a few piles of mildewed carpet tiles and some battered old shelf units. It smelled bad – damp and sickly. From far above them came the drone of heavy rain and the warble of sheltering pigeons. They reached the foot of the stairs and started up.

'I wanna make sure they cleared everything out. Barney couldn't get here this morning, his wife's sick or something.' Barney was an ex-bouncer and former prison warden whose aggressive temperament perfectly qualified him for his position as Marrick's site manager. Unpleasant things happened in Marrick's company that Jonathan did not know about, that he could not allow himself to discover. Not if he wanted to keep his job and his sanity.

Although Marrick was young, he was considerably over-weight; the stairs were already defeating him. He reached the second-floor landing and looked up through the centre of the stairwell, catching his breath. 'You can check out the top two floors, Jon, make sure we ain't got any squatters in. Fucking hell, it stinks in here.'

Jonathan stopped on the staircase and stared out of the rain-streaked window into the centre of the block, where the backs of the buildings met.

Rooms. Something odd about the rooms. He studied the brick walls of the courtyard formed by the other properties. He felt as if he had a cold coming on. Getting his jacket so wet hadn't helped matters. He should have bought himself a new umbrella. He sneezed hard, wiped his nose on a tissue. Spots of dark blood, a crimson constellation. He looked from the window again. The bricks. That's what it was. The bricks to the right of the window. They were in the wrong place. There should have been an empty space there. It was marked on the map, but not there from the window.

There was one room too many.

'Adrian, come and look at this a minute.' He beckoned Marrick down and pointed from the glass. 'There shouldn't be another room in the centre-well. The old wall to the right, do you see?'

'Yeah, so?'

'It's not on the plans.'

'Why would that be?'

The brickwork was ancient, and the spaces between the blackened bricks were filled with bedraggled weeds. Near the top of the wall was a tiny window less than a foot long. There was no glass in it, just a single iron bar running across the gap. Jonathan frowned, trying to understand. 'The 1933 plans were drawn over much older ones, but when they traced the new buildings in, they didn't add the existing layout.'

'So what was there before?'

'I don't know. The original drawings have been lost, misfiled somewhere.'

Marrick looked at him as if he was going senile. 'I'm not following you, Jon.'

'There was another building already here at the centre of the site, or at least part of one. A very old one. Look at the bricks. There must be an entrance to it.'

'Wait, before you go off on a fucking treasure hunt, how about we finish what we came here to do?'

'This building has been cleared.' Jonathan scrubbed his fist across the filthy pane.

'We have to find a way into that room.'

'Why?' It was useless to assume that Marrick had a natural sense of curiosity, so Jonathan appealed to his greed. 'It could have been sealed off for years. There might be something of value in there.'

'If there was, it was probably nicked years ago. Someone's bound to have been in there already.'

'I think that's unlikely. There's no immediate access, and it looks like it belongs to part of another building. It's hard to even see.'

'Hmm. You have a point there.' They both started looking for a doorway. There was nothing on any of the landings, or on the second floor. At the bottom of the stairs they found a door leading to a basement, but it was locked and there was no key. Marrick picked up a chunk of discarded pipe and smashed at the lock until the damp wood around it splintered and fell away.

'Fucking hell! What died?' Marrick waved a hand in front of his nose. 'Shine your torch down there. These steps look rotten.' The beam rippled back at them. The whole of the basement was under an inch of filthy water. On the far side was an arched passage. Jonathan instinctively knew that this was the way to the room at the centre of the building.

He'd seen this type of layout in old architectural books. 'We have to go over there.' He pointed at the arch.

'You're joking. These shoes cost a fucking fortune. I'm not going down there.'

Jonathan's torch caught a stack of planks piled under the stairs. It was a simple matter to lay them like duckboards across the basement. The ceiling was low, and Marrick swore spectacularly as he banged his head. They arrived at the far side of the room, and Jonathan reached out to touch the heavy oak door set before them. He could hear running water. The torch illuminated the source through a crack in the wood; a brick channel filled with sluggishly moving liquid, cut through an arched tunnel that led off to an iron grate in the wall. 'The Fleet,' said Jonathan excitedly, 'it's a tributary of the Fleet.'

'What the fuck is that, a river?'

'Certainly a river. It was used as a rubbish dump for centuries. Runs from Hampstead down to Holborn and right across London.'

'What do you mean "runs"? It's still there?'

'It was finally channelled underground at the end of the eighteenth century, but the main part is still used as a sewer. There's a whole network of tributaries attached to it, and this looks like one of them. A lot of basements used to have access to the city's sewer system.' Marrick had lost interest. He pulled at the edge of the door, and it shifted inwards.

'Doesn't look like it's being used any more,' said Jonathan. 'The water's clean.' He shone his torch further along the channel and found another, much smaller door. This one was painted black and studded with iron bolts. 'That has to be the way to the centre-well.'

They carefully stepped across the open water-pipe and examined the door. It was set two feet from the ground, presumably to keep the area behind it dry and avoid the danger of flooding.

'It's locked. I wonder who has the key.'

Marrick dug about in his pocket and produced a handful of loose Yales. 'Take your pick, there's these and dozens more of the bastards back in the office.' But all of them proved too small to fit the lock.

'The mechanism will probably need oiling, anyway,' said Jonathan. 'We wouldn't be able to shift it by ourselves, not if it's been shut for years.' They resolved to come back down on Monday morning.

London was once settled much lower in the ground. Layers were added; strata of gravel and stone and tarmacadam, layers of bones, the residue of corpses stricken by pestilence and firestorm, three decades of cholera victims, the sickly paupers from debtors' jails and workhouses, the silent majority of the city. Denied a voice in life, how they longed to speak and be heard.

The first tunnel under the Thames was a private enterprise built by Marc Brunel and opened, after considerable loss of life, in 1843. Within fifteen weeks, a million pedestrians had paid a penny each to walk through it, but the novelty wore off fast, and for the next decade the gloomy arched passageways underneath the river became the favoured haunt of thieves and prostitutes.

Jonathan was unable to find a key which would fit, so Marrick asked his foreman Barney to take the door off its hinges. Barney did so that Friday morning, following Marrick's instructions not to go inside. Marrick, who fancied himself as a bit of an Indiana Jones, was determined to retain that privilege for himself. Later on in the afternoon, as the biggest storm of the autumn broke over their heads, Jonathan accompanied his employer back to the cellar, and they crossed the sewage channel to the door in the wall.

Barney had set the square iron panel to one side. Marrick assumed proprietorial charge of the flashlight, and now wielding a crowbar in his other fist, shone his beam ahead into a rubble-filled corridor. Jonathan followed him through, pausing beside a crumpled sheet of newspaper, *The Daily Sketch, May 18th, 1949*. He rose, disappointed, hoping to find something older. At least it was dry in here. They had to be under the centre-well of the buildings now. The room he had seen would be above them at the end of the passage and to the right.

'I don't know why I'm fucking wasting my time down here. I should never have let you talk me into this.' Marrick picked his way across the littered floor, leaving Jonathan to fend for himself in the dark. From far above them came the distant rumble of thunder, like masonry being emptied into a skip. Jonathan listened to his boss's muttered complaints, knowing that the merest sliver of hope would drive him forward. 'You never know what we might find,' he said. 'There, at the end, where you just pointed the torch. What is that?'

Twisted curlicues of iron hung from the ceiling. A number of sections had rusted through, and lay on the floor like giant fruit-rinds. Marrick cast the beam upwards. 'Looks like part of a staircase,' said Jonathan.

'Not like any fucking staircase I've ever seen. You reckon this room of yours is above here?'

'There's nowhere else it could be.' He raised his eyes to the stained plaster ceiling and saw the slightly protuberant square of plaster in the corner of the passage. It was half the size of the first door, but large enough for a man to climb through. 'There's your door,' he said excitedly. 'There should be an iron ring set flat in the front section, buried under the plaster.'

'How could you know that?' Marrick stopped and stared back at him through the glare of the torch beam. 'You haven't been down here before.'

'I've read about these things. It's a relic room. Lots of

wealthy old houses used to have them. You built a special room, just a small one, and sealed a treasured possession inside, and built the rest of the house around it.'

'Then what?'

'Then nothing. You sealed the room up from the outside and forgot all about it, and the building would have good luck all of its life. It was a pagan thing. By giving up something precious you appeased the household gods. The old Roman habits died hard. Not all Londoners were Christians, you know.'

Marrick's eyes glittered in the gloom. 'So you reckon there's something really valuable in there?'

'There could be, I don't know. They tucked away all sorts of belongings. Gold candlesticks, silver and pewter plate, chalices, they were all popular sacrifices.'

'Reading all them books of yours finally paid off, eh?' Marrick thumped the ceiling square with the end of his crowbar. The plaster coating that covered it sounded thin. A few more thumps rained wafer-fine pieces on to his shoulders. It only took a few minutes to reveal the edges of the door. When he shone the torch back up, they could both see it; a dirty iron ring, recessed into the square. 'Give me a hand here,' said Marrick, thrusting the torch at him. 'Hold that steady.' His fingers followed the outline of the ring and dug around it, pulling it down toward him. As he brought his weight to bear on it, the door grudgingly opened downwards in a shower of plaster fragments.

'Christ, this thing must be on a fucking spring,' Marrick cried, 'I can barely hold it.'

'Do you want me to help?'

'You'd give yourself a hernia. Just grab the bottom corners as soon as you can reach them.' He was right. Jonathan could feel the power of the door as it tried to close itself. Marrick moved the torch to the inside of the hole. Pinpoints of reflected light glittered back. 'There's definitely something in there all right. Keep a hold on the door.'

Marrick braced his feet against the walls and raised his arms into the open hole, pulling himself up. 'Used to – ugh – do this sort of thing in gym,' he gasped through gritted teeth. As his torso, his legs and finally his expensive Italian shoes disappeared into the hole, Jonathan shoved against the door with all his might to keep the heavy spring from slamming it shut.

'What can you see?' he called.

'Hang on a minute, let me get my breath – ' Marrick shone the torch around the room, which was less than five feet square. The air was thick and old, but breathable. His head brushed against the brick ceiling. Beside him at head-height was the tiny window he had seen from outside.

'Plate,' he called down finally. 'Silver plate by the look of it.' He shifted his feet either side of the trapdoor hole. A great mound of the stuff was stacked in a corner. Each piece was twice the size of the average dinner plate. It looked like the municipal tableware they used for mayoral banquets. He bent down and pulled the largest one free in a cloud of straw-dust. It was badly tarnished, but he could still make out the leaping stags, the coat of arms, the portrait of some ugly bird in a pointy headdress. His heart was beating faster. Even an idiot could see that this lot was worth a fucking fortune. He turned it over, and there on the reverse was an inscription, hard to read because the S's were substituted with F's, but the date was clear; 1503. Dear God in Heaven, he was rich.

'Here, cop hold of this.' He passed the plate down to Jonathan, who was propped against the trapdoor and had trouble accepting the heavy metal dish. Marrick switched the torch into the opposite corner, no more than two feet behind him. His mouth fell open.

Jonathan's arms were tiring. He was not sure how much longer he could manage to keep the door down. Beyond in the darkness he could hear the steadily augmenting sound of rushing water. The deluge above them was filtering through the pipes of the building and swelling the sewer channel. 'Hurry up,' he called anxiously. 'The storm's bringing a lot of water down.'

Marrick did not hear. He was staring back at a dead body. It was centuries-dead and dried out, so that it appeared as little more than a skeleton with yellow skin vacuum-formed across its bones. It was small, just over four feet high, its head tilted back and its jaws wide open so that it appeared to be laughing, or screaming. There were iron rings around its wrists, manacling it to the wall. They seemed unnecessarily heavy on such a small frame. A chill crept over Marrick as it occurred to him that the poor creature had been chained up alive and left to die here, and that it was most probably a child.

'Oh, Christ – '

'What's the matter?'

'They walled up something precious to bring themselves luck – '

Several things happened at once just then. An enormous roll of thunder made itself heard all the way to the basement, there was a sudden renewed rush of water through the sewer duct, and Jonathan started in surprise, moving his shoulder from the trapdoor. The spring tightened, the lid swung unstoppably up and slammed shut with a deafening bang. For a moment both men were shocked into silence. Then Marrick began shouting and thumping about in his tiny cell, but the sound of his rage was not enough to carry clearly through the heavy sealed door.

Marrick stood up sharply and cracked his head on the ceiling. His heart was pounding in the darkness. The walls pressed forward. He was unable to catch his breath. Claustrophobia hemmed him in. The dead air in his throat stifled him. He gasped and bellowed at Jonathan, every filthy insult he could conjure, and threw himself to the floor in an attempt to dislodge the trapdoor. But it was somehow arranged so that it could only be opened from the iron ring outside – and only he had had the strength to pull it down. Jonathan would never be able to manage it alone. He forced himself to calm down for a moment. Barney. Jonathan would have to go and get Barney. He might still be at the office. He wished he had not left his mobile phone in his briefcase on the ground floor.

'Jon,' he shouted at the floor, 'go and get Barney to help you! Call him! Get Barney!' He held his breath and listened, but all he could hear was the rain outside and the distant rushing water below. 'Jon, for fuck's sake what are you doing?' His voice rose in fright as the beam from the torch grew yellow and died. He dropped to his knees and scrabbled at the seams of the unmoving door until he could no longer feel his fingers.

Jonathan made his way back along the passageway in total darkness. He soaked his legs crossing the sewer duct, which was now overflowing the sides of the brick channel. A faint light showed from the distant cellar entrance. When he reached the top of the stairs, he collected Marrick's briefcase. Then he went back to the rumbling river.

Positioning himself by the water that boiled and rushed through the iron grating, he emptied the contents of the case, Marrick's pens, his mobile phone, his cocaine, his lunch receipts, and all the contracts he had drawn up for the purchase and eventual demolition of the building. Jonathan watched as they passed through the wide iron mesh on their underground journey to the city's dark heart.

'There are no kind gods,' he said aloud. 'The price of true belief will always be terrible.'

Back on the ground floor he studied the huge plate Marrick had passed to him, the lauded ceremonial plate commemorating the death of Elizabeth of York, daughter of Edward IV, sister to the murdered princes in the Tower, beloved mother of Henry VIII. On the back was engraved an elegy, written for her by Sir Thomas More. He was holding a cornerstone of history, long thought lost, finally restored to safe hands. He would never know what else the *oubliette* contained – apart from the large useless article that would now serve the birth of a new urban deity.

Several days later, Jonathan returned to the stairwell window and looked out into the centre of the building. It was a still, sunny day, and a sparrow perched on one of the sturdy weed-stems that sprouted from the wall of the hidden room. Jonathan stared at the tiny window with the thick iron bar across it, and occasionally – as if it could sense that someone was watching – a pale face, despairing and nightmarish, passed before the gap like the moon fleetingly glimpsed through clouds. It was a sight that he would never forget, an eternal penance. His skin prickling, he hastily returned to the warm city streets and the choking traffic beyond.

There is a brief respite in the sobbing, crying maelstrom. The city's agonies are temporarily assuaged. A sacrifice accepted; a building restored. For the most fleeting of moments, the tough old woman raises her crumpled face to the sun and smiles.

A century and a half ago, within the thick Wren walls of the Theatre Royal, Drury Lane, a body was discovered with a dagger in its ribs. Somebody was murdered in the theatre and quietly bricked in. Nobody knows why, or whether the victim was still alive when the last brick was cemented into place.

THE MAN WHO WOUND
A THOUSAND CLOCKS

The Sultan Omar Mehmet Shay-Tarrazin was a ruler much given to statistics, not particularly through his own choice. It was simply that he had so much of everything, there was a fascination in quantifying it. He had seventy-three concubines and four hundred and twenty-six children. His great summer palace of white and ochre wood, *Mehmet Shay-Tarrazin yali*, built between two streams known as the 'Sweet Waters of Asia' on the banks of the Bosphorus, stood on the threshold of two continents. It had nearly six hundred rooms, passages, portals, halls and courtyards. The Sultan trained fifty imported Arabian stallions, each an undefeated champion in its class. The land he owned stretched so far and wide that one could ride from dawn to sunset for six days on the fleetest of his horses and still cross no more than one fifth of his property. His political allies could be found as far afield as Britain, China and the Cape of Good Hope. He sailed fleets of gold-crested vessels laden with cinnamon, cumin, hashish and nutmeg, and fought holy wars for the reliquaries of gods, and issued stern unpopular edicts, and cremated his chancellor for dropping tangerine peel on the steps of the royal harem, which was unfortunate for the innocent chancellor, who was allergic to tangerines and still alive to protest his innocence when the execution pyre was lit. The Sultan's slightest whim became the harshest law.

How did one man ever become so powerful? Omar

Mehmet Shay-Tarrazin was the last thin trickle in a long dark bloodline winding down through the centuries from the offspring of Suleyman the Magnificent himself. His family had ruled in every shy corner of the East, and though depleted still planned to continue its rule far into the future, until fate intervened.

Shay-Tarrazin's wife, Melek (the woman chosen by Allah, his grandfather, and his father in that order) had been raised solely for the purpose of betrothal to the Sultan, and was so finely bred that she could walk no more than five paces without requiring assistance. But one hot morning she died in childbirth, and her sickly son only survived the ordeal until sunset. Now there was no-one pure enough to continue the line without polluting it, so Shay-Tarrazin made do with his plump young concubines and his ivory stallions, and watched his power slowly settle until he relied entirely on the news of couriers for his dealings with the outside world, and hardly ever left the grounds of his palace. His wealth and status allowed him a life beyond all restriction, and yet it was filled with so many rules, laws, arrangements and appointments that he became a prisoner of his own making.

It happened that the Sultan was newly fascinated by the concept of time. Like many royal rulers he was seized by fads, and longed to make sense of a world he mostly witnessed through the tortoiseshell latticework of the throne-room. Having grown bored with the wonders of astrology, biology and alchemy (and having cremated the practitioners of all three sciences whom he had invited to the palace to instruct him) he turned to more ethereal concepts, and discovered time. He liked the idea very much. It was tantalisingly intangible, unlike biology, which had required the dissection of living animals, or alchemy, which had blackened the walls of his temples and filled the orange-orchards with the stench of smouldering sulphur.

Shay-Tarrazin knew that time would only exist in its measuring, so he started collecting clocks of every size and description, from a microscopic Russian gold chimer to a twenty-two-foot-high gilded Ormolu state-clock that took fifteen men to carry it. There were Austrian clocks with dancing figures that popped from doorways and fought duels with tigers. There was a German clock featuring an enamel tableau in which an executioner beheaded his kneeling victim on the quarter-hour. There was a set of Siberian winter-solstice clocks that fitted inside each other like wooden dolls. There was a Castilian clock that predicted the weather with miniature globes of coloured water, and a Brazilian timepiece that measured the passing moments by the fall of tiny purple gems. There was a Belgian celestial clock depicting the movement of the heavens, topped with a gold-chased orrery. There were Portuguese ceramic clocks, Chinese Coptic balsa clocks, booming British grandfather clocks, imperial Ottoman clocks inlaid with mother-of-pearl and decorated with panels of Kutahya tiles, clocks in polychrome, walnut and stained glass – it made the head spin to even think about them.

There were nine hundred and ninety-nine of them.

And they all required winding.

So enamoured did the Sultan become with the concept of time that he came to rely upon it completely. Before the idea had been explained to him, the daily business of his kingdom had been ordered by the position of the sun, so that no work was ever undertaken after dark, and tasks were completed eventually, with no sense of haste or urgency. Life was allowed to run its natural, unhurried course. But once Shay-Tarrazin had installed time in his palace, he and his courtiers, their retinue, the concubines, consorts, servants, cooks and porters were all capable of being late. And as being late upset the running of the kingdom, it became an offence punishable by beheading or cremation. The Sultan was not a wise man, or a fair man, or even a good man, but his empire ran well and provided commercial intercourse with the world, advancing business and society, and making the globe spin a little faster on its axis.

So it became absolutely imperative to keep the clocks wound.

For this purpose, the Sultan sent five dozen of his guards to search the city for a reliable man, someone with a sense of routine and responsibility. Sabin Darr was such a man. He was twenty-two years old, had a wife and three small children each as handsome as he, and earned a living as a carver and furniture repairer of no small ingenuity. He dwelt in a small orange house in the green foothills of the river basin, and was taken by surprise when the king's men hammered at his front door with the butts of their daggers.

While his family cowered behind their modesty curtains, Sabin Darr stood before the guards and answered each of their questions as truthfully as he could. It quickly became clear that he was the man for the job, but as he proved reluctant to join them, three of the king's men slipped between the curtains and ran his wife and children through with their sabres. Hearing their cries above the slither of steel, Sabin ran back to find his sandals splashed with the blood of his family. Half-blinded by grief and fury he watched as the guards dropped torches of burning pitch on to the roof of his house, and bade him mount the horse they had set aside for the first part of his journey to the clockhouse of Shay-Tarrazin. For Sabin Darr, time stopped on that terrible day.

The Sultan himself came out to greet the slender caique that docked before the steps of his palace. He explained why he needed Sabin Darr. The job had to be performed by someone with no social ties. It was demanding and all-consuming. Every single clock and watch had to be wound each day, and there were so many that it would require every hour of daylight to perform the task. Those that were slow or fast would have to be recalibrated until they were as accurate as the most immaculate timekeeper in the palace. Some clocks required ladders to reach their winding mechanisms. Some had winders that were so microscopically tiny and fine that special tweezers had to be used to turn them. Some clocks had processions of mechanical figures with joints that seized up in the warm dry air, preventing their steady movement. They had to be cleaned and lubricated. Some clocks had keys that were hidden away in elaborate decorations, and required the solving of a puzzle to free them. Some could only be wound at certain hours of the day, because their winding holes were in their faces, and the hands passed over them, preventing access. Yet others were not wound by conventional keys at all, but by the balancing of vials of oil and water, by filling with sand, by the displacement of marble pebbles, by the resetting of tumblers, by the stacking of ball-bearings, and by turning upside down.

Sabin was set to work in the great hall of the clockhouse, which had been built in a raised piazza beyond the main courtyard of the palace, above the shining blue Bosphorus, and he learned how to keep time. His task was arduous. There were only just enough minutes in the day to wind every single clock before the chimes of six rang out. Each night as the sun settled inside banks of heated crimson dust, he raced to refresh the final mechanism and only just succeeded. His winding schedule was so exact that the spring of each time-piece was fully unwound upon reaching it.

After leaving the hall he was presented with an oval copper tray of bread, meat, wine and fruit. At night he washed the noise of ticking from his head and fell asleep on an arrangement of yellow velvet pillows in the Eunuchs' quarters of the *Selamlik*. As he lay looking out at the deepening sky, he remembered his wife and children, and tumbled his thoughts into salted teardrops.

The Sultan's fascination with time gradually dimmed, but the course of his kingdom was now set. With time had come punctuality, and efficiency, and profitability. It was not a concept, like the alchemical one of turning coal into gold, that he could easily discard. His guards checked on Sabin every day, and issued him with a warning; should he fail to wind just one of the clocks on one occasion, he would forfeit a digit from his left hand. This was proof that the Sultan was not a wise man, for such a punishment could only reduce the clockwinder's dexterity, but punishment was regarded by Shay-Tarrazin as a purely legal matter, and everyone knew that laws were not subject to the influence of common sense.

In time, Sabin Darr's wrath turned into the infinite sadness of resignation. He learned the art of winding the clocks, and had them rearranged in careful declension, so that he might perform his task with the greatest efficiency. Thus, Sabin was able to fulfil his daily chores, Shay-Tarrazin was able to behead any cook whose dishes arrived a minute late at his table, and everything was cared for in its fashion.

It happened that a favoured son of the Sultan's (as much as any child born of a concubine could find favour in his court), returning from an excursion in Rome, wished to ingratiate himself with his father. This was for the sake of his mother, who had reached the age of two-and-twenty and had been discarded, and now languished in a shabbier section of the harem, unloved and forgotten. Through guile and deceit the boy had been able to procure a fine Italian timepiece for presentation as a gift. It possessed six onyx clock-faces, each smaller than the last, each requiring daily winding with its own special silver key.

The new clock was the thousandth, and a straw to break a camel's back; it upset the balance of the clockhouse, since Sabin Darr's schedule operated on the thickness of a hair. After much calculation and consideration, planning and paperwork, he reordered the collection to incorporate the new clock, and rehearsed the windings through the course of one night. The following day, still weary from his exacting rehearsal, he slipped while running between the final two clocks and dropped one of the winding keys. It slid across the marble mosaic floor and came to rest beneath the case of a water-clock, and Sabin lost precious seconds retrieving it. As the clocks all began to chime six, there still remained one last clock to wind.

Moments later, two guards marched into the great room. They laid his hand on an alabaster block. One of them expertly slammed a sabre-blade down on his little finger, neatly severing it at the base. The other laid the red-hot tip of a dagger he had heated in a *mangal*, a cremation brazier, across the little stump, cauterising the wound and instantly staunching the flow of blood. It was all very efficient.

That evening, to ease his pain (for he was not a man without pity) the Sultan sent a beautiful honey-eyed and amber-breasted harem girl called Safieh to deliver Sabin's food. Abducted as a child by corsairs, she had been sold into the seraglio as an *ikbal*, a love slave, and was the most adept at her arts. She fed him lovingly, inserting her tapered brown fingers into his waiting mouth, and sweetly played to him on her *ney*, which is an instrument rather like a lute. After Sabin had eaten his fill she entwined with him on the velvet cushions, and brought alive his memories of the woman he had loved (for she knew his history), and stayed with him until one hour before dawn.

It was almost worth losing a finger for.

But lest you should think that the hero of this tale is merely some passive reed, bending this way and that with the events of his life, forgetful of avenging his poor family, rest assured that he was concocting a cunning plan.

First he made a series of careful tests and calculations, just as he had for the winding of the clocks. He knew that Shay-Tarrazin and his guards had only one way of knowing if he had fulfilled his nightly task, and that was by checking that all the clocks were working, and that he had wound the last clock before the chimes of six. So Sabin started to wind each of the clocks with a single quarter-turn less, which meant that each timepiece ran down and stopped just a few moments before he reached it. He still reached the final clock on time; in fact, he arrived a fraction earlier now that there was time to spare. This made Sabin's life a little easier, but more important, it changed time by imperceptibly stretching it. As the days turned into weeks and months became years, the Sultan's interests moved on to other concepts, such as animal husbandry and flying machines, and he visited the clockhouse less and less frequently. Sabin continued to underwind the clocks, carefully allowing their mechanisms to slow, their springs to expand, their hands to shift less sharply, so that time itself geared down to a lazier pace.

The change was so slight that no-one noticed. All of the other clocks and watches in the kingdom took their time from the clockhouse, and though it was perceived that the sun and moon had altered the times of their appearance, the kingdom was so powerful and so right that it was assumed the heavens had revised their cosmic schedule in order to be more accommodating. After all, how could one measure time but from a clock, and if all the clocks ran slow who was to say that the clocks were wrong and that time itself was right? Absolute time could not be measured in any other way, particularly if one believed that earthbound humans had more power than the heavens.

For the next eight years, Sabin slowed the pace of the world. And at the age of thirty, to celebrate the anniversary of his birthyear, he took it slower still, giving each of the thousand keys a half-turn less.

Safieh, the bountiful harem girl, stayed with him four more times. Her appearance was a mixed blessing, for it meant that he had lost another finger, but he would experience a night of love. The clocks were subject to imperfection, and occasionally broke down. When this happened the royal blacksmiths forged new cogs and wires, and Sabin replaced the damaged part once he had concluded his tour for the night.

Incredibly, it failed to come to the attention of the ageing Omar Mehmet Shay-Tarrazin that his kingdom had fallen out of step. It had grown so lethargic that his ships sat docked in the Bosphorus for months on end, their cargoes rotting, their crews drunk and asleep. His Grand Vizier, that is to say his prime minister, passed his days sweating in the *hamam* with his favourite concubine, and no longer bothered concerning himself with affairs of state, because they were resolved too slowly. Those states whose borders touched the Sultan's empire withdrew their trading agreements and found new allies. The slave girls that peered beneath the *jalousie*-screens into the *mabeyn* area of the palace grew fat and bored, for they were visited with more vigour in times of prosperity (men always sought to prove their sexual prowess after proving their trading acumen). The peacocks in the formal gardens of the palace wandered through the overgrown lawns tearing out their feathers through inattention. The very air ceased to buzz with the energy of insects, and even the battalions of ferocious ants that swarmed across the flagstoned embankments now droned as softly as bees in an English garden. Lassitude settled over the kingdom like a warm dry shroud.

Finally, when Sabin had reduced the clocks to their slowest possible rate, he requested an audience with the Sultan, and built a special royal viewing platform upon which to receive his guest.

The reply, borne on petal-scented paper from across the courtyard, took five full days to reach him. Sabin watched from his window, and finally saw Shay-Tarrazin's entourage moving as slowly as a constellation toward the clockhouse.

The Sultan had grown old and bewildered. His rheumy eyes peeped out from beneath a huge turquoise turban that had a feather dipped in molten gold attached to it with an eagle-claw. To Sabin, the Sultan's willingness to visit the clockhouse upon request was a sure sign of how far the empire had fallen into disarray. Once, Shay-Tarrazin's most gossamer caprice would have been set in stone. Now, too much time had made him lose his will and his way.

Upon sighting Sabin he slowly – so slowly – held out his jewel-encrusted hands and warmly clasped his arm.

'Ah, my loyal clockwinder!' he exclaimed. 'How – how –' But here he lost the thread of this simple exercise in conversation, and his unfocussed eyes drifted up to study a lizard on the ceiling as he sought to regain his topic.

'How runs your kingdom?' prompted Sabin.

'Indeed.' The Sultan smiled vaguely. Behind him, several members of his retinue had begun to fall asleep standing up, their chins slumping on their breastplates.

'Why, this room is the heart of your kingdom, sire,' said Sabin, bowing low. 'If you would care to step upon my platform and listen carefully, you may hear its beat.'

And with that he climbed the steps and cupped his ear, bidding the Sultan to follow his example. Unaware of the impertinence, Shay-Tarrazin followed Sabin's example and listened, and came to realise that the ticking of the thousand clocks mirrored the slow, slow beat of his own weary heart, and now the concept of time that had so long eluded him became clear. For his fogged brain realised that true time was a personal thing, the measurement of each man's life on earth.

And with that, the first of the thousand clocks stopped. The Sultan and his retinue noticed nothing, but Sabin's finely tuned ear registered the absence.

Then another clock stopped.

And another.
And another.
And another.

So that the dense sound of ticking was gradually stripped away, like members of a performing orchestra laying down their instruments one after the next. The Sultan was paralysed by the phenomenon. With each stopped clock his heart grew a thousandth part weaker. After eight years, Sabin was winding the clocks so little that time's elasticity had been stretched to breaking point.

Shay-Tarrazin's eyes widened in horror as he dimly realised that his life must cease with the stopping of the final clock, and that for him, as it eventually did for everyone, time would soon terminate altogether. The ticking grew thinner and thinner as pendulums stilled, movements stopped moving, gems and sand and water ceased to pour, suns and moons no longer followed one another, and as the hands of the last clock ceased their movement around its calibrated surface, the Sultan's heartbeat demurred to the point of extinction, his body seizing into silence. He fell gently from the platform, cushioned by his saffron robes, into the great gold-filigree case of his best-loved Ormolu clock, where he lay unaided by his snoozing retinue.

As Sabin was the only man in the kingdom who had learned to master time, he assumed the responsibility of helping to bury the Sultan and attend his mourning rituals. Even the Grand Vizier (once he could be found and woken) agreed that this was appropriate and seemly.

The clocks were never wound again. The once-great empire of Omar Mehmet Shay-Tarrazin never emerged from its reverie. Sabin Darr was finally granted the freedom of the kingdom. He resolved to return to his village, and requested the slave-girl Safieh as a reward for his unstinting loyalty to the Sultan. The Grand Vizier was happy to grant him this, and to seal good fortune on the couple's union, presented them with a golden clock.

The hands of the clock did not move. Its interior mechanism had been removed, and the case had been filled with diamonds and sapphires.

For Sabin Darr, who had lost his family and his fingers, but not his sense of time, the world started to revolve once more.

INNER FIRE

He had been gingerly attempting to unfold a copy of the *Sunday Times*, but the newspaper snapped apart in his hands and shattered into dozens of pieces. Kallie swore angrily as he shovelled the shards into a pile with his boot; some of the broken edges were razor-sharp. There was nothing else to read in the apartment except his father's books, but there was no way of getting them off the shelves without a blow-torch, which he figured would somewhat defeat the object. Someone had given him some old magazines, but these were now stuck fast to the kitchen table, their covers rippled together in a lurid mosaic.

Kallie wondered how much longer Bennett would be. He had gone to the shops three days ago – or was it four? Perhaps he'd run into friends and gone to stay with them. Well, good riddance. Bennett had been camping out on the sofa for over two months now. Not bad for a guy who was 'just passing through the neighbourhood'. He had supposedly called in to see how his old schoolfriend was faring, but in the last eight weeks all he had done was empty the larder and try to repair the refrigerator. The refrigerator! Why in the name of everything perverse would he want to do that? The only reason Kallie hadn't thrown it out into the hall was because it would not fit through the kitchen door, which his father had replaced after drunkenly burning the old one two years ago.

He walked over to the window and rubbed away a patch of ice with the back of his glove. Across the street was the bus depot where no buses ever ran. Not too many people passed by, either. Most had learned their lesson the hard way, leaving the comparative warmth of their homes only to become disoriented in the blizzards and stumble into snow-drifts. It didn't take long for a body to cool down in these temperatures. His father had been fond of describing a time when you could see the curving green meadow of Primrose Hill from the bedroom windows. All Kallie had ever seen was a perpetual ice-haze hanging in the air, obscuring a sun that at its best was as watery as an uncooked egg.

There seemed little point in trying to lead a normal life now. Everything conspired against it. The solution, his eternally optimistic father had always told him, was to stay busy. Edward had stayed busy right until the end, refusing to acknowledge the fact that he was slowing down, moving with ever-increasing decrepitude, like a clockwork toy at the end of its winding. Finally he had overestimated his stamina on a trip to town and had failed to make it back to safety before a storm of truly biblical proportions had set in. The blizzard lasted for over three months. When it subsided, the landscape had changed its proportions entirely, and his father had presumably become part of the great permafrost ridge that separated North London from the city centre.

Kallie realised with a shock that he was cold. Cold. Nor-mally the word held little meaning. It was a permanent state of being, an endless dull ache in his bones, a spiteful stinging in his nerve ends, a dead sensation that dragged at his limbs, numbing his extremities, slowing his brain and thickening his blood. He forced himself to think. It was his only defence against the pervasive cold. Physical exercise brought only a temporary respite, sweat turning to icewater. He looked about the barren grey room, as uninviting as a Soviet state flat, and forced himself to think.

The only problem with Bennett not coming back was that Bennett had taken his wallet, ostensibly to buy food. The reason for deciding to trust a man who had never shown an ounce of reliability was obscure to him now. He looked over at the telephone, willing it to ring. It wouldn't, of course, even if Bennett had bothered to note the number. The mechanism was encrusted in ice, as indeed was the entire exchange, although he had heard a rumour that certain members of parliament could still operate some kind of closed circuit telecommunication system – presumably for use in emergencies.

Well, what was it now if not an emergency? The entire apartment, the entire apartment complex, the entire city, the entire country was frozen solid, and had been for twenty-two years, and with each passing year it grew a little colder, a little more still and silent, as the national heartbeat slowed to a weak and distanced blip.

Kallie was twenty-four years old, but held no memory of those fabulous sun-soaked times before the great freeze. Like a man blind from birth, he had not even been granted the pleasure of memories. Bennett was a year or so older, and swore he could recall laying in long grass with the sun in his eyes, so light and bright it hurt to look into the sky. But almost everything that came out of his mouth was a lie. He said he had seen shops open in Oxford Street. He said he knew people who could take them South, far beyond the reach of the ice. He said if they waited inside long enough the government would find a way to make it warmer. All lies. But he was right about one thing; they could not survive without food. That was why Kallie let him go. They had been living on beans and tinned luncheon meat, which was edible if you made a couple of holes in the lid of the can and gently heated it over the stove. But ten days ago the last gas ring had ceased to work, even though the council had promised to keep the pipes clear. There was no news coming in at all now that Mr Jakobowski had stopped calling by. Perhaps it was over, the last warm body had chilled to a blue cadaver and the city was finally a postcard snowscape.

And perhaps Bennett had found a pub open somewhere and was spending his money with a bunch of his drunken mates. Kallie knew there was nothing for it but to find out for himself and go outside. He would certainly die if he stayed here. His last source of heat – the gas ring – had packed in. The electricity still worked intermittently, but there were no electric radiators to be had, not unless you were rich enough to buy one on the black market. There was nothing left to eat except boxes of dry cereal, and he hadn't any milk to put on them. In the last few days, the temperature in the apartment had plunged, although he imagined it was still a long way above the subzeros in the street below. It hadn't helped that he had thrown his typewriter through the window in a fit of temper two days ago. The keys had jammed, and he lacked the patience – and the required agility of his numbed fingers – to repair it. What alarmed him more was the fact that he no longer really cared what happened to him. It would be easy to escape this bitter place; he just had to open all the windows, remove his greatcoat and lay down on the bed for a few minutes. Perhaps that was his only choice. But not just yet. Not before he visited the outside world one last time.

He added an itchy red woollen sweater to the other layers of his clothing, then wound a scarf around his chest. Over this he struggled into his greatcoat, dug out leather gloves with split seams, tucked his jeans into the tops of his battered Caterpillar boots.

When he unlatched the front door and looked out, he was surprised to find snow drifting in the hall. It had been nearly two months since his last foray into the streets of what had once recognisably been Camden Town. The tall windows at the end of the floor had been broken by children, and the

snow had formed a drift below the sill. If any of his neighbours still lived in the building, they were not prepared to
answer his knock. Kallie rapped on Mr Jakobowski's door
and listened with his ear placed to the peeling brown
paintwork.

'Mr Jakobowski, I'm going outside. Do you want me to
get you anything?'

He was sure he could hear someone moving around in the
sitting room, but what could he do if the old man wasn't
prepared to let anyone help him? In these strange times,
who knew how people would behave? Something electrical
hummed beyond the door. It sounded as if he had a radiator
running in there. People jealously hoarded their heat sources.
Who could blame them? Heat was hard to share; if you
opened the circle it dissipated. He called a few more times,
then gave up. In the past, when he had found anything he
thought the old man might like, he would haul it home and
leave it against his door. But the good-neighbour rules were
no longer in force; now it was every man for himself.

Down the icy stairwell – the lift had not worked in thirteen
years – to the front door, which was so frozen shut that Kallie
assumed no-one had been in or out since Bennett had left
with the contents of his wallet. Deadening whiteness glared
in through the window panels. He would need to find sun-
glasses. He had tried to pick up ski equipment from
Lillywhites the last time he was in town, but – surprise,
surprise – they had sold out. Only a handful of staff still
manned the store, keeping up the old conventions. He had
worked there himself once, bored out of his mind, waiting
to seize upon the odd straggling customer who had made it
in through the snow. That was back when the market was
still trying to cope with the crisis, when the rich warm nations
were still exporting to their poor frozen neighbours. Now
that those neighbours had ceased to earn wages, there was

no point in supplying them with affordable products. The milk of human kindness had been the first thing to freeze.

Throwing his weight against the door, he shifted it wide enough to push his way through. Bayonets of ice divorced themselves from the lintel and fell about him, cutting stencils into the swathes of snow that crusted the steps. Kallie raised his face into the biting wind and looked along the street, in the direction of the city. The air stole his breath, forcing a gasp with the realisation that it was far colder than anything he had experienced before.

Snow dunes, sparkling like hills of granulated jewels, swept in great unspoilt arcs across a bleached Sahara of roads and pavements. This was a bad sign; the route had been passable the last time he ventured out. But now even those high-profile charity missions the government was fond of announcing had ceased while everyone sorted out the problems in their own back yards.

On his last trip, Kallie had seen a few heavy-traction vehicles lumbering toward town. No people, though. There were never any people. It was simply too dangerous to set out on your own. He vaguely recalled a shopping expedition with his parents, and some friends of theirs who owned a car fitted with snowtyres. His mother had bought crazy things, pointless things, floral dresses and summer blouses she would never be warm enough to wear. Anxious to be rid of their stock, the storekeepers had been bargained down to nothing. He would always remember his mother laughing in front of the mirror as she held the diaphanous chiffon material against her. Ironically, her refusal to lose hope had brought her to a protracted, painful end.

What had instilled his parents with such unreasoning optimism? Was it because they remembered a time when their world was a cacophony of movement and sound, when trees still flowered, when their vision was saturated with rainbow colours? Had they never lost sight of life's possibilities? Is that why they had allowed him to be born?

It took forty minutes to reach the deserted high street, silent but for the wind that moaned eerily around the corners of buildings like a widow at a wake. At Camden Lock the ice in the canals had expanded and crushed itself upwards into fantastic twisted geometries. Kallie pulled the fur hood of his coat tighter around his face and concentrated on placing one foot before the other. The secret was to keep moving, always keep moving.

There were no shops open at all in the high street. This was a worrying new development. Surely some signs of life still existed? In the last few years he had seen fewer and fewer people on the crystalline streets. Many had found ways of moving to the southern hemisphere. Some had chosen to stay because they were determined to rebuild their lives in the face of the changed climate. And there were the others, the ones who had no money and no way of leaving alive.

As he trudged on, staying wide of the treacherously deep drifts, he remembered a picture he had seen once, a framed tube poster from the 1930s. The fanciful painting showed a gigantic cherub with translucent blue skin, a symbolic representation of the North Wind, perched on the roof of Oxford Circus tube station, breathing icy air down over the scurrying populace. The message was something about getting in out of the cold. Such bright pigments, such warmth, all gone now, gone forever. The sheer white force of snow and ice blotted every other colour from the landscape.

He resolved to walk as far as the giant supermarket at the end of the road, and no further. Beyond lay the crusted ridge of permafrost that had built up in the warring crosswinds of the Euston Road. Passing near it always unnerved him; there were people in the ice, frost-blackened hands and faces staring out like half-uncovered statues. It wasn't right that they had been left there, but what could anyone do? After a few years the ice turned to stone, shifting and rupturing like the tectonic plates of the earth.

The Safeway car park was almost empty. The attendant's barrier was up, and from the lack of tyre tracks it looked like nothing had driven in or out for days. The long glass wall of the supermarket glittered with frost, and was covered in starburst cracks where the great weight of snow was slowly pushing it in, but at least the lights were still on inside, and that meant the store was open for business. Kallie had no money on him, but with luck there would be no staff to operate the tills. Many people continued to conduct a semblance of normal life, as if determined to prove that the British could remain polite in the direst of circumstances, but were easily turned from their daily tasks. Nothing could be relied upon any more, beyond the fact that the situation would worsen.

The only advantage of the new cold climate was that food stayed fresher. Just as well; supplies were sporadic and perverse. Trucks would deliver great quantities of razorblades or suntan lotion, but there would be no bread or meat. Sometimes fresh-looking food would prove to have been frozen for years, and was impossible to thaw.

The temperature inside the store was, oddly enough, too high. Because of the value of its vast cold storage capacity, Safeway operated on its own generator, but the thermostats must have become damaged in the recent storms. To be hit by the smell of rotting meat was one final cruel consumerist joke to play on the few half-starved members of the public who still ventured through its doors.

Kallie unbuttoned his coat and fought the desire to vomit as he tried to ignore the sweet, ripe smell of putrifying vegetables. It was no use trying to refreeze food that had thawed. He would have to stick to tins again.

'Hey, Kallie.' He looked along the aisle to see an old friend of his mother's, Mrs Quintero, waving her bad hand at him.

She had lost three fingers to frostbite last winter, and had not had the wounds properly dressed. The black stumps of her distended knuckles suppurated through filthy bandages. He was not surprised to see her; she lived here in the store. Besides, there were only a few people who visited the outside world with any regularity these days, and one tended to see the same faces.

'The heating came back on, Kallie, can you believe it? Seventy-two degrees! Everything's gone off. The one place it needed to be cold.'

'Hasn't the professor been able to fix it?'

'Are you kidding? He hasn't a practical bone in his body. I wish you would take a look.'

'Have there been any shipments lately?' he called back, ignoring her request. If he moved any closer she would come over and hug him, and he wanted to avoid that at all costs. He hated anyone touching him.

'I don't know. I've been staying in. My husband's been really sick.' She shoved a wedge of peroxided hair from her dark-rimmed eyes. He wondered why on earth she still bothered to wear make-up. 'You heard anything?'

It was the most common question of all. Everyone expected some kind of government-authorised announcement to be made. Crisis over, it's safe to come out, that kind of thing. But it had not happened in his lifetime, and he doubted it could ever happen, or that there was still a government that could make any sort of announcement. Things had moved too far away from the norm now. How could their former lives ever be restored?

'We've had a few people call in, but nobody with any news. Been ages since we had news. A crowd of rough kids came by this week, stole the coffee vending machine, really noisy types. Of course, you don't remember when the whole world was noisy.' She looked around, too sharp, too anxious. 'It's so quiet now. The snow deadens everything, but oh! it never used to be like this.'

'Things change,' Kallie shrugged, keen to move on.

'I used to work in an office,' she continued, desperate to be understood, 'I was good at my job, and always busy, no time to stop. And the noise! Telephones, typewriters, and buses out in the street, people calling to each other. Televisions just left on. Singing at Christmas as we left the pub. Sometimes you had to shout to be heard. Now you can almost hear yourself think. Noise was life.' She blinked and shook her head, too frightened to speak.

'I have to go, Mrs Quintero.'

'The professor's in the stockroom giving a class.' She had turned away, unwilling to share her distress. 'My two are in there with him.'

'I'll look in and say hi,' he assured her, even though he did not want to.

'There's tinned peaches in syrup on Aisle 6, and powdered eggs,' she added listlessly. 'Make sure you take some. You need to keep your strength up.'

Why? he thought. What the hell for? 'Thanks, Mrs Quintero. Take care.' He set his metal basket aside and decided to look in on the professor first. He wasn't really a professor; he just looked and sounded like everybody's idea of one. He must have been a school-teacher at one time, because he behaved officiously and was always holding classes in the rear of the store.

The stockroom had long been cleared of produce, and folding metal chairs had been set in rows. The metal was cold to sit on, but everything wooden had long been burned. Anyone could attend the professor's lectures. Kallie was sure he would continue to make them even if no-one showed up at all. Today he was lecturing Mrs Quintero's children, and another boy he had not seen before. He stood at the back and raised his hand in silent gesture. The professor did not take kindly to being interrupted.

'Ice cores drilled from the centre of the Greenland ice-sheet should have warned us.' His dull monotone blunted the most interesting facts. The kids looked bored, and exhibited the distracted mannerisms of the unwell. 'They proved that the climate of the earth fluctuates far more than was ever previously realised. The last ice age took very little time to occur, perhaps just a decade or two, and lasted for over a hundred thousand years. Chance plays a large part in the survival temperature of our planet. In the seas of the world there are five natural pumps that drive the great currents of the oceans. The European Sub-Polar Ocean Programme found that one of these, the Odden Feature, powers a deep cold current that helps to control the circulation of the North Atlantic Ocean. It is caused by a vast tongue of ice in the Greenland Sea.'

Kallie quietly helped himself to a tray of sausage rolls Mrs Quintero had defrosted. They tasted like putty.

'Back in February 1993, Greenland's winter ice receded due to global warming, and the tongue of ice failed to form, dissolving into pancake ice.' He paused here to write the word PANCAKE on the wall with a blue crayon. One of Mrs Quintero's boys started repeating the word aloud.

'Without a pump to drive it, the Gulf Stream, one of the sea's warmest currents, stopped almost overnight. The Gulf Stream kept Britain and northern Europe warm, and now it's gone. Then, in less than a decade, the other great pumps died, transforming the weather patterns of the world in the wink of an eye. We are in uncharted territory now. The Royal Commission of Environmental Pollution's report into the flooding of Egypt and southern china – '

But the children were all saying 'Pancake, pancake,' and the professor's lesson, always the same lesson, was wasted.

They were too young to understand, anyway. They would learn soon enough.

'You were listening, weren't you, Kallie?' he asked wearily, throwing his crayon away.

'Heard it all before, prof. Nothing we can do, right?'

'Right. A friend of yours was in the other day. Tuesday.'

Kallie could not imagine why he still bothered to work out the names of individual days. Nobody else did. 'What was his name?' he asked.

'Bennett. Sat in the beverage department all day. He was very drunk when he left. I warned him not to go outside, but he wouldn't be stopped. Wouldn't even take his jacket. Became very belligerent when challenged.' He clicked his tongue disapprovingly.

That was it, then. No chance of getting his wallet back now. It was hard enough staying alive when you were sober, let alone drunk.

'Someone else was looking for you,' said the professor, an almost playful tone in his voice. Without asking, Kallie knew who.

'How is she?' he said finally. The professor grinned. 'Missing you, naturally. She always asks after you. She still talks about the time – '

'I know.' He cut the conversation short, uninterested in hearing an embroidered account of how, a year ago, he had saved Shari's life. 'I have to go.'

'I understand,' the professor answered with mock solemnity. 'You're a busy man. You know, I think it's time you considered moving in here with us while the generator still holds out. You get used to the smell, and it's worth it to be warm.'

'Thanks for the offer,' he mumbled, rebuttoning his coat. 'I'll keep it in mind.' Moving in meant being a part of the professor's ever-changing extended family, which meant looking after sick kids and hysterical, gangrenous parents.

'Shari will be sorry she missed you.'

I'll bet, he thought. He was suspicious of Shari since the accident; she was too nice to him now. 'Say hi to her for me.' He waved to Mrs Quintero as he pushed against the exit door.

Outside, the rising wind drove the temperature still lower. He reached the bottom of the slope below the supermarket and saw what he initially took to be a pile of brown rags, but closer inspection revealed a rigid hand, its fingers clutching the gelid air as if trying to take hold on life itself. Crystals of ice had formed over the corpse's eyes like luxuriant cataracts. Kallie cracked open its jacket and felt around for his wallet, but found nothing. Bennett had either dropped it in his drunken stupor, or had been robbed.

He knelt and bowed his head for a moment. No prayer, just a few seconds of stillness. They had spent their childhood years together; he owed Bennett something. Then he rose and continued on his way.

On a suicidal impulse he decided to push further on into the city centre, something he had not done for over four years. He wanted to see the River Thames, to prove for himself that this life-channel, more ancient than the pre-Christian city that had grown on its banks, still existed. It meant he would be trapped there overnight, because it would take him until sunset just to reach Piccadilly Circus, and it was virtually impossible to travel alone after dark without being very well prepared. Still, he wanted to see Eros once more. See it, perhaps, one last time.

As he passed the cylindrical ruin of the Telecom Tower, he thought of Shari; how she had been passing him somewhere near here on her way back to the supermarket, and how the Red Cross van had swung wildly around the corner. He remembered the lethal guillotine of ice sliding from its roof in a broad oblong sheet, and how he had thrown himself at her with a shout, slamming her body to the pavement as the ice shattered above their heads. It was the first time he had touched a girl. Up until then, the thought of physical contact with anyone had made him shudder uncontrollably. Shari had hugged him tight, clinging to the life she had nearly lost. Kallie had gently disentangled himself, embarrassed. He had shunned her ever since.

The freezing wind sucked at his greatcoat as he waded knee-deep through the intersection at Charlotte Street. His right foot had gone numb; a dangerous sign, one which suggested he should at least find a warm place to rest up for a few minutes. But there was nothing open around here. He continued past the shuttered, padlocked stores, concentrating on reaching Leicester Square and the circus beyond, unable to afford the luxury of worrying about his safety. Without realising it, he had reached a decision. The river was no longer just a point in his journey, but the point of the journey. After arriving there he felt sure he would have no need of further goals.

In Rathbone Place he passed a dying dog, a red setter, half buried in an avalanche of dislodged ice. The shards that sparkled in its diamante fur lent it an air of ostentatious glamour.

Oxford Street. Once a cheap-and-cheerful marketplace thronged with shoppers, according to his father. Now a wind-ravaged tunnel of ice, black-spotted in places where the corpses of foolhardy pedestrians poked up through the snow-drifts. No life here at all. It was worse than he had feared. The blizzard cleared for a moment, and as if through flawed crystal he glimpsed two ragged figures roped together, struggling to stay upright, in trouble. They had disappeared in the fifteen minutes it took him to reach the spot they had occupied. Already their footprints were obliterated.

Soho was impassable. The narrow streets were blocked with abandoned trucks and boulders created by the sheet-ice that slid continuously from the rooftops. The upper floors were skeined with billowing crosshairs of ice that caught the dying light like the wings of giant dragonflies.

Kallie skirted around into Regent Street, the great curve of Nash's terrace pockmarked by the blown-in windows of department stores. The pale sun had descended behind the buildings as he reached the blue-shadowed end of the street. Here the wind was at its fiercest. A red double-decker Route-master bus lay on its side, almost buried by drifts. A diamond shop had lost its panes, the ground floor now extravagantly filled with iridescent icicles, so that it appeared little changed from its window-dressed heyday.

The snow in the circus was sullied by the discharges of overturned trucks and the tracks of pilgrims who had come here in the vain hope that reaching this gaudy apex of civilis-ation might somehow end their own spiritual loss. As man descended once more into beast, the manufactured tokens of a forgotten sophisticated world took on the power of talismen. Kallie watched as an elderly woman floundered past with a green plastic Harrods bag on her head. Earlier that day, at Mornington Crescent, he had seen two young men dragging an electronic exercise machine toward the tube station, perhaps intending to install it as an object of veneration.

And here was Eros, poor Eros, intended as an inspiration to Londoners, now twisted from its perch so that only a leg and an elegant silvery wing of Gilbert's famous statue could be seen thrusting hopelessly up from the dunes in the centre of the roundabout. Kallie stood before the fallen God and grimaced in despair, heaving in gulps of stinging knife-sharp air as he stared at the upturned calf and ankle, the feathered wingtip almost lost in snow and discarded chunks of scaf-folding. Then he was running at the statue, clawing at it in a desperate attempt to free it from the swamped remains of the desecrated fountain. Uncovering even another inch proved impossible. Others had tried to remove the permafrost trellis that encased it like a crystal shroud, in vain.

Kallie stumbled blindly away, tipping over into the oil-stained drifts, pushing himself back on to his feet, scrabbling around the long-abandoned traffic until he came up against the steel-shuttered doorway of Tower Records. There was nothing else for him here, and nowhere else for him to go, so he remained completely still, unable to think or move. As night fell, the warmth within him slowly faded. At his back, giant cut-outs of forgotten rock stars struck poses of defiance, icons of redundant anarchy.

Kallie started to die.

It was as easy as he had hoped it would be. You just had to do nothing, keep still and allow the insidious numbness to colonise your limbs. The crawling clouds reflected the whiteness of the city, and finally ceased to move, as if the world could no longer be bothered to turn upon its axis. He closed his eyes and rested his head against the ice-jewelled shutters, allowing life to quietly slip away.

The explosion of noise that followed blasted him to his feet. Somebody was playing music inside the building. He could feel the bass tones vibrating the windowpanes. Forcing his reluctant body into action he stepped back, trying to see beyond the reflections into the rear of the ground floor. Someone – some *thing* – was gyrating insanely to the music, raging the entire length of the store. And there were lights, bursts of primary colour, flashing sequentially.

It took him a while to discover the forced door of the delivery bay at the side of the building. He climbed over buckled steel struts – they must have been rammed with a vehicle – to the interior, and was deafened by the surrounding, saturating noise. Someone had used a bright yellow forklift truck to break in. Piles of cracked and broken CD cases littered the floor. A primitive set of disco lights pulsed red and blue diamonds at the back of the floor near the stairwell. The dancer was a short, slim woman in her forties. Her body retained the litheness and aggression of a professional performer. She swung and slammed and span, kicking out, punching the chill air with a series of guttural grunts. Her greying red hair was tied back with a green bandana. She wore a red satin leotard with the leggings hacked off above the knee, and a yellow scarf carelessly knotted around her waist. She looked ablaze with anger and energy.

Kallie dropped behind a record rack and watched as the music changed, from the techno-trance of The Shamen to the electronic heartbeat of Tangerine Dream, from the calypso rhythms of the Penguin Cafe Orchestra to the classical cadences of Michael Nyman. She danced through an eclectic melange of sound that comfortably encompassed Offenbach and Elton John. Now that there was no more culture, the abrupt changes did not shock. When the music ceased in midtrack she crossed to the DJ booth and flipped the tape – obviously an item she had personally assembled – so that she could continue to dance. The first track of the second side was 'We're Havin' a Heatwave', sung by Marilyn Monroe, and Kallie caught himself grinning uncontrollably. Wondering where the power was coming from, he searched the floor and saw that a pair of car batteries had been rigged to the system with jump leads.

Now he was able to observe her properly for the first time, bent over the light in the booth, feeling for the controls. She was unable to see, permanently blinded by time spent lost in the snowy wastes. There were no fingers at all on her swollen right hand, and just two on her left. She had deftly flipped the tape with her thumbs. He tried to catch sight of her feet, dreading to imagine their damaged state, knowing that every step she took must be agonising, but she was already off and away, pounding across the floor to the brassy orchestrations.

Finally, even the deafening music failed to keep him awake. Comforted by the great weight of sound, with his greatcoat pulled about his head, he slept on through the long, loud night.

He awoke soon after dawn to find the store silent, the lights and the sound system turned off to conserve what little power there was left. The dancer was asleep on a patchwork duvet beside the DJ booth, snoring lightly. Studying her, he was tempted to think that the tiny crosshatched lines around her mouth and eyes were caused by laughter, not fear, even though he saw that her feet were little more than swollen stumps. For a moment he wanted to ask her how she could dance in the face of all reason, when the world and her own body were steadily failing her, how it was possible to experience pleasure without hope. But waking her up, he realised, would be a mistake. Better to let her sleep on, and rebuild her energy for another dance.

Gingerly stepping between CD cases, he made his way back to the delivery bay door and left. Outside, he paused before the windows and looked back in, but could no longer see her. The floor was still and dark, as if the building would only reawaken when she did.

The sky had cleared to a deep sapphire-hard blue and the wind was keen, but at least the snow had stopped. He passed several people on his way to the river, but none of them were prepared to acknowledge him, or even look up. For the first time he began to sense just how completely the cold had closed him, closed them all, off. He was aware of being hungry, a state he normally never noticed, and grew colder by the minute, but the shimmering ebony band ahead drove him forward along the half-buried embankment, until he was standing in the silent centre of Waterloo Bridge, above the strangled stream that had once been the mighty Thames.

When he looked down into the spangled black water and saw that it still ran, determinedly chugging around the encrusted floes and over mounds of industrial debris, on through the heart of the city, he began to cry; lightly at first, then uncontrollably, great howls of despair that turned to roars of frustration, rage and joy. Ice formed on his face where the tears coagulated. Something inside him opened, fanning into faint life, slowly growing warmer until his gut was burning. He turned and bellowed from the bridge, out across the sub-zero city, up into the frozen sky where hardy white gulls still wheeled and screamed, yelling until he was hoarse and dizzy from the exertion.

And as that first great release subsided, he knew; that hope was false, a misleading hollow nonsense obscuring all that was real and true. The truth was that the world would die and take him with it, today, tomorrow, years from now, in agony, in terror, in unreadiness, and it didn't matter. What mattered was the time left to live. His rumbling stomach broke his train of thought, and he yelped with the shock of the noise after so much silence.

Kallie looked out across the glittering, foolish river, to the weakling sun climbing in a pointless sky, where a dancing madwoman whirled in scraps of fire on crippled feet, beyond the laws of gravity, the threshold of pain, the bounds of rationality. He removed a glove and wiped his eyes until they were clear and dry. Heavy grey snowclouds were amassing on the estuary horizon. It was time to head North, before the temperature fell further.

He wondered what Shari was doing, and whether, in the face of all reason, she too was laughing.

WAGE SLAVES

The office block blotted out the night sky above Canary Wharf. Walls of polished black glass absorbed all reflections, turning the building into a black hole, inhuman and infinite. The surrounding streets were deserted. At this time of night a single window was still illuminated, on the 35th floor.

Leonard Clark was in his office studying a document. He was a lifer, heavy, balding, gym-fit, a workaholic whose calculated responses and unflinching stares made others nervous. His office was clinically corporate. The only touches of humanity were a framed photograph of a lost-looking wife and a signed cricket bat – a quota-achievement trophy – mounted on the wall.

Matthew Felix knocked and entered. Another executive, but one with an attitude as yet unhardened by the vicissitudes of business life.

'Ah, Mr Felix. I've just finished checking your report. Take a pew.'

The younger man seated himself and awaited Clark's verdict. 'The style is sharp, succinct,' noted his boss. 'It's very impressive. *Very* impressive.' He paced about, studying the document while Felix fidgeted, unnerved by the rare praise.

'Thorough, that's the word. And not afraid to be critical. That's good. It shows integrity.' Felix grew increasingly uncomfortable as Clark paced behind him. 'How long did this take you?'

'Three days. Well. Days and nights.'

'It's paid off. It really has. There's just one thing that bothers me. A silly thing. It's this, here.' He held the document close to Felix's face. Too close. 'Receipt. I before E except after C. But you get it wrong every time. Every single time. Look. Receipt. Receipt. Receipt. *Receipt*.'

Clark carefully removed his prized cricket bat from the wall, giving it a few test swings. 'A foolish, tiny, minuscule mistake. Ruining *everything*.'

He took a sudden high swing with the bat. The massive connecting *crack* against the back of Felix's skull knocked him clean out of his swivel chair, sprawling him face down on the carpet-tiles. Clark examined his unconscious subordinate, then dragged him out of the office by the lapels of his suit. 'There's simply no excuse for shoddy workmanship these days,' he reflected.

Imagine an incredibly complex computer program, a physical structure, skeletal at first, then gaining a dense musculature of electronic cabling, pipework and floors and finally, an exterior skin. A monolithic mirrored cathedral, towering over the city horizon. Below the postmodern fripperies of its entrance, down in the railway station at its base, a train discharged its next batch of commuters. They marched along the platform in regiments, financial warriors heading into fresh battle.

Ben Harper's tie was knotted too tightly. He tried to loosen the knot as he marched with the crowd. Feeling something sticking in his neck, he pulled a pin from the collar of his brand-new shirt. He had yet to notice the price sticker still on his briefcase. He checked his watch and glanced up at the sombre building, its windows darkening as clouds passed.

Ben had the hopelessly innocent face of a young man on his first day in a new job. He watched the other commuters for his cues, swallowing nervously and wondering why he had ever lied in the first place. Then he crossed the half-finished road to the Symax building and entered its pristine foyer.

The Olympian marble hall appeared to have been designed by Albert Speer. A cleaner shadowed Ben, carefully wiping away his wet footprints, removing all human spoor. To access the elevator he had to collect an electronic tag from the commissionaire, who punched in its encoded number. The guards looked like American police officers. Video monitors checked his progress as the lift arrived and he entered.

'Hold the doors!' An attractive young woman slipped into the elevator and smiled at Ben. She stood on one leg and removed her shoe, then belted the base of the door with the heel. The door juddered and shut. 'There's something weird with the electrics,' she explained. 'I should keep a hammer in my handbag.' She put the shoe back on.

Ben watched her, fascinated, until the doors opened on the 35th floor.

The reception area was a gleaming shrine to the work ethic, part space station, part rainforest. A large chromium sign read: **SYMAX. The Future Is Now.** Beyond this a bank of TV screens showed corporate videos; images of wheatfields, dolphins and sunsets. The robotic blonde behind the desk noted Ben's colour-coded badge. 'Oh, new boy. I'll call someone.'

He watched one of the corporate videos. An avuncular voice intoned something about 'the first generation of environments that work for you. A Symax building is an infinitely adaptable stress-free workspace. Light, heat and climate are monitored by sensors that control your staff's constantly changing needs. One day all offices will be this way, because at Symax the future is here to stay.'

'Mr Harper.' A corporate-looking woman in her early thirties held out her hand. 'Diana Carter. We met briefly at your interview. If you'd care to follow me.'

She led Ben through the swing doors, past rows of extreme-technology work stations. The sky dominated, framed in the floor-to-ceiling windows. It gave the area a feeling of peace, as though they were on the deck of a liner coasting its way through the clouds. Staffers had customised their work spaces in odd ways, as if trying to make them cosier and less efficient-looking. All sound was absorbed but for the clicking of key-boards.

'There's been a personnel change since we spoke,' explained Carter. 'Mr Felix left us rather suddenly. The PR department isn't fully functional yet. Things are a little crazy.' She handed him a manual. 'Company bible. Read and believe. This desk was supposed to have been cleared. Mr Temple wanted to welcome you but he's not himself today. None of us are.' She gave a brief bleak smile and whizzed off, leaving Ben at his work station.

The girl from the lift was at the next desk. She looked over and smiled, appraising him. Feeling spied upon, Ben attempted to look efficient. Unfortunately, he couldn't find the switch to activate his terminal. Perhaps it needed a key or something. He checked the desk drawers. The first one contained a pair of damp socks, a bottle of painkillers and a hunting knife.

His watch had stopped. His chair-back appeared to be broken. He tried to fire up the computer again, to no avail. He studied other people for tips and got none. Amused, the girl finally came over. 'Try the button at the front.'

Ben sheepishly pressed it. The screen came on, but nothing else did.

'You've never used one of these before, have you?'

'I'm not familiar with this, uh, make,' said Ben.

She reached over and booted up the system for him. 'What are you doing here?'

He shifted awkwardly. 'I'm the new PR assistant to Mr Clark – '

'I don't see how. You obviously have no experience.'

'I've had dozens of corporate jobs.'

'Then go ahead and set your voicemail.' She sat back, amused. 'You can fool them but not me. You've never worked in a place like this before, have you?'

Ben was flustered. 'I thought I'd get a *bit* further before being found out. It's only ten past nine.'

'I won't tell anyone.' She held out her hand. 'Marie Vine. Let's cut a deal. Tell me what you're doing here, and I'll get you through. Nobody has to know.'

There was no point in continuing to lie. 'I needed the work,' he admitted. 'So I faked my CV. I was a teacher, do you know what that pays? I'm twenty-six and sick of never having any money. I can handle this. I know about people.'

'If you know so much about people,' asked Marie, 'why did you stop teaching?'

'I got fired for organising a student picket. I get too involved. This will be better for me, more – impersonal. It's just press releases. How hard can it be?'

She brought her lips close to his ear. 'Here's something for you to think about. This is the most advanced work environment in the world. Yet it gives a job to a little red school-teacher with a faked CV. What does that tell you?'

At noon, Carter reappeared to take Ben on a tour of the floor. 'Over there,' she pointed to a thin man in a tight grey suit, 'that's Mr Swan.' Swan's posture was birdlike and vaguely irritating. He slowly craned forward. 'If there's anything in the company manual that doesn't leap out at you, feel free to give me a tinkle.'

'Over there, Mr Carmichael.' Ben nodded to each of the staff in turn, but people were too busy to take much notice. 'Lucy, your shared PA. Paula, word processing.' They passed another office. The huge shape of an arguing man could be seen through the glass. 'Mr Clark, the new department head.'

Marie passed with a sheaf of papers and interrupted in a

manner that seemed to annoy Carter. 'Mr Felix was in line for the position, but he's gone,' she explained. 'Vanished like a summer rain.'

'Mr Temple is the managing director, as you know, but he's not often here,' said Carter. 'He lives on the floor above – '

' – but seeing him is like getting an appointment with the Wizard of Oz,' Marie cut in. 'Oh well, better get back to work. We're all on Candid Camera, you know. They record everything, and they're everywhere. Even in the toilets.'

'I suppose Symax needs good security if it's developing systems no-one else has,' Ben replied.

'Exactly so, Mr Harper,' agreed Carter. Marie was disappointed that Ben had chosen to side with the management. Ahead, a crowd was gathering around one of the refreshment stations.

'It's happening again!' called one of the office boys. People were watching a half-filled water cooler that was emitting an ominous rumbling sound. The water inside swirled around in an impossible whirlpool, climbing the sides of the plastic jar. It whirled faster and faster, and suddenly the jar ruptured, spraying water everywhere. The secretaries squealed and jumped back.

Ben turned to Carter but found her place taken by Marie. 'A bug in the system,' she explained. 'Look, my little bogus friend, I know it's your first day but I'd like to speak frankly with you. You confided in me. Not here, though. The walls have ears and eyes. You have to be careful who you talk to. Over lunch.'

They crossed an acre of grey marble floor to the restaurant, passing a pair of security guards with vicious-looking guns in their belts. 'Private security firm,' noted Marie. 'Those things on their belts are tasors.'

'Is that legal?'

'This place is beyond the jurisdiction of the police,' she

explained. In the restaurant there were vegetarian dishes, roasting chickens, trays of ham and beef. They shared a quiet table away from the chatter-filled main section.

'Three weeks ago Matthew Felix walked out of here and never even came back to collect his belongings,' she explained, talking through a mouthful of chicken. 'His car's still in its usual parking space under the building, but he's gone. He was my friend. And your predecessor.'

'What can I do?' Ben shrugged helplessly. 'I just got here.'

'The secretaries are always off sick. They say there's something in the air that makes you ill. At this height the windows can't be opened because of the winds. Then there are the phone lines. They randomly switch themselves around, like they've got poltergeists or something.'

'It's my first day,' he pleaded.

'The staff can sense that there's something wrong even if the management can't, but no-one – NO-ONE – is willing to talk about it.'

'This suit is brand new, Marie. And the tie.'

'I'm trying to find someone who's not just a management sheep.'

'I'm not a sheep!' Ben protested. 'I've been in the business world for four hours! Management must be able to do something. Temple, he's the boss-man.'

Marie speared a piece of asparagus. 'He won't see me. I've already had two official cautions from Clark. One more and I'll lose my job. They all think I like to stir things up.'

Ben grew more exasperated. 'I should stay away from you. I fought hard for this job and I'd really like to keep it.'

'It's not like I'm asking you to do anything illegal, just keep your eyes and ears open, and tell me if you notice anything strange. Do it before the place gets to you and you become like the rest of them.'

Ben lowered his fork. 'Which is what?'

'You know. Corporate.'

'What's wrong with that?'

'You're an individual.'

He thought for a moment. 'Maybe I don't want to be.'

Marie rose to leave. She was frustrated by Ben's attitude. 'Maybe you don't. But I think Matthew Felix is dead. The police found his cat half-starved. Maybe he had a heart attack and it was stress-related so they quietly took him away. Somebody here knows more than they're telling. For God's sake, look at them!'

'Why would they hide something like that?'

'This is a new company. Maybe they're scared of bad publicity. Oh, forget it. Just forget I said anything.' Ben watched helplessly as she rose from the table and left. He looked out of the window at the power lines which passed close to the glass. He could hear their eerie hum beneath the moaning wind. There were dead pigeons all along the window ledge, neatly aligned in a row. He thought, *I've entered the Twilight Zone.*

Aided by a bank of video monitors running interactive graphic devices, Clark was giving a talk to a group of potential Symax investors. Ben found a chair and watched his new boss in action.

'This is the first fully operational smart building in the United Kingdom. Created by computer to minimise employee error and maximise profit potential.' On the screens behind, Ben could see diagrams of the building's nerve centre, the antiseptic, unmanned sensor room filled with gauges and cylinders. 'A Symax building is designed for every temperature, atmosphere and movement change. In a non-smart building, company staff have to find a way of fitting around the architecture. Symax systems learn from staff habits and adapt to create a unique environment for each company.'

As the meeting ended, Clark walked with the leader of the group, Ben following alongside, listening in.

'I want New York to see this,' said the client. 'I'll need a full presentation on Friday. Can you handle it?'

'I have no problem with that at all,' Clark replied, seeing him into the lift. After the doors had shut, he eyed Ben suspiciously. 'You heard him. Four days to the biggest presentation we've ever had. This place is going to be jumping, and you with it.'

Dusk brought a lurid red glow to the windows, which automatically darkened to reduce the glare. Ben attempted to set up a stack of books on his desk, which appeared to be perfectly level, but each time he balanced them they shifted and fell over. He took a marble from his drawer and set it on the white melamine desktop. The little glass ball rolled first one way, then abruptly another. He tapped his teeth with a pencil and looked back at Marie, thinking. Nothing made sense here. Was that normal in the world of big business? He knew he shouldn't get involved, that it would only lead to trouble, but decided to talk to Swan anyway.

'My predecessor seems to have left very suddenly,' he prompted.

'Mr Clark fired him,' Swan explained. 'They had a terrible row.'

'What about?'

'I don't know. Work, I suppose. They didn't get on.'

'I thought everyone got on here. Isn't that the point?'

'In theory, yes. Did you ever hear of a theory that fully worked in practice? Thought you might like a copy of this. More useful than the office bible.'

Ben accepted the proferred pamphlet and turned it over in his hands. It bore the title GOD IN THE WORKPLACE.

'Er, thanks.'

Swan pointed to the small gold crucifix he wore over his tie. 'The devil and his works are all around us, Mr Harper. Better safe than sorry.'

✦

That night, as everyone worked late, an exhausted secretary swept into the office of her supervisor, Mr Meadows, and dumped a stack of papers on to his overflowing desk. The executive argued into his headset while signing papers and returning them: 'I know it was late because I checked with security, and if it doesn't reach me in time my client won't pay so we all get shafted. Well, fuck-you-very-much but an apology isn't recognisable in fiscal terms – you're hovering, what is it?'

'Accounts on 2,' said the secretary. 'Wife on 3 and Mr Clark on the internal.'

'I'll call them all back. Close the door, Norma – close it.'

She reluctantly left, pulling the door shut behind her. Meadows kicked back, yanking off the headset and thumbing the remote on his stereo unit. Classical music began playing, Smetana's *Libuse*, the volume increasing. He stared at the phone, still trilling, and suddenly yanked it out of the wall. Then he shook the buzz from his ears, locked the door and returned to his desk, slipping off his jacket, removing his tie, kicking off his shoes and unbuckling his trouser belt.

Outside the office, two secretaries noticed him through the glass and started to giggle. Meadows continued to strip until he was completely naked. A crowd gathered as he stood at the picture window behind his desk. Everyone yelled when he raised his chair and hurled it through the glass. They hammered at the locked door as Meadows climbed over the broken shards on to the ledge.

He raised his arms high. It was a hell of a drop. Balancing on the balls of his feet, he executed a graceful swan dive out over the glittering city. The office door caved in seconds too late. The secretary screamed. Bouyed by the crosswinds, Meadows fell slowly through the starry sky – fell and fell – and laughed, until he smashed thunderously through the glass canopy of the station roof amid hordes of homegoing commuters.

✦

Ben pulled open the glass doors. Far above him in the sensor room, electronic dials registered the change in temperature and compensated for the sudden fall with a boost. In the reception area, the screens continued to run endless plugs for Symax. Already the words sounded repetitive and hollow. The receptionist was holding her head in her hands. It looked like a bad start to Tuesday.

'You okay?' asked Ben as he passed.

'The monitors are giving me a headache,' the receptionist replied.

As Ben reached his work station he could see staff members discussing something very intently. The broken glass in front of Meadows' office was being swept up, the area sealed off.

'What happened here?'

'Just after you left last night, Mr Meadows went for a walk outside the building and missed his train. By about three feet,' Marie explained. 'Thirty-five floors. They scraped him off the tarmac like a dab of strawberry jam. The police are still looking for his teeth.'

'He must have been – really stressed out.'

'That's an understatement. They're sending people to coun-sellors. Perhaps now you'll believe me. I have to talk to you.'

'Not again.'

'Remember, I know your little secret.'

Reluctantly, Ben followed her away from the steady gaze of the cameras to the stairwell, and then up four flights of stairs to one of the deserted floors. Heat dials and movement recorders flickered as they crossed the grey carpet tiles. 'They haven't sold this floor yet. No-one can hear or see us.'

Ben felt guilty. 'We shouldn't even be here.' He paused and looked down at his shoes. Dozens of tiny dead insects were arranged in neat curving rows across the floor.

'I need to trust someone,' said Marie. 'I don't want to spoil your chances with the company. I mean – look at you. All freshly scrubbed and innocent.'

'Matthew Felix didn't go missing, he got fired.'

'Nobody knows that for sure. I was due to meet him that night, but he never showed up.'

'Did you talk to the police?'

'They said they'd let me know if they heard anything. It's not like I'm a relative. I'm sure something terrible has happened to him. You're new, you could ask around.' The big appealing eyes swayed him. 'Please?'

Mr Carmichael was a fussy time-server most people avoided, and today he had an appalling head-cold. 'Of course he was stressed,' he told Ben, 'he'd just had a terrible argument with Clark. I don't know where he went, nobody knows. I liked him, he was a nice man. Punctual. I liked Meadows, too. Never thought he'd do something like that. They say it's always the quiet ones, but Meadows . . . Mind you, everyone else hated his guts.'

In the ceiling corners, gleaming cameras recorded all movement as the air-mixers raised and lowered their pitch. Ben tapped the pencil on his teeth, trying to work it out. Worry made people overdose on sleeping pills, but what could make you hurl yourself to your death? Rainclouds the colour of drain-water rolled past the windows. He looked over at Marie's work station. She briefly glanced up and gave him an absent, tired smile.

'Want to go for a drink tonight?'

'By the time I'm through there won't be anywhere open. Besides, we shouldn't be seen together. Office fraternising is discouraged.'

Her changes of mood were unpredictable. The day passed at a crawl. Ben concentrated on drafting the press releases Carter had outlined to him. When he left the building that night, the thousand storm-streaked panes that looked down on him seemed far more sinister than they had yesterday morning.

✦

Clark had been summoned to the director's office, an elegant low-lit suite that was more like a private apartment. Inside, the greying, debonair Temple was checking his watch impatiently, ready to leave.

'I hear the police were trying to get in again, Leonard. This is getting to be a habit.'

'I've told them this is private property,' said Clark, 'that we have our own security force.'

'We're still subject to the laws of the land. Anyone know why Meadows did it?'

'I've asked around. He seemed fine, a little hyper, but so is everyone else with this presentation looming . . .'

'It's not a wonderful advert for a stress-free environment, is it?'

'An unfortunate coincidence. And now these rumours . . .'

'You're saying we have – grumblers?' Temple made the word sound sinister. 'If we do, keep an eye on them, report back to me. New York is the big one, the make or break contract. Nothing must jeopardise that. Do you understand? This is more than war. This is business.'

In the reception area of the 35th floor, the monitors were still spewing out their 'Peace and Harmony' sales pitch. Ben passed two managers who were shouting at each other, and another dropping papers everywhere who looked like she'd been up all night.

Lucy, his PA, startled him. 'Can cellular phones give you cancer?' she asked.

'I don't know,' Ben answered. 'Why?'

'I get these headaches all the time. Can you get cancer of the head?'

'Have you seen the company doctor?'

'He thinks I'm faking. Maybe it's these things.' She tapped his monitor.

'Tell me something, Lucy. What was Mr Felix like?'

'Really cute. She soon got her claws into him.' She pointed at Marie's chair.

'Before he left, did he seem strange to you in any way?'

'Not strange. Angry. He'd had an argument with Mr Clark.'

'They didn't get along?'

'Mr Clark hated him. He hates everyone. He already hates you.'

Later that morning, Ben attempted to requisition a file from a harassed Human Resources Officer. 'I told you,' insisted the officer, 'you can't see Mr Felix's medical history without proper authorisation.'

'What about absenteeism?' asked Ben. 'Does Symax have many people off sick?'

'What do you expect? Germs travel through the heating system. There are a few repetitive strain injuries. Always more when we're busy. There's a flu virus decimating the place. All companies get them, but this is particularly bad. We've a bigger health problem, but it doesn't make any sense.'

'What do you mean?'

'Hard to explain.' The officer pulled a pen from her hair and scrubbed something out on a form. 'I don't have any figures. Deadlines produce stress, which increases blood pressure, causes headaches, heartburn, sleep disorders... standard stuff. But there's an instability here. People over-react, flare up, lose their tempers, burst into tears. It's something peculiar to this building. You know the hand dryers in the toilets? They're supposed to be more hygienic. They're not. They incubate bacteria. You can get pneumonia from them. Nobody really knows what's good for you. Or what's harmful. And my clock's running backwards.'

Ben was momentarily thrown. 'Sorry?'

'My computer clock. They shouldn't do that, should they? Run backwards?'

'Could you give me a print-out of the sickness figures?'

'It's against regulations. Haven't you read your manual? Head office don't like it.'

Ben fooled around with his computer, but any management files of importance were sealed with passwords. He tried different keys of his own devising, but nothing worked. He watched Marie at her desk. Knowing she could be seen, she crossed her long legs and gave him a sexy look. He drew a heart on a piece of paper and folded it into an airplane. Throwing it in her direction, he was dismayed to see it sucked into the air-conditioning unit that sat between them. The sun suddenly broke through the clouds, causing the photo-sensitised windows to compensate for the changing light density and darken, while the illuminated ceiling panels grew perversely brighter to compensate for the windows.

Ben despairingly studied his monitor, typing slowly, but his attention drifted to Felix's belongings. Rechecking the desk he felt something, a flat square stuck at the back of the bottom drawer. The computer disk was labelled *Property of Matthew Felix*. He pocketed it just as Clark appeared beside him.

'You never seem to be doing any work, Harper.'

'I was – going to ask your advice on the press releases,' said Ben. 'I take it we gloss over Mr Meadows' first diving lesson?'

Clark glowered at him. 'I don't like you, Harper. Why is that?'

'You haven't tried my cooking yet?'

'Just do your job and I won't have cause to lose my temper.'

Marie helped Ben load the disk after Clark had moved on. 'You'll need the password,' she warned. 'Everyone is expected to enter and remember their own five-letter code.'

'Didn't he tell you what his was?' asked Ben. 'I mean, you were friends.'

'I liked him, but I didn't exactly get inside his mind. Besides, we aren't supposed to tell each other things like that.'

'Then maybe he kept it written down somewhere. You okay?'

'It's nothing, just a headache. We'll have to keep looking.'

He studied Felix's belongings again, trying to make sense of it all. In a travelbag beneath the desk he found a dog-eared book of horoscopes. 'You'd think the police would have taken his belongings away.'

'They never came up here. Our security firm wouldn't let them.'

'What birth-sign was Felix?' he asked Marie.

'Gemini, I think.'

He flicked through the horoscope book to Gemini, and found a drawing of Janus. *The Twin-Faced Guardian Of Doorways, Entrances And Beginnings*, read the asterisked caption. He typed in 'Janus' and pressed ENTER. The disk started to open its files, but as quickly as it did, the contents corrupted. Damn the magnetics in this place . . .

One newspaper clipping was legible before the screen contents vanished. A photograph of the building captioned *Father of 'smart' architecture commits suicide*. Then the item dispersed into the ether.

'Maybe he realised something was wrong with the building and killed himself,' suggested Marie.

'Maybe somebody else realised something was wrong and shut him up.' They exchanged alarmed looks.

Swan suddenly appeared beside them, looking pleased with himself. 'Want to see something really strange?' he asked. Before they could reply, he unclipped the steel biro he kept in his jacket pocket and slapped it against the wall above Ben's desk. When he removed his hand, the pen stayed there by itself. 'Some days the whole blessed place is magnetised.'

'We need your help,' said Ben. 'Who designed this building?'

'That kind of information isn't available any more,' Swan

complained. 'I'd be breaking company rules. Punishable by instant dismissal.'

'Who's going to know?'

'In an environment with total information control? Are you nuts? Look, it's not a good idea to get too involved with the work. You could lose your job, your credit rating, who knows what else. Those cameras up there probably lipread.'

'You're being paranoid.'

'You're right,' agreed Swan. 'That's good. It's healthy to be paranoid.'

The sun set beyond the vast windows as Paula, the typist, put down her coffee and slopped some of it on to her desk. Tutting with annoyance, she dug out a paper towel and started mopping up the mess. At her feet, one of the recessed floor plugs emitted sparks. Just beyond her field of vision, a wall circuit was scorching a live path to her computer, tiny white flashes jumping across the keyboard. The spilt coffee reached her mouse just as she mopped it. The resulting electric shock threw her across the room.

Several people saw the burning lines shortcircuiting in the walls, passing from one computer to the next, rendering each one live. 'Where's the mains switch?' someone shouted. 'Keep away from the machines!' Others just looked confused. Nobody moved.

But everyone stared at Ben as he stormed into Diana Carter's office. Carter was on the phone, and not pleased by the interruption. 'A girl just got electrocuted and everyone's carrying on as if nothing happened!' he shouted, pointing through the glass. 'Look at them!' The workforce was busily going about its business. 'This is gross negligence. There's something wrong with the electrics. We had to unplug the terminals.'

She eyed his dirty knees. 'Everyone is working very hard here, Harper. It's bad enough that half of my girls are off sick without you causing trouble. You're not allowed to tamper with the machines. It's against company policy.'

'We'll see about that,' said Ben, slamming out.

'One of my staff members, Mr Swan, brought the matter to my attention,' said Clark. 'He overheard Harper telling someone he'd lied his way into the job.'

'Christ, don't you think I have enough to worry about without this?' demanded Temple. 'We're taking orders from all over the world and yet our figures are down. How is that possible? The efficiency of our workforce is plunging. *Inside the world's most efficient building.* What the hell is going wrong? And now you tell me we have some kind of a spy in our midst. Well, you'll have to deal with it. Nothing can screw up this presentation.'

The small chipboard door opened in the basement wall and a troll-like man of around sixty looked out. Snowy bristles sprouted from his eyebrows, nose and ears. 'I haven't seen you before,' said Hegarty, the caretaker, in a high, strangled voice. 'What are you?'

'Who am I?' asked Ben.

'No,' said Hegarty laboriously, '*what* are you? Are you a drone or an executive?'

'Oh. Well, I've only just started.'

'Unsullied, eh? You'd better come in, then. Name?'

'Ben Harper.'

'Oh, the troublemaker. I've read the e-mail on you. How did you find me?'

'Oddly enough,' said Ben, 'I thought of the Wizard of Oz. The man behind the curtain operating the levers. Why would this building need a caretaker?'

'Well of course it doesn't, but they couldn't think of another job title for me.' Hegarty's hut was as cluttered as an allotment shed. The caretaker boiled tea. 'All buildings will be like this soon,' he said. 'Self-regulating. Auto-balanced. Remote-logic. If you break wind it'll spray Atar of Roses over you. Sugar?'

'One please. You sound as if you don't approve.'

'You hear anybody say what a great place this is to work? I thought not. Know why? It's no good.'

Ben accepted a cracked, murky brown mug, eyeing it dubiously. 'There are bound to be teething problems.'

'Listen to me: *It's no good*. The wind changes, the building shifts, the compensation mechanism causes all kinds of leaks. For every action, a reaction. The bigger the action, the bigger the reaction. They haven't allowed for that. Old buildings are lived in, cherished. This one changes people. Causes breakdowns.'

'I'm not sure I understand.'

The caretaker sighed impatiently. 'A building is not just a box made out of bricks. It's organic. Shaped by the needs of the people within. This building responds. People cause disorder, no matter how well controlled they are. The Symax system is responding to human chaos with counterbalancing chaos. Action, reaction. People break down – what happens to buildings?'

'You think it's already started happening?'

'You tell me. People are jumping out of windows. Did you know there are live spots all over the building? Come over here.' He pointed to a narrow air-shaft, cocking his head to one side. Voices carried from somewhere far above. 'You can hear them quite clearly, yet there must be thirty floors between us. Odd, isn't it? There's a gap in the centre courtyard where tiny magnetic tornadoes form. Why? Buildings are like women. Each one has a special mystique.'

'Why did the architect kill himself?'

'Ah, you know about that. Well, fair enough. Carrington Rogers was my partner. This building wasn't really his, of course. Computers designed it for Symax. Optimised his sketches. Wasn't much left of the original plans. He knew it would go wrong, even warned them, but there was nothing he could do to stop it. By that time he'd taken the money, you see. There was no other way out for him. His suicide, my breakdown, the end of all our dreams. I came to work here so I could keep an eye on the place, keep the bosses' secrets safe for them.'

'Do you still have the plans?'

'Yes, but they're all classified. In case of industrial sabotage.' He reached into a battered grey steel filing cabinet and withdrew an amorphous mass of documentation. Maps that consisted of curving dotted lines. Scrawled notes. Clipped articles on the architect and his plans for Symax. He splayed the huge drafting papers across the table. 'I shouldn't be showing them to you, but – ' he smiled, his beady eyes glittering ' – into every ordered system prances the imp of chaos. What do you know about electromagnetic fields?'

Grinning, the old man set a metal company biro on the concrete floor and watched as it started to spin, faster and faster. Finally it shot across the room and embedded itself into the skirting board. At the same time Ben could feel his hair lifting and prickling. He remembered the insects lined in rows at his feet.

'No wonder my watch stopped.'

'It's a vortex, a turbulent area where opposing electromagnetic fields overlap. A modern office building is filled with electrical fields. Every machine you use provides its own forcefield. The only reason why they don't cause havoc is because they're shielded. They have to be. Electromagnetic forces affect brain patterns. In moments of stress they can cause someone's least stable traits to surface violently. Nobody knows the full effects of unshielded mag-force. Symptoms are everything from stress-related stuff like headaches, to terminal disease. Cancer patients have been suing cellular phone companies lately. It's now thought that overhead cables may cause leukaemia.'

'But if these machines are all shielded, how can they cause any harm?'

'I think something must have upset the system's balance.'

'Surely they'll have to evacuate the building until the problem's located?'

'That won't be enough,' said Hegarty. 'Look at this.' He dug out a dusty diskette and pushed it into an ancient terminal hidden behind tea towels. The screen quickly filled with typewritten newspaper files.

'People's Architect' to initiate designs for 'ultimate human environment.'

'Architect warns of hidden dangers in computer-assisted designs.'

'Unshielded electrical fields cause massive electro-turbulence, says top architect.'

'The board of directors know there's a problem, but they have no answers. All they can do is bury their heads in the sand and act like nothing's wrong. These systems are on the verge of being sold across the world. Rogers was concerned that the use of so much electronic equipment might have an effect on human occupants. When the computers "enhanced" his designs, he was worried that they would allow for human error, but not human nature. People are perverse. You try to streamline them and they develop odd behavioural quirks. The computers made improvements which were, by themselves, acceptable. Except that they completely changed the building's electro-radiation levels.'

'Surely someone checked for this sort of thing?'

'Computers checked. Their programs change the pressure, the temperature, the chemical composition of the air, calming when the atmosphere is charged, energising when things are too relaxed. But you can't program people. Every time the computer reacts, they react back and the whole thing escalates. The result is a potential madhouse. And the more electronic equipment that's turned on, the more devastating the effect.'

'But if the building's so dangerous,' asked Ben, 'why aren't we all affected?'

'We are,' replied Hegarty, tapping the side of his head. 'We don't all feel it yet.'

On Wednesday the weather worsened. The wet workforce shook out their umbrellas and entered the building ready for their toughest day. Ben wondered how much longer he could get away with not doing his work, but people were too preoccupied to notice. He sat and shuffled papers, trying to look busy.

'Clark's making everyone go through the night,' said Marie. Behind her, the wall lights glowed like waxing moons as the sensors adjusted to the displacement and warmth and movement of stressed-out humanity. The recycled air smelled musty and bitter. By mid-morning everyone was operating at the double. Phones rang, screens flashed, staff swept past in a frenzy of hyperactivity. The sense of collective unease was palpable.

He had been aware of the humming for some time now, a dull rumble that vibrated in his bones. The very air was shimmering. A maelstrom of electromagnetic activity, caused by every damned machine in the place operating at full capacity. Marie had gone missing. He'd only left his desk for a moment. He checked all the work stations calling her name, and missed her as she passed him heading toward the elevator banks.

Marie stepped into the lift and pressed a lower floor button just as Ben spotted her. The doors shut and the lift started off smoothly, but suddenly stopped. Inside, the lights began to flicker and fail. The lift walls snapped and sparkled with cobalt streaks of electromagnetic energy. Ben watched the overhead panel to see where Marie would alight. The panel indicator illuminated 34, but when he took the stairs there he found the doors shut. He held his breath and listened. Something weird was happening in the shaft.

He tried to force the doors open, but they wouldn't budge. The entire lift shaft was suddenly filled with electrical fire. There was a sharp crack as it shorted out, and the lift started moving again. Ben pulled Marie clear as the doors slammed open before him with a vicious, deafening bang.

'Where were you going?' he asked.

'I don't know.' Marie rubbed her eyes. 'I had some kind of panic attack.'

Through the open swing doors they caught sight of Clark, whose efforts to concentrate and compose himself were undermined by his left eye, which twitched uncontrollably. 'Harper,' he called, 'my office, right now.'

'Go and get your coat,' said Ben. 'Wait for me in reception. We're getting out.'

Clark ushered Ben into his office and closed the door. 'My staff are falling apart,' he complained. 'Half of them have barricaded themselves in the toilets. The rest have gone mad. It's all coming true, everything Carrington and Hegarty warned the board about.' Then, as if suddenly jabbed with a pin, he started shouting. 'Stress doesn't touch you, though, does it? Because you're not corporate material. You don't fit the profile. You lied to get the job! A teacher, fired for breeding insurrection!' He reached for the nearest telephone and punched out a number. 'Why did you come here?'

'I wanted something with potential.'

'But you've just destroyed your chances. Why would you do that?'

Ben thought for a moment. 'Human nature.'

A huge security guard filled the doorway. 'Escort this man off the premises.'

Ben was pulled from the room. Wary of the tasor strapped to the guard, he went quietly. As they reached the lift he broke into a run, the guard following close on his heels. Suddenly they were confronted by a demented-looking Swan, who forced his way between Ben and the guard. 'Been up to see the boss, have we? Reporting back on the workers? Everything was all right 'til you got here.'

'I've no quarrel with you.'

'So innocent. How do you know what it's like to keep having your quotas raised, to still be working long after your children are in bed?' He furiously poked Ben in the chest. Ben pushed him on to the guard, who immediately grabbed Swan by the tie. As this happened, Ben pulled the tasor from the guard's pocket and fired it, dropping him to his knees like a felled bull.

Swan's eyes widened in surprise. He smoothed his tie into place. 'That's more like it,' he said. 'A little respect for a decent Christian. *All hail the Lord.*'

The guard's jacket was smoking. 'Christ,' said Ben, dropping the tasor.

Swan turned on him. 'Blasphemer!'

This is not going to look good on my CV thought Ben as he kneed Swan in the testicles and pushed him down the stairs.

The 35th floor was devoid of life. Somewhere in the distance were screams, moaning, the sound of breaking glass. The monitors droned on in the reception area, but the tape of sunsets and dolphins was slurred and distorted. The receptionist was sitting on the floor with her legs straight out, nursing her head like a character from a Laurel and Hardy film. Marie ran to her work station and collected her coat. She tried to telephone the police, but watched on her display unit as the call was diverted to a dead line. She punched out a 9, then 100. 'Hello, operator, I'm trying to get connected to the police. Why can't you? I know we're not under police jurisdiction, that's because the company has its own security services, but surely a 999 call is still – well, yes, it is an emergency.'

She cradled the receiver under her ear, looking around.

Lucy had set fire to a wastepaper bin and was standing on a chair holding it near the ceiling, trying to set off the sprinkler system. One of the other typists was seated at her keyboard printing out hundreds of pages of Z's. Carmichael had over a dozen biros protruding from his back, and lay sprawled on the floor beneath his desk. Everyone else had fled to darker corners.

Clark wandered about his office clutching his face. The muffled cries and scuffles emanating from the floor outside made him look up in a state of dementia.

'You killed him, didn't you?' said Marie as he hoved into her eyeline.

'Felix's report suggested delaying everything while we investigated the problem,' Clark moaned. 'The shares would have plummeted. I didn't mean to kill him. But I – get – these – headaches.'

Marie slowly replaced the receiver. 'What did you do with his body?'

'Put him in a cool place, somewhere off limits,' he replied dully. 'The sensor room.'

'My god, that's supposed to be a sterile area. You left a corpse in there with the building's sensor units?'

'I wasn't thinking too clearly. I'm better now.' The heavy executive suddenly lunged at her, and they fell back on to her desk as Marie desperately cast about for something to hit him with. Grabbing wildly behind her, she smashed a 'You Don't Have To Be Mad To Work Here But It Helps' breakfast mug over his head, which briefly dazed him.

Clark scrambled after Marie as she fought to get away. She rammed her chair at him, and while he was tipped back against the desk rubbing his head she pulled the plastic bottle from the water cooler beside her and flung it at him. From the way he suddenly grew rigid and began grinding his teeth she could only assume that her keyboard, too, was now electrified, and that he was sitting on it in wet trousers.

Marie and Ben stumbled into the building's deserted atrium and made for the main doors. They had been forced to use the stairs down, as people were making love in the lifts. Fights had broken out on every floor. 'I'm sorry I took so long to find you,' wheezed Ben, 'but a gang of bookkeepers ambushed me in Accounts.'

'The system won't let us out,' said Marie. 'These things are locked.'

'What do you mean, locked?' he said stupidly, staring at the steel deadbolts that had slid across the inch-thick tinted glass. He hurled himself against the door but it did not even vibrate under his weight.

'We'll never get out now.'

'What are you talking about? The police, fire, ambulance, emergency teams, they'll all turn up here any minute.'

'No, they won't,' shouted the elderly caretaker. Hegarty was hobbling toward them using a desk-leg as a stick. There was a thick smear of blood on one side of his head. 'The phone lines are all diverted. The entrances and exits are all sealed. The building will deal with the crisis without enlisting outside help. That's what it's designed to do.'

'So what happens now?'

'In an emergency situation – a Code Purple – the system can attempt to restore balance in the building by starting all over again.'

'And how will it do that?' asked Ben, dreading the answer.

'By sucking out all of the air, purifying the structure with scalding antiseptic spray, flash-freezing it and then slowly restoring the normal temperature. The process won't harm office hardware. Of course, it's never been used on humans.'

Ben looked up at the flashing purple square on the atrium wall and listened as the warning sirens began to whine. 'I guess now would be a bad time to ask for a salary increase,' he said as the great ceiling ventilators slowly opened.

ARMIES OF THE HEART

Looking down at the child, he realised he had surprised himself with his own strength. The boy lay face down in the litter-strewn grass, his hands twisted behind his back with the palms up, as if he had fallen to earth while sky-diving. His jeans were torn down around his thin ankles, his pants and buttocks stained carmine. His baseball cap had been caught by the thorns of the gorse bush that hid them both from the road.

His attacker rose and wiped the sweat from his face. It was getting dark. He would soon be missed at home. He had not meant to be so rough. At his feet the boy lay motionless, the focus of his eyes lost in a far-off place. Thin strands of blood leaked from his oval mouth to the ground like hungry roots. An arc of purple bites scarred the pale flesh below his shoulder blades where the cheap cotton T-shirt he wore had been wrenched up. His life had been extinguished four days before his eleventh birthday.

There was nothing to be done for the lad. Readjusting the belt of his trousers and shaking out the pain from his bitten hand, the man stepped away from the cooling body, walking back toward the path that bisected the waste ground. His main concern now was relocating the Volvo and getting home to his wife and children before they started to ask where he had been.

◆

'You won't.'

'I will.'

'You won't.'

'I *will*.'

'You bloody won't.'

'I bloody will.'

'Wait, I forgot what you two are arguing about.'

'She says she'll get in, and I say she won't.'

'Well, we'll just have to see, won't we?'

The venue was five hundred yards ahead of them, a large Victorian pub standing by itself at the junction of two roads. It appeared derelict; the windows were covered with sheets of steel and wood, painted matt black. No lights showed. The tenebrous building reared against the stars like a great abandoned ship. On either side of it apartment blocks curved endlessly off into darkness.

'We should get off the street, man,' said Bax. 'This is not a good area to be seen in.' There were three of them, Bax, Jack and Woody, whose real name was Claire Woodson. There was no-one else around.

'It's okay for you,' Woody complained. 'We're white. We stick out like neon bulbs.'

'Fuck you, Woody. You wanna know something? There's as many white people living here as black. You're just scared of being around poor folks. You wanna hang out with your low-life friends so you can piss off your mummy and daddy. They ain't gonna let you inside, anyway.'

'If they don't,' said Jack, 'Bax and I are still gonna go in, okay? That was the deal.'

'I know. I agreed, didn't I? Well, you don't have to worry about me. I'll just head somewhere else. There must be plenty of other places.'

'Around here?' Bax released a guffaw. 'Right. Gangsta bars full of guys with spiderwebs tattooed on their elbows. I don't know why you have to do this, Woody, it's like you got something to prove. You just hanging out with us 'cause it makes a change from shopping. You need to get something goin' for yourself, girlfriend.'

'Hey, this is a new experience,' said Woody as they reached the side-entrance of the pub. 'Something I haven't tried yet.'

'Yeah? So's having a kidney removed, don't mean you gotta do it.'

Jack reached over their heads and rang the doorbell. They waited outside the dingy crimson doors, their breath distilling in the chill November air. Bax and Woody were dressed in padded jackets, track-suit bottoms and Caterpillars. Jack hitched up a pair of baggy combat trousers. All three wore black hats over shaved heads. There was a specific reason for their loose clothing. From inside came the sound of a bolt being drawn back. Heat and thumping techno ballooned out at them as the door opened and the knuckle-dragger on the ticket stand stepped back to allow them entry.

'That's five quid each.' His gimlet gaze shifted from one to the next. His eyes lingered on Woody, who lowered her head as she pretended to have trouble unbuttoning her jacket. The other two held their breath. The doorman accepted fifteen pounds from Jack, who held all the cash, and pointed them to a stack of green plastic bags on the floor.

'Okay, in you go, bags are over there.' Jack scooped up three and passed the other two back as they walked on along the corridor.

'What are these for?'

'To put your clothes in,' Bax explained. 'Check 'em behind the counter in the corner.'

'Where are you putting your wallet?'

'Down the side of my boot.'

The corridor had opened out into a large bar area. Beyond this were the flashing greens and violets of a dance floor. The interior was also painted black. As Woody's eyes adjusted, she could see men in their underwear lounging around the bar drinking, smoking and talking just as if they were fully dressed. Some wore jockstraps, but most sported white designer-label pants and boots. Men were undressing beside powerful radiators in the gloomier corners. Jack stopped and turned to watch Woody. 'This I've got to see,' he said, grinning. 'You know they'll go nuts if they find out there's a girl in here.'

'Well, they're not going to find out.' Woody removed her jacket to reveal a tight-fitting khaki combat vest.

'What did you do with your tits?' Bax was amazed.

'I strapped them down with tape.' She pulled down her track-suit bottoms to reveal a pair of men's Calvin Klein Y-fronts. Her breasts were small, and suppressing them gave her the appearance of having developed pectoral muscles. She bundled her discarded clothes into the bag and stepped back with her hands resting lightly at her hips. 'So – do I look okay?'

'You look like Valdez in *Aliens*.'

'But do I pass as a man?'

Jack pulled off his nylon cap and carefully stuffed it into the front of Woody's pants. 'You do now.'

'You wish.'

'I *know*.' He and Bax stripped down to their underwear and headed for the bag-check. The bag-man handed them three reclaim tickets and took their clothing out into the small annexe behind the bar that housed the cloakroom. Jack wasn't entirely sure how he had been persuaded to smuggle a girl into a men-only club on Underwear Night of all nights, but now they were inside together he decided to make the best of it. She had been nagging them to take her for weeks, ever since she'd heard about the place. Jack and Bax were her best friends, and the fact that they happened to be lovers never deterred her from hanging out with them wherever they went.

The club was called The Outlook, and attracted men who

were prepared to take a walk on the wilder side of life, partly because the activities that took place beyond the dancefloor were apt to get a little raunchy, and partly because the pub was situated at the edge of South London's largest and most trouble-ridden public housing estate. In the mid-1850s the Skinner's Arms had been a boxing pub with a glass cupola above a sweat-stained ring, where workers gathered to cheer and bet on the neighbourhood's finest fighters. The matches had been halted by an unavailability of suitable pugilists in the Great War, and the old glass roof had been demolished by a stray bomb in the next. In the seventies the ground floor had been cleared of its separate Snug and Saloon bars to become a disco, and in the late eighties it had turned into a crack den. No matter how many times the police held raids, the local hoods continued to trade drugs both inside and on the street. By the time it was turned into a gay club the exhausted police and the desperate residents were happy to leave it alone because, in their eyes, anything was better than pushers, even queers. Just so long as no-one could see or hear what was going on inside it remained under a flag of uneasy truce, on the frontline of a no-go area. People entered and vacated the building quietly, and the smart cars that parked outside were left alone, because even the local kids could figure out that if they started smashing quarterlights and boosting stereos the bar would close down and the junkies would return, and nobody wanted that.

'What have you got in your briefs, a pound of sausages?' Woody released a high laugh, then quickly lowered the timbre, looking guiltily around.

'This is all me,' said Jack, looking down at his underpants. 'Can I help it if God was bountiful? This is yours.' He passed Woody a pint of strong lager, which she had ordered in the belief that it would provide her with additional gender-camouflage. She took a sip in a way that showed she was unfamiliar with holding such a glass, like a non-smoker drawing on a cigarette. As she did she took covert glances at Bax's sculptured torso.

'I'd drink that slowly, if I were you,' said Jack. 'There's no ladies' room in here. You may be able to pass for a man but I doubt even you can convincingly pee standing up.'

The room was starting to fill. The temperature had begun to climb with the volume of the music. Woody clutched the glass to her flattened chest and took a deep breath, drawing in the smell of bitter hops that had soaked and impregnated the surrounding wooden bar for more than a century. All old pubs had this odour, but here there were other scents; traces of aftershave, cologne and the musky maleness of nearly a hundred stripped, sexed-up and overheated men. She felt herself becoming aroused, even though she was aware of the paradox; they would only be interested in her if she could successfully prove herself to be male, and that was the one thing she could not do. In the dark beyond the dancefloor she sensed naked torsos touching, arms and legs shifting across each other. Maybe she had made a mistake coming along, and they were right when they asked her what she was trying to prove.

'You okay?' Bax laid a hand on her shoulder.

'I have a faint suspicion,' she said, narrowing her eyes, 'that there may be people fucking in here. It smells like fucking. Don't you think?'

'A fuck's just a way of celebrating life, princess, like a champagne toast. Look, you asked to come along with us.'

'I know, I just didn't realise I was going to end up in the House of Testosterone. Who's Jack talking to?'

Bax looked over his shoulder. Behind him stood a vague, thin-limbed boy of about nineteen. He had carelessly cropped blonde hair, watery blue eyes and the self-absorbed stance of a piece of minor Victorian statuary. He also had a dog-chain tightened around his pale cigarette-burned neck. 'His name's Simon. He knows us from evening classes. Gives me the creeps. He's into humiliation. Likes to take punishment. They say his dad sexually assaulted him for years, and nobody found out about it until after the old guy was dead. I don't know why Jack talks to him. I never do.'

'You mean he's a masochist?'

'Yeah, why? You wanna interview him for your thesis?' Bax drained his beer and set the glass down on the cigarette machine. 'He won't be very interesting. People who are into role-playing never are.'

'Why's that?'

'Because they're selfish, working out their childhood shit. They just take what they want from sex.'

Woody peered around Bax's chest. The boy was flirting shamelessly with Jack. 'Perhaps he has no choice.'

'You're right there. Kids like that are just whipping boys, put on earth to suck up all the bad vibes and take the blame.'

'Don't you get jealous when guys flirt with Jack?'

Bax looked surprised. 'Me? We've been together for six years. I hardly think he's about to run off with someone else, and if he did I'd like to think he'd choose someone attractive. Besides, we have a deal. It's simple; if he ever leaves me, I'll kill him. You want another beer?'

'I can keep pace with you, no problem,' she said defensively.

'Come and give me a hand.'

The two bartenders were ignoring customers in order to conduct some kind of odd argument with each other. Something was clearly wrong for them both to look so worried. 'What's going on?' Bax shouted over the music as one of the boys distractedly took his order.

'They found some little kid on the wasteground this afternoon,' explained the barman. 'Dead. Raped. A little boy.'

'Christ. That's terrible.'

'Yeah. One of the customers just told me there's a crowd hanging around outside.'

'What do you mean?'

'A bunch of people who live on the estate. At least, that's where he thinks they're from.'

Bax was appalled. 'They don't think the person who did it is in *here*?'

The barman looked at him as if he was stupid. 'I wouldn't be surprised – would you?'

News of the boy's death had swept around the estate with electrifying speed, and as it passed along each street it gained gruesome new details. The boy was local and liked by all. Some other kids had seen him talking to a man, not someone from around here, a visitor, a stranger. The only people who came to this area did so to frequent *that* pub across the road. The pub was just five hundred yards from the wasteground, the perfect sanctuary. They were shielding him inside, protecting one of their own. In the minds of the growing mob, deviants of that nature knew no difference between love and rape, between adults and children.

At first there had only been a handful of people on the pavement outside, but over the last hour the numbers had swelled until there were more than a hundred restless men and women. The police had been called to control the crowd, and at the moment were nervously discussing the problem in the next street while they awaited the arrival of the two Armed Response Vehicles they had requested. Their relationship with the estate residents had never been an easy one, and at this point one wrong move, one misunderstood command, would start a riot.

They lingered outside, the dark faces of the multitude, muttering to one another, cupping matches in their hands to light cigarettes, shifting back and forth from one group to the next trying to glean details, waiting for news, waiting for action, and not prepared to wait much longer.

'When you think about it, this is really silly. A bunch of

grown men standing around in their underclothes.' Woody slid her arm around Bax as they watched the dancefloor, but her eyes kept straying to the dark recesses beyond. Jack was still at the counter having an intense conversation with Simon and the barman. 'Oh, I don't know,' said Bax. 'It's kind of like having X-ray vision. Didn't you ever see Ray Milland in *The Man with the X-Ray Eyes*? Anyway, nobody's hurting anyone else, so where's the harm?'

The noise of the brick cut through even the fuzzing bass sound of the track playing over the speakers. It clanged against the steel shutter next to the entrance and the bruit echoed through the club. A moment later the DJ cut the music. Muffled shouts could be heard outside. A chunk of concrete resounded against another of the shutters. Scuffles and angry yells broke out behind them as the rear door to the bar was hastily slammed shut. One of the barmen crashed a heavy iron rod across the door and locked it in place.

'What was that?' Woody looked back, shocked by the noise.

'They've broken in through the window of the corridor between the bar and the cloakroom,' said Bax. 'They can't get in here. But we can't get in there.'

'What does that mean?'

'It means, my dear, that we can't get our clothes back.'

'Let me get this straight,' said Woody, raising her hands in rising panic. 'We're locked in here, in just our underwear, with what sounds like a lynch mob outside howling for someone's blood.'

'*Our* blood,' said Bax. 'You're one of us now. Congratulations. You always wanted to be one of the boys.'

'Well, someone will have to go out there and tell them there's been a mistake.'

'Good idea, Woodson. You wanna handle that?'

Jack reappeared beside them as another hail of rocks clanged against the shuttered windows. 'I don't think they can get in. This place is built like a fortress. Besides, the cops should be here in a minute.'

'Well, *that's* reassuring. I feel better already. Let's have another drink, turn the music back on and dance.' Bax raised his glass just as – incredibly – the technotrack really did resume, bleeding a thudding beat through the speakers. 'Jeezus, I don't believe these queens!'

'It's like I said, they could tango their way through the stations of the fucking cross.'

'Somehow I think it's gonna take more than a sense of rhythm and a pair of cha-cha heels to get us out of this situation.' A few guys had returned to the dancefloor, mainly the ones who were tripping. Everyone else was standing back by the bar, watching the sealed-up windows with increasing nervousness.

'How many of them do you think are out there?' asked Woody.

'A couple of hundred by now,' replied Simon, who had appeared beside them.

'Oh yeah?' Bax wasn't prepared to allow the newcomer into their circle just because Jack sometimes spoke to him. 'How do you know that?'

'I'm sensitive to shifts of mood. A bit psychic. My mother, my *real* mother, was a medium.'

'Just great,' moaned Bax, 'we've gone from the *Twilight Zone* to the *X-Files*. I'm gonna see what's happening.' He headed off to the entrance, where the club's bouncer was watching the street from his peephole in the door.

'What's going on outside?'

'Some kids just climbed that pole over there and cut our phone lines. Now they're all just standing around like a bunch of – lemmings – or something. Like they're waiting for a signal.' The bouncer motioned him away. 'I'd get back from the door if I were you.'

Another hurled chunk of concrete hammered against the

panels, shaking the air. The noise level on the street was rising as the crowd gained confidence and found its voice. 'Can't someone call the police on a mobile?' asked Bax.

'You won't get reception in here. The cops are probably waiting for ARV's. They're equipped to deal with stuff like this. Nothing for us to do but wait.' The sound of glass exploded on the other side of the door, and suddenly a pool of burning petrol was fanning through the gap beneath it, illuminating the room and turning the air acrid.

'Fire over here!' bellowed the bouncer. Bax jumped back, grabbed at the stack of listings magazines behind him and stamped a pile of them over the searing patch, spattering gobbets of flame over his boots and bare calves. The bouncer, the only fully clothed man in the building, found a small CO_2 extinguisher just as another burning cocktail shattered across the plywood-covered window to the left of the entrance. The wood panel quickly heated and caught fire, then the inner window cracked with a bang and burning petrol began to drip down the interior wall. They could hear the mob outside cheering each direct hit.

This time the dance music stopped for good. Some clubbers were arguing with the staff, others were shouting at each other, but most were just standing around in shock, unable to go anywhere or do anything. Woody looked around to find herself left alone with Simon, whose face had drained of blood. He had the exotic look of an albino.

'Are you all right?'

'He wasn't frightened,' he said in a clear loud voice, as if answering a distant enquiry. 'Not until the very end.'

'Who wasn't frightened?' she asked in alarm. The boy's skin was prickling, his eyes staring off at something, a view, a tableau she could not see. He was breathing too fast, starting to shake. 'Here.' She grabbed a plastic bottle of Evian from the bar, snapped off the cap and made him drink.

'It's too late,' said Simon, water spilling from his mouth. 'The man has gone now.'

'Which man?'

'The one who hurt him, who made him bleed. The one in the big car.' He was shaking uncontrollably now, edging into spasms. 'He said he only wanted to look, to touch. He lied, he lied – '

'Can you help us?' she called to a man standing behind her. Simon was thrashing violently in her arms and then, before anyone could come to her aid, he was still once more and breathing normally. The attack had ended as quickly as it had begun.

'I'm fine now, really.' He disentangled himself from her embrace and rose unsteadily to his feet, a look of mild surprise on his face.

'Are you quite sure?'

His colour was returning. He gave a wan smile to show that he was fine.

Frustrated by his own inaction, Jack was asking one of the barmen what he could do to help. 'Is there any other way out of this room?'

'No, only through the bar and upstairs on to the roof.'

'We can't stay in here. We'll be burned alive. Do you have a sprinkler system we can turn on?'

'No,' said the barman helplessly. 'The place still qualifies as a pub, not a music venue. It's not big enough to require one. The only water supply is in the sinks and dishwasher behind the counter, and out with the clothes-bags.'

'Then I guess we'll just have to hold out until the police take charge.'

'There are enough of them outside to murder us all,' said Simon softly. 'They won't stop until they've performed a sacrifice.'

'That's bloody cheerful,' snapped Woody.

He threw her a sudden odd look. 'Why are you pretending to be a man?'

'Just give me a hand with this.' She and several of the others shifted one of the heavy drinks tables away from the wall and set it on end, blocking the broken window nearest the entrance. Bax and the bouncer were training extinguishers on the fiery fluid seeping through the windows from more burning Molotovs. People were motivating into groups, at work on separate sections of the room. It was as if a collective intelligence had kicked in to make them perform the necessary protective actions. The explosion of wood and glass that erupted near Woody caught everyone by surprise.

'Fuck me, what are they using?' Jack straightened up and looked out through the jagged hole that had been punched through the shutter by some kind of large calibre ammunition. Following its flight path he found one of the barmen clutching his shoulder as blood pumped between his fingers. The bullet had passed through the boy's T-shirt, grazing the soft flesh of his armpit, and had gone on to explode a bottle of Schmirnoff above the bar. Within moments, two customers had torn tea towels into strips and were staunching his wound. Another gunshot blast ripped through the steel sheeting on the main window of the dancefloor, but failed to find a target, smashing into the plaster ceiling rose in the centre of the room. Surprisingly, nobody screamed.

'Everyone seems so calm,' said Woody as Bax reappeared. 'Never underestimate the balls of a queen, honey. Half these guys grew up getting punched out by parents who won't speak to them until they're on their deathbeds.' He didn't say whose deathbeds he meant, and Woody didn't ask. The rending noise that began at the farthest window alerted them to the fact that someone outside was levering the sheet-steel away with a crowbar. 'Oh shit.'

Suddenly the sheeting was off and the inner window was being smashed out with boots and batons. Wood and glass splintered everywhere as dark figures struggled to climb in through the gap.

Jack swept the beer glasses from the other huge drinks table. He and Bax upended it, and with the help of four others ran it face-out at the breach. The heavy oak top crashed down over the limbs entering from outside. There were yelps of pain and rage as injured body-parts were withdrawn. Everyone fell against the back of the table, determined to hold it in place by sheer weight of numbers.

'The cops aren't going to get here in time, are they?' said Woody, pushing with all her might.

Another gunshot exploded the piece of window that still showed above the table edge. The bullet ploughed into the ceiling, and a shower of plaster cascaded over them. Bax wiped his hand across his neck to find flecks of blood from the fragments of glass. The guttural roar from outside sounded like football fans raging against a missed penalty. The table swayed and rocked but remained in its place. More petrol bombs were being thrown at the windows beyond the bar. The bouncer left his post at the doors and ran toward the spreading flames with his extinguisher. The room was filling with dense smoke. There was an explosion of glass on the floor above them, but they had no way of knowing whether it was caused by a rock or a petrol bomb.

'Simon?'

The boy drifted through the crowd and passed Woody like a wraith, staring hard ahead. He was moving quickly toward the club's temporarily unguarded entrance.

'SIMON!' Woody left the others rammed against the great table and ran toward the boy, who was reaching up on tiptoe to release the bolt at the top of the door. He had drawn it halfway down when she barrelled into him, knocking him aside. '*What the hell do you think you're doing?*' she heard herself screaming.

When he turned his translucent eyes to hers, his serenity was the peace of inner madness. 'Let me open the door.'

'They'll come in and they'll kill us, don't you understand? You can't reason with them!'

'I don't need to reason with them. I have the boy within me.' He ran bony fingers across his chest. 'I reached out to him and took his pain. It's safe inside me now.'

There was another terrible eruption on the far side of the room. Somebody fell back with an agonised yell. 'How can that be?' she shouted, shoving at him, '*how can that be?*'

'I know his suffering. I've lived with such pain all my life, I'm a fucking magnet for abuse and I'm dying from it, do you understand?' He tore himself free of her and stood alone.

Others had seen what was happening and were moving toward them. 'They'll kill you, Simon,' she said. 'They'll tear you apart with their bare hands.'

'Of course they will. They must have someone to blame. A whipping boy.'

'But the real culprit – '

'*The real culprit* is far away. I can't catch him. I'm not clever, all I can do is take the pain. From my father, from the crowd outside, I can absorb their darkness. It's what I do, how I survive. Feeding on the violence of others.' He held her with a look she would never forget to her dying day. 'Someone once told me about the army.'

'What army?'

'Everyone has an army in their heart, an army that rallies when its host is most in danger, an army that fights back with all its might until every last one of its soldiers is dead. But I don't. I have no army. There's nothing inside me fighting back, there's just a black hole.' He smiled at her. 'Don't look so worried. I know how to make the most of it.' As he had been talking to her, he had raised the entry-door's floor-bolt with his boot, and now he shrugged himself away to release the top bolt in one swift, simple movement. The door suddenly opened inwards and he slipped through it before anyone could realise what was happening.

Woody screamed after him but the others had crashed forward to slam the door shut once more. She begged them to open it, screamed and pleaded until her throat was raw, but they carried her away to the side of the room, where Bax gave her water and sat her down. She regained her breath, stopped crying and waited.

They all waited.

Outside, Simon stood before the seething crowd with the placidity of a medieval child-saint, a sickly hermaphrodite that raised its arms in preparation for final absolution. His moon-blanched face was tense with sexual anticipation, his body illuminated by dozens of flashlights as the figures around him surged and erupted forward. In the distance the riot vehicles could be heard arriving. The mob took the sound of their sirens as a call to action and fell upon the boy, slashing and punching at him with everything they were holding, machetes and carpet-cutters, butchers' hooks, bread knives, daggers and carving-forks. Obviously those inside the club were unwilling to take the rap for the murderer and had forced him to step out in the open. They had no loyalty to one another and probably all deserved to die but this one, *this* one had to suffer properly for what he had done.

But then the swinging boots and arcing knives slowed their rhythm. Gradually the shouts died down and stopped. For a few moments total silence descended on the neighbourhood. Then a few of the women started to scream. The crowd slunk back from the grotesque remains of their victim, slipping in crimson mire. A sense of shame and horror descended over them as they listened to those inside the building putting the remaining fires out. Weapons were released from bloody hands as men began to cover their faces and weep. Some fell to their knees. Others stumbled into the arms of their women like lost children. As the police disembarked from their grid-covered vehicles, one of the wives came forward and laid her coat across the shattered skull of the boy who had drained their rage away.

Inside the club, the sudden silence was eerier than anything they had heard so far. Woody put her eye to one of the bullet-holes and watched as nearly three hundred men, women and children were herded back to the far side of the street. At the corner of her vision she could see the edge of the pavement, and a pale leg lying in a pool of blood, its foot severed at the ankle.

Bax had been standing up at the window. He had seen the boy hacked apart, and was crying uncontrollably. Jack and the bouncer were opening the club's main entrance doors, trying to clear away the suffocating smoke. Woody stepped numbly down and walked off through the guttering fires of the club, toward the chill clean air outside. She pulled her vest over her head and let it drop, then tore away the strips of tape and released her breasts from their confinement. She looked back at Jack, who returned her rueful smile. They both knew that she wasn't one of the boys any more.

She didn't need to be.

She had her own army.

FIVE STAR

Celia wiped her forehead and checked her watch again. Sweat was dripping in her eyes. 'If the worst comes to the worst,' she said, 'we could go down to the crossroads and wait for the local bus. They're apparently quite reliable.'

'Don't be ridiculous,' said Trevor, 'the whole point of booking a cab is to avoid having to mix with the locals. I've seen enough locals to last a lifetime. All those deformities.'

Celia shuddered. A drip of sweat fell from the tip of her nose. 'That blind man with the flying snakes. Ugh.'

'Exactly. That's the whole point of staying in a five star hotel. They make their ice cubes with Evian. They have French chefs. Shower-caps. Fruit baskets. Slippers under your bed. If it wasn't for the outside temperature you'd think you were at home. The beach and the bar are for the use of residents only. Safety is not in numbers, safety is in five stars. Ah.' Trevor looked up at the sound of the vehicle and tilted back the brim of his straw hat. 'Better late than never.'

The filthy taxicab that hoved into view was Russian in origin. It looked like a child's drawing of a car, a grey tin box with squared-off corners and bashed-up fenders. The dashboard was filled with every kind of gaudy religious icon imaginable, the centrepiece being a bare-breasted madonna with a pale green wobbly head that looked suspiciously as if it might glow in the dark. The vehicle slewed to a stop in a spray of brown dust and its driver alighted. He batted his sweat-stained shirt with his cap and opened the trunk so that their Louis Vuitton luggage could be stowed beside the greasy pumps and jacks, then stepped back to watch while the couple struggled to fit their cases. He spoke good English but had no intention of revealing this talent, for if he did so he would inevitably be drawn into arguments about lateness, overcharging and the unavailability of change. Instead he picked his teeth with a match while the skinny pale English lady fussed and tutted around her useless-looking husband.

He knew at once that they were upper class. They had that pinched look the posh English so often had, a look created by a lifetime of making false economies. The upper-class English always found new corners to cut while clinging to the lavish lifestyles they felt were their birthright, as if a reduction in the porter's tip would somehow pay for their next trip to Gstaad or Glyndebourne. The woman was bitching at her husband now, something about getting grease on her dress, and he was just nodding apologetically. Poor bastard. If he was any kind of a man he'd shut her mouth with a slap. Wearily the driver reached in and adjusted his wooden-beaded seat cover before heaving himself back into the car. They trundled off and around the corner, surprising a goat who was searching the road for a cool spot to give birth.

'Well, check-in time is two hours before departure, which already makes us over half an hour late,' said Celia, checking her compact mirror for facial anomalies.

'That's for passengers in Economy,' said Trevor, staring from the window as they passed a herd of perilously undernourished cows. 'We can turn up mere minutes before the flight if we wish. They have to wait for us. We're the ones who keep the airline running by paying full fare, not those lager-swilling chimps you see on the bargain package tours. Christ, it's hot.' The sea was a wall of blue at their backs, the air stagnant and still beneath the sun. The taxi wound its way inland, past derelict mills and bleached fields of dead brown crops. 'If only we could have gone to the house in St Raphael,' said Celia, fanning herself, 'instead of having to come here.'

'You know very well we couldn't do that. The press would have been expecting it. We'd have had no privacy.'

'Do you honestly think things will be better back in England?' she snapped. 'I've had people come up to me in the street and make accusations to my face!'

'Darling, you'll be surprised how quickly people forget. They have the attention spans of goldfish. We're yesterday's news. Trust me.'

He knew he was right. Twenty-four days ago his name had been dragged across the front pages of all the national dailies, but by now the press had already moved on to the next big scandal. He'd been in some tight squeezes before, but damage limitation was easy if you knew the right people, and no minister worth his salt got far in the cabinet without making decent connections. He made sure that the rumours about his private life could never be confirmed. The call-girl who had sold her story to the press about their sexual escapades had been paid to recant her version of events, and the whole thing had been parlayed into a photo opportunity featuring Trevor Colson, stalwart Conservative MP, hugging the loyal wife who stood by him. There had been the exposure of his vested interests with the nuclear lobby, the accusation of insider trading, and the homes-for-votes cover-up, but all of it had remained innuendo, and any journalist who had dared to suggest otherwise was vigorously pursued into the courtroom.

But this last business was a little more serious. Colson had acted as financial adviser to a banking syndicate that had run foul of international trading barriers. As an MP he had been expected to foresee such problems and remove them for his partners. But he had failed to read up on the new laws and take appropriate action in time to prevent the bank at the centre of the syndicate from going bust overnight. Investors had lost fortunes, institutions had collapsed, and the Right Hon. Trevor Colson and his wife had decamped to the sun, to spend three weeks incognito in their five star hotel waiting for the fuss to die down.

The taxi swerved on to the two-lane blacktop leading to the centre of the island, and the airport came into view. It consisted of little more than one runway, an oblong white box which housed arriving and departing passengers, a few concrete sheds and an unfinished air traffic control room with rusted iron rods sticking out of one end. There was also a dead pelican. It had been lying on the verge of the runway when they arrived, and was still there.

As the cab pulled up behind a cluster of hotel minivans, Trevor watched the disembarking passengers with a scornful glare in his eyes. Looking at their sunburned faces, their smutty-joke T-shirts, their shoddy luggage, their hideous screaming children, he almost felt glad that many were returning to find their savings wiped out. It would teach them to invest more wisely in future.

The collapse of the bank had affected the common man in the street, about whom he cared not a jot, but it had also damaged some businesses it didn't pay to annoy; the collapsed bank was, after all, built on Russian and Sicilian money, and the further back you followed the paper trail the murkier the finance connections became. Still, he was confident that his long-term prospects were unharmed; a few lunches with the right people had seen to that.

There were holidaymakers sitting on the airport steps, which seemed odd. It looked as if they'd been there for quite a while. Inside, Trevor's worst fears were confirmed; their plane had failed to arrive, and the ground staff had no information as to the current whereabouts of the inbound flight. Stephanie, the hard-faced little airline representative who was striding around the check-in area with her clipboard, informed him in the most extraordinary nasal voice that it was likely the flight had not yet left London, so the delay would be considerable, and as there were no other flights available they would just have to sit tight. Leaving the vicinity of the airport was impossible once they had checked their bags, and if the plane failed to turn up within the next three hours they would probably all have to stay overnight as the airport was not licensed for flights during the hours of darkness – but, she promised, they would be issued with vouchers for a free lamb stew and complimentary glass of house red.

Stephanie had a tough time making herself heard before the Economy passengers, several of whom had stripped down to shorts, climbed up on the roof of the departure lounge and were now dancing to blurred techno from their portable music system. The island had a healthy rave culture that attracted clubbable youngsters from across Europe.

'Look at this shower,' spat Trevor. 'The roof's covered in pirouetting queers. Presumably they have no future appointments arranged in their empty lives and don't need to worry about reaching Heathrow on time.' He mopped his forehead angrily. 'Stay here, Celia. I'll find out what the hell's going on.'

'You're entitled to a complimentary sandwich from the buffet,' promised Stephanie, her hard little face and voice hardening still further as Trevor glared at her. 'And a Sprite.'

Trevor looked suddenly lost. There was no social order here in the airport. There seemed to be no-one with overall authority, and there was no foreseeable escape route that could be accessed with the wave of a credit card.

'Well, we can't stay here,' he snapped, and found he was talking to himself. Celia had wandered over to the gift shop, which was selling mutated ceramic donkeys, headsquares printed with out-of-register pictures of the island's hotels, phallic bottles of sickly yellow liquor and week-old copies of El Pais. 'Celia, for God's sake!'

'I was looking for stomach pills. If we're going to be eating – '

'We're not going to be eating anywhere,' hissed Trevor. 'That stupid girl has no idea what's going on.'

'So what do you suggest we do?'

'Excuse pliz?'

A short, overweight taxidriver was standing behind them in a sweat-stained tropical shirt. 'Are you speaking to me?' asked Trevor, horrified.

'There will be no plane here tonight.'

'What do you mean?'

'This happen every week.' He held his thumb and forefinger together, counting out the words. 'There – will – be – no – plane – tonight. It come in morning, eleven or twelve, not before. Never before this hours.'

'Are you quite sure?'

The taxidriver smiled, revealing an unbroken row of gold teeth beneath his ratty moustache. 'You smart gentleman. Would I lie to you?'

Trevor queued to use the only pay-telephone that was working, and eventually managed to speak to their hotel manager. 'But you must have a vacancy,' he shouted, 'if my plane doesn't turn up, you'll have no guests arriving on the incoming flight, will you?' The argument ended with Trevor slamming down the receiver.

'What did he say?' asked Celia, fanning herself with a postcard.

'They're overbooked. Some sort of conference. He's already installed new guests in our room.'

'You should never have tipped him so much,' she sniffed. 'It gives them airs.'

'Don't you see, if our own hotel can't put us up for the night, that ghastly woman will try and put us in one of her disgusting tavernas.' Suddenly aware that their conversation was being overheard, they turned to find the little taxidriver watching them happily.

'And what on earth is *he* grinning about?' asked Celia loudly.

'Pliz, I have a cousin.'

'How very nice for you.' Celia snapped her sarcastic smile off and turned back to her husband. 'Well? We can't just stand around here with all these appalling people.'

'Pliz, I have a cousin who has hotel, very nice, very clean. Everything else booked.'

'We're not interested in your – '

'Wait,' said Trevor, gingerly touching his sweat-slick arm. 'Why is everything else booked?'

'Start of high season,' came the reply. 'School holidays.'

'Why isn't your cousin fully booked, then?'

'Hotel not finished yet. He can't get his licence until government inspection.'

'Then he's not supposed to take in guests until then.'

'He needs the money. Don't worry, no-one knows you stay there.'

'Where is this place?'

'Trevor, you're not seriously thinking of – '

'Do you have any better ideas?'

Behind them, Stephanie was organising a queue for sandwich vouchers. Celia shuddered as she watched the sunburned line shuffle forward.

'My name is Gregor.' The taxidriver wiped his hand on his shirt and proffered it. 'You like my cousin's hotel, I promise. If not I drive you back here, free of charge, okay?'

'Okay,' commanded Trevor, as droplets of sweat bulged on the tip of his nose. 'Lead on.'

Unlike the earlier driver, Gregor was happy to load their luggage into his ancient Mercedes without assistance. As the thumping from the speakers of the airport's unconcerned revellers dwindled into the distance, they turned from the main road on to a pot-holed single-lane track and spent the next twenty minutes bouncing around in the back of the car until they felt sick. The sun had passed its white-hot zenith, and a kind golden light now swathed the banks of dessicated eucalyptus trees. The rasp of cicadas sounded like a hundred lawn sprinklers. Celia tried to wind her window lower, but it was stuck. God, how barren the land was before irrigation! Ahead lay a gentle downward slope to the sea, but no sign yet of a hotel, unfinished or otherwise.

Gregor did not speak as he drove. He had no need to. He knew all he needed to know about the discomfited couple jiggling in the back of his car. Without a doubt the man was Trevor Colson, the crooked financier and British member of parliament who had been featured on the front page of his *Daily Mirror* nearly every day for the past two weeks. The pinch-faced woman next to him was too plain to be anyone but his wife.

Gregor had many, many cousins. He also had quite a few brothers, two of whom operated a chain of highly successful takeaway shops in England. Every month they sent money home so that Gregor and his cousin could complete the building of their hotel in time for the start of high season. But this month no money had arrived, because the brothers had lost every penny they had ever earned when their bank – their sensible *English* bank – had collapsed and vanished overnight.

Thanks to the tabloid press, Gregor knew all about the fiend in human form who had triggered that collapse, and now the gods had miraculously delivered him into his hands. He knew that revenge was a dish best served cold, but in this land nothing was cold for very long. He prayed he would at least be able to keep his temper until justice had been meted out.

Justice was the problem; Gregor was a civilised man, not given to violence. His creed was a simple one. He believed men made their own destinies. It was not in his nature to be cruel, or to encourage cruelty in others. How, then, to take revenge fairly?

'It's beautiful,' whispered Celia, nodding to the white-washed villa that had appeared to the right of the car. Bouquets of scarlet bougainvillea were stippled across a curving white entrance, before which stood the empty marble basin of a fountain. Trevor returned a pout and a raised eyebrow, meaning *perhaps we're not being ripped off after all*.

The hotel's open-fronted foyer was deep in shadow, its tiles cooler to the touch. An emerald lizard skittered across the floor like a clockwork toy and vanished behind the check-in desk.

'I'm sorry no lights,' puffed Gregor, setting down their luggage. 'But hot water and electric fans all work. You sign in please.' He pointed to the guest-book on the desk, mentally improvising possibilities; Colson's signature might prove useful to him at a later point. Trevor dug a ballpoint pen from his jacket pocket and scrawled his name across the top of the page.

'We're your first visitors, I see. Quite an honour.' Beware my husband loud and jovial, thought Celia. He sounded so false when he was being nice to the natives. She never bothered; it required too much of an effort. 'Is your telephone working?' she asked. She wanted to call Sebastian at his boarding school and warn him of their late return.

'No, not yet, next week maybe. This way pliz.' Gregor hoisted their bags and led them off along a gloomy marble corridor, thinking frantically.

'How many stars will the hotel merit when it's finished?' asked Trevor, addressing their host's back.

'Pliz?'

'Stars – how many will this hotel rate?'

'I don't know yet. But now I already have one star here,

yes?' Gregor chuckled softly to himself – a good joke that Colson clearly did not get, which was probably just as well.

The room was spacious, cool and very white, with red Moroccan rugs and long white cotton curtains that billowed across an elegant Louis Philippe bed. 'Are all the rooms like this?' asked Trevor, taken aback.

'Not yet. This is – how you say – show-room. Please – make yourself comfortable. I see to dinner.'

'Are you going to cook, Mr – ?' Celia had decided to reward their host by asking his name, even though she had been told before.

'Gregor. I make traditional dish for you tonight, my special guests. You would like to eat at – ' he consulted his watch, ' – eight o'clock?'

'That would be convenient, yes,' agreed Trevor with a flicker of a smile as he gently closed the door in Gregor's face.

'You see, it won't be such a hardship after all,' said Celia. Her mouth was a coral O as she reapplied her lipstick in the mirror, 'although I would have liked to call Sebastian to tell him where we were. Absolutely nobody knows we're here, and we don't know this man – he might be anyone.'

'That may well be a blessing.' Trevor stepped on to the balcony, buttoning his cuffs. A warm zephyr ruffled the leaves of the eucalyptus bushes that grew beneath their windows. It was the kind of air that soothed the sinuses and freshened the eyes. The night sky was diamond-dust tossed on to velvet. The reflections of the stars spackled the sea like mica drifting through oil. He felt safe here, far from the baying hounds of the press and the querulous complaints of his constituents. If only this tranquil, luxurious privacy could last for ever . . .

'I feel overdressed for tonight,' said Celia, realigning her decolletage. 'I mean, he's a taxidriver, for heaven's sake.'

'He's a property owner,' Trevor replied, feeling his moment slip by.

'*Part*-property owner. He barely speaks English.' She, of course, spoke no other language. 'Well, I hope they manage to make a go of it, he and his brother, cousin or whatever. This could become a very smart place providing it attracts the right sort of clientele. I hope he's not cooking anything too exotic. Earrings?' She held the glittering clusters either side of her head.

'A little too much. We'd better go down.'

The dining room had calibrated glass panels that opened on to a series of small mosaic pools. Wrought iron candelabras set at either end of the room threw wavering aqueous reflections on to the ceiling.

'What a clever idea,' said Celia, waiting for Trevor to pull out her chair. 'I must remember this for the new conservatory.'

Gregor entered bearing a large metal baking dish, which he set down on a cream marble side table. He had changed into a clean white shirt. 'This very special local dish I make for you.'

Celia smoothed a napkin into her lap. 'I hope we didn't put you to too much trouble.'

'Is no trouble. My cousin and I, we catch fish here every morning. I make for you the fish baked in special herbs, with garlic.' He removed the lid of the tureen and a rich aroma flooded the room. Gregor's gold front tooth shone in the candlelight as he grinned at them. 'I hope you are very hungry.'

Celia watched as her plate was filled, then waved her host away. 'Goodness, that's ample.' It looked and smelled very foreign indeed.

The fish was delicious, light and flaky to the touch of Trevor's fork, leaking pungent juices. Gregor brought over a huge glass bowl filled with a crunchy absinthe-green salad that smelled like fresh-cut grass. He poured them generous measures of an agreeably chilled Chablis.

Celia eyed the white meat on the end of her fork suspiciously. Her stomach was delicate at the best of times. Her husband was shovelling his food down, so she supposed it had to be safe. She took a bite, savoured the sauce and found herself pleased.

'A very decent wine,' murmured Trevor appreciatively as he examined the bottle's label. 'Rather out of fashion these days. I fear it's been elbowed aside by all these overpoweringly fruity colonial Chardonnays.'

'My cousin – he chooses the wine. I show you list.' He passed Trevor a handwritten sheet. The MP beamed with delight as he read it. 'Well, well! Small but perfectly formed, as they say.' He handed it back.

'Pliz?'

' – A good list.'

'Ah. Thank you. My cousin – his hobby.'

'Ah.'

The limits of language had made themselves felt, and silence prevailed. Celia picked up the conversation effortlessly, just as she did on a thousand other dining nights in London. 'You have a lovely view here. Was the land expensive?'

'He does not own the land.' No, the land was owned by a British company, thought Gregor, a company that would have no compassion about foreclosure as soon as it realised the payments had ceased.

'Are you married, Mr – um?' asked Celia.

'Yes, but she died.'

'Ah.'

They ate peacefully, listening to the distant sea as the conversation lulled. Gregor cleared away the plates and brought them strong dark coffee, which he served on the verandah with a selection of almond biscuits. Trevor had drunk a fair amount, and seemed intent on explaining the benefits of a capitalist society to Gregor, who merely smiled and nodded.

'People have to build their own lives,' he insisted. 'Then, if they make a hash of it, they only have themselves to blame.'

'But what if – something – go wrong beyond their control?' asked Gregor.

'It's up to them to find a way of putting it right, of course. Like you and this place.' Gregor's heart skipped a beat. For a moment he thought that his guest had seen through him. 'You and your cousin could have decided to buy a little one star Bed & Breakfast hotel, but no, you went for the best, borrowed – a considerable amount of money, I imagine – and good luck to you.' He drained his coffee cup and looked around, smacking his lips. 'Time for a *digestif*? A drop of brandy, perhaps.'

'Pliz, on the side table, help yourself.'

Celia watched as her husband rose unsteadily to his feet and headed for the array of amber bottles gathered at the rear of the room's marble serving board.

'Darling, a snifter for you? Help you sleep?'

'Just a small one.' Trevor was one of those men who preferred his alcoholic company to keep pace with him. 'Gregor, will you join us?'

The little taxidriver stood beside the man who had ruined him, and poured himself a grappa. 'This is very good. You should try.' He held up the bottle for his guest to see.

'Rather too rough for the European palate, I fear,' said Trevor dismissively, ignoring the fact that his host was also European. 'Good heavens! This cognac! Do you know what you have here?'

Gregor shrugged. 'I know nothing of brandy. Is good?'

'Good? This is – ' He stared down at the bottle in amazement. He had been about to say, *this is the best, a quite unique '34 that stands head and shoulders above any other costly cognac in the world*. But then he saw the amount that was left and knew that he could – would – easily finish it, and changed his remark to 'this is a very pleasant drink. May

I?' And of course Gregor agreed with a hospitable smile, sipping his grappa as Trevor brought the bottle to the table and carefully poured a measure for his wife, then filled his own glass to the brim.

Celia and her husband finished a bottle of the most expensive cognac either of them had tasted in a very long time. Trevor rested his head on the back of his chair and listened to the hushing sea. It seemed to be speaking to him – calling – soothing – beckoning. Gravity was crushing down on him. His lips felt numb. Something was dripping on them. He raised his hand to his face and his fingers came away stained with spots of blood. As he slid from the chair and fell heavily to the floor, cracking his head on the flagstones, Celia gave a little scream and was shocked to find that she, too, was suffering from a nosebleed.

'What's wrong?' she gasped, staring incredulously at Gregor. A hot brick of pain thudded into her chest. She could feel blood pouring down the back of her throat. Trevor was convulsing on the floor beside her.

'All I could find was poison for the rats,' Gregor explained apologetically. 'Very strong taste. But hidden in brandy, I think. Especially after spicy food. Mrs Colson. I let your husband choose.' Gregor raised his hands in a gesture of personal absolution. 'He chose the best.' He turned the label of the cognac bottle to show Celia the row of golden stars, but her eyes stared past him, reflecting only pain, terrible endless pain. 'Five Star, see. Very good. To be fair, this bottle was the only one I put poison in, out of so many. Always a man like that has to have the very best, no?'

Gregor waited for the bodies of his two guests to stop twitching, then stripped and dragged them to the open basement door, kicking them down into darkness. His cousin was due to have the area pumped full of cement in a week, to stop the foundation piles from shifting. It would be an easy matter to bring the delivery date forward. He wondered how long it would take him to forge Mr Colson's signature from the visitors' book. A man like that always came abroad with plenty of travellers' cheques. After locking the door, he walked down to the jetty and plunked the empty brandy bottle into the sea. A terrible waste of a fine cognac, he knew.

Tonight, though, a glass of homemade wine would taste just as well.

SCRATCH

It was too wet and too cold to go all the way into town for such a trivial purpose, but as Ann pointed out, he might regret it if he didn't. Somebody had to win, after all, and there was a double rollover this week.

He had tried to point out the folly of buying the tickets at all, had explained that the odds were so astronomical she was more likely to be struck by lightning ten times in a row than win the national lottery, but she would not be told. Somebody has to win, she would say, I've seen them on the telly, grinning brickies, office workers in syndicates, housewives, don't tell me that they've all been struck by lightning ten times.

She was missing his point. To say that they were short of money was an understatement. They were living in a limbo somewhere beyond bankruptcy, about to have their electricity cut off, about to lose their house and all its contents, and hoping against hope that everything would be neatly sorted out by winning an unimaginable amount of money seemed, well, unrealistic to say the least.

But he went, because she wanted him to and he loved her. That was what you did, wasn't it, if you loved someone? Things you didn't want to do yourself. The engine of the little Fiat sounded as if it was suffering from tuberculosis. He crested the hill and looked down on the wet rooftops of the town, the ashen carparks, the hideous plasticky shopping centre and the inhospitable moorland that butted against the new estate beyond. How he hated what he saw, how he longed to get out, even though he knew he was imprisoned here as surely as if he was locked inside a cell. Money could do that, just lift him up and set him down somewhere better. A simple row of numbers marked down in biro, the work of a moment. But the odds! The astronomical odds! He'd read that each week 30,000 people picked the numbers 1 to 6 in consecutive order! Ann had read an article on the subject which advocated ringing the number 1 – infrequently chosen for its proximity to the top of the sheet – and multiples of ten, which did not look random enough for the public to select. But how could anyone really know? Second-guessing the laws of chance would require understanding how life itself was shaped.

As he entered the tobacconist's shop, a spark of elation jumped within him at the prospect of winning, even though he knew the impossible, absurd odds and loathed the irrationality of hope. They could not afford to waste money, and yet here he was gambling it away. He ran a hand through the back of his shaggy blonde hair and waited for a pair of ancient women to shift from the counter. Queuing for the lottery had taken the place of queuing in the post office for sheer annoyance-value. He snatched up a pair of forms, grimly aware of the syndicates up and down the country that were each filling in dozens of such forms, thought for a moment and began marking off numbers. The age of his dog, Boots (12), the size of his shoes (9), the age of Ann's mother (56), and so on, until he was done.

He posted the slips in the white plastic box and started to leave the shop when he felt a loose pound coin in his jacket pocket. At the same moment his eye caught a separate scratchcard dispenser beside the main lottery ticket display. Dropping the pound coin in the slot released one of the scratchcards, which he slipped into his jeans intending to scratch off when he reached the car. But the rain had begun falling in slate-grey sheets, the traffic was bad, the DJ on the radio annoyed him and he forgot all about it.

Ann insisted on seeing the lottery draw live on television, so that he was forced to miss the end of the programme he was watching in order to stare at some capering ninny and his simpering sidekick while they made a big deal about reading the numbers from coloured ping-pong balls – *ping-pong balls*!

'Doesn't it amaze you that we have all this modern technology, and the best random-number selection device they can come up with is running a hairdryer under a box of ping-pong balls?' he asked, but was shushed. Ann excitedly checked each number, and even managed not to reveal her disappointment when she failed to match a single digit to the winning line. Her innocent enthusiasm never ceased to surprise him; it was one of her most charming qualities.

It was then that he remembered the scratchcard in his back pocket. And it was only when he looked at it properly that he realised what an odd item it was. One word was emblazoned across the top of the card in crimson: WIN! Win what it didn't say, almost as if the promotions company could not be bothered to put details on the card. Underneath this were six grey panels, and beneath these were instructions: **Scratch off each of the boxes in turn. Each one will reveal a word, WIN or LOSE. The more you WIN, the bigger your prize. To be the Prizewinner Of The Week you must uncover three WIN boxes. To be the Prizewinner Of The Month you must uncover four WIN boxes. To be the Grand Prizewinner Of The Year you must uncover all six WIN boxes.** On the back was an address where you had to send the card to by registered post if you were a winner. He rested the cardboard oblong on his knee and began scratching across two of the boxes with a five pence piece while he was still talking to

Ann. He stopped talking as soon as he saw the words revealed beneath the plastic coating, **WIN**, both.

Then a third.

'Ann?' He looked down at the card on his knee, and she followed his gaze. 'How many do you need?' she asked.

'Not sure. All, for the grand prize.'

'Keep going, then.'

He placed the edge of the coin against the corner of the fourth square and scratched. **WIN**.

And the fifth. **WIN**.

He swallowed and looked across at Ann. She gave him a puzzled look, a suspicious *this couldn't happen to us* look. 'Well, do it.'

He scratched at the sixth square, but could not bring himself to look. Slowly, he opened his eyes.

WIN.

'It's a trick, it's not a real card,' he said, 'it must be selling something.'

'No, you paid for it, didn't you?'

'Yes, but – '

'Then you've won, Gary. My god, you've won. Does it say how much?'

'No, it just tells you how to do it, and there's no company name, it's weird. I've never seen cards like these before.'

'Maybe they're new, maybe the money goes to some special charity. Fill in your name and address, send it off.'

'I'll put your name down, if you like.'

'That's sweet of you,' said Ann. 'But you picked that particular card, you were chosen fair and square.' So he filled out his own name and address, and on Monday morning drove back into town to send it off by registered post.

The next few days crawled by in agonising torpor. They had agreed not to mention the win, not to even think of it, but to behave in such a way would have been a defiance of human nature. They'd pay their bills, thought Gary, be prudent, clear all their debts, start anew and not make the same mistakes. Find somewhere decent for Ann's mother to live instead of her damp run-down flat. Find himself a job that paid a proper salary. Maybe they could even think about starting a family ... The locks seemed to be falling away from the sealed gates of their fate, and some kind of decent future beckoned beyond. But Gary could not allow himself to think of such a thing; the more he dreamt, the greater would be his disappointment if it turned out to be a con, if the company was, say, a double-glazing firm attempting to hook customers.

He did not even believe in the lottery. Surely somebody less contemptuous should have won, a true believer who slavishly worked out the odds of various numerical formulations in order to maximise winning potential, someone who paid visits to the ticket dispenser with the regularity of a devout churchgoer? When it came to the divine power of chance, Gary was an agnostic. The idea of fate was unnerving; it contradicted natural laws. Someone had to win, Ann told him, but that meant someone had to lose.

One odd thing happened four days after he bought the ticket. He had stopped in town to pick up some shopping, and entered the tobacconist's to buy a newspaper.

'Where do you get your scratchcards from?' he asked the young Asian man stacking shelves.

'We don't sell 'em, mate.'

'Yes you do, you've a machine – ' he indicated a space just past the regular lottery ticket dispenser, ' – just over – there.' His words dwindled away as he found himself pointing at nothing. 'It was there on Saturday,' he ended lamely.

'No, mate,' replied the boy, 'we've just got the regular one.'

'But I saw it, a red box near the door. I bought a ticket from it.'

'If there was anything like that there, someone must have brought it in from outside and then taken it away again.' He chuckled, shook his head and returned to aligning boxes of tampons.

Maybe it had been a scam. He had heard of bogus cash-points being set up in empty shops, then removed at the end of a busy Saturday, filled with credit card details. As the days passed he grew convinced that he had been abstractly victimised – but then the postcard arrived.

It had been mailed inside a plain white envelope, presumably to preserve his anonymity. The frank-mark indicated that it had come from London. The address was computer-typed, and the back took the form of a generic tick-box reply, the kind you found attached to the guarantee when you bought a toaster. The top of the card bore the legend **GRAND PRIZEWINNER**. It asked a variety of simple questions, his age, marital status, if he was a houseowner. At the bottom it read **Our representatives will call you to arrange a time when they can visit.** There was no other information on the card, or in the envelope.

'Don't you think they're being rather mysterious?' he asked Ann over breakfast on the morning the card arrived. 'No company name, no details, no picture of cars, or cash, or sundrenched beaches . . .'

Ann shrugged and gathered up the plates. 'They obviously have their own system,' she said, 'you'll just have to be patient.'

'When I was a kid there was a special offer on the back of a packet of cereal,' he recalled. 'Something called a 37-In-One-Scope, a kind of – instrument – that had 37 separate uses, magnifying glasses and knives, all sorts of stuff. You had to send three and six – '

'My god, old money,' laughed Ann.

' – to get this wonderful *thing*. I'll always remember how excited I was when the postman called to deliver it, but when I opened the box I found this tiny, badly made piece of plastic. The illustration on the cereal box had been greatly exaggerated, and the magnifier was blurry and the knives were plastic. It was junk.'

'Poor Gary.' She reached down and gave him a kiss on the head. He seemed melancholy today. She decided not to show him the final demand from the gas board that had arrived with the card. 'Well, you never know. Maybe your luck has changed.'

'Not me,' he replied, 'I never get chosen for anything.'

'But you have been,' she said, waving the card at him. 'You're a good man. Why shouldn't you get what's coming to you?'

A man rang that evening, to arrange the visit. He and his colleague would come to the house on Saturday night, one week after Gary had scratched the card. He thought it odd that they operated outside of normal office hours, but said nothing to Ann; she had quite enough on her mind. On Saturday evening, shortly after a watery sun had set behind the trees, there was a knock at the front door. Two gaunt, unhealthy-looking young men stood side by side in matching black ties and raincoats. They looked like eastern European government inspectors, he thought, or Bible salesmen.

'You are Mr Gary Chapman?' asked one.

'Yes, I am,' replied Gary. 'Do you want to come in and have a cup of tea?'

'The same Gary Chapman who filled in this form?' He held the card up between thumb and forefinger.

'That's right.' Gary held the door wide, but neither of them showed signs of accepting his invitation. 'What have I won?'

'Will you be available to receive your reward here, say, tomorrow afternoon?' one asked, ignoring his question.

'I suppose so, yes.' He felt vaguely put out by their dour, unsmiling behaviour. Wasn't this supposed to be something to celebrate? Shouldn't he be congratulated on his luck?

'Shall we say four o'clock?' The man took a small black notebook from his colleague and jotted down the time.

'Yeah, fine.' He nodded at them defiantly, looking from one to the other.

'You'll be ready tomorrow, then.' They turned to go. 'Good day to you.'

'Wait, will it be you coming back tomorrow?'

'No, not us, sir – someone else. Well, good day to you.' They walked to the corner of the street in perfect step – as though they had rehearsed the movement together – and were gone.

'Why didn't you ask them anything useful?' Ann was watching from the kitchen, waiting for him to shut the front door.

'How could I? You saw what they were like.' Something they had said bothered him. The word *reward*. Surely they'd meant *award*?

The forecast for the day ahead was stormy. By noon on Sunday the sky had blackened and the wind was flattening the grass in the fields behind the house, making the moors resemble billowing green sails. There was an uncomfortable, heavy atmosphere in the kitchen. They barely spoke to each other as they sat studying the newspapers, watching TV, eating lunch. At five minutes to four they began surreptitiously watching the kitchen clock. By a quarter past four rain was falling in a light fine drizzle, and Gary had begun to feel as nervous as a condemned man in his last hour. He tried to read an article in the paper, something about the Church of England revising their definition of hell, but found it impossible to concentrate for more than a sentence or two.

'Nobody's coming,' he concluded finally. 'Look at the time. It's gone half past now.'

'Perhaps the weather has set them back.' Ann put down her book. 'Pacing about isn't going to help. If someone's coming up from London, the traffic's probably bad on the motorway.'

At five o'clock he could stand it no longer. The house felt

small and suffocating. He had to go outside, to look down on the town and see for himself. He pulled his old gaberdine raincoat and boots from the cupboard under the stairs. Boots, the labrador, leapt to his feet.

'Where do you think you're going?' Ann asked wearily. 'What do I do if they turn up before you get back?'

'How do I know?' he snapped. 'I need to go out for a while. Take Boots for his walk.' He snapped a lead on to the panting dog.

'But it's raining.'

'I just need to – see for myself.' He opened the front door and looked back at her, seated calmly in the armchair with a book in her lap, a frown of concern creasing her forehead. 'It's to do with fate. It can't be helped.' She did not answer.

'Well, goodbye, then,' he said.

'I love you very much, Gary.' She gave him a gentle smile, and watched as he went out into the night.

He had not meant to alarm her. Of course it was fate, like meeting a woman or becoming ill. The dog pulled him across the rising moor, the wild wind buffeting his back. The sky was a roaring black morass now, sparked by distant cracks of lightning. As they neared the dark woodland at the hill's brow, the sound of thrashing leaves drowned out any other. But then there was another noise, the shrieking howls of icy air sucked through branches that sounded like a psychotic raging choir.

He reached the edge of the wood and slipped Boots from his lead, but the labrador ran off fast and hard in the opposite direction. In moments he was lost from sight in the flailing grass.

When Gary looked over at the trees he saw something shifting back and forth, as if trying to free itself from the foliage. He stared harder. It was moving toward him, an immense black shape wavering between the oaks. It was almost as tall as the trees themselves, but hunched over, like a man searching for something beneath a table. When it raised its great head against the sky, above the treetops, he gasped. It had a face, not human at all but with small eyes set far apart, reflecting the night like an animal. It was hunting him, sensing him, unsure of its direction, and then it had his scent and was crashing through the undergrowth toward him, uprooting bushes in showers of earth and shoving aside great trunks, splintering them in its fury.

Gary turned and began to run then, back through the slippery wet grass until – as he knew he would – he stumbled and pitched over, and the great roaring darkness of the Fallen One's shadow swept across him like a cloak, and the satanic stink of his pursuer burned deep within his throat.

The wind dropped as it drew back for a moment, the better to build its strength.

Then it blasted down and roared through him, smashing his ribcage into pieces, shredding and pounding with such force that parts of him were buried deep in the hillside, and other parts, whipped dry of blood, were tumbled away across the moor so that his obliterated body looked like the remains of an air crash victim. His skull was separated so completely that it later proved impossible to identify his remains. His bones and teeth were split and ground into a pulpy dust that turned to mud and was washed away by the thundering torrent. He was there and then gone, like a bolt of summer lightning, a swatted mayfly, a sunray caught in the painted saints gracing a church window, and like all of those, it mattered not that he had been there at all.

Ann found the labrador shivering and crying on the moor, loping in uncertain circles. She saw no sign of her lover in the turbulent fields, and knew instinctively that only her memories of him now survived. The dog cried for his master so often that she was finally forced to give him away. Ann made a vow that she would never enter the lottery again. She saw no point in having to win at someone else's expense.

Even fate, she reasoned in the terrible empty days that ensued, was expected to maintain a sense of balance. There was no joy without pain.

The following week, a ten-year-old child was found dead from malnutrition in a block of luxury flats, and a woman who ran a successful clothing company in Oldham won ten million pounds. She told the clamouring press that her good fortune would in no way change her lifestyle.

STILL LIFE

Outside, the bell clanging, the rain falling. Inside, the cat, gingerly picking its path through the clusters of chair and table legs. Black as the coal in the dented copper scuttle standing in the corner. Its tiny tongue rasping the parquet floor, collecting the few crumbs of rock cake that remained.

'Beryl, take a broom under table four. We'll be having mice in here next.'

'Yes, Mrs Bagot.'

The woman behind the counter cracked upright, tall and pale and dry as a stick, cardigan pulled tight about her flat bust, colourless hair scraped high. 'For the life of me I really don't know why people can't use their napkins properly.' A bony forefinger ran around the rim of the cake dish on the corner of the counter. The edge of an apron was applied.

'I said to Mr Sanders, you ought to put down linoleum what with people traipsing in and out of here in all weathers. I might as well have saved my breath.'

A coal popped in the grate. Beyond the tearoom, drizzly twilight faded into darkness. A brisk stamping of boots on the platform outside and Mr Godby entered, his station-issue raincoat buffeted by the wind. With him came cascades of rain and the chill of the October evening. Faced with the imminent attack of Beryl and the broom, the cat fled from beneath a table out into the night.

'Are them Bamburys fresh? If so you could do worse than let me 'ave a couple with a nice cup of tea.'

'Most certainly they're fresh.' Myrtle's height grew with indignation. 'And you can take just one. I've got my customers to think of.'

'Customers?' asked Mr Godby with a wink to Beryl, 'I don't see any customers. Wouldn't be surprised meself if your rock cakes hadn't driven them out into the rain.'

Beryl turned her giggle into a cough and concentrated hard on the floor.

'I'll thank you not to be so cheeky, Mr Godby. We had newlyweds in this afternoon, off on their 'oneymoon. Pretty as a picture, she was. No complaints from them, I noticed. Haven't you got the boat train to let through?'

'It's not due for another ten minutes, so it's a cup of tea or a kiss, which?'

'I'm sure I don't know to what you are referrin'.' Myrtle turned over a cup and stood it beneath the urn. 'You can have a cup of tea and welcome if you keep your sauce to yourself. Beryl, put some more coal on. That wood's too damp to pick up.'

All along the platform, the light shades clanged rhythmically against the girders of the station roof. Rain cascaded down the tobacco-coloured sloping glass. Laura stepped through the swinging pools of light toward the butter-glow of the refreshment room windows, coat knotted tightly around her, Boots library book tucked high under one arm.

Inside, she waited for a break in the conversation to order. The reedy, tittle-tattle voice of the woman behind the counter faltered as she acknowledged her customer. This is how I want to remember it, thought Laura, the pop and crunch of the fire in the grate, the rain outside. I shan't be coming here again.

'A cup of tea, please.'

'Certainly.' Myrtle turned a cup. 'Cake or pastry?'

'Perhaps a Bath bun. Are they fresh?'

Mr Godby shot a knowing look at Beryl.

'Made this morning.' Myrtle removed the glass dome and tonged a bun on to a thick white plate. 'That'll be fourpence.'

Laura dug into her purse, the volume of Keats sliding from beneath her arm toward the floor. Mr Godby stopped it, placing it on the counter.

'Thank you so much.' Laura awkwardly removed her purse, tea and cake to a nearby table, returning for the book.

The tea grew cold in her hand as she idly turned the pages. How many times so far this week? Six or seven at least. Soon, perhaps, it would only be once or twice. Perhaps his earnest face would only come to mind on rainy Thursday afternoons, describing a routine day at the hospital until the whistle for the boat train gave him pause. Sometimes she played a game, staring hard at the book until she was convinced that he would be standing there when she looked up. She played it now, closing the cover and wiping it dry with the back of her glove. Now she would look up and see –

'Laura! Goodness, we *do* seem to be running into each other a lot these days! My dear, you look frazzled. I'm not a bit surprised, this ghastly weather is enough to tire anyone out.'

Dolly Messiter, bustling with chat, garlanded with packages, dropped into the chair opposite. Laura forced a smile of recognition, if not welcome. Dolly failed to notice. She scraped her chair around and addressed the counter.

'I say, could I have a cup of tea, not too strong, and a bar of Nestles?' She turned to Laura. 'It's for Tony. I'm surprised he still has a tooth in his head.'

'Sixpenny or shilling?' Myrtle was displeased at having to call from the counter. Dolly showed no sign of rising to collect her tea.

'Oh, the sixpenny, plain if you have it.' She lowered her

voice and turned back. 'Laura, you really do look rather peaky. Would you like a fresh cup, buck you up?'

'No, really, I'm fine thanks, just a little tired.'

'Iron pills. They're the answer. Margo swears by them, not that they've done her much good, poor soul.'

Beryl brought over the tea and the chocolate.

'Thank you, dear.' Dolly handed her eightpence and plopped in the cube of sugar from her saucer. 'Who would have thought that the shops would be so crowded on such a beastly day? My dear I'm all done in, and soaked thanks to the pavement outside McFisheries.'

Laura's gaze had returned to the back of the library book. *If you have enjoyed this book, why not try these other fine –*

'These stockings were a present from Tony, and now of course they're quite ruined . . .'

In the distance, machinery rattled. Rails pinged with the weight of a locomotive. 'Could you tell me, is that the Ketchworth train?'

Mr Godby looked up from his *Daily Sketch*, propped against the cake stand.

'No, it's the express, the boat train.' He set down his cup of tea. 'Early too!' and hurried out of the door.

'Really, Laura, you ought to see a doctor. You looked exhausted the last time I saw you. But of course, you were *with* a doctor, weren't you? Doctor . . .'

She searched the air for a name, waiting for Laura to supply it.

'Doctor Harvey. Alec Harvey.'

'Harvey, that's right. What a charming man. There are so few about these days. Didn't he go to India?'

'Africa. He moved his practice there.'

'Africa, that's it. He should have prescribed you something. Have you heard from him?'

'No, nothing.' Laura drank the last of her cold tea. The

express roared through, beating a tattoo on the sleepers, halting conversation.

She's going to ask how Fred is now. What can I tell her? Fred will be sitting at home listening to the wireless, doing the crossword. Fred is writing in the answer to a clue, checking his watch, waiting for his dinner. Fred is Fred. Not Alec.

'Well, much as I hate to brave the cold, I'd really better heave these parcels on to the platform or I'll never board the train in time. What time *is* it?'

'Twenty to six. It's due in three minutes. They don't bother to close the gates between the two trains. Here, let me give you a hand with those.'

Dolly thankfully handed her one of the smaller packages.

'You go ahead,' said Laura, 'I'll bring the rest.'

Dolly staggered out of the tearoom clutching her purchases while Laura rose and folded up the fur collar of her coat. As she pulled on her gloves she gazed around the refreshment room for the last time. The door had closed on Dolly. Myrtle was attending to her accounts, squinting over the top of her spectacles as she made ticks on a list. For a moment the only sound was the shifting of fireplace coals.

Laura tilted back her head and closed her eyes. Until now she had not felt it was truly over. They had parted without saying goodbye. How could they have, with Dolly and her confounded congregation of parcels plumping down between them at the last minute? But now, in the quiet of the tearoom it felt finally over. With the closing of its door the memory would be sealed inside forever.

Across the room, Beryl set the scuttle down with a bang.

Laura's eyes snapped open, wide and brown. She pulled out a handkerchief and blew her nose in an annoyed fashion. Gathering the parcel and book, she opened the waiting room door and propped it with her foot. The bright empty room with its familiar window table now seemed like any other. In the distance the whistle of the five forty-three sounded, and Laura let the door swing shut.

Once Dolly's parcels were safely loaded on to the luggage rack, Laura smoothed the seat of her coat and took a window seat. Spread across the centre of the carriage, Dolly prattled. Tony had been ill, Derry and Toms were having a sale, she still hadn't found a replacement for Phyllis. Laura nodded amiably and sympathised without hearing a word.

With a push of steam and a lurch the train moved forward and began to pick up speed. Laura cleared a patch of glass. Beyond the window, green enamel signs rolled past, posters and benches flashing by. Milford Junction sped away.

'Of course I was sorry to see her go, she was a treasure and heaven knows it's hard enough finding a replacement these days . . .'

They were pulling level with the underpass entrance at the end of the platform as someone – a lanky figure running awkwardly, fawn Dunn & Co raincoat flapping, trilby pulled down tight, missed the train. For a second, really just a second, the loping gait seemed so familiar, the bony hand raised to hold the hat, the long legs striding up the slope, something forlorn and lost – but the image was gone, replaced by the bare wet branches of the elms that lined the cutting.

Laura slumped back in her seat and closed her eyes. Dolly had ceased her chatter and was now pulling at a magazine wedged in her handbag.

The beat of wheels on metal, over wood, lulled Laura to sleep. There had been no-one running for the train. Beneath her body, the points switched. The train swayed, bearing her back to Ketchworth and home.

The door of the refreshment room flew open, spraying rain with it, as the figure strode across to the counter. 'I'm sorry, could you tell me, was that the Ketchworth train?'

Myrtle peered over the top of her glasses and set aside her

fountain pen. Instead of setting down his trilby with a pinch of his hand, the enquirer pulled his hat tighter on to his head and refused to catch her eye.

'Indeed it was. You've only just missed it.'

The man tugged open his raincoat and pulled at a pocket. He moved oddly, as though he had been wounded. The war had done terrible things to the country's men.

'I'll have a tea please.'

'Cake or pastry?'

'Just a tea.' He still refused to catch her eye. Perhaps there was something wrong with his face. Myrtle slipped two cubes of sugar into the saucer. In the distance, thunder rumbled. Alec fumbled for money and placed two pennies on the counter. He felt the weight of the book dragging at him. After a brief moment of hesitation he withdrew it and took his tea to the window table, sitting in the opposite chair to where she had sat.

Myrtle glanced over once or twice and could tell he was writing something. There was a strange smell in the room, drawn from the damp wood in the fire.

When she next looked up, he was standing before her.

'I say, you didn't happen to see a lady in here earlier, small, brown hair, a coat with a fox-trim collar?'

'Why, yes. She just left. In here every Thursday, like as not. Catches the Ketchworth train.'

'The thing is, I have something of hers, and I wanted to give it to her. I can't – be here – again. I wonder if I could ask you a favour, seeing as she comes in each week . . .'

Myrtle studied the book on the counter and narrowed her eyes. 'I must say it's most irregular,' she began. 'This is not a lending library.'

'Could you give it to her? I really would be most grateful.'

'Well, all right. I'll keep it back here with my accounts. Just this once, mind.' She'd do him the favour. He didn't look well.

'It's awfully kind of you.'

He finished his tea back at the table, sipping slowly, like an invalid taking soup. When Myrtle next looked up, he had gone, splashing off through the underpass no doubt, and Beryl was clearing the crockery.

The book was a volume of Victorian poetry, awful sickly stuff, the pages bordered with faded roses. The letter was folded inside the flyleaf and addressed to Laura Jesson in scratchy, broken script, as though someone very ill had written it. Myrtle turned it over in her hands. A Billy Doo, and she was in charge of it! The urn steamed and bubbled. She looked over at Beryl.

'Get the broom, Beryl, and run it under table two. There's rice everywhere. Sweep it up.'

'Yes, Mrs Bagot.'

All very well for newlyweds, thought Myrtle, *they don't have to worry about the mess*, as she allowed the envelope to stray in front of the steam. It wasn't her fault that the flap popped open. Barely glued down, it had been. The letter virtually slid out by itself.

'And mind you don't miss any,' she said loudly, scanning the page.

Left Madeline behind – desperate to see you one more time – life meant nothing without you – wanted to die –

'Mrs Bagot—'

Knowing we could never be together – no other choice – wrong of me, I know – a dreadful sin to take one's own life – wanted to die thinking of you – prayed that would be the end of it – who could have known that love would prove stronger than death – now this awful pain will never end – only once we are reunited –

'Mrs Bagot—'

– love stronger than death –

Beryl sounded frantic. 'Mrs Bagot, it's not rice.' She slammed her broom at the floor. 'It's maggots!'

✦

Each swing of the train bore Laura further away from Milford Junction. Dolly Messiter tapped her on the shoulder and offered her a handkerchief. 'Are you all right?' she enquired. 'You looked as if you were having a bad dream.'

'No,' said Laura firmly. 'I just had a piece of grit in my eye, that's all.'

THE CAGES

'Look,' said Albert, 'they're beating up Mrs Tremayne.'

'She's not done anything wrong, has she?' asked Dr Figgis.

'No. Perhaps that's why they're beating her up.'

'Doesn't follow, does it? God, she's making a lot of noise.'
He shouted through the bars. 'Hey, keep it down!'

'This thing's hard on my arse.' Albert fidgeted on the rungs.
After a few hours they cut into your buttocks and forced you
to change position. At least, that was the effect they had on
Albert. He noticed that many of the others never seemed to
move at all.

'There's a technique to sitting.' The doctor demonstrated,
bouncing up and down on the balls of his feet. 'It's all a
question of balance. It took me a couple of months to really
get the hang of it. You've only been up here – how long?'

Albert counted on his fingers. 'Let me see, I was still in the
bright yellow cages last Thursday.'

'Ah,' the doctor nodded, adding redundantly, 'Sunflower
Section. This is Waterlily.'

'They must have come for me on the Friday morning,
which would make it about a week.'

'There you are, then,' confirmed the doctor. 'You haven't
found your sea-legs yet.'

'We're not at sea, are we?' asked Albert, alarmed.

'It's just an expression.'

'Because that would account for the swaying.' He pointed

along the lines of cages. Each grey steel-runged box was suspended by four heavy oiled chains, and shifted slightly in and out of his vision. Each cage contained one person. Albert could count thirty-four in front of him and perhaps sixty behind. The occupants were mostly silent, so that the only sound was a faint musical tinkling of link against link, diminishing with distance. The fetid grime-filled air prevented him from seeing clearly in any direction.

'I'm glad we're not at sea. That would mean we were going somewhere, and I'm not ready to go anywhere yet. I've still got the shits.' He dropped to the floor of the cage and tried to find a comfortable position by lying on his stomach. 'I thought I might do a workout. Strengthen my abs. Do you ever wonder what these cages are for? Who built them? Are there many more underneath us?'

'Oh, yes,' replied Dr Figgis, authoritatively. 'There's someone just a few yards below you, but you can't see him. He used to have a light, but it burned out. When you dropped your soup bowl last night most of it went through the bars on to his head. He didn't say anything, but you could tell he wasn't pleased. Mr Whitely is seventy-two and never complains, but then he fought in the war. Didn't even yell out when we had the rain of spiders. Everyone else did.'

'I'm quite looking forward to my dinner tonight.' Albert winced and shifted his position. 'You appreciate your food more when you only get one meal a day. We used to get two in Sunflower.'

The doctor moved closer to the bars. 'You know what it is, don't you? In the bowls?'

Albert thought for a moment. 'Some kind of beef and marrow mixture in gravy stock?'

'Oh dear, no.' Dr Figgis shook his head and chuckled. 'If only it was. No, I'm afraid you've been eating something rather more verminous.'

'How unimaginative.' Albert sighed, nursing his knees. 'I'm

not squeamish, though. You can get used to anything. Make the best of a bad job. We had nice food in Yellow, and in Blue before that.'

'Ah, Iris Section.'

Just then an anguished howl rose from one of the cages on their left. An elderly man had slipped over, trapping his bony leg between the floor bars. As he fell it cracked with a sharp snap, and was left dangling uselessly beyond reach in its pouch of pallid skin while the old man cried and cried.

'I hope he doesn't think someone's going to come rushing along to help him,' said the doctor. 'He shouldn't be down here in the first place. He and Mr Whitely were supposed to be put somewhere up at the front in Tulip. But I've noticed sometimes they put the wrong ones in here. Like you.' He came to the edge of the bars. 'If you don't mind my saying so, you're far too young to be in this division.'

'What about Mrs Tremayne?' asked Albert. 'She has to be fifty. I don't think there's a greater power at work, you know, deciding where we all go. You just get put wherever you get put, and there's nothing at all you can do about it.'

'Hmm, you're probably right. You have to make the best of things, don't you?'

'I used to get a bit bored, though, in Sunflower. Of course, you had solid concrete floors there, which made life a lot simpler. Keeping your balance, and that. I had a nice bowl of flowers in my cage. Chrysanthemums. Nothing like that here. You can't help feeling a bit trapped in this thing. There's no room.' He stretched his arms out, touching either side of the cage with his fingertips. 'I'm sure this is much smaller than the last one.'

'They do get smaller,' agreed Dr Figgis. 'You should see Crocus.'

'Have you been put there, then?'

'No, but I have a friend who has. Whenever they move you, it's never to better conditions. The beatings get more frequent. And the food gets worse. They don't cook it at all in Hydrangea, which is two after this, and they don't serve it until it's turned rotten in Nasturtium. But someone told me there are fewer and fewer bars on the cages as you move down.'

'Oh, that's good.'

'Not really. The air is much murkier below, it's harder to see and breathe properly, and because of the bars it gets more difficult to stay inside without falling out into space.'

'Mind you,' said Albert, 'that means you can probably get out.'

'Get out? Oh, you can get out whenever you want. You probably never thought about it much before now. Anybody can get out, whenever they're ready to go. Look at this.' The doctor reached through the bars of his cage and pushed against Albert's door with the palm of his hand. 'See, it's not locked. It's never been locked. All you have to do is take a mighty leap into the dark.'

There was a shower of rust, and the iron grille swung wide with a slow painful creak. The space revealed before Albert was awesome, dark and eternal. Albert gingerly moved forward and looked down. There were men and women vertiginously suspended in cages below him as far as he could see, crushed humanity in every direction, all the way back to his childhood and infancy.

He contemplated the scene for a moment.

'It's an awfully long way down, isn't it?' he exclaimed. 'Probably bottomless. Just space forever. Fair makes you dizzy to look.' But Albert could not resist the looking. After a few minutes, though, he nervously reached forward and pulled the cage door shut until it shifted back in place with a firm, satisfying click.

'You can open it any time,' reminded Dr Figgis.

'Out there. The fall – '

'The fall would kill you.'

Albert glanced uncomfortably between his feet. 'I'm sure it would.'

'But while you fall, you'll be completely free.'

Albert considered the idea for a moment, then returned to the rear corner of the cage and rubbed against his bars appreciatively. 'I understand what you're saying,' he told the doctor, despair creeping into his voice, 'but I think on the whole I'm better off staying in here.'

'Now you know who built the cages,' said the doctor, smiling sadly.

THE GRAND FINALE
HOTEL

'Good Lord In Heaven,' gasped Mr Satardoo, eyeing the great golden lounge clock as he scuttered past it, 'if he cared for us at all he would allow sixty-one minutes in an hour today, just today, and our gratitude for his temporal lassitude would be expressed in renewed endeavour.'

The under-manager's language echoed the convoluted structure of the Delhi civil service, in whose foreign office he had been trained. He had migrated from his native India just after the war and had worked here at the Grand Finale Hotel ever since, longer than most of the house staff, but not so long as the senior housekeeper Mrs Opie, or the septuagenarian manager, General Sullivan.

Mr Satardoo barely slowed his pace as he wheeled into the main hall to inspect his troops.

Before him stood a battalion of chambermaids in crisp monochrome, their caps of fluted white linen seated upon their coiffures like matching baby doves. Beside them a regiment of stiff-backed waiters stood to attention, the diagonal planes of their noses held at exactly forty-five degrees to the icy blue marble floor, their haircuts macassared in perfect geometry, their hooded eyes impossible to catch. The waitresses had their own division, their flared black dresses cut low and short, edged in white to give them the appearance of mischievous angels. Then came a squad of veteran porters as stooped as question marks, their jacket sleeves subtly altered to incorporate an added length of bone caused by lifetimes of lifting great leather cases.

An infantry of bellboys flanked the sides of the sunlit hall, their brass buttons glittering like crocodile eyes, their caps set at an angle that suggested jauntiness without jocularity, disarm without disrespect. Their emerald suits were sectioned with silver piping that ran from collar to spats, a uniform as proudly worn as those of Wellington's men, and much admired by the hotel's female guests, who always watched discreetly as the lads scurried past on their errands.

Mr Satardoo clapped his hands together, and even though the sound was muffled by the white kid gloves he habitually wore, everyone snapped to attention.

The only members of staff not represented in the hall were the cooks, who could not risk leaving the kitchens so close to the hour set aside for luncheon.

'Now,' began Mr Satardoo, 'I want you all to pay careful attention. In a few minutes the Archduke Fernandel Aracino will arrive with his entourage, and it is imperative that he receives the kind of service that a man of his reputation would expect from our hotel. Although it is the first time he has taken a suite here – and of course for every one of our guests who takes a suite it is always the first visit – I want you to make him feel that he is among old friends. Where is Mr Mack?'

'Here, Mr Satardoo.' The little concierge stepped from behind an enormous potted aspidistra and coughed softly into his fist.

'Ah, there you are. I thought perhaps we had lost you in the loamy confines of the foliage.' Mr Satardoo was fond of teasing Mr Mack about his height. The concierge did not mind. He was happy and confident in his job, because he knew that the staff greatly respected him. Even Mr Satardoo would have admitted it, were he not so obsessed with honouring the hierarchy that placed him technically above Mr Mack in the hotel's complex chain of command.

'How long does the Archduke plan to stay with us?' asked Mr Mack.

'As long as it takes, of course.'

'And he has specifically requested the Virginia Woolf Chamber?'

'I am given to understand so.' Five gigantic suites at the top of the hotel were currently available for royal ranks. There was a sixth, but it was permanently reserved for the Princess Arthur of Connaught, in recognition of a great favour once performed by that esteemed house for the hotel's first owner.

Its real name was the Imperial Rex, but the less respectful staff had nicknamed it the Grand Finale Hotel. It had one hundred and fifty rooms, of which forty-seven were themed suites of unrivalled opulence, and like the world's most truly special hotels, it had many more staff than guests. However, the Rex was unlike any other hotel in the world, and for this reason remained hidden from the pages of those glossy volumes listing the finest places to stay. Under certain conditions its bar and restaurant were open to the casual visitor, and its rooms could be booked by families whose tiered generations were well-known to the management. Rooms were occasionally available to newcomers who made it through the deliberately labyrinthine booking procedure, but its special suites were the exclusive province of those who fulfilled more exacting criteria. Despite this seeming elitism the hotel was surprisingly egalitarian in its guest list, and so long as its conditions of stay were followed to the letter, even the poorest struggling artist might eventually be admitted to one of the suites. Its rooms were a different matter; they, and the items on the restaurant menu, remained unpriced, the tacit understanding being that if you had to ask the cost of anything at the Grand Finale, you could not afford it. It was normal for those who booked one of the forty-seven special suites to be served their meals in luxurious privacy. These suites were only full in times of great crisis, after wars, plagues and depressions, and, due to the vicissitudes of modern life, were never entirely empty.

The Rex occupied a rocky bluff overlooking the rolling jade ocean. There was a private beach, and teak-decked motorboats rode the tide in a cave cut into the ivory cliff-face, accessible by a flight of stone steps leading down from the basement. Throughout the years, it remained a dazzling white fortress of taste and calm, with an elegant double bow-front, striped emerald lawns, pergolas and a maze, and garish red and blue flags fluttering brazenly between pyramids of hyacinths all along its battlements. The hotel was simply unique, a home to great joy and sadness. A testimony, Mr Satardoo was fond of saying, to the bravery of the human soul, although there were those who were appalled that such a place should exist at all.

Mr Satardoo checked his watch and dismissed the ranks, but kept Mr Mack behind. 'I fear,' he intimated, 'we shall not be spared the distressing dilemma presented by the Crown Prince of Jhada's recent stay. The Archduke is renowned for harbouring similar proclivities.'

Mr Mack nodded sagely. While it was perfectly usual for royalty to arrive with a small army of personal staff, the Crown Prince had appeared with two dozen of his favourite concubines, giving rise to all manner of problems in protocol. 'I daresay we can solve the problem,' he replied, 'without having to resort to such drastic tactics as before. The Archduke is a man of greater sensitivities.'

'We shall have to see.' Mr Satardoo gave a grim little shake of his head, as if expecting the very worst. 'We shall have to see.' His eagle eye alighted upon the faintest smear of brass polish beneath the dolphin-handle of one of the entrance doors, and he set off with great relish on a mission to box the culprit's ears.

Malcolm Bridger did not come from an old-money family. He was not a knight or a lord or even well-connected, but the Imperial Rex had agreed to rent him a room. True it was one of the smaller chambers to the rear of the building, but it was a room nevertheless, and you could even glimpse the sea by leaning perilously from the bathroom window. Forsaking his former career as a tabloid journalist, Malcolm was now a biographer of international renown, and something about him had appealed to General Sullivan, whose snobbery was only surpassed by his admiration for biographers (it was no secret that the general hoped to persuade someone to transcribe his own history). And so here he was, seated in one of the great plush velvet armchairs in the Disraeli Lounge making surreptitious notes as the Archduke arrived.

First two liveried footmen in ash wigs and gilt epaulettes entered the lobby. They were followed by two young valets and a senior servant dressed in midnight blue. After this arrived a secretary who acted as the Archduke's liaison with the hotel staff. Mr Satardoo, Mr Mack and Mrs Opie headed the welcoming committee which stood to attention in two smart rows flanking the great staircase. The Archduke himself was as tall and frail as a bamboo pole. His white goatee thrust from his bony chin like a spurt of gun smoke, and matched the pale plume of his tricorn hat. He walked with the careful delicacy of a flamingo, an ascetic figure who whispered to his secretary as if he could hardly bring himself to discourse with the outside world. He wore presentation battledress of black and gold, for he had travelled here directly from an inspection of his troops.

Behind him, bearing all the earmarks of discretion that the Crown Prince of Jhada's concubines had lacked, were two demure women in the late bloom of their youth, dressed in matching bonnets and reticulated gowns of deep grey silk. Malcolm noted everything he saw, and was so adept at committing pen to paper that none saw him write. He knew that the Archduke's story was a sad one; he had seen one son shot dead and another blown to pieces in a terrible battle, and within two months had lost his wife during a plague that reached far within the walls of his palace, so far that he himself had only survived by sacrificing his right arm and replacing the appendage with a limb of gleaming steel.

He was ashamed of outliving his children, and of receiving his only injury from an illness instead of a war. He was disappointed by power and tired of the lies of men. So what on earth, wondered Malcolm, brought him here?

As the ladies of the Archduke rustled past and the entourage passed on to the staircase, spreading across it in a rising river, the biographer recapped his pen and sat back among the downy purple cushions, pondering the question. Fernandel Aracino's visit was just part of the puzzle. There was a sense of mystery here, of omission and discretion. The Imperial Rex withheld its true purpose from casual gaze. It went without saying that Mr Satardoo refused to allow him to interview the guests, but he could not even be shown inside any of the suites, and bribing a chambermaid had brought an indignant Mr Mack to his door.

There was something going on in this sunbeam-trellised hotel, this haven of calm and peaceful repose, that earned it a hushed reverence from outsiders. Mention of the hotel's name was enough to create a gap in the conversation, as if a talisman had been evoked. That evening, Malcolm spotted Mr Satardoo in the supper lounge and seized the opportunity to speak with him.

'Ah, Mr Bridger, I trust you do not find the nocturnal ozone too piquant?' he asked, referring, Malcolm assumed, to the fresh wind emanating from the open French windows that led on to the cliffs.

'Not at all, Mr Satardoo.' He seated himself opposite the plump Indian under-manager, who made a little rising gesture to acknowledge his guest. 'I've been meaning to ask you something.'

'Please feel most free to do so.' Mr Satardoo's corsets creaked like sea timbers as he leaned forward in his seat.

'Has no-one ever offered to write a history of this marvellous hotel?'

'The board of directors would, I feel, be less than willing to draw unnecessary attention to our little haven.'

'But many of your rooms are empty. Some good publicity would fill them.'

'Goodness, this hotel was not built simply to turn a profit,' said Mr Satardoo, shocked. 'It was constructed with the purpose of providing an oasis of tranquillity in a world that I fear is tipping into insanity.'

'I appreciate that, but perhaps a discreet brochure, with some tasteful photographs . . .'

'General Sullivan has indeed spoken of commissioning such a prospectus in the past,' sighed the under-manager, 'but the problem has always lain with authorial suitability.'

'You mean you haven't been able to find someone who could write such a thing to your satisfaction?'

'In a nutshell.'

'Then you need look no further,' said Malcolm. 'I'm your man.'

Mr Satardoo stared at him for a moment, then emitted an eager squeak. Clearly he saw an opportunity to ingratiate himself with his superior. 'I'll attempt to initiate the introduction of such a proposal into my next conversation with the general,' he informed the biographer with unconcealed delight, 'I am most certain of success.'

He was as good as his word. In the space of an interview that lasted for exactly ten minutes, no more or less, General Sullivan approved Malcolm's appointment on the project, agreed a handsome fee, and instructed Mr Satardoo to provide him with all the information he might require for such a task, with one proviso; that he would not be allowed to interview any of the guests who were staying in the forty-seven special suites, for their privacy was sacrosanct. This seemed reasonable, and Malcolm embarked upon the project with enthusiasm. Truth to tell, although he was enjoying his stay at the Imperial Rex immensely, inactivity made him fractious and caused his mind to dwell on certain morbid preoccupations. He missed his wife, who had divorced him almost a year ago, and had grown increasingly dissatisfied with the world around him, a world that provided poor recompense for his occupation and even less spiritual comfort.

The morning after the general had given his consent to the commission, Malcolm rose early and took breakfast outside on the broad white curve of the first-floor balcony, high above the shimmering green sea. Running his hand lightly over his thinning chestnut hair, he rose as the sedate ladies of the Archduke picked a path between the tables and took their places with the regular guests. Theirs was a gesture of respect to the hotel; the Archduke could have allowed his concubines to remain in the suite with him while he broke fast, but, choosing not to draw attention to their status, sent them instead to observe normal mealtimes in the correct fashion. Malcolm smiled at the stern bodices and severe skirts that gave no hint of the fleshly passions laced within. Mr Satardoo had no need to be alarmed; the Archduke was clearly a gentleman given to the employment of tact and delicacy. He was one more part of a rich dramatic tapestry being daily woven throughout the hotel, both on its public stages and behind the scenes. It seemed a shame that part of the tapestry would remain permanently hidden from the biographer's view.

Malcolm drew up a list of practical questions about the

hotel. He was less concerned with facts and figures, which were easily obtained, and more anxious to convey the unique ambience of a stay at the Rex. As the sapphire rawness of the morning tempered itself into a golden windswept summer's day, very possibly the last of the year, he strolled through each of the hotel's public spaces, watching and listening, filling his calfskin notebook with neat square writing.

But the suites which lined the top two floors of the hotel remained forbidden territory, and their exclusion nagged at him. Even the lifts would not go there without a special key. Something was being deliberately hidden from his gaze, and he wanted to know why. What on earth could a hotel such as this have to hide?

Malcolm was a man whose curiosity sometimes extended beyond common sense, and now his former tabloid skills represented themselves. Once he had ascertained the whereabouts of the silver lift keys, it was a simple matter to slip behind Mr Mack's counter and borrow one. That afternoon he had it copied in the town and returned to its hook before nightfall.

By itself, though, such a key was useless without further access to one of the suites, and this could only be gained by breaking the general's rule about fraternising with their occupants. That evening, Malcolm sat down to formulate a plan.

His main problem was finding a point of contact. The suite-guests did not mix with the other residents, and even sunbathed on a separate peninsula of rock away from the hotel's exclusive pebbled beach. The rubescence on the cheeks of the Archduke's concubines suggested that they took a little sun, and as this seemed a good enough place to start, Malcolm set about observing their movements.

He soon saw that there were two sides to Marisia and Therese (as they addressed each other in conversation). They gave courteous smiles as they rose from their morning table, nodding to the waiters and the other guests, but when they felt themselves to be unobserved, their mansuetude faded and expressions of the utmost dolour fell upon them. Indeed, they looked so sad that Malcolm felt ashamed to be spying on them. But his curiosity drove him on.

As the weather began to disappoint, the ladies took to sitting inside the glass-walled sun terrace until luncheon, writing in their commonplace books or demurely reading until the gong sounded. Within the space of a few days Malcolm was a familiar figure to them, always doffing his cap as they passed. Finally he was bold enough to sit beside them one morning as they shielded their eyes from the sun to watch several tiny white yachts cresting the waves.

'The Archduke hopes to sail tomorrow if the fine weather holds,' Marisia told him.

'But it is due to change,' warned Therese. 'Mr Satardoo tells me that the barometer is dropping.'

It was all the information he needed to know. Malcolm continued to work on his history of the hotel that afternoon, and prayed that the pressure would remain high enough for the Archduke to take out a boat.

He awoke next morning to a glorious sunny day. Rising early, he sat in the lobby reading the newspapers until he observed the Archduke and his men leaving. They were dressed in blue and white striped sweaters and flapping cream trousers, unmistakable yachting gear. Malcolm carefully folded away his copy of the *Times* and made his way to the sun lounge.

'I don't like that man,' Mr Mack confided to Flora, one of the third-floor chambermaids. 'There's something altogether too furry about him, the wispy hair and beard, the woolly jumper and corduroy trousers. He's sly. Forever creeping about behind people's backs, padding around in those horrible brown suede shoes, it's not natural.'

'What, brown suede shoes?' laughed Flora, giving him an

affectionate pinch on the bum. 'He's a writer, he watches people for ideas.' She checked to see if her cap was back on straight. The concierge had knocked it awry when he had pulled her into the pantry for a kiss.

'He's up to something.' Mr Mack narrowed his eyes, then let the fronds of the aspidistra fall back in place. 'Well, he may have got around Mr Satardoo, but he won't get around me so easily. Have one of your girls keep an eye on him.'

Malcolm watched the dazzling gold and crimson ranks assemble and launch tipsily into the overture from *Orphee Aux Enfers*. Marisia and Therese were seated in a pair of striped deckchairs nearest the bandstand. An empty chair stood five feet from them.

'Good morning, ladies,' said Malcolm, tipping his cap as he tugged the spare chair closer. 'Perhaps we'll be lucky with the weather after all.'

'I do hope so.' Therese looked out to sea, where the yachts were bobbing on a fresh swell. 'The Archduke is an enthusiastic sailor but not, I fear, a good one.'

From where he was sitting he could see the suite key lying in the top of Marisia's needlework bag. Malcolm smiled generously as he shuffled closer. 'Please, ladies, do not allow me to interrupt your appreciation of the music.'

The band struck up a languorous piece by Sibelius, the sun reappeared from behind a small cloud and the ladies settled back in their chairs. Within minutes, their eyes were fluttering shut. Malcolm raised himself from the deckchair as quietly as possible and, as he passed Marisia's back, pretended to attend to his shoelace. The ladies usually fell asleep during the day. Presumably their night exertions took a certain toll. With the suite key deftly slipped into his left palm, he quickly walked to the hotel steps.

Malcolm waited until the coast was clear and boarded a lift. The two floors on which the suites were housed were marked by a pair of unlabelled brass buttons. The first took him to a curving blue corridor with recessed doors, but here the numbers fell short of the one on Marisia's key, and a maid eyed him suspiciously as he examined the doors, so he continued up to the second. Alighting, he soon found himself facing the door of the Archduke's suite. With a pounding heart he inserted the key and twisted it in the lock. Surely there had to be something extraordinary within. Why else would the General and his staff have such a need for secrecy? The door swung silently wide, and he stepped into the room.

General Sullivan sat in his office with his head in his hands, as a sense of infinite sadness settled upon him. He supposed it was inevitable that such a thing should happen, that the outside world would finally invade his kingdom. He had been taken in by Malcolm Bridger. A simple routine check on the biographer's background told him that five years ago Bridger had been dismissed from a notorious tabloid newspaper for breaching their code of ethics, such as the publication had. And now he was being allowed to snoop around the hotel, peeping and prying. The general had made his first foolish mistake, and it had to be put right immediately. With a heavy-hearted sigh, he summoned Mr Satardoo.

Malcolm stared about him. Nothing was out of place here – quite the reverse, in fact. The Archduke's suite was luxurious beyond all imagining. The furnishings were more suited to a Moorish summer palace. Great teak-framed windows, swathed in fine gilt silk, ran from floor to ceiling, and the light from the sea threw brilliant undulations on to the arched sapphire walls. The rooms around him swayed blue and gold, gold and blue, like a tropical aquarium in the sky. Each room, it was said, had its own style, one like a winter palace in Samarkand, another like an Egyptian seraglio. Why would the management wish to hide such magnificence? Puzzled, he began a systematic search of the rooms.

Mr Satardoo tipped himself on to the points of his shoes and looked about the sun-lounge. 'I understand our elusive gentleman biographer was briefly sighted here earlier. Have you been vouchsafed such an epiphany?' The head bellboy dreaded being asked anything by Mr Satardoo because he rarely understood a single sentence that issued from the under-manager's lips.

'I'm sorry, sir?'

'Mr Bridger. Have you seen him?'

'Oh yes, sir. He was sitting with the Archduke's ladies, out by the bandstand.'

Mr Satardoo flickered a smile of grim satisfaction and headed outside. His eagerness to please had caused a betrayal of the General's trust, and now it was up to him to win back his reputation.

The lounge contained a dark-mirrored cocktail cabinet better stocked than the American Bar at the Savoy. Malcolm poured himself a small whisky, swilling it around the tumbler as he conducted his investigation. From the window he could see the distant bandstand and the silk dresses of the slumbering concubines. He failed to notice that the weather was changing out to sea, however, and that the yachts were reluctantly returning to their harbour. Allowing the malt liquid to spill around his tongue, he wandered from room to room, his journalist's eye searching for the slightest hint of something untoward.

There was nothing unusual in the bathroom, if one ignored the fact that it was carved from lazurite the colour of a night sky. The bedrooms of the Archduke's courtesans were painted in delicate yellow-green shades of topaz, a gemstone that hung in heavy pendants from the lamps on their writing tables. The master bedroom was similarly opulent, if more alarming. The bed itself was carved in the shape of an enormous black swan, perhaps twelve feet long and as many wide, the mattress covered with a glittering onyx bedspread. It was more like a Stygian vessel than a couch of temporary repose. Frowning, he drew closer.

It was while he was examining this particular item of furniture that he discovered the brass-lined holes, ten of them on either side of the base, and another six set in the headboard of the bed. They were evenly spaced along the wood, none of them more than half an inch across.

What on earth, he wondered, could they be for? He touched them lightly with his forefinger and tried to reason; these rooms were only available to the few clients who met certain criteria demanded by the hotel. Nobody spoke of the situation, but everyone knew it to be true. Why did no-one probe deeper? If something wrong, something *bad* was going on, why wasn't it exposed?

What was the Imperial Rex trying to hide?

'Elise insists she saw him get out of the lift on the seventh floor, Mr Mack.'

'I don't see how that's possible. He's not in possession of a key.'

'She says she saw one in his hand, sir, not more than ten minutes ago. She didn't think nothing of it, until she saw him searching the door numbers. Was going to ask him what his game was, not being allowed on the floor and all, but he got back in the lift just as she went up to him.'

As Mr Mack listened to the girl, his eyes widened.

Malcolm Bridger racked his brains. What was it about the Archduke that set him aside from other men? Was his stately mantle of melancholia simply an attitude donned with his status? Or was there a deeper purpose that drove him here to the gilt mirrored halls of the world's most luxurious hotel?

Pondering the question, he climbed up upon the great black swan and lay back on the bed, his hands resting lightly on the ebony coverlet. Gulls wheeled past the great curved windows, driven inland by the changing weather. The room grew darker with his thoughts. Lying here, Malcolm found that there was something conducive to introspection. The pulsation of lightwaves on the ceiling, the dull glitter of gold mosaics in the Gustav Klimt murals, the gentle harmonies of musical instruments as delicate as celestial windchimes, the mingled scents of fresh-cut grass and ozone, of a woman's perfume lingering on a warm pale neck . . .

Women. No more women in my life, he thought, remembering the wife who had left him, the child she would not allow him to see. He asked himself why he had refused to let her into his heart, questioned the path that had finally brought him here. How, he asked himself, did I ever come to be so alone?

And when he raised his head at the noise, he found them all looking at him, Mr Satardoo, Mr Mack, Mrs Opie and the General himself, their faces a mixture of pity, kindness and infinite patience.

'I assume you understand now?' Mr Mack gently asked. Mrs Opie appeared by his side and wiped his eyes with a white linen handkerchief.

'I . . . I'm not sure.'

'These suites are only for those who are sure,' said Mr Mack as the others quietly left the room, pulling the doors shut behind them. 'They are reserved for guests who have definitely decided. Perhaps you have decided, and don't realise it yet. You are all alone in the world, aren't you? Try to tell me how you feel.'

Malcolm tried to marshal his thoughts. 'I'm tired,' he said finally.

'Then you have come to the right place,' smiled Mr Mack. 'Our lives begin in such high spirits, but once we see the world for what it is, it fatigues us. Disappointment is a tiring emotion, Malcolm. Where we had hoped for understanding, we find only cynicism, where there once was love is only selfishness. Our lives empty out with the passing years, until sometimes there is nothing left but our corporeal form. It is in this state that our special guests arrive, and here find final peace. Just as you shall.'

He walked around to the side of the bed and pressed a switch recessed in the headboard. His voice was a monotone as soothing as a calm sea. 'It is important for you to relax, Malcolm, to find serenity at the end, just as the Archduke will when he is ready, just as hundreds of others have.'

He's right, thought Malcolm, his eyes welling with tears. He felt the pinpricks brush his skin, and his body began to lose its tension. From the ten holes on either side of the bed, and the six in the headboard, the steel filaments had snaked out, piercing his clothes and entering the flesh of his neck, his arms, his torso, his legs, nipping into his veins, pumping fluid in, draining away his fears and doubts, filling his head with visions of tranquillity.

'No more unhappiness, Malcolm, no more uncertainty, and you have the General to thank. He wanted to provide a haven for those who wished to end their lives. He is shocked by the sordid, disordered way too many people reach their final moments. You come into this world in peace and warmth and love. Why is there no provision for leaving it in the same manner? Well, there is, Malcolm, but of course people aren't allowed to decide such things for themselves, and such a wonderful service is deemed not to be in society's best interests. Why not, Malcolm, answer me that? Where is the harm?'

Malcolm was numb. His mind was alert, but all panic had ceased. He realised that from the moment he had lain on the bed, the very air above him had changed. Tiny jets had been triggered by the pressure of his body on the mattress. He remembered his childhood, running in the park with a blue paper kite, being lifted in the air by his father, endless summer days, storms over the downs, the deaths of his parents, the loss of his faith, his wife at the door with her son in her arms, the grey days that had replaced his hopes, and nothing mattered any more. Nothing.

His memories faded into sleep, and the sleep deepened into death.

Mr Mack studied the departed biographer with a sad sigh. He walked to the telephone and rang Mrs Opie. 'Tell the Archduke we're still cleaning his room,' he said, his voice filled with reverence for the departed. 'Have Mr Bridger's bill made up and lose it in the Archduke's dining expenses. And see what you can get for his luggage from the usual source.'

'One hundred and fifty rooms, of which forty-seven are themed suites of unrivalled opulence' reads the new brochure for the Imperial Rex. 'So many guests have found peace with us.'

MIDAS TOUCH

(Author's Note: In the process of developing the character of Judy Merrigan for a new multiple-plot novel called 'Soho Black', I wrote her part out as a short story. If you're planning to read the novel, you may wish to delay reading this tale, although the two versions are substantially different.)

Everyone knows about the Midas touch, right? Those M's are among the few pieces of mythology one still remembers; the Medusa, the Minotaur and Midas – the man with the golden touch. I should have been warned by his name.

My name is Judy Merrigan, another M and no myth, just an ordinary Mrs. I was thirty-two when I moved from Arizona to England to be with my husband for the four inglorious years our marriage lasted. Michael and I met in Phoenix, where he taught classical history at the university. He took me out to dinner and asked if he could take me home. It turned out he meant *all the way* home. From Phoenix to Sussex, England, quite a culture shock. It was my first trip to Europe, only I didn't see any of the things you're supposed to see. Even Texas boys get to visit Paris when they graduate, but I found myself marooned in a silent English suburb with funny little front gardens and round red mailboxes and bay windows, looking after a man who needed a mother more than a wife.

I had given up a successful career as a graphic artist to do this. There was no way I could keep my clients from my new overseas base, and I couldn't start afresh without contacts. Besides, Michael didn't like me working. We separated because he wanted more children, and I wasn't crazy about the ones he already had.

I had no intention of returning to Phoenix and subjecting myself to my father's barbed remarks about the failure-rate of modern marriages; I decided to stay on in England so long as I could move to London. My divorce papers came through and suddenly I was on my own in a city I hardly knew. Most people would have been thrilled at the prospect of independence, but I was scared. Michael had spent four years bullying the confidence out of me. As I walked down an impossibly crowded Regent Street, I realised just how much I had distanced myself from the world outside.

When my mother died she left me a little money, and as there wasn't much forthcoming from the divorce settlement, I used her bequest to fulfil a dream. I bought my own property. Not the kind of place Michael or my father would ever have approved of – that was part of the charm – a town apartment, cosmopolitan and chic and central to everything. The third floor of a renovated two-hundred-year-old building with polished hardwood floors and large airy rooms, in Great Titchfield Street, part of the area they call Fitzrovia (I loved those names), where the sidewalk cafes and corner pubs and late night stores steeped with trays of exotic vegetables make it the closest you can get in Central London to a New York neighbourhood.

This was the first time I had a place I could truly call my own, and I spent every last penny fixing it up. I thought I could use part of the lounge as a studio and resume my interrupted career. Got myself a deal with an illustration agency, made a few contacts, but the industry had changed while I'd been away – computers had replaced illustration work with photo-composites. I didn't get downhearted. At the start of that hot, thundery summer I leaned out of my window watching the world pass below, convinced that somebody somewhere would still need watercolours, gouaches and pencil sketches, and that I could produce them from my penthouse eyrie.

There were others in the building; a woman in the apartment below, and an old Greek couple in the first-floor flat with its ground-level grocery. There was one more apartment, opposite mine, separated by a small dark landing. The brass sign on the door read *Midas Blake*, but I never saw him. Maria, the Greek lady, told me he was strange. 'What kind of strange?' I asked her.

'Very quiet,' she explained, 'keeps his door closed. Comes and goes late at night. Doesn't have a job, but always has money.' That didn't sound so bad. 'A nice man, though?' I asked.

'Oh yes,' she said, smiling with her big white false teeth, 'very nice.' And then one night there he was, rattling his key at the lock as I arrived, looking over his shoulder at me. I didn't introduce myself. We just nodded to each other and turned our backs. He closed his door and I closed mine. I didn't see him again for an age. Never heard his latch click, or any sound from his apartment. For a big man he had to be very light on his feet.

Then one hot Monday morning in June I had my bag snatched on the tube platform by this – *child* – no more than fourteen I swear, but strong and fast enough to break my shoulder strap and hightail it out of the station. The policeman I complained to at Tottenham Court Road took details indifferently, another statistic to be tallied. I cancelled my cards, bought a new wallet, then realised I was missing my spare keys. When I got home, Maria's husband Ari stopped me on the gloomy landing, where he was repairing a junction box. A tiny man, as soft and grey as a waterlogged potato, very gentle. Always giving advice, not all of it good. He told me I should change my locks just in case.

'More expense,' I complained. I was up to my limit for the month, with still a week to go, so the lock stayed as it was.

The good thing about London is you don't get brownouts. The bad thing is, I didn't know how to fix an English fuse. On the Thursday of that week I came home late to find the stairway in total darkness. I managed to grope my way up to the second floor, then heard someone on the landing above, and there was something about the sound that told me it wasn't right. I felt my heart beating faster and set my shopping bag down, listening. There was an angry shout, a scuffle of boots, the sound of someone being punched or slapped, and suddenly that someone was coming toward me at great speed, stamp stamp stamp, crashing past me and downwards, out of the door at the bottom of the stairwell.

'Are you all right?' asked a deep male voice, cultured, out of breath, and I said yes, and in the flare of a match I found myself being introduced to Mr Midas Blake.

He had long dirty-blonde hair to his shoulders, a stubbled chin scarred at the jawline, pale sensitive eyes. My God. Beautiful, but big and crazy-looking, at least a foot taller than me.

'You sure you're all right?'

'Yes,' I said again, puzzled now.

'Your shopping got knocked over.'

'Did it?' I couldn't see – too dark. How could he tell?

'I'll fix the lights. I'll bring up your purchases.'

And that was it. He showed me to my apartment and waited with another match while I dug around for my key. As soon as I was through the door he pulled it shut behind me. A few moments later I saw the hall lights go on and found my shopping stacked neatly on my doormat. No sign of my neighbour. I nearly crossed the landing and rang his bell, but decided to let it go. In cities it's hard to figure out where privacy begins.

The next morning, just after eight o'clock, there was a knock on my front door. Naturally I was looking as unattractive as I could possibly make myself, face cream, bendi-curlers and old sweatpants, and there he was, a big gold god, smelling of something fresh and citrus, standing awkwardly in faded shorts, a grey T-shirt and Nikes, unsure where to place his great hands.

He explained that someone had tried to burgle my apartment last night, and pointed out scratchmarks on the front door. He'd seen the guy off before he could do any real damage. This morning he had reported the matter to the police.

I offered my thanks, made coffee, told him more about myself than I intended. His size was daunting. The palest eyes stared out beneath a heavy brow, so that he appeared permanently angry. I explained about losing the keys, how the police would blame me for keeping my home address in my purse, how I couldn't afford to change the locks let alone install a proper security system.

'You have to do something,' he said. 'These front doors are as thin as cardboard. You could put a fist through them.' When he asked me to come and see the security set-up in his own apartment, I accepted his offer.

I found myself standing in a mirror image of my own rooms – but the decor was radically different. The flat was filled with talismen and mystical paraphernalia, found-art, totems, prayer-wheels, trompe l'oeil wall paintings, mandalas and plants, greenery everywhere, thick green stems bursting from all the corners of the lounge, explosions of red petals, terracotta pots of every size. The kind of place a hippy would have if he was rich and had taste.

I was enchanted by Midas Blake, placed under the spell of a charismatic man. His speech was slow and earnest, his manner accidentally charming, as though he had no idea that he was attractive. He seemed aggressively prepared to protect his privacy. A simple question would crease his brow in fury, as if he would hit you for daring to pry. He was the first man I'd ever met who looked capable of killing. We spent over an hour together. He told me he was good with plants. He enjoyed 'helping people out'. He was Greek by birth, but had been raised in London. I left knowing little more than this.

I returned to my own apartment, to the tiny studio I'd built with its drawing board, racks of pens and – concession to modern technology – computer, and attempted to immerse myself in work. But with no freelance projects coming in I knew I would soon have to consider a full-time office job. The break came when Daniel Battsek, one of the few friends I'd made during my marriage, called me with a commission. He'd taken over a key position in the marketing department of Buena Vista in Kensington Village, and had some ideas for a movie poster he wished to explore. He was prepared to pay half up front, which would allow me to cover my overdue mortgage repayment. I was off and running.

Much about London puzzled and bothered me. Ari warned me that conmen targeted single women in the nearby flats, and that many of the victims were nurses working at the Middlesex Hospital. He said these men could sense when a woman had been hurt, and gave me a funny look, as though he figured I was especially vulnerable.

Maybe I was. I know I spent too many evenings in with the cable remote and a tub of Marks & Spencer's Chocolate Chunk, which is the ice cream for depressed women who need to move up from Haagen Dazs. The clouds held in the heat all week, and I kept every window in the apartment wide open, the British summer not lasting long enough to require the purchase of an air-conditioning unit. On Saturday night the weather broke, thunder rolled and great fat raindrops began to fall. I was running around shutting the windows when Midas Blake knocked.

'Why close the place up?' he asked, looking around. 'What's a little warm rain on the floor?'

And I thought, he's right. Why do I always act on the instincts my father bred in me? I leave the windows open, it gets a little wet . . .

He said, 'I've just opened a bottle of very cold Chablis. I shouldn't keep it all to myself.' His eyes stayed on mine as he spoke. I accepted his invitation and followed him across the landing. Shifted from my territory over to his. He poured the wine into glasses that released the faint glissando of evaporating frost. We drank, and he talked in a strange soft way that made me listen to the rhythm of his voice but not the words. When he went to the open window and leaned out to look at the sky, fat spots of rain stained his shirt. He turned and spoke so quietly that his words just appeared in my head. I remember little of what passed between us, but before we parted he said something odd, something about how we mustn't be scared of going out into the night because there were darker places in our hearts. It sounded familiar, a Robert Frost quote paraphrased. He smiled, and something about his expression chilled me. It was the only time I saw him look helpless, imprisoned by his own image. At the end of the evening – against my better judgement – I kissed him goodnight.

Well, the high heavens didn't fall, but I'm pretty sure the earth moved when my lips brushed his cheek. The trip home across the landing was like stepping between worlds.

Gloria, my agent, warned me against being too cautious with men. 'You wait and they're gone,' she said over lunch the next day, 'and let's face it, you're not getting any younger. What's the worst that could happen?'

'He lives in my building,' I said. 'The worst that could

happen is I date him and it goes horribly wrong and I end up regretting it until the very day I die.'

'There is that, I suppose,' she admitted.

Mr Midas Blake sent me flowers. Wild carmine orchids, followed by a tree of fat, petulant roses. He left glistening, leathery plants on my doormat. He invited me to lunch. *Lunch*. A woman can build dreams around a man who takes her to lunch. Plants and flowers arrived daily. He called me over to dinner. He was a great cook. He told me he'd learned in the galley of a yacht when he had sailed around Europe. Pointedly mentioned that he'd settled now because he was tired of being alone. There was something about him that was so foreign, exotic and yet familiar, as if he had always existed in a root-memory. Studying his still eyes gave me heatstroke.

The dreams started when I began sleeping with him.

This would be around mid-July. I hadn't intended to sleep with him and they weren't normal dreams. The sheets stuck to my body as I tossed and turned beneath the carved headboard of his bed, my mind awhirl with scenes from a heat-drowsed pagan past. In the ruins of a Grecian temple I saw something scamper between vine-clad columns, watching me with small red eyes. Little boys, naked and plump, with the legs of brown rats, sat in shadowed corners patiently observing. Panpipes and birdsong filled my head. Fever reveries, I decided, born of hot nights. I would wake to find him raised on one elbow, watching me.

And then there was the sex. My God, the *sex*. His charm became licentiousness, his energy, violence. He knew he could hurt me, and took pleasure in teasing me across the threshold. But before you think this was some kind of stroke-book fantasy – and I'm the first to admit it was less romantic than pornographic – mitigating his power was something else, another dimension to the experience. While he was inside me my mind became drenched with fantasies, saturated with

images of a forgotten tropical paradise. When we were com-
bined the city around us disappeared, the old bursting
through the new, flora and fauna reclaiming the streets until
all brick and stone had been replaced with dense choking
greenery. I felt drugged, transfigured, hauled back to something ancient and dangerous.

He told me his semen contained the power to open my
mind. I told him I'd heard that line before, put slightly differ-
ently. I wanted to introduce him to jealous girlfriends who
would throw him sidelong glances over dinner and whisper
behind his back. My agent Gloria, who was so independent
everyone assumed she was a lesbian, would be reduced to
coy girliness beneath his intense gaze. He was a *new* new man,
unashamedly masculine. But when it came to the ordering of
a normal social life, Midas remained elusive. One lunchtime
he failed to show up when he knew I had specifically invited
Gloria to meet him, then called three hours later with a half-
hearted apology. He had no interest in civilised conventions.

Was it a coincidence that my artistic ability began to germi-
nate? The Disney designs I'd been commissioned to produce
became such a delightful riot of colour and chaos I was
hired to develop artwork for an upcoming jungle epic. My
confidence grew with my prowess. The drabness of my suburban imprisonment was blasted aside by this new fertility
of mind. Thanks to the endless gifts of plants, my apartment
grew into a tropical jungle. It seemed that even flowers
responded to the Midas touch. Our lives became idyllic; the
building took on an oddly Mediterranean atmosphere,
becalmed and pleasant, drifting above a summer sea of traffic
fumes. Only Ari and Maria failed to notice the change. Midas
and I carefully maintained separate apartments, awaiting invi-
tations from each other before crossing thresholds, a matter
of territorial privacy. I painted the overgrown cities of my
dreams, filling my bedroom with lush acrylic vistas while
Midas –

That was the problem; what did *he* do? Where did he go to late at night? Could he be seeing other women? Where did he get his money? Why did he have no friends? He'd told me his parents were dead, but surely others were close to him? There were no family photographs in his apartment, no personal mementoes, just things he'd collected on voyages. He drank vast amounts of red wine, as if trying to blot out bad memories, and would behave like a reprimanded schoolboy when I asked questions, dropping his head to his chest, his hair flopping down to shield unforgiving eyes. He occupied my every thought.

My prying developed subtlety, and when that failed I tried snooping around his apartment, only to find locked drawers without keys. I complained; our relationship was based on little more than a feral sex-life. Midas was content with the way things were, happy to float on the summer tide. His moods were a series of heatwaves inexorably rippling toward a storm, which broke when he drunkenly barged into my flat one night and accused me of trying to emasculate him.

Emasculate! His fury frightened me; we argued over whether he should have my keys, and the matter added to the mysteries between us. Questions of trust. What did I really know about him? No more than if I had passed him in the street. I had held nothing back; why should he keep secrets?

We entered August in deepening bad feeling. The more I complained, the drunker and more unreliable Midas became. On the first Saturday of the month he failed to show for a dinner party, only to appear at three in the morning smelling as if he'd been dropped in a vat of Chianti.

'Where have you been?' I calmly asked.

'Where I always am at night,' he slurred, sprawling heavily into an armchair.

'And where is that?'

His eyes held mine. 'Where do you think?'

'Midas, I'm tired of playing games with you.'

He turned his attention to his boots, trying to loosen one and failing. 'I work,' he said. 'I'm not the layabout you think I am.'

'What is it you do?'

'I wonder if I should tell you. You wouldn't approve.'

I called his bluff. 'Try me.'

He stared long and hard. 'I inherited certain – powers – from my parents.'

'What kind of powers? Healing powers?'

'In a way. Abilities that stem from my virility. People need my help.'

'What sort of people? Where do you meet them, Midas?'

'At parties. Specially arranged parties. I am in great demand, especially with older women. And some men. They pay me well. My sex gives them strength. It opens their senses. As it has done to you.'

'Are you trying to tell me you're paid to attend *orgies*?'

'They're ceremonies. Ceremonies of pagan veneration. I don't see why I should have to explain this. It has no bearing on our relationship.'

'Think again,' I said, attempting to drag him from the chair.

'But we're good together,' he said, 'you know that. Don't spoil it now, Judy.'

'I'm a pretty liberal person,' I explained, 'but I draw the line at allowing other people to worship at the shrine of your dick.'

He shook his head in disgust. 'You cannot forsake me now. I cast spells. I can help you. Your life would be much less pleasant without me.'

I didn't want to believe what I'd heard, but I knew it was true because the role fitted him so perfectly. I just wanted him out of my flat. I would never have managed it if he hadn't been so drunk. By the time I had slammed the front door and double-locked it I was shaking with anger and fright. This, I told myself, was my reward for trusting too fast.

I avoided him. There was no question of moving out, or of coming to terms with what he had told me. I would not be bullied, and anyway I couldn't afford to leave. He put a note through my door begging to talk to me. I tore it up and posted it back through his letterbox. The next time I passed him on the stairs, I warned him to leave me alone or I would tell the police I was being pestered.

Two nights later, the real trouble began.

I was trying to paint, staring at a great blank sheet of Daler Board. Nothing was coming out right. I told myself that the idea of Midas affecting my artistic ability was simply some form of psychosomatic suggestion. Just then, the walls of my flat started shaking with the sound of Greek music. Midas held a party that carried on until dawn. People were still arriving at four in the morning. I donned earplugs and went to bed, but didn't sleep a wink.

'You missed a great night,' Ari said the next day when I passed him on the stairs, 'a great night! How we danced and laughed! Midas is a wonderful host.'

'I thought you said he was very quiet.'

'Yes, but a party, that's different! Such singing! It's a pity you couldn't come.'

There were seven binbags filled with wine bottles by the front door.

Hey, I figured, live and let live. Maybe this was his way of coping with rejection. But it was just the first of the parties. From being the quietest guy in town, Midas suddenly became the neighbour from hell. Crashing and banging, deafening me at all hours with music, howls of laughter and even what sounded like screams of pain. People came and left at three, four, five in the morning. Sometimes I went on to the landing and saw them climbing the stairs, dangerous types, criminal lowlife, drug dealers, crazies, whores. Each week it got worse. Several times I got up the courage to hammer on his door, but he would never answer. I angrily complained to Ari and Maria, who were dumbfounded.

'But you must be able to hear the noise, even two floors away,' I insisted.

'No,' they said, shaking their heads, 'we haven't heard a thing. As far as we know, Midas only had one party.'

'But the rubbish he throws out on to the landing, the people, the mess . . .'

'You see any mess around here?' asked Ari defensively. 'I think maybe you're overreacting. We never have any trouble from Midas.'

I was *not* imagining it. The woman in the apartment below mine was spending summer at her daughter's house in Cornwall. That just left me.

The noise and the mess continued. I asked the residents in the buildings on either side of mine if they had suffered disturbances, without luck. I visited a harassed young man at a council advice centre and was told that nearly fifty per cent of all flat owners move because of problems with neighbours. He outlined the alternatives, patience or the police, and counselled the former. I was reluctant to involve the law, as I had done during the stormy end of my marriage, and finally persuaded the community officer to call on Midas. The report he sent me after his visit made me wonder if we knew the same man; it was virtually a love letter. My neighbour, my ex-lover, had certainly turned on some full-strength charm. As the community officer was almost certainly gay, I found myself wondering if he had done more than that.

I felt like selling my story to the *Enquirer*: I DATED A PAGAN GIGOLO. Surely he was just an ordinary man with a smart line in seduction. Could Midas have found a way of preventing others from hearing his noise? If he really could cast spells, perhaps he wasn't just directing them at me. Legally my hands were tied. No previous problems had ever been recorded at this address. If anything, *I* was the nuisance. Perhaps I was going crazy. I could imagine the community officer's official report: *Ms Merrigan complains that her neighbour is bewitching her.*

My patience was pushed to the limit. My relationship with Midas became a war of nerves. Thunderous music that no-one else ever seemed to hear played all night. Bags of stinking rubbish split and spilled against my front door. Creepy characters sat at the top of my stairs drinking, picking their teeth and flirting; a smacked-out kid who played with a knife, a laughing fat whore with gold teeth, a sickly bald man who constantly hawked and spat – Midas's acolytes. Ari and Maria swore they saw nobody pass them, but how else did these sleazeballs get on to the staircase, by flying in through the skylight? The first few times I saw someone sitting there I raced down to the ground-floor apartment and dragged Ari upstairs, only to discover the landing deserted. It was like living in a carnival funhouse. I could feel my ordered life cracking apart as quickly as the plants in my flat were drying and dying.

One hot evening I heard a noise outside my door and opened it to find Midas drunk and nearly naked, smeared with paint and slumped on the landing smiling at me.

'I'll call the police if you come any closer,' I warned, trying not to panic.

'And I'll send them away with love in their hearts,' he replied, smoothing his stomach, allowing his hand to brush his genitals. 'Don't you know the story of the wind and the sun, and their wager to remove a traveller's coat? The wind tries to blow the coat off but the traveller pulls it more tightly around himself. The sun just smiles and warms his victim until he sheds his clothes . . .'

He was tumescent now. I yelped and darted back into my apartment, slamming the door with a bang. There was no point in ringing anyone for help. I knew Midas would be sober, clothed and full of charm by the time they arrived.

That night my dreams betrayed me, conjuring him into my bedroom, pacing before my bed, whispering happy obscenities. Wherever his bare feet touched the carpet, grapevines sprang up in verdant knots. Wherever his strong hands touched me, silvery green tendrils traced lines of moisture on my skin. I reached between his broad brown thighs and buried my face there, at the source of his heat, to fill my head with searing comets. In the morning I awoke feeling spent and sluttish. Later I passed Midas on the stairs, smartly attired, going out. 'Sleep well?' he asked with a knowing smile.

I was going mad. I sought Gloria's advice over lunch, and after trying to persuade me to go to the police she produced a more workable idea. 'Find out about him,' she said. 'Make him your quarry. The more you discover of a man like that, the less strength he has over you.'

I knew Midas often received mail from a woman. Her unwanted letters, handwritten in purple ballpoint, accumulated in the hall. When I returned home, I made a note of her return address.

Her name was Danielle Passmore. She lived in Notting Hill, on the top floor of one of those grey Victorian houses large enough to garrison a regiment. The front garden was filled with dead rhododendrons, the ground floor boarded with corrugated iron, so that at first sight it looked as if nobody lived there.

I rang the bell and stepped back, squinting up at the filthy windows, wondering what I would say. She took so long to come to the door, I was about to leave. Danielle was small and shy, thirtyish, fair and very pale, probably once attractive. It was hard to tell now, because her face was disfigured. A livid crimson scar traced a series of crescent-shaped indentations from forehead to chin, as if someone had tried to cleave her skull in two. She was missing her right eye. Skin had dried dark and tight across the socket. I tried not to look too hard.

'I hope you don't mind me just turning up like this,' I said, but before I could continue she interrupted; 'It's about him, isn't it? You've come about him. I knew someone would eventually.'

I asked her what she meant, and she invited me to the silent heart of that shadowed house. We sat facing each other in faded armchairs, in a shuttered room that showed too many signs of a woman living long alone.

'He is still beautiful, isn't he?' she asked. 'Did he touch you? He did, I can tell. You smell of him. Have you felt his power? He places people beneath the spell of his fertility, the spell of the satyr. You knew he was a satyr, did you? The distilled essence of everything male. A priapic satanist, a pagan. A god.'

While I was trying to form a response to this she continued. 'I tried to leave him. We were lovers for months but he frightened me. He showed me things inside myself that I couldn't bear to think about. He lived in South London then, in the great old house he used for ceremonies. I told him I'd have no more to do with him. He was very gracious. Said he was sorry I felt that way. Kissed me on the forehead as I left.' She touched the first of her scars, retracing his lips. 'When I reached home it was late and the hall lights were out. The timer wasn't working. I made my way upstairs, let myself in and boiled the kettle. Then I heard a noise in the lounge, a clanking sound. Metal on wood. Couldn't think what it was. Went in to see, but there was nothing to see.

'There was a chest of drawers against the far wall, and that's where the noise was coming from, a steady rhythmic knocking, the only sound in a silent house. It was where I kept a few tools for home repairs. Curious, I opened the drawer and a wooden-handled claw hammer flew out at me, smashing into my face. Each time I shoved it away it flew back, hammering at my eyes, my nose, my teeth. I saw it returning through a curtain of blood, over and over. Eventually I passed out. In the morning I awoke and managed to call someone. I was in hospital for nearly a month. They wired my jaw but couldn't save my eye.'

'My god, what did the police say?'

'It was just a hammer. There were no prints on it except mine. There was nobody else here, Miss Merrigan. What could the police say?'

'Who else knows about this?'

'No-one. I knew he wouldn't want me to speak of it.'

'But we have to tell someone. If he has some kind of – power – over people, he must be stopped.'

'You don't understand,' whispered Danielle, wiping her good eye with the heel of her hand. 'He refuses to see me. He ignores all my letters.'

'It sounds like you're safer if he does – '

'I still adore him. I pray for us to be together again. Why else do you think I call and write? I have no control over this awful – desire. He has left me with a thirst that can't be quenched. I worship him. That's what he wants.'

I left the poor thing shortly after that. In the dessicated garden I looked back up at the window and saw her crooked face staring down at me. I believed in darkness then. Perhaps her wounds were self-inflicted and she was simply deranged. It made no difference. Her suffering was real. I understood now. The price of the gifts Midas bestowed was slavery. Every god needs to be worshipped. And those who lapse are cast into damnation.

I couldn't just walk out of the apartment. Aside from the financial problems it would involve, those rooms represented every shred of independence I had mustered for myself. I wearily returned home to find the landing at the top of the stairs sombre and silent, but when I listened at Midas' door

I could hear a faint chanting of madrigals. I dreaded to think what he was up to in there.

Two days later my ex-husband came to London to discuss the maintenance payments he had failed to keep up. When I returned from the station with him, Midas was lying in wait, standing casually outside his front door as if keeping a pre-arranged appointment.

'Judy's told me so much about you,' he said, extending his hand, which was shaken in puzzlement. 'She and I are neighbours but I like to think we share much more than just a landing.'

I attempted to shepherd Michael into my apartment, but Midas caught his arm. 'Before you two go off and talk business, I'd love to offer you a drink.' Michael looked at me unsurely, but I could tell that he was prepared to be swayed.

'Judy says you collect science fiction. I have quite a decent collection myself.'

His door was open. His arm was extended. His smile was wide. Michael was lured inside, and I followed like a fool. Over the next half-hour, Midas exuded so much sincerity that I nearly passed out with the strain of smiling back. The two men sat cross-legged on the floor pulling books out of racks and laughing together. Michael was completely taken in and proved reluctant to leave, even when I insisted on keeping our restaurant booking. The neighbours of serial killers never notice anything unusual. What do they see? Smiling strangers who quietly close their doors. Good citizens. Likeable men.

My personality withered beneath the force of Midas' onslaught of charisma. How could I be expected to compete? He was more believable than me, more fun to be with. All I did was moan through dinner. It didn't take a genius to see that Michael would rather have spent the remainder of the evening bonding with my neighbour. I had no allies. Midas could direct his fury at me and shield others from any awareness of it. I realised with some alarm that I had a less forceful personality than the enemy plaguing me. When Michael left, he told me I was lucky to have someone so interesting living next door, and that I should see a doctor about my depression. Perhaps I should try Prozac. I told him to mail me a cheque or I'd see him in court.

I wish we hadn't parted on bad terms. It was the last time I saw him uninjured. He shouldn't have been driving; he was way over the alcohol limit. His car ploughed into the outer lane barrier on the M2 at the Medway Bridge, a hundred feet above that black river. Midas stopped me on the landing to tell me that my ex-husband had not been wearing a seatbelt. Shocked into silence, I tried not to imagine how he knew. Michael was hospitalised. They wouldn't let me see him for days.

The last week of August was unbearable, the hottest for years. The icemaker in Ari's store broke down and all his vegetables spoiled. The days were stuck together, melting into nights. In the height of summer a London night has but five hours of darkness. Many of the clubs and bars in the area close with the rising sun. Midas' guests stayed long after that. I lay sleepless and lost in an empty hot bed, listening to the obscene laughter of the revellers on the landing. I could feel my nerves fraying further each day. The most I could ask was for Midas to leave me alone. And he did until the first Friday in September, when there was a familiar knock.

'I must talk to you,' he said quietly. 'May I come in?' I held open the door. He had lost a little weight, looked great. I felt a wreck, not up to confrontation.

'You've changed things around.'

'I had to,' I said. 'All the plants you gave me died.'

'I can't afford to lose you, you know. I've never lost anyone.'

'Oh? What about Danielle Passmore? Do I look as much of a victim as her? Did you think I'd be easier to convert?'

He showed no surprise. 'I can do so much for you, Judy, if you believe in me.'

'Oh, I believe. You're no crank, I'm sure of that. But I prefer to rely on myself.'

'Then I must make you realise your mistake.' He disclosed a clear plastic tube in his hand and snapped open the cap, allowing the milky contents to leak on to the doorframe. 'Just as my seed can bring fertility to the barren lives of others, so it can be used in other, more persuasive ways.' As soon as I realised what he had in the tube I shoved him out of the doorway. He allowed me to do so. He knew his strength. 'Let me know when you're ready to reconsider,' he called.

I had no idea what he meant until the next morning. I had taken two sleeping tablets, and groggily awoke to another cauldron-hot day. The bedroom was stifling; the window had slid shut in the night and wouldn't budge when I tried to open it. None of the lounge windows would open, either. I thought perhaps the paintwork on the sills had become sticky – until I tried the front door. The latch refused to move even a tenth of an inch. The wood had become sealed in its frame. There was no other way in or out of the apartment.

Determined not to panic, I picked up the telephone receiver to call Ari, but found the line dead. The junction box in the skirting board looked as if it had been damaged. Okay, I thought, I'll break a window. At first I considered using a hammer, but remembering what had happened to Danielle I decided to stay out of the storage-closet where I kept the toolbox.

Instead I entered the lounge with a tea towel wrapped around my arm, clutching a hiking boot, and whacked the window with all my might. Nothing happened. No sound, no shatter, nothing. The glass didn't even shake. That was when I started to lose it. I screamed my lungs out for a while hoping that someone would hear me through the walls, but no-one came running up the stairs. In the boiling streets below, pedestrians passed without stopping to look up and listen.

By midday the temperature in the flat was 105 degrees Fahrenheit, and I forced myself to stop panicking long enough to take stock of my position. I carried out an inventory of supplies; I had half a day-old loaf, a little butter, some yoghurt, a tin of beans, a packet of sliced ham, an almost-empty jar of peanut butter, some breakfast cereal but no milk. That was it. I usually stocked up on Saturday. At least there was an unlimited supply of tapwater. I tried the windows again, this time hammering them with a steel-framed kitchen chair, but they seemed to absorb the sound and impact of every blow.

The computer. I ran to it and switched on the modem. I tried E-mailing Gloria through the internet but my message just rerouted itself back to me, endlessly scrolling down the screen until I was forced to shut the monitor off. The next time I tried it, it didn't work at all.

My clothes were stained with sweat, so I took a shower. I do my best thinking in the shower. There had to be a way out. I figured I'd be wasting my time taking the floorboards up or burrowing through the walls with the puny hand-drill Michael had left me. There was an attic above the apartment that might be able to get me to the roof – except that the entrance to it was set in the landing ceiling, beyond the front door.

If I was truly under an enchantment, I wouldn't be able to escape so easily. I thought about the few friends I had made in London. They never came around without calling first; how long would it take them to report my dead telephone line? How long would it take an inquisitive friend to climb my stairs?

The first night seemed to last forever. Through the front door I could hear Midas' damned madrigals and the imbecile laughter of his debauched acolytes. Secured in my baking cocoon, I began to consider the possibility that he had decided to let me die here.

I tried a few other ruses to attract attention; turned the TV, the radio and the CD player way up until the collective volume was ear-splitting. No effect at all. He was keeping the sound in, just as he kept others from hearing his celebrations. It was like being sealed away from the world in an impenetrable bubble. On the third day my food supply, with the exception of a few items like gravy mix and maple syrup, ran dry. I had carefully bagged my garbage but the flat was still starting to smell funky and I was out of ideas, trying not to panic. What could I do but sit and wait for someone to find me? I watched TV, read books, played music, listened at the sealed front door as Midas prowled back and forth, laughed, partied. I couldn't believe I was being held prisoner in the middle of a city of eleven million people. It was as if nobody knew I was still alive. Perhaps they didn't; the thought flipped my stomach. Perhaps he had changed their perception of me. Perhaps, like an unloved octogenarian, my bloated body would be found weeks after my death. That night, the fourth night, I lay in bed and cried myself sick.

The following morning I rose unrefreshed and switched on the TV. The weatherman promised that the summer's endless heatwave would end in the mother of all storms, then a game show host unveiled a cheap-looking car to a collective wave of oohs and aahs. I tiredly followed my track around the apartment, trying to think of ideas and clutching at even the most foolish, like running to the radio for a phone-in number, only to remember that the phone wasn't working.

I carried out my daily inventory; I was out of soap, shampoo, washing powder and suddenly I was out of water. Turning on the faucet produced a thin trickle, then nothing. He must have turned it off at the mains supply in the attic. I had half a can of flat Sprite in the refrigerator and nothing else. How long, I wondered, could a person survive without water? Three days, four, more? I lay on the floor of the lounge, drained of energy, watching as simpering couples won video recorders on the game show. The thought of giving in to Midas no longer occurred to me. I knew now that this apartment was to be my *oubliette*. I would die here, an unremembered martyr.

That afternoon I carefully scooped the water from the toilet cistern into a saucepan, boiled it, then stored it in the fridge. Going to the bathroom wouldn't be a problem; there was nothing to eat. My stomach growled constantly, but there was no pain. I told myself it was like going on a diet. But I knew it wasn't. It was dying by degrees. I felt myself slipping into a fugue state, aided by the incessant drone of the television and the stifling heat of my cell. The door and windows remained unbudgeable. I lay with my burning forehead pressed against the window as the tide of passers-by ebbed and flowed. Day faded to night and back to day. I could feel myself wasting away, stomach shrinking, tongue swelling, muscles atrophying, and I no longer cared.

The heated, hallucinatory hours crawled by. In a brief moment of lucidity I noticed the appalling state of the apartment. Empty food wrappers littered the lounge. One of the wastebags had split, a dark stinking residue leaking on to the kitchen floor. And at night, all night, the satyr sang his song. It pounded against the walls, rattled the crockery cabinets and shook the windows, a high, atonal wind instrument rising beside his voice – and nobody heard it but me. I no longer slept, existing instead in a perpetual mental twilight as his delicate, persistent jungle sprouted around me; phosphorescent sprays of greenery shielding my body, the fragile tracery of ferns brushing my bare flesh. Bright insects buzzed around engorged shoots pulsing with rhythmic growth, rooting me into dank hot earth. More than anything, I remember the suffocating heat that made me tear off my clothes with the little remaining strength I possessed, a humidity perfect for succumbing to an orgiastic pagan past.

And like a true pagan, I decided that I needed a totem, a spear, something primitive to carry beside me. In my weakened condition it took the next few hours to loosen and remove the wrought-iron embellishments from the coatstand that stood beside the front door. By the time I was left with just a five-foot bevelled metal rod in my hands, it was nearly midnight. It was then that I called out to him. I had no need to summon loudly. A whisper would have done as well, providing it was done in good faith. I called softly again, then held my breath and listened at the door, knowing he would come . . .

. . . and heard his boots scuffing together, just outside the sealed entrance to the apartment. 'Judy,' I heard him murmur, 'oh, Judy.' Behind me, one of the lounge windows gently slid down from its jammed position. The door lock loosened and unclicked. The spell was waning with his arrival, and my acceptance . . .

And with my last ounce of strength I ran at the door, ramming the point of the stand through the thin plywood panel until it met with resistance. There was a shout on the other side as the rod passed through and struck him a damaging blow to the stomach. The iron shaft I retracted was smeared with blood. I was beset with a feeling of infinite loss, a terrified animal trapped in the heat-death of the rainforest. The sudden exertion had been too much for me. The room shifted. There was only blessed oblivion.

And then nothing until – raindrops on my face.

That's the next thing I remember. Fat wet baubles bursting on my parched skin. A cool zephyr traversing my arms and exposed breasts. More rain. And thunder, blessed deafening thunder as the promised storm finally broke above me . . .

'Miss Merrigan.'

An elderly woman with too-large teeth, upside down. Ari's

wife, Maria. She was holding out a mug of tea. I tried to raise my head. I could hear the rain falling steadily. The air was cool. My mouth and throat were dry, too parched to speak. I gulped at the tea, scalding my tongue.

'How did – how did you get in?'

'The front door was wide open. We could smell something. We thought you'd gone away. Are you all right?'

'I – think so.' Ari was at the other end of the flat, opening the windows. Clouds of flies were resettling on the rotting bin-bags beside the sink. One thought passed through my disordered mind. I had to confront Midas in the company of Maria and Ari, to prove to someone that I was not mad, that I had not done this to myself. I pulled my shirt down over my breasts, staggered to my feet and all but dragged them across the landing to his door.

'Are you *sure* you're all right?' Maria was asking, and Ari was saying something about getting me to a doctor when the door opened and there stood a small grey-haired man in a patterned cardigan and slippers. He had a pot-belly and rimless glasses. He looked like a retired accountant.

'Where's Midas?' I shouted. 'Is he in there?'

The little man shot a puzzled look at Maria, then back at me. 'What does she – ?'

I was hysterical now. 'Where is Midas Blake?'

'I'm sorry, Mr Blake,' Ari was saying, 'she's not been well and she – '

'Young lady, I am – '

'*Where the hell is he?*'

' – I am Midas Blake. I don't believe we've met before.'

'You're lying, you're all lying!' I pushed past the little accountant. 'He must be in here!' But the apartment was completely different, floral wallpaper, cheap padded leatherette furniture, no plants at all. 'You know where he is,' I screamed, 'why are you protecting him?'

They're all in it, I thought, *he's got to all of them*. But he hadn't; I know that now. The grey-haired man in spectacles really was someone called Midas Blake, and he'd been living there for years. We'd never met. He'd only ever had one party, the one Ari had so enthusiastically attended. If I had gone as well I would have realised the truth, but we had never bumped into each other.

The man I had known as Midas was someone quite different. I suspect he has many other names. He is the stranger who comes to lead us into temptation, the one who can give us everything we need in return for blind allegiance. He may appear at a certain co-ordinate on the map, to a certain type of person, when the skies are strange and the time is right, and to many people, stronger people, he may never appear at all. An arid marriage, four years of loneliness, how ripe I had been for his attentions! There was no point in returning to Danielle Passmore and asking to see a photograph; his likeness would not be the same. He would never adopt the same guise twice.

One thing puzzled me. Why was I released from his power? Why did he allow the door to open, why did he not let me die? I can only assume he plans to come back for me. He thinks I am still weak enough to accept him. He is in for a surprise. Through the changing seasons I watch from my windows and calmly await his return, armed with a faith I never knew I had.

PERMANENT FIXTURE

No man is an island, but quite a few are peninsulas. I guess if you really hate people, it's easy to cut yourself off. You move into the countryside, never go to the cinema or a football match, avoid casual arrangements, lock yourself away. But it won't make you a happier person. A friend of mine called Margaret told me this story over lunch the other day, and I'm still not sure if all of it's true, although she swears it is.

In 1972 Margaret upset her entire family by marrying a man they all felt to be unsuitable for her. She was nineteen years old, an only child who had just moved to North London from the kind of small Hertfordshire village where everyone knows everyone else's business and doesn't approve of it. She knew nothing of city life and very little about men. Kenneth was her first boyfriend, and the courtship lasted just four months. They were married in a registry office in Islington, and no-one was allowed to throw confetti because of the litter laws. The ceremony was reluctantly attended by Margaret's father, who barely bothered to conceal his disappointment and left immediately after the photographs were taken. Margaret's mother telephoned during the reception to wish her well, but turned the call into a catalogue of complaints, and only spoke to her daughter on one further occasion before she died of a stroke seven months later.

Kenneth Stanford was thirty-one. He drove a Ford Corsair, collected Miles Davis and Buddy Rich recordings, worked in a town planning office and promised to love Margaret forever. He decided he had enough money saved to buy a house, and carefully chose where he wanted to live. The location he picked was in Avenell Road, Highbury, right opposite the gate of the Arsenal football ground. He had supported the Gunners since he was a kid, and had recently bought himself a seat there.

In typical London style the area hid its surprises well, for who would have thought that such an immense stadium could be tucked so invisibly behind the rows of little houses? In an equally odd arrangement, famous film stars and directors often visited the road to check on their feature prints at the nearby Metrocolor film processing labs, but the child who ventured to suggest that he just saw Mel Gibson passing the fish shop usually received a cuff about the head for lying.

So it was that Margaret moved into a damp Victorian two-floor terraced house in the shadow of a great stadium. She became pregnant twice in quick succession, and saw very little of her husband, who worked late, spent his nights drinking at Ronnie Scott's and his weekends attending football matches with his mates. In accordance with the social etiquette of the day he never introduced his wife to his friends – the people he met at the jazz club to whom he wished to appear cool – or his mates – the people he met on the terraces to whom he wished to appear laddish.

Margaret had no interest in football. She regarded the red and white hordes who periodically trooped past her bay window as some kind of natural phenomenon, like a plague of frogs. She learned not to invite friends over for lunch on Saturday afternoons. She grew used to being segregated from fans in the Arsenal tube station, watching guiltily as they were herded into the separate tunnel of their rat-run. She became accustomed to the closed-off streets, the suspended parking bays, the colour co-ordinated families, the makeshift souvenir stalls selling booklets, flags, scarves, T-shirts and rattles, the neighbours who ran out into the road to collect the horse-droppings from the mounted police for their gardens, or who turned the fronts of their houses into tea and sandwich shops. The fans were just another vexatious and slightly mysterious part of life, like wondering why garages sell charcoal briquettes in winter or why Rolf Harris never gets any older.

So she lived with the sharp smell of frying onions and beefburgers, the nights being lit as bright as day, the packets of chips chucked over her gate, the cans of Special Brew left on her front windowsill, the local supermarkets bumping up their prices on Saturdays, the Scots boys for whom her bedraggled front garden held eerie allure as a urinal, the spontaneous outbursts of singing, the great endless flow of generally good-natured people. She accepted it all as something that came with the house, a permanent fixture, like having a pylon in the garden.

Eventually she rather liked it. She liked watching fathers pass by with their hands on the shoulders of their sons. She had given birth to two beautiful daughters. It was no coincidence that Kenneth's interest in football and marriage ebbed from this point. Soon he became indifferent to the point of vanishing altogether, and Margaret raised her children alone. He let her keep the house, which was falling into disrepair, and moved into the more spaciously appointed Westbourne Grove residence of a sometime nightclub singer who appreciated his record collection.

And through the years Margaret watched from her window as the great red and white sea trudged back and forth. It seemed strange that such a vast cross-section of humanity could remain so placid, but there was rarely any trouble in the street. A grudge match against Tottenham Hotspur would occasionally create a small explosive pocket of anger ending with shouts and the sound of broken bottles, and on one late summer afternoon somebody slipped a hand through her open bay window to steal the handbag she had foolishly left lying on a chair, but such incidents were spaced far apart across the seasons.

The girls grew tall, developing in a curious way that mixed coarse humour with immaculate behaviour. By the age of ten they were already growing familiar with the works of Lewis Carroll and Conan Doyle, but also knew the words to popular songs like 'You're Going Home in the Back of an Ambulance' and 'My Old Man Said "Be an Arsenal Fan", I Said "Fuck Off, Bollocks, You're a Cunt".' They weren't really fans, but so much of their lives had been played out before the audience that ebbed around the house, they knew more about the Arsenal and its people than seasoned veterans.

Times remained hard for Margaret and her children. Her maintenance cheques had to be extracted with threats. She feared the future. One Saturday afternoon she sat in her front garden in the slanting autumn sunlight and cried a little. The girls were both out with friends, and she was feeling alone and saddened by the knowledge that she would one day lose them when a grinning young man called at her from the ocean of people shuffling past, 'Hey, cheer up missus, can't be that bad, come along with us and have a laugh!' and she smiled and wiped her eyes and got up, and got on.

After that, she never felt alone on Saturdays.

But she met a man, a red-headed minicab driver seven years her junior called Malcolm, and in her desperation to overlook his faults she ignored his worst; his disrespect for everything except her sexuality. After the first time he hit her, he apologised for hours and even cried, and quoted the Bible, and treated her nicely for several weeks.

The girls stayed out of his way. He was infuriated by the creativity of their swearing (something they did naturally as a consequence of where they lived) and forced them to attend services at a bleak little baptist church near his cab office in Holloway, although they only managed to go three times. It seemed to Margaret that he stared at her girls too hard, sometimes with dead-eyed hatred, and sometimes with a little too much liking. He was an unhappy man, embittered by his lot in life, yet he could be kind and supportive, and she needed him, and the affair drifted on long enough for him to be given his own front door key.

But there came a time when she wanted it back, and she wanted him out. She knew that he looked upon the three of them as godless and doomed. He nagged at Margaret to be a better mother. He complained that she was disorganised, forgetful, useless, a lousy housekeeper. He worked nights and slept days, forcing her to creep around and hold her breath each time she dropped something. He warned the girls against forming undesirable friendships after school, then enforced the warning with a curfew. He did not approve of Margaret's friends, who were Caribbean and Greek and Indian and nothing at all like the suburban couples his parents invited over for barbecues. Little by little the house in Avenell Road became a prison with limited visiting hours. During the day its atmosphere was sepulchral, colder and quieter than the street outside.

Then the new season began. The Gunners played well and ascended the league table, swelling the gate and filling the streets with more fans than ever before. There was to be a midweek charity match for a beloved retiring player. By half-past six that Wednesday evening the tide of fans had risen to a deluge. Gillespie Road and Plimsoll Road were at a standstill. The floodlights had given the backstreets the brightness of Las Vegas. Malcolm strode about the living room shouting, and Margaret became frightened that he would smack her again. He was annoyed that she had allowed the girls to bring friends to the house while he was trying to sleep. She knew he took 'jellies' – tamarzepam – to sleep, and suspected that this addiction was the cause of his mood-swings, but she could not bring herself to discuss the matter with him.

'If I don't sleep I can't work, and that means no money for any of us, do you understand?'

'I don't take anything from you,' she complained. 'I provide for the girls.' To cut a long story short, she asked for the front door key back and he refused to return it. Margaret's oldest daughter was away on a school trip, and Caroline, the younger one, was hovering by the kitchen door chewing a fingernail, listening to the escalating row. When she heard the screech of furniture shifting and something – a vase? – knocked over, then silence, she ran into the room to find her mother sitting on the floor with a look of surprise on her face, as if she had just slipped over while learning to ice-skate.

When Malcolm advanced on her again she yelped and scuttled into the hall like a frightened dog, and Caroline was ashamed of her mother's cowardly behaviour. 'Fucking kill you,' she heard him say, and now he had something in his hand, a poker she thought, but by this time she had opened the front door and was calling out for help. He said something about 'everyone knowing our business' and made to hit her because she was embarrassing him, but Caroline pulled her mother through the door into the front garden and stared desperately into the relentless crowds.

Which must have helped because there he was right in front of them, the grinning young man in his red and white scarf, him or someone very much like him, calling out 'Oi, you wanna hand? Is he botherin' you?', and she must have looked grateful because here were outstretched hands, dozens of hands, lifting her and her daughter over the garden wall and into the crowd, over the heads of so many fathers and sons, cresting the human surf faster and faster, bearing them away from danger on the same surf that turned to crash against her attacker, to push him back, and the more Malcolm tried to struggle the more they pinned him down, so that it appeared as if he had been thrown into a boiling river with his clothes stuffed full of rocks.

Margaret and her daughter were borne aloft by the living wave, away into the beating heart of the maelstrom. The crowd was singing as it worked to protect them. It was here that she saw she had entirely misunderstood the football match. The centre of this mighty organism was not the pitch, not the game itself but the surrounding weight of life in the stands, in the street, a force that made her dizzy with its strength and vitality. Yet the centre was as hushed and calm as the eye of a hurricane, and it was here that the crowd set them down. Watching the men, women and children dividing around them like a living wall she momentarily felt part of something much larger. She somehow connected with the grander scheme for the first time in her life.

Of course, the crowd had also connected with Malcolm, or to be more accurate had connected with his collarbone, his left ankle, his skull and four of his ribs.

Margaret tells me that this is why she now goes to football, to experience that incredible moment when the crowd becomes a single powerful creature, when for a split-second it feels as though anything in the world is possible just by needing it.

She tries to tell me that here is something mystic, deep-rooted and inexplicable, but I point out the simple truth: when you have so many thousand people all concentrating on one man's ability to plant a ball in the back of a net, you harness an energy that can shift the world from its axis.

Margaret's children can tell you what life is really like. It smells of frying onions, and will beat the shit out of you if you resist it.

LOOKING FOR
BOLIVAR

There are a number of ways you can change your life in a week.

You can fall in love with the wrong person. Career-switch from banking to wicker repair. Experience religious conversion. Get caught shoplifting. Change your barber. Undergo an epiphanal moment when you realise that you'll never drive through Rio in an open-top Mercedes unless you stop spending your weekends drifting around the shops looking at things you don't really want. What I mean is, at some point you either realise who you are and act toward the grain of your personality, no matter how unpalatable that might turn out to be, or you end up in a kind of bitter emotional cul-de-sac that eventually leads to you machine-gunning thirty people dead in McDonald's.

I saw this ad once for running shoes or CDs that said 'Whoever you are, be someone else.' I was twenty-four when I realised I could no longer imagine being someone else, and decided to make a change before it was too late. I moved from London to New York, and ended up looking for Bolivar.

As a child I was sickly, timid, sensible. Rejected by other kids, adored by adults. 'So grown-up!' my aunt would marvel, pinching my face between her fingers as if reaching a decision on curtain material. I left college with unimpressive credentials and was employed in the customer relations department of Barclays Bank, a job with an interest factor equivalent to staring at mud. To spend an evening in the pub with my colleagues was to grasp a sense of the infinite.

I rented a dingy flat in North London. 'It's not a lower-ground,' my estate-agent brother informed me, 'it's a basement. I should know.' I failed to meet the Right Girl. 'Plenty of time for that,' said my mother, who had a mouth designed for holding pins, 'after you've done some hard work.' When the possibility of a transfer came up I took it without quite knowing why, although shifting from such a domineering family to a place where my nearest relative would be several thousand miles away seemed the sensible thing to do.

Maybe I was sick of living in a city that looked like a fish tank whose owner had forgotten to change its water. Maybe I went to New York because the streets were wide and the light was high, because the wind swept in from the sea, because at night the town looked like Stromboli's fairground – how many reasons could there be?

On the day I left, I found myself at the departure gate surrounded by relatives vying with each other to impart advice. I boarded the flight with a head full of rules and lectures, and forgot them all before we landed.

The big things about New York were over-familiar before I'd even seen them. Vertiginous chromium avenues and yellow cabs were so instantly commonplace that they were rendered curiously unimpressive. Rather, I remember being struck by ground-level details. The colours of old Manhattan, faded reds and browns, interiors painted a dingy shade of ochre peculiar to the city. Those little iron hoops that bordered all the trees. Racks of vegetables sprayed with water. Basketball courts on the street. Smelly subway gratings through which could be heard the distant thunder of trains. Vending machines chained to the ground, but trusting you enough to take just one newspaper.

The bank rented me an apartment in Hoboken. My first mistake was to lease a flat where the bedroom window was situated above a bus stop. I had no idea people would actually sit on the bench below all night long, talking and playing ghetto-blasters. I wasn't about to go down and ask men with grey cotton hoods protruding over leather jackets to turn the music down.

After six weeks I was desperate. I am a light sleeper at the best of times, but this was impossible; I arrived at Union Square each morning lurching into work like a zombie. Finally I arranged to break the lease and move to another apartment in a quieter neighbourhood, but there was a short-fall between the dates of about a week, when I would have nowhere to stay.

One evening in early June I went out with some people from the bank. They were more conservative in conversation than their London counterparts, but spoke frankly of their careers and finances – subjects we tend to regard as slightly taboo. They were sending off a teller named Dean Stanowicz, who was leaving under some kind of cloud nobody wanted to talk about. We went to this little Jewish restaurant and they gave him a gaudy iced cake, a tradition for every staff birthday, anniversary and wedding. For some reason I found myself explaining my housing problem to Dean, and he told me about a woman he knew who owned an apartment on West 44th Street. It seemed this woman – I couldn't decide how the two of them were related – was going into hospital for a hip operation, and she needed someone to take care of her apartment for a week. It was perfect. Our dates matched exactly. Her name was Mary Amity, which sounded friendly.

Until then it hadn't occurred to me that people lived in the centre of Manhattan. On Saturday morning I arrived at the front door of Miss Amity's building carrying a bag of clothes, a bulky set of keys and a page of scribbled instructions. Dean was supposed to have taken me around the place on Friday evening, but didn't seem very reliable. I had called his home number, but his message service was switched on.

I don't know what I was expecting to find inside that tall terraced house with brown window frames and black railings. I had not yet been invited inside an American home – my colleagues worked hard and kept to themselves, valuing their privacy and guarding it accordingly. I suspected they considered me unfriendly, and back then perhaps I was.

A deep brown hallway – that colour again – smelled of freshly polished boots, and led to four gloomy flights of stairs. At the top of these, a firetruck-red front door sported three hard-to-open locks. The keys weren't marked, and the elimination process took me twenty minutes. I resolved to label them before I attempted to regain entry. I was a tidy man, and liked labelling things.

Inside, a narrow hall led to a disproportionately enormous lounge that smelled strongly of cigarettes. There were dozens of scruffy plants dotted in between comfortable pieces of furniture, and as many stacks of books. In the corner was an easel with an odd half-finished painting of what appeared to be a three-legged cow, or an overweight hairless cat, on it. There were a number of seventies' new age items scattered about, including a blue glass bong and several sets of redundant wind chimes. Miss Amity had been admitted to hospital two days earlier, so I had the place to myself, or so I thought. No sooner had I set my bag down when a man in white overalls wandered out of the kitchen with a mug of tea in his hands, real PG-Tips-tea, not those perfumed things on strings you get in New York cafes.

'Hi,' he said amiably, 'do you know if there's a toy store around here?'

Thrown, I shrugged. 'I'm new in town. I don't know where everything is yet.'

'See, I gotta get my kid this troop-carrier spaceship for his birthday and I ain't got time to get to FAO Schwartz. Sixty bucks for something that'll be broke in a week. Crazy, huh? Makes me wish a bunch of real mean aliens would turn up and blast the shit outta the place just so kids would stop wanting models of 'em.'

I wasn't in the mood to conduct a conversation about spaceships with a total stranger when I had been expecting to be left in peace on my own. Just then, an extraordinary clanging noise started up in the next room.

'I'm Charles,' I shouted, holding out my hand and hoping for some reciprocal information.

'And I'm Carlos. Hey, Chuck.' He slapped my fingers.

'Charles, actually.'

'You the guy looking after the joint while the lady of the house is away?'

'Yes, but I don't know – I mean – I wasn't expecting anyone else to be here.'

He looked amazed. 'You mean Dean didn't say anything about me and Raoul?' He aimed a paint-spattered thumb back at the kitchen. 'Raoul's in there trying to get the waste-pipe loose.'

'Not a word.'

'You want some tea?' He filled a mug from a large brown pot and returned with it. 'Miss Amity's kind of like the mother Dean never had. When he found out she'd have to go into hospital and miss her birthday, he arranged for us to come in and rebuild her bathroom, kind of a surprise for her when she comes out, so if she calls, don't say nothing about it. She's got this old bath that ain't plumbed in right, and the tiles are all cracked, so we're putting in a load of new stuff.'

'Then why does she need someone to look after the place if you're here?'

'Because we're only gonna be here a couple days, and Bolivar gets lonely.' Skittering in across the polished floorboards came a bulky brindle bull terrier with a grinning mouth that looked wider than his body. He was wearing a broad leather collar studded with spikes, the kind of dog that looks like he's owned by the manager of a bar. I stepped back, alarmed. As a child, I'd had a bad experience with such an animal.

'Nobody said anything about a dog.'

'Hey, he's no trouble. Eats anything, waits till he gets outside to piss, spends most of the day snoring and farting. Not like a dog at all. More like an intelligent pygmy with a big appetite.'

The bedroom was filled with dusty velvet swagging and framed photographs crammed on to unstable tables. Miss Amity appeared to be a sparky, photogenic woman in her early fifties, well-preserved, compact, her hair a range of different colours from copper to blonde. She was strangely beautiful, in the way that very kind people eventually become. She seemed to attend a lot of charity events, and across the years had been photographed with an unlikely range of guests, including a couple of mayors, Zsa Zsa Gabor, Joe DiMaggio, Sylvia Miles, Joey Buttofuoco and someone who looked like – but surely couldn't be – Malcolm X. There was also a picture of a man dressed as a giant carrot.

She wore a lot of junk jewellery – the room looked like a dumping ground for Mardi Gras beads. It wasn't tidy, or very clean. Nor was the rest of the apartment. The refrigerator contained mostly items past their sell-by dates. There was something growing in a Tupperware tub, and a half-chewed plate of lasagna had a kind of pubic mould springing from it. While I was unpacking, Raoul wandered in chewing a chicken leg. He transferred the grease from his hand to his thigh and slapped his fingers against mine. 'Yo – Chaz, how ya doin'?'

'Er, Charles, actually.'

'Listen, you got no hot water tonight.'

'Great.'

'We're not plumbers.'

'I'm sorry?'

'You don't have to be all hoity-toity with us. We're not plumbers, we're just helpin' out, okay?'

I didn't wish to appear stuffy but they both seemed overfamiliar, with me, and with the apartment. Carlos was sitting with his legs hanging over an armchair watching NBA highlights on cable. Raoul was chugging a beer in the bathroom, hammering on the pipes again. Wandering uncomfortably from room to room, I announced that I was going to take the dog for a walk.

'A word of advice,' called Raoul. 'Let him lead you. He'll go the route Mary always takes him. Bolivar knows the way, okay?' Bolivar stared at me knowingly, then rolled back on his haunches and began licking his absurdly protruberant testicles. I slipped the heavy chain around his muscular neck and seconds later was dragged out to the stairs.

Ron's Lucky Silver Dollar Bar & Grill did not possess a grill, although there was a giant silver dollar in the window above a hand-painted sign that read SUBS & GYROS. Where I came from, a gyro was a cheque. I asked the barman if he was Ron.

'Nope. Ron's dead. He ate a bad scallop. Not here, somewhere else. I'm Bill.'

'Charles.'

'What can I get you, Chuck?'

'I don't really – the dog pulled me in here.' I pointed at my feet. Bill leaned over the bar. 'It just – wouldn't stop pulling.'

'Hey, that's Bolivar! Hey boy!' The dog hoisted itself clumsily on to its hind legs and began scuttling back and forth with its tongue lolling out. Bill poured two shots from a bottle with a lot of signatures on it. He raised his glass. Not wishing to seem rude, I drank with him. The shot tasted like chillis mixed with liquid soap. I noticed that Ron had arms like a weightlifter, or someone who'd been in prison. His biceps were as big as his head. He had a tattoo of a scorpion stinging itself.

'So where's Mary?'

'She's in the hospital. I'm apartment-sitting for her.'

'She comes in most nights. Her son, Randy, used to work here.'

'He was a barman?'

'Well now, that's not for me to say. Randy operated for himself, kind of a one-man business.' Ron suddenly found something to do behind his bar. A crease of concentration ran across his forehead. Then he brightened. 'But you're welcome here any time. No friend of Mary's will ever be a stranger in the Lucky Dollar.' He grasped my hand warmly, grinding several bones to powder.

When I returned to the apartment, Raoul and Carlos had gone, locking up behind them. It took me ages to open the door again. They had left behind the remains of their dinner. I was washing their plates in cold water when the phone rang.

'Hey, Mary,' yelled a woman's voice. 'I have the armadillo. Do you realise Dan had to bring it in the back of his car from Tucson?'

'This is Charles,' I replied patiently.

'Oh. I must have the wrong – '

'This is Miss Amity's apartment.'

'Then who the hell are you?'

I explained. It was something I was obviously going to be doing a lot.

'Shit. Look, I'm gonna have to bring this damned thing around because it's making a hole in its box. You're Jewish, right?'

'How can you tell? Did you say an armadillo?'

'I can spot a nice Jewish boy like an eagle can see lambs in a canyon. Are you married? Don't answer. I'll be there in twenty minutes. No, don't thank me, just pour me a drink. Whisky, rocks, Jim Beam if there's any left.'

I replaced the receiver, puzzled.

'Mary paints,' said Melissa, setting her glass on to a paper coaster I'd found. She stifled a giggle.

'What's funny?' I asked.

'She'd get a kick seeing you put down coasters. She's not that kind of person.'

'What do you mean? What kind of person?'

'You know, like Tony Randall in *The Odd Couple*. She lets her drinks leave little rings on the table.' Melissa crossed long, jean-clad legs. 'She likes to paint animals, but it's tough painting at the zoo with so many people around, so I told my brother to get her something. Well, he drove up from Tucson to see me, and he brought this.' She pointed to the armadillo. It was scratching around in a corner of its straw-filled box. The creature was about a foot long, and had funny bristling ears. It looked mechanical, hardly a living creature at all. 'I can't keep it in my apartment because I have cats.'

'What about Bolivar?' I asked. The dog was whining in the kitchen, scrabbling at the door.

'Oh, he'll be fine. You take good care of him, he's Mary's pride and joy. The armadillo can look after itself, trust me. It's nocturnal, and that's when it'll try to dig its way out. I've left it a box of insects and vegetables. You just top it up with broccoli and cockroaches. But tell me about you, you adorable thing. You're English, single obviously.' She sat back and waited for me to talk.

Melissa originally came from Kansas, 'The Dorothy State', as she drily referred to it. She was as thin and brown as well-worn leather, her bony wrists covered in fat gold ropes, someone who'd had a hard life and then found money. I liked her from the first, which was just as well because she out-stayed her welcome and got completely drunk. When I tried to get her to the door, she made a grab for my balls. 'Mary would like you,' she announced, 'but you need to get out more. Put that adorable face in the sun.'

I had to give the cab driver an extra ten dollars to take her. But that night I had my first decent eight-hour sleep in weeks.

The next morning was Sunday. I had a hangover, and was looking forward to a lie-in. There was a smell in the apartment beneath the ground-in cigarette smoke that I associated with my own childhood. It took me a while to realise that it was dampness, something I didn't associate with American homes, yet it made me feel comfortable and secure. Burrowing back into the blankets, my rest was rudely awakened by the front door slamming. I figured Carlos and Raoul were back, but then I heard different voices.

'*Xanadu*'s fabulous. Olivia Newton-John as a Greek muse, all lip gloss and roller skates? It's been waiting fifteen years to be recognised as a classic, but the world is still not ready. You can learn so much about hair maintenance watching her.'

I pulled myself out of bed and opened the curtains. The day was warm and wet, the sidewalk empty and every bit as Sundayish as a residential English backstreet. The sky had a dead, exhausted look. I listened to the lounge.

'Donald loses all his dates because of his terrible taste in movies,' said another voice. 'Just as they're starting to get along fine, he drags them off to see a double bill of something like *Grease* 2 and *Yentl*.'

Making sure my pyjamas were not exposing anything, I ventured out of the bedroom. There were three strangers in the kitchen making coffee. A muscular young man in a black nylon T-shirt, a slender Asian boy wearing rather a lot of make-up for this time of the morning and an attractive, overweight girl with dyed black hair. They seemed as surprised to see me as I was them.

'Oh my God, we woke the maid,' cried the Max-Factored one. 'Who are you, honey? Did you know you got no hot water?'

'I'm Charles,' I explained. 'Yes, I did know. I'm looking after Miss Amity's apartment for her.'

'Well, Charlene, I'm sorry we woke you but Mary never mentioned anyone was staying here.'

'That's okay. I should be getting up anyway. Who are you?'

'Donald.' Mr Black T-shirt thumbed his chest. 'That's Jaffe, and Val's the female, gynaecologically speaking. Jaffe's still undergoing some kind of sexual identity crisis but the men are rooting for him, so he may get through it with just a few mascara burns. Your armadillo has escaped.'

Jaffe was wearing an extraordinary badge on his jacket, little pieces of broken mirror, an old Andrew Logan design from the eighties, and it kept catching the light, shimmying specks on to the nicotined ceiling like a disco ball. I saw that the armadillo was trying to dig its way out through the kitchen cabinets, away from the light. Fascinated, Bolivar was taking gentle snaps at the creature, as if trying to cradle it in his enormous jaws. I wanted to separate them, but I'd never touched an armadillo before.

'You can join us for brunch if you like,' Donald offered. 'We'll be discussing the movie career of Brad Pitt in depth, and you may wish to contribute something to that. Are you from Harvard or something? You have a funny accent.'

'I'm English,' I said apologetically, as you do. I wanted to ask why he had access to Mary's apartment, but could find no way of phrasing the question politely. At my feet the dog was whimpering in frustration and the armadillo was noisily butting its head against the units.

'So, Charlita, you going to join us for a glass of second-rate champagne and a Spanish meal presented between slices of cantaloupe?' asked Jaffe.

'Thank you for the offer,' I replied, offended, 'but I have things to do.'

'He's so polite. I *love* it.'

'We're old friends of Mary's,' Val took the trouble to explain. 'We always come by on a Sunday. She reads our tarot, then arranges my astrological week. I can't go out of the house without it.'

'Well, she won't be able to do it for you today.'

'She already did.' Val held up a scroll of paper. 'She left it out for me. What star-sign are you?'

'I don't believe in the stars,' I said testily. 'You have your own door keys for the apartment?'

Jaffe was defensive. 'Mary gives her keys to everyone. Don't think you're special.'

'What's she like?' I asked Val.

'Mary? A sweetie. Prickly as a cactus, soft as a pear. Bad at keeping secrets. Her parents were imprisoned by the Nazis. She's had a wild life. Come with us, we'll tell you all about her.'

'No, really, thank you, I can't.'

'Your choice. You're gonna miss the dish.'

Laughing, they left. I don't know why I refused their offer. Their over-friendliness unnerved me. In such situations I invariably retreated. After they had gone I wandered about the apartment wondering if I should clean it. I decided to wait until the bathroom was finished. The shower stall was filled with weird oils, dried flowers and glycerine soaps, none of which smelled very pleasant. Even in here there were buckled photographs taped on the walls. She seemed to have so many friends. I had virtually none. Bolivar was whining for a walk, and I was just about to take him when the telephone rang.

'Is that you, Charles?'

'Yes, it is,' I replied, instinctively knowing that this was Mary Amity.

'How are you settling in, dear?'

'Very well, thanks. I just wondered – forgive me for asking – how many people have you given your front door keys to?'

'I've never really counted. I could probably work it out. Do you need to know?'

'No, I was just thinking about security.'

'Darling, I have nothing worth stealing. My most precious possessions are all inside my head. Although if a woman called Sheryl-Ann tries to let herself in, you must stop her.'

'How do I do that?'

'Just put your foot against the door until you can get the chain on, that's what I always do. Then call the super. You'll recognise her easily, she looks like a hooker but I swear I had no idea she was when I gave her the keys. How is my Bolivar?'

'He's fine. He's – fine.' I looked down at Bolivar, who was trying to choke himself to death on the lead, torn between conflicting desires to torment the armadillo and get out on the street. 'How are you?'

'Thank you for asking. So polite. I've had the operation, I just have to lie here and heal. Take good care of him, won't you? Don't let him overeat. He'll eat absolutely anything. He ate a shovel once. Give me your work number, just in case.' She didn't explain in case of what, but I gave it to her. I was a guest in her apartment, after all.

'I wasn't able to get hold of Dean,' I explained. 'He was going to show me where everything was.'

'You're a big boy, you can find things out for yourself, can't you? You won't be hearing from Dean for a while. He's gone away.'

'Oh? He didn't tell me he was going – '

'Well, the truth is he's starting a jail sentence. It's not his fault. He's a good boy who's had some bad luck. Take my dog for a walk, will you? He likes walks.'

✦

'Hey, Bolivar, c'mere you big hunk of muscle!' screamed the waitress, pulling Bolivar's front paws up on her apron. It seemed unhygienic. This time, the dog had stopped sharply on a corner three streets from the apartment, then dragged me into a coffee shop called Manny's Freshly Brewed Sip 'N' Go. The waitress, a slender, pretty Puerto Rican girl with smoky eyes, butted heads with the dog, then dropped him back down.

'I'm Maria. Listen, the manager'll piss blood if he sees the dog in here.' She laughed carelessly. 'The health board already hate him. They closed us down in '95 for having mice in the pan racks.'

'You know Miss Amity?'

'Oh sure. She used to teach tap over at this crummy little studio on West 46th. I wanted to be a dancer, but I really wasn't good enough.'

'Was she a dancer, then?'

'Once, long ago, out in Hollywood. Chorus stuff. Way before she took her accountancy exams and married that maniac, that crazy pianist.'

'She was married to a pianist?'

'Her second husband. The first one shot himself, but then I guess he had a good reason. Not that the pianist turned out any better. That was all before my time. Mary was sub-leasing the studio from this guy who turned out to be some kind of gangster. He ran a luggage shop near the Marriot that was a front for a gambling syndicate, one of these places that sold suitcases, statues of Jesus and flick-knives, and had old Turkish guys in the back playing cards. He had to get out of town quick, and robbed the studio while everyone was in the tap class. Cleaned the place out of wallets, purses, jewelry, took all Mary's savings from the apartment. But he didn't get out in time, and they cut one of his feet off. The right, I think. Sure slowed him down. Mary says it made him a better person. She's always in trouble, one of those people, y'know?

make sure you don't get caught up. It has a way
oping everyone. It's because she has this instinct, she
nows stuff about people and sometimes they don't like it.
You ready for a coffee?'

On the way home I met another half dozen people who were
acquainted with Bolivar and Mary Amity. A Greek couple in
a dry cleaners. Two old ladies in ratty fur coats who finished
each other's sentences. A thin horse-faced man in a floor-
length plastic slicker. A cop. I would have expected this sort
of thing in an English country village, but it did not seem
possible that one woman could be so well known in such a
cosmopolitan neighbourhood. From each of them I gleaned
another curious piece of information about my hostess, but
they confused my picture of her instead of clarifying it. The
cop mentioned her recent divorce from 'that writer, the guy
who caused all that trouble at Rockaway Beach'. Was this
the pianist, or someone else? The couple in the dry cleaners
professed themselves glad that Mary had gotten her eyesight
back. The horse-faced man asked me if she still had 'the
singing hen'.

I returned to the apartment half-expecting to find another
stranger sitting in the lounge, but for once it was empty, and
I could concentrate on going through the figures I needed to
prepare for work the following morning. Or I would have
been able to, had the armadillo not clawed them all to pieces
and pissed on them. It took me the rest of the day to put
everything right, during which time I fielded over a dozen
phonecalls from borderline-crazies asking for Mary. Apparently she ran some kind of astrology hotline on her other
number Sunday evenings. I don't know the details but I think
there was some kind of gambling element involved because
one guy asked if he could put thirty dollars on Saturn.
Deciding to set her voicemail in future, I finally got to bed

just before one, having first locked the rewritten papers safely inside my briefcase.

Sleep did not come easily. My head was full of questions. Why had Mary's first husband killed himself? Why was the second one a maniac? Why was Dean in jail? Why couldn't I just ignore all this stuff and quietly get on with my own life?

On Monday, Bolivar had to stay behind in the apartment while I went to work, but Raoul and Carlos arrived just as I was leaving.

'Yo! The Chuckster!' bellowed Carlos. 'The new tub is arriving today. Gonna be some banging.'

'That's fine,' I said, relieved. 'Do your worst. I won't be here.' I stopped in the doorway. 'As a matter of interest, how do you know Miss Amity?'

She had helped the pair out of some difficulty when they were little more than schoolkids, in trouble with the law. Carlos now worked for a security firm and Raoul was a hot-diver. That is, he explained, he was paid to jump into radioactive water at power plants, in order to fix things. 'It hasn't done a hell of a lot for my sperm-count and my pants glow in the dark,' he laughed, 'but the money's good.'

The great thing about the location of Mary's apartment was its proximity to the bank. I could be there in a few minutes, not that I particularly wanted to. It wasn't a very interesting job. That evening I was back by five-thirty, and returned to find the front door standing wide open. Carlos was on the floor doing something intricate with spanners. His portable cassette recorder was playing a mutilated tape of mariachi music.

'You know the front door's been left wide open?'

'Raoul, I asked you to shut it, man.'

'Where's the dog?' I asked.

'You didn't take him to work with you?'

They looked from one to the other, then back at me.

I asked the neighbours. I walked the streets. I reported the loss to the police. Bolivar was nowhere to be found. He could have left the apartment at any time during the day. By ten o'clock I was in a state of panic, but there was nothing to do except return home and see if he had managed to find his way back.

There was no sign of him. I fed the armadillo, which by this time was making the kitchen smell strange, and went to bed, if not to sleep.

When I awoke the following morning to find yet another stranger in the apartment, I was glad to have someone to talk to. He was a very large black man named Gregor, and was washing his underpants in the kitchen sink.

'You have something wrong with your water.'

'What are you doing?' I asked.

'Your basement washer-dryer is being overhauled and I couldn't get in the bathroom, there's pipes an' shit everywhere,' he explained.

'I mean, what are you doing here in this apartment?' I noticed an aggressive tone in my voice that I could have sworn wasn't normally there.

'See, Mary lets me use her utility room because mine is full of hookers.' He wrung out an enormous pair of Calvin Klein Y-fronts and draped them over a radiator. 'They work the street a block down from here, right outside my building, and we have a deal with them to be off the sidewalk by seven in the morning, when our kids start getting up, but in return they get to wash all their stuff in the utility room, and I don't want to be sharing a drum with all their split-crotch shit. So Mary gave me her – '

' – apartment keys. I understand. I'm Charles. You want some coffee?'

'Sure thing, Charlie,' he said gratefully. 'I hope I'm not putting you to trouble or nothing.'

'Oh, it's no trouble,' I said wearily, reaching for the coffee pot.

I could hardly concentrate on work that day, I was so worried. There had been no word about Bolivar, and I wondered how long a dog could survive by itself on the streets of Manhattan. He was wearing a collar, but to my knowledge there was no address on it. I called the police again, but finding a lost dog came a pretty long way down their list of things to do today. I resolved to leave work early and continue trawling the streets. Naturally, by five o'clock it was raining so hard that you couldn't see more than the blurred red tail-lights of the nearest retreating cab.

By eight o'clock, soaked through and in despair, I ended up back at the apartment. I had just managed to get the door open when the telephone rang.

'Oh, I'm so glad you're there,' said Mary. 'I tried you at work but they said you'd gone for the evening. I spoke to a nice young lady named Barbara. Such a nice voice. She broke up with her boyfriend, did you know?'

'No, I didn't know that.'

'You should talk to her. A good soul, but lonely. When she's not with someone she puts on weight. You can tell just by listening.'

'Yes, she's very nice,' I agreed, pulling off my wet raincoat. 'I was just taking the dog for a walk.'

'In this terrible weather? Oh, you didn't have to do that. Put him on, will you? Let me hear him.'

I desperately looked around. 'He can't come to the phone right now. He's eating.'

'He'll come when he hears my voice. Bolivar!' She began shouting his name over and over. I hoped she was in a private room. With no other choice available, I was forced to impersonate the bull terrier. I interspersed ragged breathy gasps with some swallows of saliva.

'Good boy! Good boy! Put Charles back on now.'

I wiped my mouth. 'Hello, Miss Amity.'

'Oh call me Mary, everyone does. I just wanted to thank you for being so kind to me, Charles. Lying here in hospital you start worrying about all sorts of things, and it's such a comfort knowing that someone responsible is taking care of my precious baby.'

Fifteen minutes later I was in Ron's Lucky Silver Dollar Bar & Grill, chugging back beers and telling the barman my problem. I had to tell someone.

'I've let the poor woman down, Bill. She allowed me to stay in her home, not because she needed someone to look after the place but because this guy I know told her I needed somewhere to stay for a week. She trusted me out of the goodness of her heart. I see that now. But I let her down. I lost her prized possession, her best friend! How could I do that? How could I be so irresponsible?'

'Strictly speaking it wasn't your fault,' said Bill, flicking something out of a beermug. 'The builders, they should have kept the front door shut.'

'You don't understand. It's a matter of good faith.'

At the other end of the bar, one of the patrons switched on the wall TV. *Lady and the Tramp* was showing. The film had just reached the part where the unclaimed dog in the pound was walking the last mile to the gas chamber. All the other dogs were howling as it went to its lonely death.

'Hey, turn that thing off!' shouted Bill. 'Jeez, sorry about that, Chuck.'

'How am I going to tell her, Bill? I mean, Dean would be able to break it to her gently, but he had to go to jail.'

'I know about that.'

'You do?'

'Sure. He comes in here with Mary.'

'Why is he going to jail?'

'He used to do a little – freelancing – for Mary.' He seemed reluctant to broach the subject.

'Oh? Was he handling her accounting work?' I knew she'd sat accountancy exams, and Dean was a teller, after all. The thought crossed my mind that they had been caught working some kind of financial scam together, and that Mary was not in hospital at all but with him in jail.

'No,' replied Bill, 'dancing.'

'What do you mean?'

'She has this entertainment company that supplies dancers to office parties, you know the kind of thing, sexy girls coming out of cakes, stuff like that. Meter maids, nurses who strip, all above-board and legit. And she has some guys who take their clothes off. Well, Dean owed some money and needed to get cash fast. She persuaded Dean to earn it by doing this act where he was dressed as a cop, and he'd turn up in some chick's office and tell them they were under arrest, and they'd ask why, and he'd say for breaking men's hearts, and then he'd whip out his tape deck and play *Stop! In The Name Of Love!* and strip down to a sequined jockstrap.'

'So why was he arrested?' I asked.

'He was coming out of the Flatiron Building after a birthday appointment and saw somebody being mugged. Well, he was still in uniform, and saw this guy off, but get this, the victim reported him for not being a real cop. And it turned out this wasn't the first time he'd used his outfit in public. They found him guilty of impersonating a police officer. That's taken very seriously around here.' He saw my mug was empty. 'Let me fill that for ya?'

I sat in the apartment, staring at the spot where Bolivar had spent his evenings happily assaulting the armadillo. When he wagged his tail, his entire body flexed back and forth like a single muscle, a grin on legs. I missed him.

Mary owned the fattest telephone book I had ever seen, but as I only knew the first names of her friends I couldn't find any of them listed within its pages. Raoul and Carlos had finished the bathroom and gone, leaving a bunch of red roses behind in the sink, and the armadillo, which seemed to have discovered a prisoner-of-war method of getting out of its box and back in before I got home, had eaten the piece of paper bearing the number of Carlos's mobile phone. I was trying to figure out my next move when the telephone rang.

This time it was Donald. Apparently, Mary had rung him and asked him to call me. I hadn't liked his attitude the other morning, but now he seemed a lot friendlier. Still, it seemed odd that he should call. I decided to break the news to him about losing Bolivar. He told me that the first thing I needed to do was duplicate a stack of posters and staple them on telephone poles around the neighbourhood.

'You think it's wise putting Miss Amity's number on them?'

'You worry too much, anyone ever point that out to you? Listen, it's easy, I'll help if you want.'

My first instinct, the one that came all too naturally, was to say no. Nobody in our family ever accepted help of any kind. Then I thought, this is crazy, and accepted his offer. That evening we put up nearly a hundred posters. The rain didn't stop for a second, but it was fun walking around the backstreets, past the glowing restaurant windows, talking to someone so alien that everything we spoke of began from opposite points of view. We didn't find Bolivar but at least I had done something positive, and that felt good.

The next day was Wednesday. Mary was due out of hospital on Friday. She called again that evening, and this time I managed to avoid bringing the dog to the telephone for a conversation. She wanted to know about my parents, and I had to admit I found it easier talking to someone I had never met.

'Families. They mean well but they're blind,' she said.

'I miss my dad.'

'Of course you do. I come from a very big family. My father planned to bring us here for many years, but by the time we finally reached New York there were only a few of us left. So I made the city my family. It was the most logical thing to do. A little assimilation is good for you. How's my doggie?'

'Uh, he's fine. He's in the kitchen, eating.'

'Then I won't disturb him. And I won't keep you from your evening. Nurse Ratchett is about to come around with my knockout pills. I hide them down the side of the bed. It drives her nuts. What birth sign are you?'

'Pisces.'

'Ah.' I could hear her smile. 'That would explain it.'

The rain had stopped. The street glittered and beckoned. As a European I find it impossible to watch American network TV because of the commercials, so after a quarter-hour of fidgety channel-hopping I headed back outside. I tried to imagine where Bolivar might have gone, but the dog knew so many stores and bars in the neighbourhood I had no idea where to start. He had a better social life than me. Deliber-ately ignoring my boss's advice – 'If you have to walk in New York, pick a destination and home in on it like a Cruise missile' – I wandered aimlessly for half an hour, then headed back to the apartment.

On the front steps I collided with Melissa, who was coming out of the building.

'I left you a Dutch Apple cake. I baked too much for myself. You need more flesh. Oh, and I topped up the armadillo's box with some cabbage leaves and a mouse. Manny can get them for you, from his coffee shop.'

I was touched. 'Thanks, Melissa, that's really sweet of you. Do you want to come up for a drin—coffee?'

She waved the offer away. 'No, I can't stop. Besides, you already have a visitor.'

'Who?' I'd been hoping for a quiet night.

'I didn't catch his name but he looks like one of Mary's emotional cripples. She does this course, this therapy-thing. Did you know she's a qualified therapist? By the way, this came off.' She put the top of the bathroom's hot-water tap in my hand.

'No, I didn't,' I replied, pocketing the faucet. 'If someone told me she was a freelance lion-tamer, it wouldn't surprise me.' Wondering who or what I was in for now, I ventured upstairs.

'Bad luck doesn't make you a loser. Do I look like a loser to you? No, you give me respect, 'cause what you see is a chick-magnet, a pretty sharp guy. Not a loser.' He wore Ray-bans on top of his head, silver-backed Cuban heels and a blue tropical shirt covered in marlins. Slick-black hair, a hula-girl tattoo on his forearm, jiggling above a diamante watch 'with a rock so big it could choke a fucking horse' (his words). He was settled in the armchair I had come to think of as Carlos's chair, nursing a large whisky. He seemed edgy and anxious to get something off his chest, and I wasn't about to argue. For all I knew he was carrying a gun. He looked the type, only more weaselly, like if he shot someone it would be because the safety catch had accidentally come off.

'Yeah. So. I got this debt around my neck from some stuff I'd picked up in the Keys. Not drugs, man, everyone thinks drugs in Florida but this was a shipment of French silverware, like cutlery and salt cellars and stuff, I figured from some Louisiana family. And I can't get rid of it because, get this, it's too valuable. I called Mary and at first she told me to return it, like I could just waltz back and cancel the deal.'

I could sense it was going to be a long night, and that I wouldn't like whatever it was this guy was working toward, so I poured myself a whisky. I never used to drink.

'She already knew what I was holding 'cause she'd seen it

on the news – the *national* news – on account of the silverware once belonged to some French bigwig or something.
Now a guy in Harlem called Dolphin Eddie is offering me a
cash deal so low it's a fucking offence to nature, but I figure
okay, I won't make a profit but it'll wipe the slate on my
debts.' He held up his glass. 'Can I get another one of these?'

'Look here, Mr—'

'Randy. Randy Amity. This is my mother's apartment. I'm
her only kid. I guess you think that's weird, considering how
many times she's been married, but something went wrong
with her tubes after she had me. You're Chuck, right?'

Now I saw the family resemblance. God, she must have
been disappointed.

'Anyways, I'm leaving the stuff here.'

'Here?' I exploded. 'Are you crazy? Where is it?'

'Relax.' Randy sat forward and drained his drink. 'It's
safely stashed away.'

'What if your mother finds out? Good Lord, she could get
hurt.'

'I don't think so. It was her idea. I was just gonna stop by,
stash the silverware for a couple of nights and take a bath,
but the hot-water faucet is missing.'

'Can I at least see this – merchandise?'

'Sure.' He reached beneath the armchair and pulled up a
large inlaid gold and blue leather case. Inside the silk-sewn
lid was a brass panel faced in dense scrollwork. I tipped
the case to the light and read the owner's name. *Donatien-
Alphonse-François, Comte de –*

My jaw dropped. 'You mean to tell me you stole the cutlery
of the Marquis de Sade?' I asked, appalled. 'Do you have any
idea how valuable this stuff is?' The carvings on the bone-
handled fish-knives, in particular, were outrageous.

'What can I tell you?' shrugged Randy, 'I'm the black sheep
of the family. Only Mama loves me, even though she won't
introduce me to her friends.'

'You don't look like her.'

'That's good. I guess I'm more like my pa.'

'Which one of her husbands is that?'

'The one she didn't marry,' he replied thoughtfully.

Just then, the door buzzer went and we both flew into a panic, shovelling the knives and forks back into the canteen like a pair of kids caught smoking dope in their bedroom. Randy stowed the case and signalled the all-clear, and I answered the door to find myself looking at a very frail elderly man in a ratty cardigan, holding a ficus tree almost as tall as himself.

'I want you should give this to Mary,' he said, shouting at the top of his voice. 'I don't want it no more. It ain't the plant, it's the money.'

'I – what? Wait.' I held up my hand. I didn't want him to repeat what he had said. He was extremely deaf and possibly half-blind, for he seemed to be addressing a spot several feet above my head.

'The tree, it's full of money,' he bellowed. 'I don't want it no more.'

I looked back at Randy, who was hiding behind the couch. He gave a puzzled 'Wassamatta?' look.

'I want you should give this to Mary,' the old man repeated. I felt like asking him why he hadn't used his keys like everyone else. 'I'm not crazy or nothing. You're looking at me like I'm crazy.'

'I'm sorry, I don't mean to,' I apologised. 'I'll give her the plant.' I wanted him to put it down before he fell down.

'It's her damn plant anyway. She lends her plants to people. I'm in her Thursday night group. Every week since my wife died. Exploring The Senses. I told her I was depressed and she gave me the plant, but she stuck money in the pot, like this way I won't think it's charity or a handout or nothin', but I saw through her, so I'm bringing it back. There's sixty dollars there and you can tell her I ain't touched a damn penny.' He thrust the battered tree into my arms and started off for the stairs. How he ever got up them in the first place I'll never know.

'An' tell her from me,' he yelled, looking back over his shoulder, 'that's a great plant she has there. Tell her it did the trick.'

Much to my relief, Randy left at midnight. He was staying at his ex-girlfriend's mother's house in Queens. From the way he was talking, I had a suspicion that he might be sleeping with her. He promised me the cutlery would only remain in the apartment for a few days, but I knew that someone with eyes like a starving boa constrictor would be capable of telling anything to anyone.

I put the ficus in with the other plants, made myself a coffee and sat by the window for a while. The room seemed oddly silent now. For the first time in ages I thought about sharing my life with someone. No-one in particular, just someone.

On Thursday I called the police again, with no luck. Miss Amity was due home the next evening, and I dreaded to think what I would say to her. I played back her messages; the usual assortment of normality-impaired individuals, someone asking her about selling a speedboat – she seemed to be acting as the middleman in a deal – someone else wanting to know if you could put a copyright on planets and sell them as brand-names.

Someone had also been in the apartment. I could smell cigar smoke. There was a squashed-out butt in the sink, and a pair of half-empty coffee cups beside the sofa. Worse still, it looked to me as though they had made love on the bed. The covers were rumpled and the room smelled stale and faintly perfumy. There was a time, just a few days ago, when the discovery would have shocked me, but my accumulated indirect knowledge of Miss Amity told me something about these new occupants. That, trapped perhaps in loveless relationships, they had fallen for each other and were unable to meet anywhere else, so she had allowed them to use the apartment for their trysts.

When Miss Amity called, I told her my suspicions.

'Damn,' she cried, 'that filthy whore has been dragging her johns in again. I warned you about Sheryl-Ann. Once I came home and found some poor businessman tied naked to a chair with duct-tape. It took hours to get it all off because he was so hairy. A nice man. I had to lend him cab fare because she took his wallet. His wife couldn't see they had a problem. Listen, I must tell you my news. Barbara has a date. Aren't you pleased for her?'

She never waited for you to catch up. 'Who are we talking about now?'

'Oh, Charles! The girl in your office. I fixed her up with my cousin Joel. He owns a chain of hardware stores. Is two a chain? He's taking her dancing. Isn't that great? Do you like mariachi music?'

She seemed to be moving in circles around me, making waves, brushing against the lives of others. This was beyond my experience. 'I'm very glad for her,' I replied. 'How did you – '

'If somebody calls about a speedboat, don't talk to them. I checked it out, and I get the feeling it was not acquired legally, if you know what I mean.'

I took Friday afternoon off. I was so nervous about Miss Amity coming home, I wanted some time to myself to figure out how to handle it. She called from the hospital at four to say she was just leaving. At half-past, there was another call.

'Guess what?' shouted Donald, out of breath. 'We found the dog.'

I leapt out of the armchair. 'My God, Miss Amity's due back any minute. Where is he?'

'In your building. He's been there the whole time. Mrs

Beckerman's been looking after him. He stays with her whenever Mary goes out of town.'

'Why on earth didn't she bring him back?'

'I guess she thought she was meant to look after him, what with Mary in the hospital. She called me to ask when Mary was getting out. Ground floor, apartment 1b. Go get 'im.'

'Donald, you are a lifesaver.'

'So buy me a drink sometime, Mr Snooty Englishman.'

'Tomorrow,' I promised. 'Tomorrow night.'

'Deal.'

The other line rang. I switched across and answered. 'Hello?'

'It's me, Mary. I stopped to get some groceries on the way. Listen, I can't get in. I don't seem to have my keys. You will be there, won't you?'

'Of course. I'm looking forward to meeting you.'

'Did you get the dog back from Mrs Beckerman?'

'You mean – you knew?'

'That you'd lost him? Of course I knew. From the moment you performed that ridiculous impersonation over the phone.'

'But if you knew, you must have had an idea where Bolivar had gone.'

'Well, of course,' she replied.

'Then why didn't you tell me?'

'I would have thought that was obvious. I wanted you to spend some time with Donald. Charles, I have something to tell you. I was talking to your mother earlier and – '

'My mother? My mother in England?'

'You have another?'

'How did you get her number?'

'Barbara found it in your address book. She's seeing Joel Saturday. I hope they get on. They're the same height; it's a start. I called your mother because I wanted to ask her something, that's all. She thinks an awful lot of you. We talked for quite a while, her and me, and one thing led to another, and I accidentally let slip – '

The other line rang.

'There's another call.'

'I have a feeling that'll be her now. Don't be mad.'

'Hold on.'

I gingerly switched to the other line.

'Mary Amity tells me you're gay,' said my mother. I nearly dropped the phone. Regaining my composure, I switched lines back.

'I didn't mean to out you,' said Miss Amity apologetically, 'I wasn't sure you even knew yourself, but it was obvious to me. Families. We shock and disappoint each other, but there's still love. Look at Randy. Pour a drink. Brandy is good. Talk to your ma, don't fight, just run with it, she's fine. I'll be there soon.'

I talked to my mother.

I collected the dog.

I waited for Mary.

But Mary Amity never arrived. We never did meet.

She hadn't been in the hospital for a hip operation. The doctors had removed a tumour. She didn't want to worry people. In the cab she developed a cramp and asked the driver to take her back. She died a few minutes after being re-admitted. She was the only person who ever got my name right.

I no longer work at the bank. I have an apartment of my own now, a modest place in Brooklyn. Two floors up, with four rooms, one bull terrier and far too many sets of keys.

LEARNING TO LET GO

Everyone has a story to tell, he reminded himself. Whether it really happened, to them or to someone else, is irrelevant. What's important is that they believe some part of it, no matter how small. The most ludicrous and unlikely narrative might yield a telling detail that could lodge in a person's mind forever.

Harold Masters smiled at the thought and was nearly killed as he stepped off the kerb on the corner of Museum Street. The passing van bounced across a crevice in the tarmac and soaked his trousers, but the doctor barely noticed. He raised his umbrella enough to see a few feet ahead and launched himself perilously into the homegoing traffic, his head clouded with doubts and dreams. Why were his pupils so inattentive? Was he a poor storyteller? How could he be bad at the one thing he loved? Perhaps he lacked the showmanship to keep their interest alive. Why could they create no histories for themselves, even false ones?

Fact and fiction, fiction and fact.

What was the old Hollywood maxim? *Nobody knows anything.* Not strictly true, he thought. Everyone has some practical knowledge, how to replace a lightbulb, how to fill a tank with petrol. But it was true that most information came second-hand, even with the much-vaunted advent of electronic global communication. You couldn't believe what you saw on the news or read in the papers, not entirely, because it was written with a subtle political, commercial or demographic slant, so why, he wondered, should you believe what you read in a washing machine manual or see on a computer screen? A taxi hooted as he hailed it, the vehicle's wing mirror catching at his coat as he jumped up on to the opposite kerb.

Dr Harold Masters, at the end of the twentieth century:

Insect-spindled, grey, dry, disillusioned, unsatisfied, argumentative (especially with his wife, whom he was due to meet on the 18 40 p.m. train from Paddington this evening), hopeful, childish, academic, isolated, impatient, forty-four years old and losing touch with the world outside, especially students (he and Jane had two of their own – Lara, currently at Exeter University, and Tyler, currently no more than a series of puzzling postcards from Nepal).

Dr Harold Masters, collector of tales, fables, legends, limericks, jokes and ghost stories, Professor of Oral History, off to the coast with his wife and best friend to deliver a lecture on fact and fiction, was firmly convinced that he could persuade anyone to tell a story. Not just something prosaic and blunted with repetition, how granny lost the cat or the time the car broke down, but a fantastic tale spun from the air, plotted in the mouth and shaped by hand gestures. All it took, he told himself and his pupils, was a little imagination and a willingness to suspend belief. Peregrine Summerfield disagreed with him, of course, but then the art historian was a disagreeable man at the best of times, and had grown worse since his girlfriend had left him. He made an interesting conversational adversary, though, and Masters looked forward to seeing him tonight.

Thank God we persuaded him to come out and spend the weekend with us, he thought as he left his taxi and walked on to the concourse at Paddington Station. Peregrine had suggested cooking dinner for the doctor and his wife this weekend, but his house doubled as his studio and was cluttered with half-filled tubes of paint, brushes glued into cups of turpentine, bits of old newspaper, pots of cloudy water and stacks of unfinished canvasses. Besides, they were bound to argue about something in the course of the evening, and at least this way they would be on neutral ground. Or rather, running over it, for they had arranged to meet in the dining car of the train.

Masters spent too long in the station bookshop quizzing one of the shelf stackers on her reading habits, and nearly forgot to keep an eye on the time. Luckily the dining carriage was situated right at the platform entrance, and he was able to climb aboard without having to gallop down the platform.

'Darling, how nice of you to be on time for once.' Jane, his wife, kissed him carefully. 'I felt sure you'd miss it again. Perry's not made it yet, either. I bribed the waiter to open up the bar and got you a sherry. God, you're soaked. I thought you were going to get a taxi. Do you want me to put that down for you?' She pointed to his dripping briefcase.

'Um, no, actually, I've something to show you.' Masters seated himself and dug inside, removing a handful of yellowed pages sealed in a clear plastic envelope. 'Thought you'd be interested in seeing this. I might include it in the lecture.'

Jane had hoped for a little social interaction with her husband before he plunged back into his ink-and-paper world. Concealing her disappointment, she accepted the package and slipped the pages from their cover. She was good at masking her emotions. She'd had plenty of practice. 'What's it supposed to be?'

'It was found in a desk drawer in a Dublin newspaper office when they were clearing out the building. Miles passed it to me for verification.'

With practised ease, Jane slipped the yellow pills into her cupped hand and washed them down with her sherry. 'You really want me to look at this now?'

'Go on, before Perry gets here,' pleaded Masters. He was

like an irritating schoolboy sometimes; he would hover over her, driving her mad if she didn't read it straightaway. Reluctantly, she perused the battered pages.

'Obviously it's meant to be a missing chapter from Bram Stoker's *Dracula*, revealing the fate of Jonathan Harker. But if it was real, it would have to be part of an earlier draft.' Jane tapped the pages level. 'The quality of the writing is different, too coarse. It wouldn't fit with the finished version of the book at all.' She studied the pages again. 'It's a fake. I think it's pretty unlikely that Bram Stoker would write about oral sex, don't you? The ink and the paper look convincingly old, though.'

'Damn.' Masters accepted the pages back. 'You saw through it without even reading it properly. Miles went to the trouble of using genuine hundred-year-old ink, too. It's his entry for a new course we're starting called "Hidden Histories".'

'Did you really expect me to believe it was the genuine article?'

'Well, I suppose so,' he admitted sheepishly.

'Honestly, you and Miles are as bad as each other.'

'Well, I believed it,' he moped. 'But then, I always believe the stories I'm told.'

Jane smiled across the top of her glass. 'Of course you do. Remember how convinced you were that the Hitler diaries were real?'

'I *wanted* them to be real. To learn about the inside of that man's brain, didn't you?'

'No, Harold, I didn't.' She looked out of the window. 'We're moving. I hope Perry got on board.'

'Jesus, that was a close thing. I wasn't expecting it to leave on time.' Peregrine Summerfield was standing beside them, attempting to tug his wet tweed jacket away from his body while a waiter pulled ineffectually at a sleeve.

'Perry, you're getting water over everything.'

'I was trying to choose a paperback. Nearly missed it. On Hallowe'en, too, that would have been an omen, eh? It's pissing down outside. Hallo, darling.' He kissed Jane. 'The tube smelled like an animal sanctuary, all wet hair and coats. Anyone ordered me a drink? What have you got there?' He pointed at the plastic-coated pages on the table as he sat down beside Masters' wife.

'Something for my lecture on fact and fiction.'

'Oh?' Summerfield thudded down into his chair and eagerly accepted a drink from Jane, carefully guiding the sherry glass over his beard.

'Yes, it purports to be – well, it's actually – '

'Jane, you're looking bloody gorgeous, as ever,' Summerfield interrupted, 'beats me how you do it on a shitty night like this. What's on the menu apart from their god-awful watery vegetables, I wonder? Let's see if we can get one of these pimply louts to open some wine, shall we?'

He made a beckoning gesture at Masters. 'Come on, then, I know you're dying to tell someone about your talk tomorrow. What have you got planned for these poor students?'

'I thought I'd talk about how fact and fiction have switched places since the war.'

'What do you mean?'

'Well, you have to look at the history of storytelling. For me, one of the most important dates in the last century was the 28th of December, eighteen hundred and eighty-one.'

Summerfield gave a shrug. 'Why?'

'On that day the first public building was illuminated with electricity for the first time ever, at the Savoy Theatre.' Masters leaned forward conspiratorially. 'Just think of it. With the click of a switch, twelve hundred electric lamps cast darkness from the room. The myths and mysteries of the past were thrown aside by the bright, cold light of scientific reason. No more shadows. No more hidden fears. No more cautionary tales of bogeymen and ghouls. And in the week of the winter solstice! As if man was determined to prove the dominance of light over darkness!

'Fiction once involved the telling of tales by candlelight. With electricity to help us separate fact from fiction, everything was clearly designated. Before the advent of television life was simpler. You went to work, you came home, you listened to the radio, you read a book; it was hard to mix your home life with your fantasy life. Now, though, the lines are blurred. People have phoney job titles and meaningless career descriptions. They spend their days lying to each other about what they do for a living, trying to make their work sound more interesting than it is, then they go home and watch gritty, realistic soap operas on TV. No wonder their kids are confused about what's real and what isn't. People write to soap stars as if they were real characters. And with so many companies spoon feeding us entertainment, no wonder we're losing the power to create our own fantasies. No wonder that we're not believed even when we've achieved the fantastic. Inexplicable mysteries occur every day, in every life. It's how we choose to read them that defines us as individuals.'

'Oh please,' Summerfield exploded, 'you might as well ask me to believe in Roswell, Area 51, crop circles, Nessie and all that Fortean stuff. You want to believe in the paranormal because you secretly think there has to be something more to the world than just this.' He pointed out of the window. It had grown dark outside. They had already left the suburbs. A glimmer of buttery light showed above the brow of a passing hill.

'Perhaps I do, but that's not the point. It's important to keep an open mind.'

'Then you'll never make any decisions in your life. You'll be like a child forever.'

'Wait a minute, let's simmer down a little.' Jane Masters held up her hand for peace. The table was becoming rowdy earlier than usual. A pair of diners in black plastic witch-hats were staring at them. 'Where are we?'

'I'm not sure. It's too dark to see.'

'Besides,' Summerfield ploughed on, 'getting someone to believe in something is simply a matter of theatricality and good presentation. If I wanted you to believe a strange story, I could easily make you do it. Especially on a night like tonight, of all nights.' He emptied the wine bottle. At this rate, thought Masters, we'll be crocked before we reach the coast. The air pressure in the carriage altered as they entered a tunnel, sucking out the flame from the little orange pumpkin-candle the waiter had placed on their table.

Summerfield turned to the others, his command of the table absolute, and raised his hands. For the next few minutes he told a tale, the odd affair of a businessman who became imprisoned within an ancient London building. At the conclusion he sat back and drained his glass. He looked from Jane to Harold Masters and permitted himself a satisfied smile.

'Well?' he asked. 'You do believe me, don't you? I hope you do, because Jonathan Laine is an old friend of mine, and the story came from his own lips. He couldn't live with the guilt of his secret, and subsequently killed himself. They found him at the bottom of the Thames, somewhere down at the Dartford estuary. So stick that in your pipe and smoke it.'

They broke the conversation as their starters arrived. The train seemed to be travelling at an unusually laborious pace, and was lumbering through the flat open countryside toward the lights of a distant town. Heavy rain began to thrash the sides of the carriage. It was as if they had entered a car wash. Toward the end of the meal, Masters raised his glass. 'I'd like to propose a toast, seeing as it's Hallowe'en and the perfect time for creepy stories. Jane, perhaps you'd like to tell one.'

'Oh no, Harold, I'd rather not,' begged Jane, throwing a desperate glance at Summerfield.

'Don't tell me all these years of hearing my stories hasn't

rubbed off on you just a little bit.' Masters gave a pantomime wink.

'I can't help you, Jane,' said Summerfield. 'Go on, join in the spirit of the thing. Show us what being with Harold has taught you.'

Jane shot him a look of betrayal that had the force to knock over a large piece of furniture.

'All right, then,' she conceded, 'I'll tell you a story I first heard many years ago. I was a young girl, impatient to become an adult. It taught me something about the nature of time.'

As the train crept on through the rain she began her story, about a powerful sultan and the winding of a thousand clocks. By the time she had finished, she looked close to tears. 'I always liked exotic stories,' she explained, blowing her nose. 'They let you forget mundane things for a while.' Harold had already lost interest, and was looking over at the next table. She followed his eyeline and saw three students, a pale-faced girl and two boys, staring at them as if they were mad. 'Godby, is that you? And Saunders?' asked Masters.

'Yes, sir.'

'Good God, lad, am I to have no privacy? As if I don't see enough of you during term. How many more of you are there?'

The first of the group spoke up. His accent was American. 'Just me and Kallie, sir. And this is Claire.' A bony, whey-faced girl seated between them gave an awkward smile.

That's all we needed, thought Jane with a sinking heart, *to be stuck with Harold's students for the rest of the journey.* They were doomed never to have time to themselves. These days it seemed that there were always other people in the room all talking at once, colleagues from the museum, hyper-active pupils, aged academics, never any of her friends, never any special private moments together, no wonder she –

'Are you going to tell any more stories?'

'I can't believe it,' Masters announced to the rest of the group, 'surely we're not in the presence of students displaying an interest? They don't noticeably do so in any of my lectures. Yes, we may well tell more stories,' he replied, 'but you can only join in if you bring a tale of your own to the table.'

'Preferably a true one,' added Summerfield, just being awkward. He did not enjoy the company of the young; they tired him with their fatuous observations, and made him feel fat and old and unattractive. 'And you must present it in the form of a proper story, with voices and acting and everything. And most important of all, you have to bring your own wine.'

Outside, sheet lightning illuminated the fields, like someone momentarily flicking on a light. 'We're drinking cider,' the first student replied, holding out his hand. 'I'm Ben. From Colorado originally, but I'm studying here now.' The introductions continued around the table. 'I've got a story from my creative writing course. It's based on something I read in an old newspaper.' Ben dug into his backpack and pulled out a folder filled with scissored articles. 'Here's the original clipping.' He held it up for everyone to see. ' "*Human civilisation, it seems, has flourished during a 10,000 year climactic ceasefire. Hostilities may be about to resume. – Independent On Sunday, 18th February 1996.*" We had to develop a story from a factual starting point, and this is what I came up with.'

'All right, but you have to convince us that it might really be true,' warned Masters. 'Let's hear what today's youth have to offer in the way of narrative ability. The floor of the carriage is yours.'

Ben cleared his throat.

'You could have warned me it was set in the future,' complained Harold Masters after he had finished. 'That counts as science fiction and I don't like science fiction.' The student sheepishly returned the clippings to his bag.

'So you didn't like the story, Harold?' asked Summerfield, surprising himself with his decision to defend the boy.

'I didn't say that. It's just that it can't be true because it hasn't happened yet.'

'But it's a possible future, one of many. Who knows what will happen to us? And who's to say it isn't happening right now in a parallel universe?'

'Well, I liked it,' said Jane, refilling her glass. 'Although I think the wine has gone to my head a little. Maybe that's making me more susceptible.'

'Perhaps.' Summerfield checked his watch. 'It's getting late. We should all be growing susceptible. The floodgates to the supernatural world are open tonight, remember. What time do we get to the coast?'

'A little after eleven,' Jane replied. 'I informed the hotel of our arrival time. They weren't terribly happy about it.' She turned to the students. 'Where are you three off to?'

'Hallowe'en party. We have friends who rent a house on the edge of Dartmoor.'

'I bet your pals have some interesting tales to tell about mysterious goings-on on the moors, eh?' said Summerfield.

'No.' Claire grimaced as though the idea was the stupidest she had ever heard. 'They just smoke dope all day and play video games.'

'Couldn't you revive the tradition of oral history and get them to make up some stories?' asked Masters.

'Oh for God's sake, Harold,' Jane exploded, 'that's not what young people want to do with their time.'

'As the father of two children, Jane, I think I can safely say that I know how the juvenile mind operates.'

'Do you? I find that hard to believe. Our offspring are certainly not children, they're not even teenagers any more, and not only do I not know who Lara has been seeing lately or where Tyler is, I'm not entirely sure I would recognise either of them if they sent me recent photographs.' She was referring to the snapshot their son had mailed from Nepal earlier in the year. The emaciated young man with the shaved head and the wispy beard seemed to bear no resemblance to the thoughtful child who used to sit beside her at night writing endless fantastic stories in his school exercise book.

'I'm working on a story at the moment,' said Kallie.

'It's not set in the future, is it?' asked Masters cautiously.

'No, London Docklands, in the present day. I read about electromagnetic pollution somewhere. Microwaves can create hot spots, areas rippling with forcefields stronger than the most powerful ocean cross-currents. The story's about a corporation that accidentally creates them in its offices.'

'Sounds a bit far-fetched.' Summerfield wrestled another wine bottle away from the concerned waiter and overfilled everyone's glasses as the train hammered over a set of points.

'Big business as the evil bogeyman, it's an ever-popular target for student paranoia,' complained Masters, unimpressed. 'There's no human dimension in the stories of the young. Too many issue-led morality tales, the sort they have on American television shows, nothing from direct experience.'

'Oh for God's sake,' snapped Jane, 'people can only reflect the times in which they live. There are no traditional heroes left, no explorers, no captains, no warriors. I don't know why you expect so much from others. One thing that years of listening to you has taught me is that you're incapable of telling a decent story. It's a talent you singularly lack, because you have no perception. You're best off leaving it to other people.'

Shocked by her own honesty, she stopped herself from saying any more. An uncomfortable atmosphere settled on the table. Stung, Masters stared out into the rainswept darkness, avoiding his wife's angry gaze.

'Come on, chaps, let's not get personal.' Summerfield clapped his hands together and startled Jane, who was gazing glumly into her wine, hypnotised by the steady movement of the train. Most of the carriage was deserted now. Even the guard was dozing in an end seat, his head lolling on his shoulder. It was as though they had been freed from the shackles of time and place, the co-ordinates that underpinned their lives slipping quietly away into the night.

Claire shifted across the aisle to the opposite seat and faced them. 'I've got a story,' she said mischievously. 'About some friends of mine who got locked in a pub.' And she told it, although it didn't sound true.

'Well.' Jane cleared her throat at the end, slightly flummoxed. 'That was certainly *frank*. Although I'm not sure it's really a fit subject to turn into a dramatic piece.'

'Some people are uncomfortable around the subject of sexuality,' mumbled Claire, meaning older people, meaning her. The senior members of the group were a little embarrassed by the girl's intensity, although it obviously did not bother Kallie or Ben. Jane drained her glass and pushed back into her seat, unsettled by what she had heard. Masters cleared a spot on the window and peered out. 'My watch has stopped. I thought we'd be able to see the sea by now. Doesn't the train run along the coast for the last hour?'

'There's not much of a moon.'

'Even so, you should be able to see something.'

The carriage shifted across a set of uneven points, and the overhead lights flickered. Electricity crackled somewhere beneath their feet.

'Maybe we're on the Hallowe'en train to hell.' Summerfield looked around. Jane was half asleep. Suddenly the train lurched hard and shuddered to a hard halt, its brakes squealing. Wine bottles and glasses toppled on tables, and several pieces of luggage bounced down from the overhead racks.

'What on earth . . .'

Jane blearily pulled herself upright. 'Are we there?'

'God knows where we are.' The doctor pressed his forehead against the window. 'It's pitch black out there. I can't see a thing.'

Ben retrieved his backpack from beneath his seat. 'I'm going to ask someone.'

'You needn't bother asking the guard,' said Masters, pointing. 'He seems to have wandered off.'

'Maybe he's dead,' Summerfield stage-whispered, 'drugged, shot with a poison dart, a minor character in an Agatha Christie play, someone whose Rosencrantz-like role exists simply to fulfil a duty to the plot.'

'Now who's muddling fact and fiction?' Masters asked uncomfortably. He turned to his wife. 'Are you warm enough?'

'You've noticed it too, then.' The heating had gone off. They could hear the steady tick of the radiators cooling all along the carriage. Jane sensed that there was something wrong, as if the world had slipped a notch deeper into darkness. Panic was descending on her like a cold veil of rain. She dug into her purse for the tablets Dr Colson had prescribed, but could not find them. She had taken two earlier. What had she done with the rest of the packet? When she turned to her husband, she found that he was making his way along the aisle toward the exit.

There *was* something wrong. She needed the tablets to stop her from worrying. She dumped the purse out on to the table and began scrabbling through the contents. The foil sheet glittered between her fingers as she popped out two of the yellow capsules. Claire pulled a mobile phone from her bag and checked it. 'No reception,' she said casually. 'Anyone else?'

'Wait.' Jane retrieved a small black square from her coat and flipped it open. 'None here either. The service isn't reliable in heavily wooded areas.'

At the front of the carriage, Masters pushed down the

train window and peered out into the darkness, his breath condensing in the invading night air. He looked back along the curving track, but could see nothing until the moon cleared the clouds.

When the lunar light finally unveiled the landscape, he saw that there were no other carriages behind them. Theirs had been uncoupled from the main body of the train, and released into what he could only assume was a siding. It sat by itself on a gravelled incline, with low hills rolling away on either side. The sea was not in sight, not where it should have been.

He tried to see ahead in the other direction, and could make out a vague dark shape beside the track, a large, squat building of some sort. Clearly there had been a mistake, some kind of accident. He decided to head back and give a cautious report to the others.

'Well, we have no power to move by ourselves,' said Summerfield, when the situation had been explained. 'As I see it, we have two choices. We can stay here and freeze our nuts off, hoping that somebody finds us, or we can head for the building you saw and try to find a telephone that works.'

'I don't understand how this could have happened.' Jane looked over at the students, annoyed that they could be so calm and still, and by the way they sat apart, implying some kind of private pact of solidarity that did not exist among their elders. 'Isn't anyone worried at all?'

'There's not really much to worry about,' said Summerfield. 'This sort of thing happens all the time. You always read about trains overshooting their stations and passengers having to walk down the track in the dark.'

'I'm not walking along the track – we could be electrocuted!'

'I'm not saying we all do, but someone should. This looks like an old branch line. Suppose a connection came loose and we got separated when we went over the points back there? It could happen, even with advanced information systems.

Perhaps nobody will be aware that there's a carriage missing until the train reaches its destination. Maybe not even then.'

'Harold, I think your imagination is bypassing your common sense,' Summerfield admonished. 'Let's face it, you've never been much good in a crisis. Let's try and be logical about this. The carriage coupling must have made a noise when it disconnected. Doesn't anyone remember hearing it?'

Masters looked around. 'And what happened to the guard? When I last saw him he was asleep in the end seat there.'

They searched the carriage, not that there were any places where someone could be concealed. The toilet was empty. The six of them were the only passengers left on board. Kallie pulled his coat down from the overhead rack. The others began donning their top coats. As they were doing so, the lights began to dim to a misty yellow. Jane released a miserable moan.

'I was going to stay in tonight,' said Claire, checking her hair in the window. 'There was a weepie on TV. But I decided to join these two. Right now I could be snuggled up indoors with a tub of ice cream watching Bette Davis going blind.'

'Was *Dark Victory* on tonight?' asked Kallie. 'I love that film.'

'Yeah, but I think it was sandwiched between *Curse of the Demon* and *Tarantula*.'

'How can you people just chatter on as if nothing is wrong?' Jane snapped.

'Yeah, you're right,' Claire agreed, 'let's all panic instead. What exactly is in those little pills you're taking, by the way?'

'I also suggest we make for the building further along the line,' said Masters. 'Unless anybody wants to stay here.'

'I've got a torch in my bag,' Kallie offered.

'Well, I'm not stepping foot outside of this carriage.' Jane dropped back into her seat just as the overhead lights faded completely. 'Oh, *great*.'

'Jane, you cannot stay here.'

'Can't I? Watch me.'

'I just don't think we should split up, that's all.'

'Yeah,' Claire cut in, 'look what happens when they do that in movies. Somebody gets a spear through them.'

'Please, Jane, you're making things awkward.'

'Do whatever you want,' snapped Jane. 'I'm staying here. You can make your own decision for once in your damned life.'

'Then I say we go,' said Masters, hurt.

'You can't leave your wife here by herself,' Summerfield protested.

'You're right, Peregrine. Would you mind staying with her? We shouldn't be gone too long.'

'But I was going to come with you.' He looked hopelessly at Jane, who was clearly anxious for him to stay. 'Oh, all right. We'll wait for you to return.'

'Okay, who else is coming?' asked Masters. The students already had their bags on their backs. 'Are you sure you'll be all right, darling?'

'I'll be fine, I'll settle once you go – '

'This is Southern England in autumn, Harold, not Greenland in January,' said Summerfield. 'Go on, piss off the lot of you, and come back with a decent explanation for all of this.'

The four of them made their way to the end of the carriage, leaving behind Jane Masters and Peregrine Summerfield, who layered themselves in sweaters and nestled beneath an orange car blanket that made them look like a pair of urbanised Buddhist monks.

It was lighter outside. The moon gave the surrounding wooded hills a pallid phosphorescence. A loamy, wooded scent of fungus and decayed leaves hung in the air. The track appeared as a luminous man-made trail in the chaotic natural landscape. They saw that the carriage must have rolled by itself for at least half a mile before coming to a stop at the bottom of the incline. The grass around them was heavily waterlogged, so they stayed in the centre of the track. Kallie kept his torch trained a few feet ahead.

'How far do you think it is?' he asked, pointing to the distant black oblong beside the track.

'I don't know. Half a mile, not much more.'

'We could have a sing-song,' said Masters. 'Claire, what kind of music do you like?'

'Trance techno and hard house,' Claire replied. 'You don't "*sing*" it.'

'Anyone else know any songs?'

'*Please*,' she begged, 'the first person to start singing gets a rock thrown at them. Ben, tell another story, just a short one.'

'Okay,' said Ben. 'The woman it happened to is a friend of my mother's, and she's not nuts or anything. At least,' he added darkly, 'she wasn't until this happened.' And he told the tale of the lottery demon.

'Sounds to me like her boyfriend left her and she couldn't handle it,' said Masters.

Claire gave a scornful hoot. 'Typical middle-aged male viewpoint.'

'So what are we saying here, that for every positive action there is a reaction?' asked Kallie, 'like you can't win without making someone else suffer? Thanks for the morality play.'

'No,' said Ben defensively, 'just that luck works in both directions. Look at tonight. If we hadn't booked the dining car and then stayed late over our meals, if we hadn't joined your table, we wouldn't be in this fucking mess now.'

Something hooted in the rustling hillside at their backs. The black bulk loomed a few hundred yards ahead. Masters was freezing. His left shoe was taking in water. He hated leaving Jane, but knew she was not strong enough to walk through unknown terrain in the dark. 'Don't worry, there will be a logical explanation for this,' he assured the others. 'There always is.'

They reached a concrete ramp and began to climb. 'It's a station,' said Ben, shining his torch ahead. '*Milford*. Ever heard of it?'

They climbed on to the platform and approached the low brick box that functioned as the main building. Masters tried the door of the waiting room, but it was locked.

'Do you think it still operates?' asked Claire. 'It's unmodernised. They've got wooden slat benches instead of those curved red steel ones with the little holes. And look at the lights. They've got tin shades.'

'It can't still be used,' said Ben, shining his torch through the window of the ticket hall. 'Take a look at this.' The others crowded around in the halo of light. The ticket machines inside had been vandalised. The timetables were heavy with mildew and drooped down like rolls of badly-hung wallpaper. Several of the floorboards were rotten and had fallen through.

'Can you see a phone?' asked Claire.

'You're joking. If there is one, it's going to be out of service. Try your mobile again.'

A silence. Only the sound of their breath and the wind in the trees while Claire tried to get a service signal. She tipped the device to the light. 'Still nothing.'

'We should at least try to work out where we are. Did anyone see if we passed Exeter?'

'I don't know, Ben,' Kallie suddenly shouted, surprising everyone. 'This was your idea, remember? I'm from the city, I don't visit places with trees unless they're the indoor kind in big pots, like the ones you get in malls. If you told me to expect rabid fruit-bats and rats the size of Shetland ponies I'd believe you because I don't *know* about outdoor stuff, this is not *me*, all right?'

'You might have told us before you decided to tag along,' said Claire. 'I'm freezing. What are we going to do?'

'I guess we either walk back to the carriage or pass the night here,' Masters replied.

'I'm not walking all the way back. Anyway, there's no more heat or light in the carriage than there is here. Oh shit, listen to that.' From above came the sound of rain on slates.

'That does it, we all spend the rest of the night in the waiting room,' said Ben firmly. 'It makes the most sense.'

'Oh, you get to decide what's good for everyone, do you?' Claire snapped. 'Of course, you're *American*.'

'Just what is that supposed to mean?'

'Just that you always boss people about.'

'Only if we know what's best for them.'

'You're trying to make up for being beaten in Vietnam and the Gulf by telling everyone else what to do.'

'At least we're capable of making life-decisions, which is more than you guys. I suggest you try it sometime.'

'Great advice coming from a country where people eat with their fingers and send money to TV evangelists.'

'Now you're being offensive.'

'Come on, you two, give it a rest.' Kallie pushed between them and led the way back to the waiting room. They had to break the lock to get the door open, but found a dry fireplace with dusty bundles of wood stacked beside it.

'I read that bird-watchers use places like these as hides,' said Masters, digging out his lighter. Outside, the rain began pounding the roof. It took a few minutes for the wood to catch, but soon they had a moderate amount of light and heat. Paint hung in strips from the ceiling, but the floor appeared to have been recently swept.

'I'm going to use the john,' said Ben, rising from the corner where he had been seated glaring balefully at Claire. 'If you hear a crash it's me kicking the lock off, okay? Give me your flashlight.' He pulled the waiting room door open. 'Hey, listen to that rain.'

'This is like the station in *Brief Encounter*.' Claire hunched down inside her overcoat. Kallie had already fallen asleep. 'I've seen it dozens of times on TV and I always want the ending to be different.'

'I'm surprised you like it at all,' said Masters. 'Surely your generation prefers more recent stuff. You'd rewrite the ending, then?'

'Only in my head. Don't you ever do that, change the endings of things?'

'All the time, Claire.'

Kallie fell asleep in front of the fire. The rain was still pounding the platform roof. 'Ben's been a long time. Do you think we should go and look for him?'

'No, it's okay, I'll go,' said Masters, forcing his aching limbs into action. He checked his watch but condensation clouded the face. As he picked his way along the dark platform, he tried to imagine what had been responsible for stranding them here. The carriage had been coupled at both ends. There had been a guard in the carriage with them. None of them had been paying much attention – they'd been too busy grandstanding each other with crazy stories. Perhaps they'd missed some kind of emergency announcement. But didn't the staff always come around and check the carriages if there was a problem? In this day and age surely people were protected from accidents of fate? Wet leaves plastered the backs of his legs as he walked. He reached the door of the ladies' toilet, but found that it was still locked. There was no sign that Ben had ever reached this far.

He turned slowly around and studied the dim forms about him. No sound but for wind and rain. But there was a faint glimmer of light, no more than a pencil beam, from somewhere near the far end of the platform. As he reached it, he realised that it had to be from Ben's torch, and it was coming from the underpass to the other platform. Wary of slipping on the wet steps, he descended.

✦

'They've probably found a telephone by now and called someone,' said Summerfield vaguely. 'There's really nothing to worry about.' He and Jane sat side by side in the pitch-black carriage, protected from moonlight by the hill behind them, as the art historian emptied the last of the wine into his glass. At least she had stopped crying now.

'I want to know why this is happening,' she said finally.

'That's like trying to explain the moon, or the course of people's lives.'

'It's all so random, and it shouldn't be. We've been telling each other stories all night, but they're not like life because they have plots. Nothing is left to chance. All this – there's no plot here, just a stupid accident, someone not doing their job properly.' She wiped her nose with a tissue. 'I don't want to be worried all my life. I'm tired of always thinking of others. When the children were ill, when my mother died, when Harold had his breakdown I was always the strong one. I had the answers and the energy to go on. It seems like there was never a moment in my life when I wasn't prepared to face disappointment. I feel like a fictional cliché, the academic's neurotic wife, and only *I* know that I'm not in someone else's story, that I'm real. Well, I don't want to be like that any more. I want someone else to take care of the worrying for a while. I want to go away somewhere warm and quiet. Where could I go, Peregrine?'

'I know a story about a special place,' he whispered.

'Is it real, though?'

'No, of course not. I don't know anything about real places.'

'But you must do. You're so much more practical than Harold.'

'Darling, I'm not real, any more than you are. In your heart you must know that.' And she knew he was right, for she remembered nothing before boarding the train.

✦

Masters reached the bottom of the dripping tunnel and peered ahead. He could see nothing but the glare of the flashlight. 'Ben?' he called, and the reverberation of his voice was lost in the falling rain.

The torch lay in a shallow puddle. He picked it up and allowed the beam to cross the walls. There was no sign that anyone had been here. He continued through the underpass to the other side, but a rusted iron trellis barred the way to the opposite platform, so he made his way back.

When he reached the waiting room once more, he found it deserted. The fire burned low in the grate. Kallie's jacket was still lying across one of the benches, but the three students had disappeared as completely as if they had never existed. Masters was a rational man. He tried to remember their faces, but found he could no longer conjure their features in his mind. Shocked, he dropped down into the nearest seat and tried to understand what was happening.

They had been on a train, and the carriage had become separated, and they had walked to the station . . . Jane and Peregrine were still waiting for him, that much he remembered. He had just decided to walk back to them when he heard a distant pinging of the lines. Impossible, of course, but it sounded as though a train was coming. He ran out on to the platform and peered into the murky night as the sound grew louder.

Now he saw the bright, empty carriages swaying around the bend ahead, heard the squeal of brakes as the locomotive pulled into the station and came to a sudden stop before him. The green-painted carriage threw yellow rectangles of light on the platform. It bore the initials GWR on its doors. The compartments were separate and lined with colourful prints of British holiday resorts. The seats had anti-Macassars on their backs. The train was a flawless reproduction of one from his childhood, but why? And how? And surely it occupied the same line as their poor stalled carriage?

He had barely managed to climb inside and shut the door before it lurched off once more, running to its timetable as surely as Alice's white rabbit, and as Masters fell back into the seat he thought; this is a memory, an idealised moment from the past, correct in the details down to the curious acrid smell of such carriages and the itchy bristles of the seat, but not something that's really happening now – merely a culmination of fragments seen and experienced, not fact but fiction, someone else's fiction.

He pushed down the window and leaned from it, searching the track ahead. Where the stalled carriage should have been was nothing at all, no carriage, no track, no hills or sea, no night or day, just nothing.

And he thought; I've fallen asleep like one of my students, that's all it is. There's nothing to be afraid of. It's simply that I've lost the ability to tell reality and fantasy apart. Right now it seems I'm fictional but I know I'm real, for I have real memories. He thought hard and tried to recall something, a moment so exact and specific to his life that it would prove he was real, so that the fiction would break up around him like an unfinished short story. He tried to think of Jane and Peregrine, whom he knew had been having an affair for nearly two years, but could not conjure a single past memory from either of them. He thought about this evening, and the way it conformed to the most absurd conventions of a typical Hallowe'en short story; the stormy night, the train ride, the mystery destination, the tale-telling guests. Stay calm, he told himself, and remember, remember, he repeated as the train hurtled toward a stomach-dropping oblivion, remember something real and true, remember the last time you were truly happy.

And then a real moment came to him.

A dead, hot day in mid-July. The air is countrified, dandelion spores rising gently on warm thermals, the lazy drone of a beetle alighting on dust-dulled hedge leaves. A suburban summertime, where the South London solstice settles in a sleepy yellow blanket over still front gardens.

Westerdale Road has its characters; the bad-tempered widow who appears in her doorway at the sound of a football being kicked against a wall, the deaf old couple whose pond freezes over every winter, so that they have to thaw their goldfish from a block of ice in a tin bath beside the fire. Some of the houses have Anderson shelters in their gardens, converted to tool-sheds in time of peace. Others still keep chickens, a distinctive sound and smell that excites the neighbourhood cats. Further along the street is a 'simple' man who sits on his front step smiling inanely in the bright sunlight.

Masters forced himself to remember, to stop himself from ceasing to exist. These weren't his memories, he realised with a shock, they belonged to someone else entirely. What were they doing in his head?

Many street names conjure pastoral imagery; 'Combedale Road', 'Mycenae Road', 'Westcombe Hill'. At noon the silent sunlight scorches the streets. Housewives stay deep within the little terraced houses, polishing sideboards, making jellies, listening to wirelesses in cool shadowed rooms. Their men are at work, mopping their brows in council offices, patrolling machine-room floors, filling out paperwork in dusty bank chambers. Their children are all at school, reciting their tables, catching beanbags, and in the break following lunch there is a special treat; the teacher unlocks a paddock behind the playground of Invicta Infants, and here is a haven from the hot concrete, a small square meadow of close-cropped emerald grass hemmed in with chicken-wire. Here we are allowed to lie on our stomachs reading comics, passing them between each other. It is peaceful, warm and quiet (the teachers do not tolerate the vulgarity of noise) and although we are in a suburban street, it feels like the heart of the countryside. And here is the heart of all remembered happiness.

Confused, Masters began crying as the carriages dissolved around him and tumbled away through the night sky, the foundations of his life evaporating as he fought to recall anything at all that made him human.

What was it about this area, what did it possess to make it so special, so irreplaceable and precious? A few roads, a pond behind a wall where sticklebacks were trapped in jars and dragonflies skimmed the oily water, a railway line with a narrow pedestrian tunnel beneath it, a station of nicotine-coloured wood and rows of green tin lamps along the platform. Some odd shops; a perpetually deserted furniture showroom, damp and dark, its proprietor standing ever-hopefully at the door, a model railway centre, a tobacconist selling sweets from large jars, a rack of Ellisdons Jokes on a stand, none of them living up to their packet descriptions, a chemist with apothecary bottles filled with coloured water and a scale machine, green and chrome with a wicker weighing basket, a bakery window filled with pink and white sugar mice, iced rounds, meringues and Battenburg cake. An advertisement painted on a wall, for varnish remover of some kind, depicting a housewife happily pouring boiling water from a kettle on to a shiny dining room table. Cinema posters under wire. A hardware shop with tin baths hanging either side of the door.

This confluence of roads and railway lines is bordered by an iron bridge and an embankment filled with white trumpet-flowered vines, and populated by families with forgotten children's names; Laurence, Percy, Pauline, Albert, Wendy, Sidney. No ambitions and aspirations here, just the stillness of summer, the faint drone of insects, bees landing on flower-beds in the police station garden, tortoises and chickens sheltering from the heat beneath bushes, cats asleep in shop windows with yellow acetate sunscreens, and life being lived, a dull, sensible kind of life, unfolding like a flower, the day loosening as slowly as a clock spring – an implacable state which children thought would never change, but which is now lost so totally, so far beyond reach that it might have occurred before Isis ruled the Nile.

The lecturer had no memories of his own because he did not truly exist. Just like any flesh and blood human being, the creation that was Harold Masters reached his time unexpectedly and without resolution, and so dissolved into a tumble of threadbare tissues. With no plot momentum to drive him and no memories of his own, just borrowings from the mind of his creator, he turned over and over into nothing and was gone. And in that moment, he was the most real.

The storyteller in the mind's eye of Harold Masters sits at his chipped writing desk staring up at shelves of books, his eye alighting on an old 78 rpm record, and it dawns on him that he took Masters' name from the label, which features a dog and a gramophone. He wonders how many other characters' names came from spines of books and recollections of friends. A video of *Brief Encounter*, a copy of *Dracula*, a photograph of New York, a lottery ticket, a drawing of a phoenix, a brandy bottle, a hotel brochure, a dog's collar, an Arsenal scarf, childhood notes. He looks for the patterns that shape his own life and finds only tarmac, concrete and steel, the dead carapace of something lost to all but his mind's eye.

His own past is as dead as his – and Masters' – recollection of it. *Dr Beeching closed the branch lines, road planners cut the streets in half, smashed down the houses, constructed swathes of concrete through the hills, the roads, the railways, the gardens, and like a bush cut through at the root, everything familiar died. The shops of his childhood were boarded up, homes falling to the wrecking ball, friends divided, families relocated. Now oil-drenched vibrations pulse the once-still air. A bright patch of pavement remains where once he stood with his face to the sun, free as the sky.*

That was his reality.

Everything now is fiction.

They feel different, he notes, fact and fantasy. The former rooted in observation and experience, the latter bound by publishers' conventions. Sitting in the small cold study, the storyteller determines to leave behind his outmoded world of locked-room mysteries and vampire soaps in search of something real. But how hard will it be to leave such a cosy niche for a place with endless horizons and no perameters? Even letting go has a learning process.

He pushes back his chair and goes to the open window, inventing as hard and as fast as he can. It is a beautiful spring morning, and the breeze causes his eyelids to flutter. There is brine in the air. He looks down from the window-ledge at the thin white clouds racing far beneath, then loosens his belt and steps out of his trousers. It only takes a moment to remove his T-shirt, pants and socks. Drawing a deep breath, he walks confidently out on to the rope-covered surface of the springboard, determined not to show that he is scared.

How the releasing of shackles makes his body feel lighter than air.

Poor old Harold Masters, not being allowed to finish his story. It was so obvious to see where his tale was going that there was simply no reason for the author to finish it himself, not when his readers could put together the clues and do the job for him. The burden is always on the author to rediscover ways of surprising his audience, and that task has been fulfilled, albeit in a rather unorthodox manner.

It's good to be standing at the edge, he tells himself, bouncing lightly on the balls of his feet. There's a new world ahead. As the old century closes, he can leave behind his plots and characters. There are some excellent practitioners of the art who seem more than happy to close up the store behind him. There will always be the attraction of lies.

His body is pale and unused to such exposure. The clouds below appear as if seen from an airplane window. He moves further to the end of the board and gives a few experimental bounces. Then he bends his knees, jumps into the air, comes down on to the board and straightens his legs. The tension released in the board springs him high into the air, so high he feels he could punch a hole in the sky. For a brief moment it seems as if he could stay like this forever.

And for those who are left back on the ground, blinking in the sharp sunlight, those who are all too familiar with where they have been, the question for them now is how not to look back, how not to look down, but where to begin.

Where to begin.

And the answer, of course, is right – here.